Crimson Groves

By Ashley Robertson

Copyright 2013 Ashley Robertson Books

**Paperback Version 2 Edition,
License Notes**

Table of Contents

1..4
2...13
3...24
4...34
5...42
6...46
7...58
8...69
9...75
10..80
11..92
12..105
13..114
14..124
15..135
16..151
17..164
18..171
19..178
20..181
21..190
22..197
23..202
24..209
25..215
26..220
27..230
28..240

My eyes shot open wide, instantly seeing what my new body craved. A disturbing thirst grew inside me as I watched tiny droplets of blood trickle down her neck. I stared at the crimson rivulets, mouthwatering, my fangs struggling to stay confined inside. My tongue stroked across my new canines—sharp and hungry. My refusal to bite her and drink her blood had been much easier before I saw it, smelled it, felt it sticking to my taste buds like honey. Sweet, scrumptious honey made of blood.

1

The Call

FOR THE PAST SIX MONTHS I've been in a really bad mood. Today was no different. I walked with an empty purpose along the streets of downtown Clermont, staring at the scuffed black tops of my Dr. Martens boots. The empty part I blame on John and Mandy, the purpose...well that was because I was on my way to work. The tall buildings around me were older, some red brick, some gray cobblestone, and a few of them were just bland shades of white, slightly worn down from the weather. They were linked like a cut-n-paste project at school. Chunky, uneven brick pavers decorated the front of each business and cracked, distressed pieces of sidewalk filled the gaps in between. Distracted by my thoughts, I tripped over a huge dip in the walkway pushed up by a swollen tree root. I skipped twice, not so gracefully, but luckily regained my balance before falling. Thank God I wasn't wearing heels or I would've just eaten the sidewalk. Some days you just can't catch a break. Maybe I just caught one?

Letting out a deep, "woe's me" kind of sigh, I looked up. The descending sun hung in the corner of the sky like a big round drop of spectral yellow paint, fighting to keep its place on a dusky blue canvas. A cool gust of air brushed past and my hair flew sideways, sticking to my face. Wrestling with it momentarily, I strained to see beyond the soft blond wisps, and as I turned a corner the breeze shifted gears, sweeping my long hair behind me. At least I could see where I was going now—not that it helped my state of mind.

A slightly overweight woman jogged past me wearing typical running attire: black leggings, skin tight neon green tank, and white Nike sneakers with a black swoosh. Her copper hair, pulled in a ponytail, poked out the top of a white sun visor. A chill brushed against my arms through the paper-thin poly-cotton material of my, black button-up shirt and I wrapped my arms around my chest, rubbing my hands up and down my arms trying to create a little heat with the friction. It was unusually cool for Florida this autumn—maybe that meant we'd actually get a real winter this year. "Yeah right," I mumbled under my breath.

The street was getting busier, cars and trucks hurrying to beat the impending rush hour traffic. Some of the restaurants around here offered great happy hours to attract those who didn't want to brave the streets, or that just wanted to get cheap drinks and bar bites. Even though the restaurant I worked at was upscale, they'd decided to start offering the same types of specials. My boss blamed it on the bad economy.

A group of men in suits walking in the same direction as me, but on the other side of the street, fit the profile of the mid to upper class business professionals my restaurant catered to, and I wondered if that's where they were going. As I reached the intersection, I hit the button and waited for a signal to cross the street. Instantly, a light in the shape of a plump stick person lit up bright white. Lucky me! Could my day possibly be looking up? Letting out a heavy sigh, I stepped off the edge of the sidewalk. Suddenly a horn bleated. Tires shrieked. It was loud. So loud, I knew it was close—too close. I swung my head up in a panic only to find a red Volvo heading straight toward me.

It came to a stop just a few feet away. I gasped, fighting for breath as my pulse hammered in my head, my attention on the smoke drifting up from the tires. Then as I raised my gaze slowly, a Latino woman in the driver's seat came into view. She looked young, barely out of her teens with a braid of long, dark hair draped over her shoulder. Her mouth gaped open, her eyes wide with panic. Swallowing hard, I tried to focus on steadying my breathing but the air seemed thin. My adrenaline was pumping as if I drank a can of rocket fuel, yet my limbs were frozen and I couldn't move.

"Ma'am, Ma'am! Are you okay?"

Looking like she'd seen a ghost, I stared at the Latino woman through the windshield and I couldn't help but wonder if something bad really *did* happen and I was having some type of out-of-body experience. Maybe she *did* hit me? Maybe I *was* a ghost?

"Ma'am!" The voice was closer and this time I registered it sounded more like a man than a woman—deep and baritone.

Slowly looking around, I saw one of the men in suits walking toward me, the wind blowing his dark hair sideways, and his suit jacket flung open. "Are you okay?" he called out, worry hardening his expression.

"Y—" I choked up, feeling shaky all over. If I really were a ghost, he wouldn't be able to see me. Right? "Yes, I'm okay," I finally managed.

Suit man smiled as relief washed over his face. When I looked back at the Latino lady, she was giving me one of those "move out of my way" looks. And she was texting on her cell phone. No wonder she'd just about run a red light and hit me. Fighting the urge to flick her off, I followed behind suit man as he headed back to his group on the sidewalk.

If you've ever had a near-death experience then you know how your life flashes right before your eyes. I would've died sad, desperate, and alone. My tombstone would've read, *Abigail Vaughn Tate – Beloved bartender.* Isn't that just a great way to go? And I thought I was having a bad day before this. No, I won't ask what else can go wrong. I really don't want to know.

The Beacon was just a little farther up ahead. With a silent prayer, I pleaded with God to let it be a busy night. Busy enough to keep my mind off John... and Mandy... and my near-death rendezvous.

"Hey, Abby," a soft voice called out as I walked in. Jamie was just out of high school, not quite eighteen, but her parents were regulars here and pretty much secured the hostess job for her.

"Hey," I said, waving at her as I passed the hostess stand. With a brief glimpse, I noticed how nice she looked with her mousy brown hair neatly tied in a bun and the deep red dress she wore hugging her slender frame. As the hostess, she was the only employee that didn't have to wear all black, but at least I made more money.

Turning left, I moved through the bar area in the front of the restaurant. A wooden countertop stretched across the entire back wall with several barstools crowded around it, two of them holding up older men. Behind the bar, there was a mirrored wall that held every type of booze you could imagine, along with two flat-screen

TVs. I headed straight behind the bar and stashed my purse in a cabinet by the floor. Then I stood back up, still a little shaken, and smiled at my coworker Justin.

"Abby, it was a slow lunch shift so I'm getting cut. Tonight's all you," Justin smarted. He didn't look away from the wine glass he was rinsing in a small sink beside the icemaker. His tall, thin frame towered over me, at least a foot taller than my five-foot, four-inch height, and his short hair was a color somewhere between blond and brown. He was one of the few people I still bothered to call a friend.

"Sorry, life could always be worse." Brushing his arm as I went past him, I added, "Like getting hit by a car and killed on your way to work?" then looked back to see his reaction.

He swung a curious look at me, one eyebrow arched higher than the other. "You what?"

"Yep. I can't believe it's still legal to text and drive. How many more people have to die before they outlaw that?"

"Well maybe you should've taken one for the team." His thin lip arched slightly upward, releasing a sly-looking smile.

"Well, it's the perfect time for me to be a human sacrifice," I mumbled under my breath, half hoping he didn't hear that.

"Let me guess...you're still pissed about John and Mandy?" spoken with a sarcastic lilt in his tone.

"Shut up," I hissed. "I don't want to talk about them!" Remembering we weren't alone, I looked toward the end of the bar where the old men sat, thankful their attention was on the football game.

"Sorry. I didn't mean to piss you off." Justin ran his fingers through his hair leaving no proof that he'd ever touched a single strand of it. "I mean, you still haven't talked to them, right?"

I absolutely hate how Justin tries to pry into my business. He's not much of a gossiper, thank God, but sadly (for me), he doesn't know when to leave things alone. "No, I haven't."

And just as if their ears were burning, here they came, walking straight toward me. John was 5'11"—slender, brunette, hazel eyes, charming—and the sight of him still caused my heart to do somersaults. He was wearing the jeans I'd bought him for his birthday last year and an off-white polo. He grinned at me: dazzling, breathtaking. Then I glanced over at Mandy, which instantly brought me back to reality. She was just a smidgen shorter than John. Her drably ash blond hair dangled slightly below her shoulders and some kind of clip held a large hunk of it to the side. A pair of faded skinny jeans and a tight red top with spaghetti straps completed her look.

"Abby, please come talk to us," pleaded Mandy. She wore so much makeup, I thought she was made of plastic. At least her hooker red lips matched her shirt.

"Get the hell out of here!" Trying to keep my voice down, but anger surging up like a tidal wave, I exclaimed more loudly, "Now!"

John shook his head. "Please just step outside and hear us out."

Seeing red in my mind, I stared daggers at the man I'd once wanted to share my life with forever, blah, blah, blah. "There's nothing to talk about," I ground out. "Please leave now or I'll have you both removed."

With watery eyes, Mandy took a small step forward. "Please," she begged. Her voice was broken, desperate, pathetic—just like her.

"Look, you guys need to leave. Now." Justin came over next to me and slid his arm around my shoulders.

"We don't want any trouble," John said. "We just need five minutes with Abby. Please."

I slowly swung my head to the right, then the left. "The answer is *no*! Please leave!" Now my voice was borderline hysterical. Another quick glance around the bar confirmed the customers weren't watching me, though without a doubt, I knew they could hear everything going on.

That was all it took for Mandy to start crying. I sure didn't remember her crying this much when we were best friends. "But Abby," she wailed, "it's been over six months. I miss you! You need to hear our side of the story."

"I already *saw* your side of the story. I don't need to hear anything else." A flashback of walking in on them having sex in the same bed I'd shared with John burned in my mind, and my stomach clenched as I pushed away that horrible image.

Letting me go, Justin turned on his heel and headed out of the bar area. "When I get back," he declared over his shoulder, "the manager will be with me, and your asses will be thrown out!"

"Don't worry about it. We're outta here." John's gorgeous face crumbled a little as he took Mandy's hand and pulled. She resisted at first. Halfway between the exit and me, Justin watched them warily, his gaze warning, challenging. John tugged again and Mandy gave up, letting my former boyfriend—her sloppy seconds—lead her out of the restaurant.

Shaking his head and looking relieved, Justin said, "What a bunch of freaking jerks! Can't they take a hint?" He meandered back to the bar and sat down at one of the stools. "You're better off without them, you know?" His tone was louder than I liked, but I let it slide since he had just saved my ass.

"Thanks for helping me, but I really don't want to talk about this."

Placing his elbows on the counter, he said, "I don't blame you. You've had quite a night so far." He looked away, seemingly heavy in thought. When he turned back with an inquisitive gaze, I knew I was in trouble. "So do you think you'll ever listen to what they have to say?"

Tossing my hands in the air I exclaimed, "I don't want to talk about them. Please. There's nothing more to say."

Justin sat there for a moment, speechless, watching me with his moon-shaped brown eyes. Then moving his arms from the counter to his lap, he said, "You look like crap. Your eyes are bloodshot, your hair's a mess, and you never smile anymore. I can't believe you're letting them get to you like this. What happened to my dear sweet friend? You remember her, right?"

Now I was the speechless one. Turning around, I stared at the mirror nestled behind the wall of alcohol. My reflection gazed back at me between the Grey Goose and Kettle One vodkas and that's when I realized Justin was right. What a sad, pathetic, lonely person I'd become. Over the last six months, I'd managed to distance myself from anyone who cared about me. Losing my boyfriend to a backstabbing best friend was too much for me mentally to handle.

"Abby," Justin called out, and once I turned to face him, he went on with his assessment. "You need to get back out there. Start dating. Maybe act nicer to the guys hitting on you. You never know, one of them might actually be a good match for you."

"I'm not interested in meeting anyone while I'm working. Especially not at a bar." I rested my hands firmly on my hips.

He looked down and hesitated for a minute, and I fought the urge to be immature and storm away. Then Justin stood up and said, "Whatever you say. Anyway, I'm out of here. Oh I almost forgot, your dad called earlier. I told him you wouldn't be in until later. He said he would call back."

I stared at Justin, feeling like he'd just slapped me across the face. He turned around and headed out of the bar. My father called? I hadn't spoken to my father in fifteen years. What would he be calling for? He left my mother and me when I was ten, and we never heard from him again. My mother didn't take it very well— years of depression turned into dark anger and loathing bitterness. Then one day out of nowhere, she started blaming me. "You were always such a brat! No wonder he took off. I should've gone with him," were the last words she ever said to me. Shortly after that, I moved out (with my good friend Mandy) and never spoke to my mother again. I'd heard "through the grapevine" that she remarried and had two more kids. Looked like she finally got her perfect little family after all.

Justin's words echoed inside my head over and over again. I couldn't help but feel anxious over the potential call I'd be receiving. Would he really call back? What would I say? What would he say? Shaking my head, I decided to put it out of my mind. The chances of him not calling back were far greater anyways.

"Excuse me, Abby," Mel called down to me from the end of the bar, "can I get another glass of wine?" Mel was older, in his late sixties, with plump high cheekbones, thin stringy white hair brushed sideways in an effort to conceal his growing bald spot, and, was very overweight. His pants didn't stand a chance of containing his oversized belly.

"Sure, sweetie." After getting a fresh wine glass from a nearby cabinet, I grabbed an open bottle of Sequoia Grove, which was our house cabernet.

Mel smiled as I set the half-filled glass on the counter in front of him. "Thanks, Hon. You're the best." His chubby fingers gripped the stem as he carefully swirled the contents inside allowing the wine to breathe a little before he raised it to his lips and took the first sip.

"No prob—"

Ring ring ring—the sound of an impatient phone wailed behind me. I turned around and stared at it, unable to move.

"Aren't you going to get that?" Mel asked.

Nodding my head, I reached for the phone and grabbed it, yanking it to my ear. "Thanks-for-calling-The-Beacon-this-is-Abby-how-can-I-help-you?" My shaky voice pushed each word out so fast they ran together, making my entire greeting sound like one long word.

"Abigail?" a deep, gruff voice spoke. "Abigail Tate?"

"Yes, this is she." My free hand found a few strands of hair and started twirling them.

"Abigail, this is your dad, if I can even call myself that anymore." A long pause went by and all I could do was wait for him to continue, my voice stuck on the enormous lump in my throat. "Look, I know how bad I wronged you. And I know how angry you must be, but I need you to listen to me. Abigail, you're in danger. He's coming to find you. Somehow, I'm not sure how, but he figured it out. He knows how special you are. You can't let him find you. You need to lay low and—"

I didn't give him a chance to finish talking. "I haven't heard from you in fifteen years and finally...finally, I get a stupid phone call. But it's not because you miss me or even because you want to apologize for walking out on me. It's not even because you care to know what I've been doing with my life. You just called to tell me some crazy story because you think I'm in trouble? Oh and let me guess, my hero father is going to rescue me? You're freaking crazy! Don't ever call me again!"

I slammed the phone down hard on its receiver and was shocked it didn't break. Lifting my gaze to the mirror behind the wall of alcohol, I saw Mel and my other customer turn back toward the football game. Obviously I'd just put on a show for them, but at least they were pretending not to notice a thing.

"Stupid jerk," I breathed. I hadn't heard from my father in so long, and the only reason he wanted to talk to me was to warn me that I was in danger. What did he mean that I was *special* and that *he* knew? Who was he talking about anyway? None of that conversation made any sense. But my dear old dad had nothing to worry about. Since my breakup with John, I'd pushed him and everyone else out of my life. There was no one left that could hurt me, and I had no desire to let anyone in my life anytime soon. Sure I was lonely, but it definitely beat being heart broken. Didn't it?

Shaking my head in disgust, I pushed my father and that deranged phone call out of my mind and tried to refocus on my work. The dining area of the restaurant was starting to seat people and that meant drink orders for me. And since I was the only bartender working tonight, I didn't have to split my tips in half. Yay for me. I stole one more minute to mentally pump myself up with some positive thoughts (okay, so I tried), and then started to make my way toward the service window. There were already a few drink orders waiting for me, brightening my mood a little.

Ring, ring, ring—the phone barged in, causing me to spill some of the Stoli vodka I was pouring. *Dang it!* I scolded myself, then set the bottle of booze on the counter and headed the few steps to the phone. My hand hesitated a moment, hovering just above it. This couldn't be my lunatic father again. No, surely it couldn't. "Thanks for calling The Beacon, this is Abby, how can I help you?" I was more confident this time—you could hear each individual word.

"Abigail, please do not hang up. Please. You have to listen—" A loud banging sound burst through the headset of the phone making me yank it away from my ear. It sounded like a fight had broken out, no doubt from whatever bar my father was in. He'd probably pissed off some other drunk and then said something stupid. I tried to put the phone back to my ear, but the ruckus coming from the other end was still too loud. I felt shivers crawling up and down my spine. My heart started beating faster, harder. Even though I had zero respect for my father, the thought of someone else kicking his ass left me feeling uneasy and confused.

Then there was a deafening shriek, and my father, or maybe it was some other drunk, screamed out in agony. The horrible noise reverberated over and over. A big swallow failed to get my heart out of my throat, and my hand felt clammy on the phone. After what seemed like forever, the screaming trailed off taking the other noises with it. Pressing the phone to my ear at last, I listened for my father to come back on the line, or anything else that would let me know he was okay. "Hello, are you there? Hello."

Then, the line went completely dead.

2

Encounter

I STILL HELD THE PHONE TO MY EAR even though there was no one on the other end. That call left me extremely unsettled, my nerves sitting on end and my mind nothing more than a jumbled mess of broken thoughts. What the hell just happened?

Finally, after God only knew how many seconds ticked by, I set the phone back on its receiver and returned to the service window, where five more orders were waiting to be filled. Like a robot on autopilot, I got busy making each drink.

After mulling it over for a few minutes, it occurred to me that the whole thing could've been a hoax. An awful prank that he'd played hoping to win me back as his loving daughter. When he realized he wasn't going to win the "hero" card with me, maybe he'd shifted gears to the "father in distress" card. Perhaps his goal now was to get sympathy from me. What a sick man my father had become. Or maybe he was like that all along and he did both my mother and me a huge favor by leaving us.

Unfortunately for him, I was unable to see any positive reasons he would call and put on such a show. If I really were in trouble, why would he care? I'd been through my fair share of hard times with no daddy around to help. So that made it even easier for me to assume that my father was a drunk, and worse, that he concocted that stupid scheme as a way to slip back in my life. What a terrible thing to do to someone, let alone his own daughter.

With shaky hands, I kept busy making drinks, trying to keep an emotional safe distance from everyone. Twice Mel asked me if everything was okay and I just brushed him off with "Sure, it's all good." Dennis, the other bar patron sitting with Mel, refrained from saying anything at all. Except, of course, when he needed a refill of his Chimay Reserve.

Over the next hour, the busyness started to die off. Mel and Dennis still sat at the bar, their attention razor sharp at whatever game was playing as they munched on a mix of cashews and almonds. I started cleaning some of the used glassware in the mini sink, all the while, my mind kept replaying the two phone calls from my father over and over again—not that I wanted it to. I was stuck in a loop, the mental torture unfathomable.

At the moment I was about to completely lose my mind, a very attractive guy came walking in. Feelings of peace and serenity drifted through me like a gentle whirlwind, blowing away those unnerving thoughts of my father. As the guy rounded a leather booth, our eyes connected and I looked down in a rush, embarrassment warming my cheeks. Though I knew it was impolite to stare, I couldn't help but slowly lift my gaze back up and there he was, still heading toward me as if we were in a slow-motion movie scene. Swerving around a couple high-top tables, he made a beeline for an empty stool at the opposite side from where my other customers sat. He was tall, maybe six feet, with a rocking toned body, angular jaw, sexy plump lips, and silk black hair framing his smooth handsome face, sweeping to the sides just below his deep, dreamy eyes. Wearing dark blue jeans and a long sleeved black shirt, he was beautiful, perfect, and he was looking right at me. My heartbeat accelerated, thumping violently inside my chest and tingles raced up my back and down my arms like sharp electric currents.

By the time his elbows found the counter and his chin came to a rest on his hands, I was breathless. His fair skin was a creamy white, ghostly, but the sexiest ghostly I'd ever seen. A thought of touching him flashed in my mind, imagining my fingertips gently stroking his cheek, gripping the firm roundness of his upper arm, and at once, my stomach clenched with need, an inferno of lust arousing me with thoughts I'd never had before. Licking my dry lips, I looked away, but the heat still burned like hot wax on my skin. My hands were shaky as I handed Dennis his beer, and as I turned to meet my new customer, a hard knot formed in my throat.

Tranquil vibes shot through me the instant our gazes locked together, easing the erratic tension to the point coherent words formed and I was able to say, "Hi, I'm Abby. What can I get for you this evening?"

His lips twisted in a wry grin as he reached out a hand. "I'm Bronx."

My fingers staggered as I reciprocated, and like a splash of water on my face, his ice-cold skin snapped me out of whatever daze I'd been in. Trying to hide my alarm as I pulled away, I stepped back, but forced myself to keep looking at him. "I would like a Crown and Coke, please." His grin widened, a brilliant display of his pearly whites, and his voice was like a cool wind in my head—relaxing, hypnotizing me back in that strange stupor.

And just like that, I was his all over again. Bizarre excitement to get him whatever he wanted consumed me. "No problem, Bronx." I nodded, smiling gently. "Coming right up." Grabbing a glass with one hand, a bottle of Crown in the other, I got busy making his drink, all the while I could feel him watching me, but he was probably only making sure I didn't under-pour the Crown and over-pour the Coke. After stirring the contents with a miniature straw, I began to garnish it with a lime.

"I do not need the lime. You made it perfect." His tongue danced over his lips, its slow stroke back and forth only seeming to entrance me deeper. My whole body felt light as feathers and I thought at any minute, I would float away.

Nodding slowly, I handed him the drink. "Here ya go then, and thanks." As he took it, his fingers laced with mine, my mind instantly registering they didn't feel cold anymore. Actually the soft, warm, touch only reawakened my attraction for him, chasing away some of those lingering doubts.

"Hey Abby," Mel called out, "I'm ready to put an order in."

In desperate need of fresh air, I pulled away and stepped back. The clenching in my stomach was more intense, but I was still able to remember that Mel had just asked for something. "Be right there," my husky reply surprised me. Was that really my voice? Releasing a long sigh, I glanced back up at Bronx who was still flashing me that same dreamlike smile.

My whole body bristled with confliction about not wanting to leave my sexy new customer, but knowing I had a job to do. "Alright Mel, what can I get ya?" A huff of words and I hoped my regular patron wouldn't notice the impatience in my tone. And though I usually made healthy suggestions on what he should eat, it seemed too much work to think about that right now. Strangely, the only thing I wanted was to get back over there with Bronx.

"I think I'll have the sliders, medium rare, and a side of the Parmesan crusted fries." The Beacon served their sliders in twos, instead of threes like a lot of other restaurants, and garnished them with fancied-up sides of tomatoes, onions, and lettuce. Unlike the countless times before, I didn't protest against Mel's order.

"No problem. Need a refill on your wine?" Even though I asked, I hoped he didn't. That would cost me more time—time I didn't have.

"Sure Abby, thanks. And thanks for not lecturing me this time about the calories and fat I just ordered." A slight jiggle moved through his waistline as he leaned forward to sip the last drop of wine from his glass. Tiny beads of sweat started to form on my forehead. Mel's lips still moved. He was saying something, but I couldn't hear him anymore. Giving him a polite smile, fake and forced, I anxiously looked back at Bronx, who didn't try to hide the fact he was watching me. Where did this gorgeous man come from and why was he staring at me?

In a rush, I was at the computer screen typing in the food order then moving even faster as I opened another bottle of house cabernet. I was cautiously aware of Bronx's presence while I poured the wine in a fresh glass, trying to remember to smile at Mel as I handed it to him. The unusual pull to Bronx was getting stronger, more urgent, like we were magnets and I needed to go to him.

Turning on my heel, I started his way.

"Hey, Abby," Dennis called out, halting me. "Can I get a Jack instead of a beer this time?" I headed back reluctantly. Dennis was about Mel's age but thinner, a lot thinner, almost skeletal, with a sunken face, dark circles under his eyes, a wrinkly bald head, and long boney fingers nudging his empty mug toward me.

"No problem," I said with a counterfeit smile, trying my best to maintain a polite composure with my loyal regulars. Neither of them had seemed so demanding earlier, but then again that was before the perfectly gorgeous guy arrived.

I moved so fast, I was lucky I didn't spill or break anything. With that fake smile plastered across my face, I set the drink in front of Dennis and turned around, heading straight to my gorgeous new customer at last. Perhaps Dennis thanked me but I didn't hear it. My mind was tangled up on Bronx and I couldn't figure out why I wanted to get back to him so badly. Heated emotions expanded in my chest, churned in my belly, and though I tried to make sense of these over-the-top feelings, my ability to concentrate remained somewhat challenged. Thoughts on how I didn't know him interspersed with wanting to know him and a need to feel close to him.

Each step closer to Bronx became more comfortable. I looked down at my feet briefly, feeling a little self-conscious, and then back up at him. That's when our gazes locked and the room began spinning, leaving me feeling dizzy and disoriented. Grabbing the countertop to steady myself, and still unable to look away, I inched closer and closer to him. Then I was there, no more than a foot away from him, standing at the edge of his event horizon, his dark eyes full of mystery—which only strengthened our magnetic attraction. Glimpsing his flawless, smooth face, I imagined touching it for the second time. Gently caressing as I ran my fingers over his cheek down to his lips. What the hell was I thinking?

He broke the silence by saying, "Is it possible for us to talk a little? I would love to get to know you better." He stretched each word out, making it last.

My cheeks flushed warm—definitely blushing. None of this made any sense whatsoever! Why was I so mesmerized by him? What the hell was I feeling? For the last six months I'd successfully shielded myself from anyone who hit on me. How did this strange but beautiful man just barge right through my barrier?

"That sounds great. What would you like to know?" was what came out of my mouth, but not what I'd been thinking. Yet I was comfortable with him and it seemed normal to feel that way. A slight tilt of my head and my hair fell sideways, sweeping over the side of my face. Some might have mistaken it for a flirtatious gesture, which, in all honesty, it was. I'd done that without thought, my body acting in some strange, trance-like autopilot. I'd never been like this before, swept off my feet by a wannabe Mr. Prince Charming. I'd also never been interested in anyone I had met at a bar. That was a rule I'd had long before my relationship with John, and it bounced straight back at me once he got caught making Mandy a friend with "benefits".

"Abby sounds like a nickname." He sipped his drink, full, moist lips brushing against the glass.

Twisting rings of my hair, I nodded. "Yeah. My real name is Abigail but I don't really like it all that much, so I go by 'Abby'. I was named after my grandma, but she passed away shortly after I was born."

"Abigail it is then. Of course, if that is okay with you?"

I nodded without thinking. Yes that name bothered me, but it was okay if he called me it. What was I doing?

He gave a graceful shrug, smile widening across his face. "You are absolutely beautiful, if I may be so blunt, and I would much enjoy learning more about you. It appears slower than usual tonight so I thought this would be a good time for me to come in and meet you."

Was this guy for real? Should I totally freak out right now? Or was this the most romantic thing that'd ever happened to me? I couldn't shake the amazing vibes I was getting from him nor could I calm my thundering heartbeat. His eyes seemed to get deeper, bottomless, and I couldn't look away, as if they were sucking me inside their depths. All of a sudden I was paralyzed, frozen, couldn't move, couldn't think anymore. I was his, mesmerized, captivated, and he was in full control—control I *wanted* him to have.

Leaning in closer, because somehow I knew that's what he wanted, my hair swept across his cheek and I glimpsed his tension in the way he compressed his lips, and for some reason that only excited me. Mouth lowering to his ear, I asked, "Have you been watching me?" in a whisper of words, then added in a soft, disappointed tone, "Why wouldn't you come inside before now to meet me?" I lifted my head back up, just enough to find his eyes again.

He half laughed. "Would you believe me if I told you I was afraid to approach you? Afraid you would not receive me the way you are this evening?"

"Well, I'm very happy you made it in tonight." I said it, I meant it, but I didn't recognize my own voice. I knew I should see a red flag and run for my life. This perfect guy had been watching me, stalking me. Didn't he have anything better to do? He was gorgeous and could probably be with anyone he wanted. Why me, an average girl that bartended for a living? How could that impress him? How could he think I was pretty enough to come in here and say that without even knowing me? He was either a total freak or this was love at first sight, which made me a total freak to even think that. "What else do you do, besides watch me?" I asked, smiling.

"I enjoy hunting...and I have gotten rather good at it. I also like long walks at night, preferably when there is no moon. Since my house is not that far away, I actually walk a lot."

I took a deep breath; it was steady, didn't tremble. "I don't live that far from here either." Didn't know why I said that, but I did.

"May I escort you home when you are finished here?"

Without thinking, I nodded.

We talked a little longer, smiling, laughing, and carrying on like we had known each other for years. I'm not really sure what we were saying. My mind felt empty, blank of thought. A few other customers came in, briefly pulling my attention away from Bronx, and I was able to breathe again, like my head had lifted out of the water. My hazy state of mind sharpened, and I took down the new drink orders with a plastic smile.

Once everyone was happy, fresh drinks in hand, I looked back. Bronx was gone. His glass was empty, except for a few remnant ice cubes, almost fully melted. My heart jumped up my throat and that horrible clenching in my stomach returned. I needed to be close to him again. Where had he gone? I couldn't believe he'd just left without even saying goodbye. Was he coming back? He'd said he'd walk me home.

The rest of my shift I was moody, and when it was finally time to go, I grabbed my oversized black purse out of the cabinet and headed out of the bar with a heavy heart. Bronx never came back. I'd probably never see him again. Releasing a deep sigh as I walked out the door, I startled when I saw *him* leaning against a streetlamp post. It shone on his face, illuminating his deep, dark eyes. Only now there was a thin crimson ring wrapped around his pupils. That hadn't been there before. What was it? Stepping closer, I strained to see him better, and instantly a hazy wave swooped over me and I forgot what I was doing.

He was beside me. I hadn't seen him move. He pulled my arm against his chest, intertwining it with his. His shirt was soft on my skin, his body hard, solid, and cool underneath. "Sorry I left unannounced," he said, voice deep, very resonate. "There was something I needed to do before I could walk you home."

My mind struggled with a barrage of thoughts, both cautious and reckless all at once. But as quick as they came, they were all gone. "That's okay," I told him brightly. "I'm glad you made it back to walk with me."

He gave my arm a tight squeeze before releasing it, then he gently grabbed my shoulders, his face lowering toward mine. I took a deep breath, held it in. His lips were there. I could see them through the darkness a split second before they brushed across my forehead, then down to my cheek. They were plump, cool, moist. They inched toward the edge of my face, hovering between my neck and ear. "Shall we get going?" his voice strained.

I nodded, couldn't speak, like my throat was squeezed shut.

He put his arm around me, pulling me against him, and then guided me down the sidewalk. Most of the shops were closed—lights out, dark inside. The streetlamps were lit, illuminating a small area around them. Craning my neck, I looked up at the black, velvety sky. There were a few bright stars scattered about, and the moon, with its wide arc of craters, looked like a smiling Cheshire cat. I guess this wasn't a good night for walking with Bronx since a moonless night would be at least a week away.

His grip around me tightened. It felt really good, a little cool, but strong and secure and I instantly started getting those crazy feelings of doing just about anything for him again. All he would have to do was ask, and I would jump at the opportunity to make him proud of me. Smiling, I nestled closer against him, feeling relieved and reassured.

Our feet moved as one as we walked. His fingers stroked my hair to the side, softly and gently. We came up to the gated entrance of my neighborhood, "The Groves". A small silver box hung on a brick wall beside the gate. Bronx punched in a code and the iron gate swung open. "You know my code?" I asked, astonished.

"I live here too."

Panic surged, breath deep and short, heart racing out of control. But then I couldn't remember why. I relaxed, shrugged my shoulders. Everything was okay again.

Following along with him, we moved down this street and then another one, dimly lit by lamps. Faint light gleamed from inside some of the houses and somewhere off in the distance, a dog was barking. A garage door opened and closed. At last, we were at my street, but when I turned, he tugged me back with him and kept walking straight ahead. Oddly, I wasn't worried, though maybe I should've been. Everything was okay. Maybe he wanted to show me where he lived first, or maybe he was taking the longer, more scenic way to prolong our walk. Whatever the reason I kept walking with him.

A house on one of the dead-end streets in the back of the neighborhood materialized as we made our way to the driveway. It was heavily treed and landscaped which gave it a lot more privacy than any of the other homes in here, including mine. One of the reasons I liked this neighborhood was because of the oversized lots every house inherited. But this home seemed to sit on two, maybe three of them. From what I could see in the outdoor lighting, it was expansive, with a turret on the front giving it a castle-like appearance.

We were at the front door, walking inside. Walking inside? I wanted to turn around and leave, but I couldn't remember why. It was okay to be here. I was okay where ever Bronx was. We stood in a dark room, darker than the night outside. My eyes struggled to focus, but I couldn't see anything. Bronx pulled my hand and I followed, completely relaxed by his touch. He squeezed me— gently, reassuringly.

My knees brushed against a soft, squishy fabric. There was a chair or sofa in front of me. "Please have a seat," he said, voice subdued and inviting. "Would you like a drink?" He leaned across me, tapping something and a light flashed on, faint and mellow. My eyes flicked back and forth, focusing on the area around me. There was a dark brown sofa next to a small table and the light came from a lamp on that table.

Sitting down as instructed, I said, "Sure."

After watching Bronx turn abruptly and leave the room, I looked around everywhere. A couple feet in front of me was a table, most likely a coffee table, and there was an expensive-looking oriental area rug on the floor showing off gray and red floral shapes. I couldn't see beyond that—the light wasn't bright enough. I turned around; there was nothing behind me, just the floor, made of some type of fancy-looking wood. It led to another room, but it was black and dark.

"Abigail."

I gasped and swung back around. Bronx was there, which created an unexpected excitement inside me. As he came closer, my pulse sped up to the point where I could feel it in my ears. My head felt swollen and heavy on my shoulders so I leaned back against the sofa seeking support, but sinking deeper into it instead. As the cushions eased me in, electrically charged butterflies took flight in my stomach.

He sat down beside me and my body leaned toward him. Getting up would not be easy when the time came.

"I hope water is okay, I did not realize I was out of everything else." His voice was like a hypnotic song.

Scooting closer, he lowered his face toward mine. Almost touching, close, so close. Then he was there, lips on my cheek, kissing me—gentle, soft baby kisses. My body froze. I tried to swallow a lump of emotion, but it seemed to be lodged in my throat. His lips trailed over to mine, then he pressed softly against them. I closed my eyes, squeezing them shut, then, instead of getting up and running for my life, I kissed him back. Throwing my arms around his neck, I kept kissing him, each one more passionate, harder than the last. In the heat of the moment he dropped the glass. I heard it thump on the rug before I felt a subtle splash on my shin through my pants. Bronx embraced me so tightly that I could hardly breathe anymore, let alone worry about getting wet. I desperately sucked at the air around his lips as he rubbed his hands up and down my back, massaging it aggressively. His kisses grew more urgent and sloppy. Moving my hands from his neck up to his hair, I grabbed big handfuls of it, lightly pulling and tugging. Then he slowly leaned back, giving me a brief moment to catch my breath—or at least attempt to.

Gasping as his fingers caressed my cheeks, he trailed his lips down my neck, then began kissing and sucking. "I have wanted you for so long," he growled, and I could feel the vibration beneath the muscles of chest. I let go of his hair, inching my fingers toward the buttons of his shirt. He sucked harder, pulling me closer. It felt so good that my insides were about to explode. Struggling with undoing his shirt, I tugged more aggressively and finally the top two buttons gave way. My fingers traced his skin to the next awaiting button.

His body tensed. A deep groan rolled off his throat, though it sounded more like a growl. Then suddenly, he bit down into my neck. His teeth were sharp, instantly puncturing the skin. Flinching, I tried to pull away but he held me too tight—I couldn't move, couldn't budge. I was in pain, but I was so scared I barely felt anything. Adrenaline raced through my veins like water bubbles floating to the surface. Then, in a rush, a wave of intense pleasure came over me. It felt good, so good, better than anything I'd ever felt before. It was absolutely incredible, sort of like your first roller-coaster ride multiplied times infinity. My body trembled, barely able to handle the intoxicating surge of emotions.

Then those euphoric feelings eased up, bringing with them a sense of awareness. I don't know how long I was out of it, or whatever I was, but Bronx was still on me, slurping and sucking. There was something wet running down my neck. Was that his saliva or my blood? I felt hot, moisture beaded across my brow and pooled at my nape. Then everything got really cold, but I was still sweating. Though I was paralyzed by fear, I knew I needed to do something to get him off of me.

Pressing my hands against his chest, I pushed, straining with intense effort, but he barely budged an inch. His body was hard, heavy, and beneath his shirt, his skin was like ice. "Please don't do this!" I screamed, voice broken, frantic. I was losing consciousness. My eyelids were like mini black curtains closing over my eyes and without a doubt I knew I was going to die if I didn't get him off of me. Pushing as hard as I could, I tried again, my fingers digging into his skin. But this time he didn't move at all. Questions crowded my mind: Who was this guy? *What* was this guy? Why was he biting me? Did he know I was dying?

Too much blood loss, body trembling, feeling weaker, frailer. A tear streamed down my face as I tried one last time to get him off, but I could sense it was too late. My emotions went numb—no more fear, no more questions. All sound faded as if the volume were suddenly turned off and I couldn't hear anything, the silence absolute.

Then, everything went completely black.

3

Transformed

BRIGHT LIGHTS DANCED AROUND ME and it felt like I was floating too, but it was impossible to know for sure since I couldn't see my feet, or anything else except for those beautiful luminous bursts of yellow, silver, and white. I was in euphoria and surely could get used to this and stay here, wherever this was, forever.

Tingles crept up my neck and scattered around my head. My body felt lighter than air, riding on gleaming, fluffy clouds. My mind thought of nothing and everything all at once, causing me to feel dazed, numb, blank. Not able to see where they ended or began, the lights seemed to go on for infinity. They were just there, everywhere around me, swallowing me inside them and then spitting me back out. They glided this way and that, pulling me along like a suction cup. I couldn't tell how long this went on nor could I grasp time itself. This must be heaven, the place I always dreamed I would go after my body died on Earth.

But as the saying goes, "all good things must come to end," and it did. The euphoric twinkling lights faded, ripped away by savage claws of darkness. Shadows lurked all around me seconds before the remnant light completely extinguished. A sensation like ants crawling up my spine made me shiver, and trepidation settled deep down in my bones. Those amazing tingles of pleasure turned into hot fire and burned me from the inside out. I screamed in agony, I cried, I cussed at it, begging for the light to return. But nothing stopped the darkness from covering me, and bringing with it the worst feelings of torture I could ever imagine. There was no way this was the heaven I'd dreamed of. This had to be hell. The place where you burned alive for eternity.

I aimlessly drifted in this hellish abyss on orange-glowing coals, my body smoldering and blistering. My gut twisted with agonizing fear—the rawest form of fear I'd ever felt. The intense pressure kept building in my head, and I was certain at any moment it would explode. That same infernal place was still there when I closed my eyes. There was nowhere to hide, nowhere to go. It was everywhere, surrounding me, taunting me.

That's when I noticed something wet slithered across my tongue, trickled down my throat. No matter how many times I tried to open my eyes, I couldn't. What was in my mouth? Was it water? It didn't exactly taste like water with its thick, velvety, texture and the metallic tang it left on my taste buds. But oh it felt so good in my parched mouth, soothing my dry throat and quenching my thirst, making me forget where I was. With each pull of the mystery liquid, I felt better, stronger, so I gulped harder, feverishly swallowing it down.

Then I felt pressure on my face, pressing down around my lips. It was smooth and hard like marble but there was a softness to it that reminded me of silk. It was the source of this refreshing drink so I grabbed it with my hands, holding it tightly against my mouth, and sucked at it fiercely, desperately. Feeling better and better the more I ingested, I clenched it more firmly, securing the continued rhythm of the healing elixir, lapping it down with my tongue. I tightly squeezed my eyes as if they, too, could help. Prickly tingles danced on my skin like goose bumps, but more intense. Happy thoughts of survival rose up in my mind and a sense that everything was going to be okay resonated inside me.

With no warning, the source of the quenching fluid was gone— as if ripped away from me. I frantically struggled to find it, wanting it back, *needing* it back. Empty air teased my hands as they waved around, aimlessly searching for whatever had just been providing the delicious drink. Panic came in a rush as the tingles increased to a level I could barely handle, scraping and cutting deep beneath my skin. Jerking sideways, I twisted back and forth.

Nothing.

I tried forcing my eyelids to open but they were weighed down like dumbbells tied onto them. *Breathe, just breathe. Take deep breaths, get a grip, and don't panic.* Sucking in as much air as I could, I startled when only tiny puffs streamed inside, as if it was blocked by congestion. *What the hell?* I tried again. Same result. Gulping the air more urgently still produced nothing. *Okay, don't freak out. You're going to be okay. Just relax. Think positive.* Musing about a warm summer day on the beach in the Caribbean, the hot blazing sun dancing atop bright blue and turquoise waters, a beverage with a little yellow umbrella garnishing some kind of frozen drink in my hand finally helped the sharp pains fizzle away. My body relaxed slightly as small breaths flowed in and out of my mouth, barely anything, but at least it was something. *If I'm not getting enough air, how am I conscious?*

That was when I heard a deep, soft voice in the back of my mind. "Do not try to get up...let my blood consume you...only a few more minutes." Was it speaking to me?

Unable to register those words, I couldn't think about them—it was too much at once. I knew I needed to open my eyes and see what the hell was going on. With a bit of a struggle, I was finally able to open them, though at first, my vision was blurry and I couldn't see much of anything. Everything was fuzzy like light in a thick fog so I closed my eyes, squeezed them shut, then slowly reopened them. This time it was better, clearer, the light less hazy than before so I fluttered my lids a few more times and a silhouette of a person standing over me materialized.

Remembering the words, instant recognition of the voice tore through me. It was *his* voice, *his...blood.* Sheer terror seized me and I gasped. My whole body felt heavy like it was filled with lead balloons, and when I tried to sit up I discovered I wasn't quite strong enough yet. Time plummeted around me, memories sifted in my mind, confusing me with their surreal vibes, yet stinging me with bites of reality. I met a guy at work. Bronx. That's right, Bronx was his name. He walked me home but never took me there, brought me somewhere else. A house...his house? Then he kissed me. No, I kissed him. He was gentle at first, but then so aggressive, so vicious. He bit me...sucked my blood. Didn't he kill me? Blinking a few more times, my vision was finally crystal clear. It was Bronx standing above me, smiling down at me, and I was still in the room he'd brought me to.

All around my mouth was wet and sticky, instantly reminding me I'd drank something that tasted strange, so I wiped my lips with the back of my hand, then looked down and found blood smeared over my skin. My stomach roiled, the putrid scent hitting the back of my throat caused my tongue to fold as I gagged. "What have you done to me? Who in the hell are you?" I glared up at him; my body trembling all over, as I ground out, "*What...are...you?*"

"Abigail, Abigail, please calm down and I will tell you everything you want to know, but you must calm down first." His voice was still, eerily still.

I swallowed hard. Took a deep breath, but nothing seemed to happen. "I can't breathe," I rasped, my hands pressed against my chest.

"Do not worry. Your body no longer requires air. It is simply acting out its old breathing pattern. In time it will stop." He smiled, big and brilliant, flashing sharp oversized canines. Fangs.

Shaking my head from side to side, I said, "Your teeth aren't human! Wh-wh-what, are you?" My voice trembled uncontrollably.

"I am a vampire, a very lonely vampire. My partner dismissed me after spending two decades together. It would have broken my heart if I had one." He chuckled, an unpleasant sound that tormented my ears. "She was bored with me and wanted a new partner, one that could bring her the excitement of passion that we no longer shared. I did not feel the same. I pleaded with her not to send me away." He closed his eyes for a few moments and I kept silent. Did he just say he was a vampire?

"One night while we were hunting, two Enforcers jumped me. Enforcers are very old vampires with special gifts in addition to being exceptionally strong. One of them had the ability to freeze the body, preventing it from moving at all. I could not stop them from taking me away from her. She laughed at me as they did. The other Enforcer could move at the speed of light. All vampires move extraordinarily fast but nowhere near as fast as that. That Enforcer brought me here to this house. He threatened that if I ever returned they would kill me but not without torturing me first." His smile was gone, eyes like black holes in space, threatening to suck me inside.

My stomach tightened as knots of fear formed in my throat.

Bronx kept talking. "It has been seven lonely years since that happened. I did what they asked and remained here, searching for a new partner. None of the other vampires I have run into have been good enough, all of them lacking some quality that I need and most important, the connection of me to her that will bind us together for eternity. Then I saw you through the window at The

Beacon. You were so beautiful. For months I walked by and watched you while you worked, waiting for the perfect time to come inside and meet you. Tonight was that special night."

When he sat down beside me, I sunk toward him and I mentally cursed gravity. He reached over and took my hands inside his. My body was frozen, numb, I didn't move, didn't fight him. He stared at me, waiting, and once I met his eyes, he pressed on, "You exceeded all of my expectations. After you spoke just a few simple words, I knew you were the one. The woman I have searched for. Your beauty exceeds far beyond your physical appearance. Your heart was full of compassion unlike anything I have ever seen or felt. I needed you to be mine forever. But you were a mortal human, and our love would never work if I left you that way...there was no choice but to transform you into one of my kind."

Nervously biting my lip, since he was clearly friggin crazy, I watched his dark eyes widen with longing, expectation. Not knowing what to say, I kept my mouth shut.

Eerie silence stretched on, all the while he watched me like he was waiting for something—a reaction maybe? Well, he wasn't going to get one just yet. My new, erratic feelings were something I couldn't quite get a grip on, let alone understand what the hell he was saying.

"Abigail, you are a vampire now. You are the one who will stand by my side as my eternal partner. I brought you back to life with my blood to complete the transformation."

That was definitely going to get a reaction—I was literally about to blow. Jerking back, I pulled my hands free, and with a *snap* the sofa conformed around me like soap bubbles in a tub. The sofa just broke? I shouldn't have been able to go that deep into the cushions yet I was clearly a lot closer to the floor. Then when I got up, the movement was crazy fast, everything around me was a blur until I stopped moving. Standing very still, I mentally assured myself everything was okay, but my ability to believe that was lost when I looked down at Bronx. His lips were curled in wry grin that concealed his teeth. "What a load of freaking crap!" I sounded hysterical, which I was. This guy was nuts and he must have drugged me with something. I'd heard about drugs that could get you into a euphoric state, and I'd also heard of ones that made you see visuals. He'd without a doubt dosed me with both.

"No. It is true. All of it."

"You're a liar," I screamed. "I'm getting out of here, now!" I turned around, started to run, but Bronx was there—I never saw him move, he was just there, holding my arm. His hard grip felt like being stuck in concrete and I couldn't budge an inch. He pulled me into him in a dizzying whir of movement, then his arms wrapped around me like an anaconda suffocating its prey. Finally able to move a little, I sidestepped him, trying to get free, but I wasn't going anywhere. I was about to have a full-on panic attack, but with my breathing still slow and a pulse I couldn't feel in my ears, I startled, trying again to step away from my captor. In my current state, I should have been gasping, my heart thundering. Shimmying a little more out of his hold, I wiggled my fingers up to my neck, pressing down hard just under my chin. Nothing. No heart beat. Extreme fear consumed me. I was so scared I didn't know what to do so I started crying like a baby. Hey, we all have our breaking points.

Eventually I calmed down, or rather I cut the crying to a minimum. Bronx's hold loosened up enough for me to finally pull away from his chest and there was an immediate whiff of something bloody, salty. My face, it was coming from my face. The scent grew sharper, more pungent and...*tasty*. But how could I possibly like the smell of blood? My mouth watered at the thought, my thirst and hunger growing. More denial whipped through me, and this time when I stepped back, Bronx let me go completely. But there was nowhere *to* go.

I was consumed with the unthinkable.

After touching my face, I lowered my hand in front of me, staring at my red fingers, mesmerized. Then suddenly loud noises shrieked in my ears, distracting me from those horrible, bloody thoughts. Everything was so much louder than it should've been, crickets chirping their nightly chorus, the swish of birds flying nearby, the low thudded vibration as the neighborhood entrance gate swung shut. The neighborhood entrance gate? How in the world was I hearing any of this?

As if things could only get worse the room started to wobble, like it actually *had* a pulse, and I frantically placed my hands over my ears as I attempted to steady myself, using my palms as earmuffs, trying to keep the noise from getting in so I could focus more on not falling. A wave of nausea slammed the pit of my stomach and pushed bile into my throat that tasted like blood. Fear gripping me, I crouched down to the floor and pressed more tightly against my ears and closed my eyes, telling myself that when I opened them, I'd be safe at home. But opening them only proved I was still here with this lunatic.

He spoke, voice ramming through my ears, which let me know my makeshift earmuffs weren't working. "I can tell you are starting to experience the enhanced senses that come with being a vampire. Seeing, hearing, feeling, smelling and most of all tasting. The taste of blood is what you thirst for above anything else, and you will need to feed again before daylight. My blood transformed you and will be enough to hold you over for a little while longer, but you will need more of it soon."

Oh-my-God, what was happening to me? A vampire? Could I really be a vampire? A make-believe being that created best-selling books and sold out movies with almost every story imagined about them. It didn't seem possible. But then again, neither did any of the crap happening to me. I was unable to move, completely frozen, immobilized by fear.

The new desires of my body were instinctive but foreign. The blood cravings, super-sharp vision, hearing so clear it was as if there was a souped-up hearing aid in my ear. And I was so much stronger, way more powerful than before. It was like I'd taken steroids—from what I'd heard about them anyway—and I couldn't deny this change in me, the knowing chill of it prickling down in my bones. All of these facts led me straight back to Bronx's crazy story. He *is* a vampire. I am a vampire too.

"Are you doing this to me? Are you making me sick? Is that your gift?" I peered up at him, and his eyes were still locked on me.

In a swish of cloth he was holding me, cradling me in his arms like a baby. I didn't see him pick me up, never even saw him move. After sitting me down on the other sofa, he sat beside me, close, too close. He held my hand, gently squeezing. His touch, our closeness, made my insides wrench in disgust. Yet when I tried to pull away his grip only got tighter, proving how much stronger than me he was. That's when I knew I was stuck. Exhaustion claimed me and I didn't want to fight him anymore. "I don't feel right," I rasped. "What's happening to me?"

"Most vampires do not have special gifts. That is what makes the Enforcers so powerful. Years ago I discovered that I could use persuasion at a level far more intense than any other. All vampires possess this ability but most are not very skilled at it, and none can use it on other vampires like I can. Persuasion enhances your emotions beyond the intense ones you are now beginning to feel as a vampire. It allows you to persuade people to do anything you want in a way that makes your victim feel like they are acting on their own. I used persuasion to make you feel comfortable with me earlier this evening; however, I am not using it on you at this time. It may have felt like you were hypnotized if you were even able to notice it at all. Most humans do not realize I am using persuasion until long after they have done what I wanted. Though most never notice it at all."

The trance-like state I was in earlier must have been this "persuasion" he spoke of. Everything had felt normal, but it wasn't. I knew something was off, but I couldn't do anything about it. I was his puppet and he was the puppet master. He controlled me—what I thought, what I felt. Getting inside my head, he made me trust him, feel completely at ease with him, and then he lured me to this place so he could destroy me, break me, and really make me his forever.

My head whipping in awareness, I tried to shake away the truth—the truth I didn't want to know. Ignorance *is* bliss. But I knew this was real. That I was a vampire. That my body was weak, exhausted, starving, and all it wanted was blood. No! Intense pressure expanded in my chest, this new reality dropping on me like an avalanche, weighing me down and suffocating my mind. Slumping back into the sofa, I closed my eyes in resignation.

"Abigail" —his voice a sadistic melody—"You are desperately in need of more blood, and you will continue to grow weaker until you get some."

"How could you do this to me?" I asked hoarsely as I glared at him. "Shouldn't I have had a choice?"

"I did not have a choice when I was transformed. It turned out to be the best decision for me." There was a blur of movement and then he wasn't sitting next to me anymore. Now he stood above me with a hint of a smile that only showed teeth, no trace of his fangs.

"But I have a life...or at least I *had* a life...and you took it away from me. What am I supposed to say to my family? To my friends? They're going to notice me missing."

"You seem to forget that I watched you long before I decided to transform you. You have been alone for the past six months."

"That's not true." I coughed to clear my throat, trying to raise the volume of my voice, but it didn't work. "I do have friends. I mean, a friend. And what about my coworkers?" Had I really let myself become such a loner? How friggin' convenient for Bronx.

"Your coworkers are hardly your friends," he said. "A phone call to your boss explaining your absence at work should buy you time to decide on a more permanent explanation. If you shall even need one."

"A more permanent explanation for what?"

"You will never see your human friends, or family for that matter, again. You are a vampire, Abigail. No one can know what you are. It is vital for our survival and theirs."

"But..."

"IF ANYONE WERE TO DISCOVER WHAT YOU ARE, THEY WOULD BE DESTROYED!" His voice was so loud I thought my eardrums would burst. I cried harder, tears falling more urgently. I needed to think of something else, I needed to be somewhere else.

After weeping in my hands for what seemed like hours, I finally peered up at Bronx. He hadn't moved an inch, his watchful eyes still on me. I looked away, squinting to see more of the dark room around me. It was much bigger than before with its wrought-iron wall hangings and tall candles with tiny dancing flames that cast shadows on the deep gray walls. Dark wood floors were distressed with cracks and creases, and a large stone gargoyle sat on top of them in a corner. The broken sofa was across me, a rectangular coffee table of wrought iron and wood in between, and I couldn't help but think what a perfect place to become an undead creature of the night.

There were footsteps, distant, across the room and I swung my head around to see where Bronx was going. He stood in an opening of what looked like a hallway. "I will return in a minute."

He was gone but then he was back—like pressing a fast-forward button. I startled at seeing a middle-aged woman held tightly in his arms. She was fifty something, short, a little overweight, wearing an oversized blue tunic with a super-tight pair of white leggings. Shoulder-length black hair streaked with gray drooped over her round, pudgy face, her inexpressive eyes peeking out at me from between thick wisps. Her arms were stretched behind her in a way that led me to believe they were restrained.

"What are you doing? W-who is t-that?" I meant it to sound more demanding, but it came out broken. More questions circulated in my mind, but I couldn't get my voice to ask them. I was beyond exhausted, too overwhelmed, and growing more impatient with Bronx and his twisted games.

Nothing could've ever prepared me for his answer.

"This human will provide you with the blood you need. Time is of the essence. Come now and drink from her."

4

Learning

I STARED AT THE WOMAN who should've looked more frightened than she did. Perhaps Bronx was persuading her, but if that was the case, then why were her hands tied? Apparently she'd already been snacked on since there were bite marks on her neck. The thought of that revolted me, and bile shot up my throat. A couple hard swallows helped get most of it back down, however the lingering taste wasn't very pleasant. Shaking my head, teeth clenched, eyes glaring, I announced in that horrible weakened voice, "I am not touching that woman."

"Yes you will, and I prefer not to use my persuasion to make you do it." He sounded calm, gentle, serious.

"I'm not going to kill her or anyone else, not now, not ever!"

"You do not have to kill her to feed on her. Some humans, known as blood donors, know of our existence and willingly allow us to drink from them. Our bite gives them a feeling of pleasure that begins during the bite and lasts for hours after. This woman has been a regular donor for a few of the other vampires around here. She would be honored for you to bite her."

"You're lying," I retorted, wanting badly to yell, but only soft wispy sounds came out. "Why are her hands tied? I know you must be persuading her to be relaxed, you can cut the crap now."

"I am not persuading her, and that is the reason her hands are bound. Persuasion should not be used the first time you feed from a human. You need to do it on your own. Her arms are tied to make it easier on you. Even willing blood donors are afraid, yet intrigued, of the bite from a new vampire. It is intensely painful at first, and most try to fight you during that time. You are too weak to keep your hold on her should that happen."

Tilting my head, I stared the woman. "Is he telling the truth? You want me to bite you?"

She looked at me, face blank, eyes empty, lips unmoving.

"Are you going to answer me?" I hardly recognized my own voice. It was hoarse and gravelly, as dry and brittle as my throat felt.

"Enough of this!" Bronx roared. He tossed the woman on the floor, clearly losing his calm façade. Her body jiggled as she landed a few feet in front of me, but I didn't move. There was no freaking way I was going to drink her blood.

"Every donor craves the bite of a new vampire. It is more potent than any other. She wants you to bite her and feed from her. She wants to feel the pleasure only you can give her." Without seeing him move, Bronx was closer to me, and I really wished he'd stop doing that.

People let vampires bite them so they can get high? This guy must be high if he thought I'd buy that crap. But the way he'd just described how a vampire bite felt, well that sure was similar to what I'd gone through when he bit me. I didn't believe him, and definitely didn't trust him, yet the only thing I had to go on was what he was telling me. Could that mean there were some tidbits of truth sprinkled inside Bronx's words? Glancing down at the woman's neck, I imagined the blood pumping in the vein within it and shook my head in disgust. Yep, that thought seemed real human, didn't it?

And to top everything off, I wasn't feeling any better. Actually it was getting worse. Not only did it feel like I'd just run a marathon, but my churning stomach demanded the one thing that made it twist harder. Blood. Fearing everything Bronx told me might actually be true, I felt a chill of fear wrap around my spine, the thought of being a stranger in my own body constricting it tighter. I licked my dry lips, fighting a swelling desire for blood, pushing it to the corner of my mind. My mouth watering, I pressed my lips together, closed my eyes, and concentrated with all of my remaining effort on anything but the woman laying on the floor in front of me. If drinking her blood was my only way to survive, then let me die again right now. And this time there wouldn't be any coming back.

This had to be the worst nightmare I'd ever dreamed, but I knew it wasn't a dream at all. This was real—*all* of it. I opened my eyes, looked at Bronx. He was smiling, watching me with anticipation. I shook my head violently, screaming "no, no, no" in my mind, then closed my eyes and started praying.

There was movement in the room. I strained to hear, not wanting to open my eyes because I was afraid of what I'd see. But that delicious aroma was already waltzing inside my nose, tickling my taste buds. On my skin, goose bumps scattered everywhere. The churning in my stomach intensified. That scent was all that mattered now, mouthwatering, irresistible, and I had to have it now.

My eyes shot open wide, instantly seeing what my new body craved. Seeing his fresh bite marks on her neck, a disturbing thirst grew inside me as I watched tiny droplets of blood trickle down from the twin punctures. I stared at the crimson rivulets, mouthwatering, my fangs struggling to stay confined inside. My tongue stroked across my new canines—sharp and hungry. My refusal to bite her and drink her blood had been much easier before I saw it, smelled it, felt it sticking to my taste buds like honey. Sweet, scrumptious honey made of blood.

Without thinking, I'd moved closer to her as if I were hypnotized by the scent of her fresh blood. It called to me, inviting me to it. Before tonight, I'd never tasted blood, but the instincts that came with my new body naturally brought with them the need for the desired blood feast.

I didn't bother asking to get the name of the middle-aged woman as I knelt down beside her. My black work shoes squeaked on the wooden floor. Bronx was close by, making some kind of growling noise, deep and guttural, but I didn't care. Everything around me went black, silent, my focus solely on this woman now, and all I wanted was her blood. *Blood, blood, blood.*

She turned her head to look up at me and regardless of any discomfort she may have felt, her facial expression was empty, emotionless. He'd assured me numerous times that this was the only way. He couldn't risk her struggling with me at my weakened state. That's why her hands were bound. He must be telling the truth, right?

Carefully placing my frigid hands on her warm, plump cheeks, trepidation spread through me, yet my hunger only intensified. My lips parted, my fangs plunged out. The woman looked shocked, her small eyes widening, though oddly I could sense she still wanted me to bite her, and the pulsating vein in her neck provoked me. I leaned down closer and closer until my fangs brushed across her soft skin just before plunging into it. The woman jerked and tried to pull away, but I was able to hold her head steady. Her blood was rich, velvety, tangy, and sweet, an explosion of goodness inside my mouth. Sucking harder, I pulled her closer, savoring every last drop. Eventually, she stopped flinching and I assumed whatever pain my bite had caused was over. She hummed and sighed, seeming breathless and high, paralyzed by the very bite she had just tried to escape. Slowly my raging hunger was satisfied, and I looked up at him in shame. The look returned, however, was one of pride and contentment, just as I'd assumed it would be.

Nothing would ever be the same for me again.

Then the woman got really quiet. Her body went limp. Panic seized me as thoughts of killing her assaulted my mind. Praying she wouldn't be dead, I quickly lifted my mouth away from her neck and searched her face for signs of life. She was breathing. The flow of air whistled faintly as it passed through her nostrils. A quick check of her pulse confirmed her heart was beating strong, alive— very alive, thank God. The woman smiled, her eyes rolling around in their sockets like a bobblehead doll. She let out a heavy sigh and I took that as an invitation to drink just a little more from her.

I felt supercharged as I stood up from my first meal as a vampire and gently laid the woman back onto the floor. She was completely out of it with a drunken smile plastered across her face. Questions began racing through my mind. I needed answers and Bronx owed them to me. I looked around, searching the room and quickly found him sitting on the sofa, face smug with a crooked grin, shoulders stiff and straight, hands folded neatly in his lap. I took a few steps in his direction, still keeping a good distance between us.

"Are blood donors ever killed?" I asked, then licked my lips. "You know, accidentally?"

"I suppose there have been accidents, but most vampires do not kill their donors as we have spent decades learning to coexist.

However, there are some that prefer not to feed this way and still hunt for their prey. They do not have an appetite for blood donors, though. Their blood is not as fresh as that of an innocent human."

"What makes them innocent?" I sucked at my bottom lip, trying to get the rest of the blood off.

"They have not been bitten yet."

"You mentioned hunting with, um, your lady friend, ex-girlfriend, whatever. Were you hunting innocents?"

"Yes," he snickered, "they are delectable."

"So, then I am not the first person you murdered?" My lips curled into a snarl. Deep growls rolled off my tongue. Wait, I was *snarling* at him? What the hell? Now I was behaving like some kind of rabid animal. I reached up, touched my lips, and then rubbed across my teeth. My top two canines were sharper, wider, extending down a little farther than before. The bottom ones felt bigger too. Their razor-sharp edges sliced into my fingertips. In a gasp, I pulled my hand away only to find my investigating fingers were bleeding.

In a flash, Bronx was here, arm wrapped around me, maybe wanting to comfort me, but it wasn't working—it was making me feel worse. I didn't fight him off. I don't know why. "Those are your new fangs," he explained, then smiled when I looked up at his face, a broad glistening expanse of teeth and fangs. I reached up and touched his lips, then inched my fingers inside, moving them slowly, gently over his fangs. They felt just like mine. Lowering my hand in a wave of shock, I stole a few minutes to let this new information sink in.

Bronx tightened his grip around me, and that sick feeling returned. In a blur of speed, I ducked out of his hold and stepped back. I was starting to get used to this super advanced pace— perhaps I even liked it. Glancing down at my fingers, I saw they weren't bleeding anymore. The wound was healed; a remnant of dried blood was all that was left. My body could regenerate? "Can we heal quicker than normal?"

He nodded slowly, eyes burning like deep, dark blue fires. "As long as you keep up a good supply of blood, you will be invincible."

Invincible? Really? Well, that could be useful.

Bronx stepped forward, voice deep as he said, "There was a time long ago when killing people was the only way for us to survive. It was not until about fifty years ago that the idea of people donating their blood grew more popular among our kind. Meredith"—his voice grew deeper upon saying that name— "refused to eat that way. She preferred killing for food just as we always had. The night I told you of, when the Enforcers attacked me, Meredith and I were hunting for our next victim. She loved finding a human and watching the fear in its eyes as she sucked it dry. They would struggle and fight to free themselves only to succumb to the pleasure of our venom. Meredith got such a rush from it, and I enjoyed watching the amusement it gave her. When the Enforcer brought me here, I realized I no longer enjoyed killing my victims and I began solely using blood donors." He ran his fingers through his smooth black hair, tucking it neatly behind his ears.

After that he inched a small step closer and carried on with his story. "There are a few clubs in the area owned by blood donors, vampires, or both working as a partnership. These clubs have back rooms where you can access the donors. They also make house calls, as you have just witnessed with our friend here." He pointed to the middle-aged woman lying on the floor. She was in a fetal position with her knees tucked into her chest. A faint sigh escaped her lips.

My shoulders were tight, and I shrugged to loosen them. It didn't work. I needed space, a few minutes to myself. But instead of getting that, Bronx flashed to me and put his arm around my shoulder. "I know this is a lot to take in," he said, "but you—"

Twisting around, I grabbed him just below the shoulders, and pushed back as hard as I could. He sidestepped twice but caught himself before completely falling over. "You're disgusting! You're a murderer! You killed people for no reason at all except the fun of it. Let me guess, it was all Meredith's fault you did it, right? You're just the victim here." My eyes were narrow, fangs extended, fists balled at my sides.

He watched me, that sadistic grin stretched across his face, and anger came at me in a rush. I wanted to beat his face in. Hey, that actually sounded like a really good idea. I sprung forward like a pouncing cat, fist tightly balled and swinging right for him. He moved to the side—one swift, graceful movement. My fist brushed past him, missing him by inches. Without hesitation, I reared back and charged, jumping higher, swinging faster, and crunching his face while still in midair. He fell to the side and then dropped to the floor, face down, blood dripping from the corner of his mouth. He wasn't grinning anymore. Good. I was already feeling better.

He pushed up off the floor and was on me. I never even saw him coming. I fell backwards and he rode me all the way down. Breaking his fall, he landed on my chest—hard. Good thing I didn't breathe anymore or the wind would've been knocked out of me. He straddled my waist and held my wrists above my head. The edge of the Oriental rug was rough, scratchy on the back of my palms as I wriggled and squirmed, trying to escape him. But he sat like a big boulder on top of me and I was trapped.

His hair swept over his face but I could still see his fiercely glowing eyes, smoldering like bright red embers. He growled, deep and guttural, fangs fully exposed. "You will never make accusations about Meredith again!" he roared. "Do you hear me? Do you understand me, Abigail? You are a new vampire. You have barely been exposed to this world. You know nothing more than what I have told you tonight. Decades ago, clubs with blood donors did not even exist. Vampires did what they had to do to survive. We die without blood! There is no other way for us to eat. There is no other way for us to live. Meredith preferred to do it the way we always did even after the donors became more popular. Yes, I would have tried one much sooner if it was not for her need to continue killing. That was how great my love for her was. That is how great my love for you now is."

His head lowered closer to me, eyes softening, and the muscles in his face relaxed. He was going to kiss me. I pulled and tugged, trying to pry my wrists out of his hands, but I couldn't. His lips trailed closer, too close. Still I couldn't get away. When I kicked my legs he just straddled me tighter. Swallowing a gasp, I jerked my head to the side and his lips landed on my cheek—soft, wet, repulsive. Gazing the middle-aged woman lying on the floor across the room, I screamed, "Help! Help me, please!"

Bronx's lips were next to my ear, close, almost touching. "That woman cannot help you," he whispered. "You do not even need any help. I have given you salvation from yourself. I only request your love in return."

Ignoring him, I kept staring over at the middle-aged woman. "P-please. P-please. H-help me."

"That woman cannot hear you. She is unaware of anything around her." His lips brushed my cheek in a back and forth motion before returning to my ear. He licked my lobe, a slow gentle flick of his tongue that only sickened me further and my whole body cringed.

"Please don't," a pleading whisper of words.

"I will not hurt you. There is no reason for you to fear me."

"You won't hurt me? Look what you've already done to me."

"Yes. Look at what I have done to you. This was meant to be. You are mine, Abigail. Always!" In a rush of motion he was off me and across the room.

"But I don't love you," I yelled after him. "I'll never love you. I hate you for what you've done to me."

"You may not love me now, but eventually you will. You need some time to adjust to your new life. We have nothing but time now. Each day that passes, the bond between us will grow. Countless days will be spent together, learning about each other. I will wait for you to feel for me as I now feel for you." He stretched each word out, making it last. Then he was gone. I was alone at last.

Only it didn't feel as good as I'd thought it would.

5

Adjusting

THE NEXT FEW WEEKS went by quickly as I learned more about my new life. We didn't sleep in coffins, or at all for that matter. Our reflection is perfectly visible in mirrors. The same applies if my picture is taken, but I hadn't really been in a picture-taking mood to confirm that. So I guess most of those award-winning vampire movies did contain fiction in them after all. Not that I'd ever really cared enough to find out before all this.

During the day we took refuge inside Bronx's extremely dark home. Most of the windows were boarded up from the inside, a few of them covered in pitch-black tinting, thick enough to look like paint. The landscaping was composed of overgrown bushes, trees, and vines to add even more protection from the sun's harmful rays. It would take hours for the sunlight to kill us, but, according to Bronx, it was a painful process nonetheless. That was one tidbit of information the vampire movies got right.

Bronx told me how the Enforcers once used the sun's potent light as a way to punish and bring justice as they saw fit. Since the Enforcers were like a vampire government, they got to make all the rules. Most of the other vampires never challenged them since they didn't possess the strength, skill, or special powers that all Enforcers had. Thankfully there weren't very many of them, and Bronx said they preferred places like Boston, Seattle, or Montreal since the overcast weather made it possible to move around during daylight hours.

The middle-aged woman had gone back to Pulse, where Bronx had found her. Pulse was one of many nightclubs around here that offered this blood-donor service. Since I was a new vampire and needed a few weeks to adjust (so Bronx said), more blood donors were sent here to the house—sort of like an assembly line. Each of them was excited to be bitten, mostly by me since I was able to give them a more intense high. What a nice girl I was, sharing my happy venom with others. Of course I wasn't just a giver; I also took from them, drinking more and more of their blood. My new senses were getting stronger, my strength more forceful. I was even getting more comfortable biting into my gracious donors. Could it be possible that everything was starting to look up?

One of the bedrooms was converted into a "training" room. There was a big open space in the center with a large burgundy floor mat. An oversized punching bag hung in the far right corner, and mirrors adorned the walls, mostly concealing the dark gray paint underneath. We spent several hours every day in this room. I hated to pay him any kind of compliment, but Bronx was an excellent fighter. Training to fight was much easier as a vampire. My ability to focus was outstanding, and that made my efforts at mimicking his moves quite simple. I paid no attention to the pleasure he obviously got from the physical contact this brought. My goal was to learn as much as I possibly could, hoping that one day I would use these new talents against him.

"Abigail, focus. Do not just try to hit me, anticipate my next move. Be faster than me," he lectured.

"But you're too fast!" My face lowered, eyes staring down at the mat. Copying his moves was easy. Hitting him, however, was not. My failed attempts to punch him in the face, or anywhere else for that matter, were gnawing at my nerves.

He grabbed my shoulders firmly, shaking me. "Look up at me."

Lifting my head, I tipped it back just enough so I could look into his eyes. They were like big sapphire flames—dangerous, threatening, with an undeniable allure. "Ask yourself this question," he said. "What is he thinking? What is his next move? Watch my eyes. Read what you see in them. I am able to escape your attempts to hit me because I see your next move inside your eyes. Concentrate on what you feel. Let your new senses guide you."

"But I am trying," I pouted. "I am using my new senses. It's not working."

He shook his head and nudged me backwards. I did the two-step, then pounced back into place. Positioning his hands in front of his chest, he motioned for me to come get him. Anger surged, those heated tendrils slicing through my head as I balled my hands into tight fists. Shivers iced my spine, while the rest of my body felt like it was inside an inferno. All I could imagine was punching Bronx square in the face. *Concentrate! Concentrate! Don't be too angry and screw up again.* We'd been practicing for nearly two weeks and I hadn't yet hit him, with the exception of that first night, but we technically weren't practicing then. That event, however, was playing a huge role in my quest to learn how to fight better. I was so thankful that Bronx had agreed to train me. He wouldn't be thankful once I learned.

Gathering myself as I studied him, I pushed all my focus on his eyes, looking for his next move. Surely he was using some of that mind control hokey pokey of his with the way those blue sapphire orbs swirled with power, pulling me into their depths. Normally, this was the part I'd look away, but obviously that little method hadn't worked. So I hardened my gaze and fought against his tug of power, hoping to see what his next move would be, predict what direction he would take to avoid my fist. Since he was mixing it up every time, dodging to the right, to the left, stepping backward, and even jumping completely over me to thwart my efforts, it was impossible to foresee what he would do now. Concentrating harder, straining, pushing myself further, I focused beyond his eyes, digging inside his mind. Suddenly, there was an internal snap and then somehow I was in. Guarded walls all around me, but I knew without a doubt I was inside his head. I could see and feel him. Waves of anger taunted me to attack, but I wasn't quite ready, needed to push a little more. I fought to resist the anger; it was one of the toughest emotions to control, but I needed to control it to succeed. Thrusting all my energy forward, I broke through his barriers at last. My anger easing, I slowly steadied myself as I mentally prepared for the attack.

Finally I was ready to take on my maker.

Releasing a snarl of warning then exposing my fangs to challenge him, I narrowed my eyes. Bronx's smile widened, returning my show of teeth, which only made me angrier. In an effort to psyche him out, I flashed forward and then back. Holding in my surprise that it worked, I watched him lunge to the right, and as he moved to duck down I rushed into him, right fist soaring toward his face and connecting to his cheekbone with a *crunch*. But I didn't stop there, a thrust of my arm moved my balled hand up the rest of his head and instantly blood squirted everywhere as he released an ear-splitting shriek I'd never forget. He fell backwards, smacking the ground with the back of his head. In a hurry, I jumped back, ready for him to get up and charge me, but he didn't. Slowly, he pushed off the ground, and when he met my gaze he smiled with pride.

"Well done." He licked his lips as he spoke, and I glimpsed those nasty wounds I'd inflicted were already healing.

I did it! I did it! I jumped up with excitement so intense it was almost intoxicating, clapping my hands together.

Another week went by, training, fighting, and kicking Bronx's butt. Of course I took plenty of beatings too. But I was getting stronger, more precise, more focused, with an unwavering motivation to keep learning. Even though Bronx looked just a little older than me, early thirties maybe, he's actually much older—a hundred thirty years to be exact. Unfortunately that means he'll always be stronger than me, no matter how hard I train or how good I fight so I'll have to be smarter than him, know his next move before he makes it, and maybe one day I just might *really* catch him off guard and get the hell out of here.

Depression would sometimes find me, clinging to me, reminding me of those I'd never see again. It's funny how you think you don't need anyone. I'd found out the hard way that that just isn't really true. I'd also get down on myself for not acquiring one of those special powers yet. I mean, if I had to be a vampire, couldn't I at least get some super cool power that no one else had? But I guess there were some perks to this life, like the fact I'd never age. I was going to look twenty-five forever. I knew plenty of people that would pay big money for that. I had to pay for it with my soul.

6

Celebration

I WAS SNAPPED OUT OF A DAYDREAM (looping thoughts of my human past) as Bronx came running up to me from the other room. It was noon on a Tuesday, and it was exactly one month ago that I had been transformed.

He grinned, eyes gleaming, spreading his hands wide, saying, "Since you have done so well this past month, I have decided we will go out and celebrate tonight. We have a midnight reservation at Pulse in one of the private back rooms."

A smile stretched across my face. "Wow, that's awesome. Thanks." I hadn't left the house since the day he brought me here to make me his vampire love slave. Now I sat in the plush leather chair in the corner of the master bedroom with my legs hung over the armrest, dangling along the side of it. I cautiously looked up at him, waiting for the joke to be unveiled. Getting out of this prison was the best news I'd heard all month.

"Abigail, get up and hug me. Our celebration starts now."

After a month of learning how to listen and obey, I'd actually become pretty good at it. I was like a robot, doing what I was told. There were never any reciprocated feelings behind my actions, but the fear of him forced me to be diligent.

Slowly standing with my fake smile still in place, I slid my arms under his and then wrapped them around his broad chest. Lowering his lips to my ear, he rubbed my back and then caressed my neck. "You do not seem very excited about this. I thought you would have leapt into my arms and showed me how thankful you were the minute I told you."

Well that was just great. He didn't like how unthankful I was acting. The academy award for best performance obviously just went to another leading lady (if I could be so lucky). Doing the best

I could to hide my disgust, I changed the subject. "Have you ever missed your old life? You know, the life you had before you were a vampire?"

I was often trapped in a loop of thoughts about my old life. It hurt to think there were only two phone calls I'd had to make to prevent any missing person reports. One was to my boss when I needed to quit my job due to a "family emergency". The other was to Justin, my coworker and probably my closest friend at the time. He tried probing for more info, hardly accepting my "family emergency" story, but in the end I left him no choice but to accept my excuse.

Bronx pulled out of my arms and of course I let him go. He grabbed my shoulders, gently, glancing down at me with soft, sincere eyes. Did I just hit one of his nerves? "It is normal to miss the life you once had when you are a new vampire. The more feedings you have, the easier it will get. The blood quenches what you thirst for and also makes you stronger. I am here to fulfill any of your other needs. You are never alone, Abigail."

Are you friggin' kidding me? He was there for me, for my needs? What a load of crap! He was there all right, but only for his own selfish reasons. I desperately wanted my old life back, the broken heart, and the bartending job—all of it. I hated this new vampire life. I'd do anything to be human and normal again.

Turning my "Abigail Tate, non-award-winning actress" mode back on, I replied, "I guess you're right."

We stood in silence for a few eerie minutes.

"You will need more blood before we go tonight." His voice was cautious, his fingers pressing deeper into my shoulders.

Knowing he was right, I looked past him at the king-size canopy bed in the center of the room. Sheer white curtains swooped between the head and footboards with an opening in the center, peeled away on both sides. My donor was lying inside those curtains, sleeping, blissful. "She's still sleeping."

"I can awaken her if you require me too?" He said it like a question, voice low and steady. He cupped my face, looking deeper into me. "You are hungrier than you think. I can see it in your eyes."

With the growing need for blood, vampire eyes form red rings around the irises. If we go without feeding too long, or if we get really mad, the crimson area will expand toward the pupils, giving them an all-over red appearance. Not very attractive. Actually, it's scary as hell to see it. I don't look in the mirror when I'm hungry— or when I'm pissed off. That doesn't leave me much time to look at myself. It's funny how Bronx always associated my warning eyes with hunger. Some people are so self-absorbed they don't even realize how much you hate them and how upset they make you.

Placing my hands on top of his, I fought the urge to yank them off my face. "Let me wake her. I'd like to stay in here for a while after I finish, if that's okay?"

"You may do as you please. Though I do have one request that would make it much easier for me to allow you the space you obviously desire."

Not this crap again. Bronx had made several attempts over the past month to kiss me again. I always turned away just in time. "Please, not now," I murmured. "I thought you could wait for me. I'm not ready." I left out the part that I'd rather he pour battery acid all over my face.

"I can and I will wait. It does not hurt for me to request this of you, does it?"

"No, I guess not."

"I desire you. My lips crave your lips. All they have is the memory of how wonderful you taste."

Gross. Yuck. Disgusting. It took everything inside me to hold back from spitting in his face. That would give him another taste, wouldn't it? I still couldn't figure out why he didn't just persuade me to kiss him again. He didn't have any trouble using that on me before I became a vampire, but hadn't used it on me at all since.

"I will come get you when it is time to get ready for our evening out." He released me, bringing his hands down to his sides.

"Thanks." I stepped to the side and walked past him, heading toward the bed. Wait a second. Get ready for tonight? I didn't have anything to wear. I'd been juggling a couple pairs of jeans and tee shirts this past month, currently wearing a lighter pair of jeans with a black V-necked tee. I was certain that wouldn't be good enough to wear to Pulse. I quickly turned around to find Bronx still standing in the same spot, watching me. "But I don't have anything to wear."

"Do not worry about that. As always, I have taken care of everything you need." He smiled slightly, a tiny dash of fang poking through his lips. Then he was gone. I was alone with my donor—for now.

When I sat down on the edge of the bed, her body rolled against me. "Hey Lily, wake up." I gently nudged her arm. She'd been in and out of consciousness for the past several hours, but I could tell the effects of my bite were wearing off.

She inhaled deeply, slowly releasing the air back out. Her face was soft, with high cheekbones, curved eyebrows, and a head full of voluminous brown hair with the hint of a widow's peak. One of her evenly spaced brown eyes slowly opened like she was winking at me. "Hey back at ya." Her other eye opened, then both of them closed and opened again. She smiled shyly, charmed. Her full lips looked like they'd been stung by a bee. It was actually a look most women paid big money to achieve. Hers were like that naturally.

"How are you feeling?" I asked, returning her smile, hoping to keep my fangs hidden.

"Like I've slept for days." She giggled and then struggled to sit up. Placing a pillow behind her, I helped scoot her back against the headboard, the sheer curtains around the bed casting broken shadows across her face.

Yesterday around six in the evening, Lily had come over with Adam, another donor. He'd left a few hours ago, and since we were going to the club tonight, Bronx told him he wouldn't need any more donor services at the house. Lily agreed to stick around in case I needed her before the big event tonight, which obviously I did.

"This will be the last time I need you today. I don't want to take too much blood from you," I told her.

She stared at me eagerly, then leaned forward, her medium-length hair falling to the sides. "I feel fine. You're always so worried about hurting one of us. Trust me, there's no reason to worry at all. I'm the one receiving the big benefit from the bite. I don't see you feel ecstasy when you bite me."

"Thanks. But you don't see much of anything when I bite you." I playfully nudged her arm enjoying our conversation. A special friendship was forming in so little time. It's rare, but when you find a bond like that, it's usually one to hold onto.

Lily leaned closer to me, brushing her hair back with her fingers, exposing her bare neck. She wore a comfy red tee shirt and dark blue jeans; her bare feet showing off her recent pedicure with light pink toe polish. Wasn't there a rule about not mixing pink and red?

The mattress dipped as I got on my knees, making her slide into me. Cupping her face with both my hands, I felt her warmth, her life force, and her trembling anticipation of my bite. With a secure grip, my fingers pressing firmly into her delicate skin, I tilted her head sideways. She was moving it more than I was. My, my, weren't we eager? No complaints here. It gave me a much better vantage point for that delicious vein as my lips lowered slowly to her neck, my fangs extended, gently grazing her skin. Her pulse sped up—*thump, thump, thump.* Tingles shot through her body like tiny electric currents. I could sense them. I could feel them.

A faint whimper escaped her lips, and excitement curled through me, my mouth opened wide, anticipating, hungry. I bit down into her hard, instantly tasting her delectable blood. Thick streams of velvety goodness swished inside my mouth, down my throat. I closed my eyes, squeezed them shut, and drank to the sweet sounds of Lily's melodic moans and sighs.

Until her voice faded, her head lay motionless in my hands. Like a kitten lapping milk, I flicked my tongue back and forth across the puncture marks in her neck to seal the wound so it would heal quickly without scarring, and, of course, I wanted to make sure there was no blood left behind.

A full-length mirror hung across the room on a wall, in between the closet and master bath. I was content with a full belly of blood, my anger just a shadow in the distance. Suddenly I stood in front of the mirror, never having felt my feet move. I was just there. Abracadabra. Magic. With normal eyes, my reflection looked back at me. They were a light bluish gray color, like the sky before it rains. They looked human, innocent, harmless. Soft, fine blond hair framed my face like thin silk curtains. A few wispy strands draped across my forehead above one of my eyes. Lily's blood smeared the corners of my mouth, still wet and sticky. I wanted to lick it. Saliva built up in my mouth. I swallowed hard, fighting the impulse to act like a monster. Sometimes it was nice to feel human, even though I wasn't. My stomach tightened, and waves of heat crawled up my back. A scream built up deep in my throat, but I held it there, couldn't let it out. Giving up, my tongue eased out of my mouth, across my lips. Back and forth, faster and faster, until all the blood was gone.

I hated being a vampire, hated drinking blood (not really), and hated being trapped inside during the day. Most of all, though, I hated Bronx.

After I finished my pity party in the mirror, I returned to the leather chair in the corner. A small table sat next to it with a bunch of books stacked messily on top, a wrought-iron floor lamp standing tall beside them. Vampires didn't need light to see, but it sure helped when you were reading.

I closed my eyes, remembering. A week ago, two blood donors had come over. Bronx thought it would be a great time to practice using persuasion. The one assigned to me was Celeste. She was forty-something, with mousy brown hair, a tall pencil-thin body, sunken cheeks, and dark circles under her eyes—obviously from years of donating blood.

"Before we eat, let us experiment with your ability, shall we?" he asked, voice eager through a childlike grin. He looked like he was going to get that lollipop from the window at the candy store.

"Okay. What do I do?"

He walked over to his donor—a petite redhead with freckles scattered around her face, big blue eyes, and oversized breasts. He asked her to wait in the other room. She turned and left without asking why. My, my, Bronx, what big *persuasion* you have. Then he focused his attention on Celeste, who seemed a little impatient with our dawdling before drinking from her. Within seconds her eyes were blank, empty, his.

"Abigail, come here and stare deep into her eyes."

I walked over and stood next to him. He placed his arm around me. Ignoring him the best I could, I turned my attention onto Celeste. Inspecting her hazily brown-colored eyes, I asked, "What do I do now?"

"It is a feeling you must release into her from yourself. Do not just look into her eyes. Feel into her eyes. Feel yourself entering into her and then make your requests to her."

"What should I ask her?"

"Anything you want." He kept his arm around me, giving me a tight squeeze. Encouraging me, I suppose.

What I really wanted was to have Celeste punch Bronx in the face. That was something I could feel from my inside out. I stared at her as hard as I could, pushing myself inside her eyes, digging deeper, penetrating beyond the surface. My head felt warm, tingly, and my hands trembled. Ignoring that sensation, I squeezed them into fists and held them at my sides. Right away, I could sense it working. I felt it. I knew it. Everything around me fell out of focus. But her eyes were clear; her mind was open, waiting for me to speak to it. She was mine. What a scary ability to have.

A smile curved my lips. You know those stupid facial expressions that give you away when you're up to something that can get you into trouble? I didn't want to smile, but it happened anyway. Envisioning Celeste punching Bronx in the face, I nudged that thought inside her mind as if getting her attention with my hands. She grinned at me, turned to Bronx, and hit him square in the nose—hard enough to make him bleed, but that was all. He let go of me, dropped his arms to his sides. There was anger in his eyes, sapphire flames building up like gasoline had just been splashed on them. I wanted to laugh, could feel it building inside my throat, but I held back. Goody for me.

But he didn't hit me. He didn't lose it like I'd thought he would. His body relaxed, head up, body straight and tall, fully controlling his anger. He reached over, placing his arm back around me, squeezing tight, a lot tighter than before. Maybe a teensy weensy bit of anger was showing. But he kept the rest of it perfectly hidden. Celeste stood motionless awaiting my next command.

"Very funny," he said, lips swaying closer to my ear. "Your attempts to piss me off are all in vain. I will always love you. You will always be mine. Soon, you will not be able to fight it any longer."

His lips trailed across my cheek. They weren't touching me, but I could feel their closeness. His eyes burned deeper; anger wasn't there anymore. It was different—not softer, too bold for that. Desire, lust, and something else, but it didn't matter. He was going to try to kiss me again. With a clenching stomach, I cringed, swallowed hard, but the lumps stuck in my throat. I jerked my head to the side just in time for his lips to connect with my cheek, a slow smack of movement on my skin, and then he lifted his head, looking down at me. He pretended not to notice my resistance, just like all

52

the other times. His hold on me tightening, I knew it was pointless to try to get away from him—until, of course, he released me.

A knock on the bedroom door jolted me out of that memory, and I quickly glanced at the clock. It was already nine o'clock at night. Since it went by much faster now, I no longer experienced time the way I had when I was human. I remembered many nights at The Beacon just watching the clock and wishing my shift was over. That kind of thing didn't happen anymore—maybe because thinking of time didn't matter when you had an eternity.

I got up from the chair and opened the door. Bronx was standing there holding a couple of bags. One was from Bloomingdales and the other from a store I'd never heard of, Foresters. Smiling as he handed them over, he said, "Here are some clothes for you to try on. I will be in the living room, please come model them for me."

Taking the bags, I thanked him and shut the door. Not in a rude way, but I was eager to see what he got me. I skipped over to the bed and turned the bags upside down. Everything inside them fell onto the mattress.

Lily was just waking up. Perhaps the rustling bags got her attention. She raised her arms over her head to stretch. In the middle of a yawn, she asked, "What's all of that?"

"I guess Bronx felt generous and bought me some new clothes. He wants me to model them for him."

Lily leaned forward and grabbed one of the dresses. After a brief inspection of the fabric, she handed it to me. "Try this one on first. You know he's crazy about you, and that dress will make him even crazier."

The dress she handed me was black, cut off just above my knees, and had a halter-shaped top. It was skin-tight, showing off all of my curves. Thank God I still had my curves. There was a pair of black wedge sandals that would match this dress perfectly. Lily must've thought the same thing since she was reaching for them.

"Thanks," I said while grabbing them from her. I put on the wedges, which were just the right fit, and then headed over to the bathroom. Running a brush through my hair, I stepped out in front of the full-length mirror, staring at my new appearance, satisfied with what I saw. Though letting Bronx see me like this was going to be challenging. I could barely keep him at bay when I wore jeans and tees. This outfit was definitely going to cause some unwanted attention.

"Hey, what's wrong?" Lily said, head tipped slightly to the side. "You look amazing. He's going to love it!"

"That's the problem." I walked back to the bed, my fingers sliding down a length of the soft, sheer curtain. "He will love it and then he'll try to kiss me again."

"And you have a problem with that?"

"Yes. Yes I do. I don't have romantic feelings for him. I just can't bear the thought of him trying to kiss me again."

Her eyebrows scrunched together. "I'm not a vampire, but that sounds like a human problem to me. It's hard to force yourself to feel a certain way. The best thing to do is stay honest with him and don't try to rush things. He's really nice, maybe a little scary, but he has always been nice when I'm around. Maybe in a while you'll start to share his feelings." She shrugged.

"And if I don't, then what? I'm kind of stuck here forever."

Lily's eyes widened, her full lips pressed in a thin line, but after a few moments I realized she definitely didn't have a come back.

So without even moving, I was back at the mirror again, staring blankly at it. Although I wanted to tell Lily how horrible Bronx really was and how I would flee from here in a New York second if I got the chance, I couldn't risk her having that knowledge. Bronx could easily persuade her and find out anything I had shared with her. Some secrets are best kept that way. Actually all of them are.

There was movement in the corner of my eye, the sound of bare feet padding closer and I didn't need to look to know who it was. Lily. She walked right up to me and hugged me, her body so warm and inviting. Her pulse was even, steady, and as I returned the embrace a flush of warmth swelled in my chest. A curiosity about all these heated feelings I'd been having bloomed in my mind. Was it normal for vampires to feel that? Surely it had to be the blood I'd drank and the warmth coming off her body now.

"It's going to be okay," she whispered. "You're going to be just fine. Plus, you should be extremely excited about tonight. You're getting out of this house and that should help you feel a lot better."

My thoughts now solely on the upcoming night, I nestled deeper inside the hug, my cheek resting comfortably against her shoulder. Lily was a little taller than me by a couple inches or so, and her skin was the color mine used to be: lightly tanned. We wore the same size, which was how I had the extra clothes here. She'd come twice in the first week after I was turned, the second time bringing me three pairs of jeans and three tee shirts. Thank God for her, since all I had before that was my work uniform.

"Okay. You're right." I nodded, pulling out of her arms.

She smiled at me with those beaming brown eyes and then grabbed the brush lying on the vanity in the bathroom. She ran it through my hair one last time. "Go on now before he comes in here to get you," she teased.

"Will you stay? I know you must want to get home, but I could really use your company. Just a little while longer."

"Adam will be here soon. I'd love to stay, but I don't think it's such a great idea. But I'll see you again at Pulse." She hesitated for a moment, brown eyes still locked on me.

"Okay. I guess that will work."

The friendship forming between Lily and I was unlike any of my friendships when I was human. It was special and wonderful, and very terrifying. The sting of what Mandy and John did still lingered inside me like a smell that never leaves your nose. And yet with Lily, I'd let most of my guard down, which was something I'd never imagined doing again.

Without lingering another moment, I headed out of the bedroom, holding my non-existent breath as I walked toward the living room. It was showtime.

Bronx admired me from across the room, tongue sliding over his lips and eyes sparkling like twin stars. Then there was a blur of speed and he was beside me, brushing his fingers through my hair. "You look gorgeous."

"Thank you." When I took a step backward, he grabbed a handful of my hair and jerked me back to him. It hurt, but not anything like it would if I were human.

"Abigail, Abigail, always trying to get away from me. The day is coming when you will no longer make those efforts."

Every insult you can imagine built up inside my throat, but I swallowed them down and just smiled. Several awkward minutes passed by and then he finally let me go. Straight away, I took off back to the bedroom where Lily helped me try on the other things while she waited for Adam to pick her up.

A black pencil skirt with a pale pink silk, button-up top—both skin-tight—presented another uncomfortable moment with Bronx. This time he leaned in and kissed my cheek. There was also a baby doll-styled dress that I liked much better than the last one. It was black with red lace on the chest area. There was a low scooping neckline that looked really sexy. It sat high above my knees, and my work shoes, the black Dr. Marten's mid-calf boots, looked amazing with it. Definitely the one I wanted to wear.

At quarter 'til midnight, I sat alone in the living room wearing the baby doll dress and black boots, hoping Bronx wouldn't make me change. Adam had picked Lily up over an hour ago and my captor was in the bedroom getting ready. The anxiety and excitement for the night ahead was overwhelming and I nervously twisted strands of my hair, making a mental note that I would most likely need to run the brush through it again before leaving.

Bronx strolled out from the hallway and made a beeline for the sofa where I was sitting. He wore black jeans and a long-sleeved, black button-up shirt with a red cross-shaped graphic on the back and extra stitching around the pockets on each pectoral. His hair was slicked to the sides and neatly tucked behind his ears. This was officially the first time I thought he looked nice since he'd turned me.

Because he loved to hear himself talk, he broke the silence and pretty much chatted my ear off until we heard a car pull into the driveway, though I was thankful he never asked me to change clothes. We were both outside in the blink of a human eye, and once I saw the wheels we were riding in, I felt my jaw drop open.

A black stretch hummer limo sprawled out, taking up most of the extended driveway. Holy crap! I'd never ridden in a limo before, let alone one that looked like a hummer. The streetlights provided minimal light, but the limo still glistened in it. A slow swing of the driver's door and a man stepped out and greeted us. He was forty-something, with thinning salt-and-pepper hair, a narrow face, and a pointed chin. The black suit he wore fit loosely on his tall, lanky frame. He guided us to the back door, the door you'd see the celebrities exit when heading to a premier event.

Bronx helped me crawl inside and I scooted down a slick leather sofa. Vegas-style neon pink and green lights lined the ceiling and around the dark-tinted windows. Bronx crawled in beside me and popped the top off a bottle of Veuve Cliquot, which conveniently sat in an iced bucket on the mini built in bar directly across from us. It was my favorite champagne.

He offered me a glass, sparkling white bubbles dancing at the top, and toasted to our evening. It was going to be a tough night to have a bad time. Cheers.

7

Pulse

OUR DRIVER PULLED UP TO THE CLUB, which was located on the bottom floor of a huge, three-story, rectangular-shaped building. The name of the club was in red neon script on an oval-shaped black sign dangling below a red awning. A line of people wrapped around the side of the building, waiting to get inside, gaped at our fancy vehicle as we came to a stop near the entrance. It made me feel nervous, and a little insecure, while I waited for the driver to come retrieve us. He motioned for me to exit first, taking my hand with his long, boney fingers. Once I was completely out of the limo, I felt a chill in the air. Out of habit, I brushed my arms with my hands even though I wasn't cold. Bronx tipped the driver and took my hand. When I tried to pull away, his grip just tightened, so I guess this wasn't an optional handholding.

Instead of getting in line behind all the other people, we walked straight up to the front. The dirty looks we got from the impatient crowd made me wonder if they'd stone us to death right here.

"Hey Bronx, this must be your new lady friend." The enormous doorman observed me with small, beady eyes. He was a little taller than Bronx, maybe six two, with dark skin, a round face, and weighed at least three hundred pounds. He was holding a tiny black flashlight with his left hand, and reached out to shake Bronx's with his right one, forcing my captor to let go of me. Thank God.

"Abigail, this is G," Bronx said. "G, this is the lovely Abigail."

"It's nice to meet you," I said as I shook his hand. His chubby fingers felt squishy.

"Likewise." G stepped to the side then hurried us in. Bronx slipped some cash into his awaiting fingers as we passed by.

"Your room's ready whenever you are," G called out to us before turning around to address the next person in line.

My eyes flitted all over, taking in everything I saw as we walked through the club. There were a lot of people already here. Candles and black lights dimly lit the darkened atmosphere. There were a couple bars, a dance floor, and a lounge area with loveseats, chairs, and tables. Royal blue, red, and black were the colors that decorated each zone.

Bronx placed his arm back around me as we made our way to the bar closest to the lounge. The glass countertop revealed black stones and white tea candles underneath. I set my arm on top and leaned down, allowing the counter to support me. A lot of people obviously knew Bronx, and he was talking to a few of them while waiting for his Crown and Coke. He ordered a vodka club soda with a lime for me. Vampires loved drinking alcohol (he'd told me on many occasions) since it took the edge off the blood cravings.

This was my first time seeing vampires aside from Bronx. There were so many of them interspersed with the humans, their scents easily discernable—dead, cold, and empty.

Overhearing Bronx saying my name, I looked back his way to find the outstretched hand of a vamp I didn't know. "Hey Abigail, I'm Brennan," gesturing to the guy beside him with his thumb, he added, "and this is William."

"Nice to meet you both, and please feel free to call me Abby."

Brennan was about the same height as Bronx and had short blond hair while William was a little shorter and had longer blond hair about down to his shoulders, kind of like a surfer. "No problem, Abby," Brennan corrected himself. "It's just so nice to meet the woman that took Bronx off the market. You wouldn't believe how many women he's turned down. You're going to make them all very jealous tonight."

"Very jealous," William agreed. He broke out into one of those annoying, pitchy laughs, slightly hunching over, hand rubbing his belly. "Where have you kept this one hidden, Bronx? There just might be some catfights tonight." Bronx elbowed William in the gut, making him step back. His laughter fading, he waved a surrendering hand. "Don't worry, man. I ain't flirting with your girl." Then he looked at me. "Sorry if I offended you, Abby."

I smiled, unable to think of anything witty to say, so I stayed quiet.

Bronx handed over my drink and apologized for William's juvenile outburst, though honestly I think it bothered him more than me. The two vampires continued to stand near us, so Bronx took my hand and pulled me away. As he led me through the lounge, I heard one of my old favorite songs playing, "Just Like a Man" by Way Out West.

Bronx sat down on a royal blue velvet loveseat, pulling me down next to him. There were two vampires sitting across from us on red, padded chairs, and I learned they were old friends of Bronx's, Damon and Valentina. We all shook hands.

"Bronx tells me that you're about a month reborn. Welcome to the new life," Valentina purred. She smiled, but it looked forced. She was tall and thin, her long legs tucked under a black leather mini-skirt; her shoulder-length red hair was so dark it almost looked black, and she was definitely in her forties when she was turned. Whatever age you are when you're "transformed" into our kind is just how old you'll look for the rest of eternity. No way to steal any youth back. Fortunately, there was no more aging either.

After taking a few sips of my drink, I said, "Thanks. There's been so much to learn and so many new experiences."

"Ah, yes. There is so much to learn," Damon added. With a silver chain dangling from the side pocket of his black leather pants, matching leather jacket, and scuffed black boots, he looked like he'd just rode in on a Harley. He wasn't wearing a shirt under his jacket, and the top of his chest looked like marble: solid, hairless, and glossy. "It's been so long I had almost forgotten."

"Abigail has done very well this past month. That is why we are here tonight." Bronx put his arm around me, fingers pressing into my shoulder.

Valentina scowled, but recovered quickly with a plastic smile. "Well good for you," she said, eyes glaring at me. "We are all so very proud of you." I didn't have to be a vampire to know she was being a bitch. That's something a woman can sense easily from other women, whether human, vampire, or anything else. I didn't need any advanced senses to determine that.

"Behave Valentina!" Damon scolded. "You should respect Bronx's decision to be with Abby." Apparently Damon had picked up on her bitchy attitude too. Was she being obvious on purpose? She was behaving like a scorned ex-girlfriend with a score to settle, but since Bronx didn't send out these vibes, I doubted they'd ever dated at all.

"Valentina," Bronx said, instantly getting her full attention. "Abigail is an amazing woman. In time you will see it for yourself. We are here to celebrate. Let us get back to that, shall we?" He pulled me closer to him. Anxiously, I kept sucking at my drink until I heard that annoying slurping sound a straw makes in an empty glass.

Turning to Bronx I said, "I'd like to get another drink at the bar." When he didn't say anything, I added, "Please."

He looked away from the other vampires, locking eyes with me. "There is a waitress that should be here any minute."

That answer wasn't good enough. I needed to get away from psycho bitch vampire and her man friend. Most of all, I wanted out of Bronx's embrace. I leaned over and whispered in his ear, "Please. The bar is close by and it'd be nice to just walk around a little more. I'll be in your sight the entire time."

He took a moment to answer me. "All right, but stay where I can see you. I will come get you shortly."

"Thanks." I got up lickety-split and dashed away without looking back. I felt Valentina's eyes all over me the entire time, and it made me want to offer her my picture since they lasted longer. But thankfully, I kept my mouth shut. I just didn't need any more drama right now.

Feeling much better at the bar, I straightened my shoulders and enjoyed a moment of pure relief. But before I could order my drink, I felt two warm hands cover my eyes. A hushed voice spoke from behind, warm breath on my ears. "Guess who?"

Excitement filling me, I jolted around and pulled Lily into a tight hug, then shook hands with Adam who stood to her left. "I'm so glad to see you guys," I said while making room for my friend to squeeze in beside me.

"I'll see you girls later," Adam said. "I've got to go meet someone."

"See ya later, alligator," Lily replied and then turned her attention to me. "So how are you holding up out here in the real world? Is it different than you thought?"

"Yes it is. I'm so nervous around the other vamp—"

Her hand rushed to my mouth, fingers pressing hard, cautious. "Shhh," she said, voice soft and low. "Be careful how loud you say that, it's a privacy thing at most clubs like this." She leaned a little closer, her lips close to my ear. "Don't worry about the other ones like you in here. They're all pretty nice—for the most part, anyway. Let me buy you a drink. It'll help take the edge off."

I couldn't talk about vampires at a vampire nightclub? Figuring there were more details to unfold, I accepted her gracious offer, and as soon as our drinks arrived, we cheered to the night's events. It was, after all, my first time out in public as a vampire, and I did look smoking hot in this baby doll dress. Lily looked pretty hot too. She wore a stretchy navy tank dress, tan, knee-high boots, and a French braid pulled back her hair, loose strands framing her face.

Glancing back toward Bronx, I saw Valentina had moved next to him and the three of them seemed enthralled in whatever they were talking about, which only encouraged me to ask Lily more questions. "There are a lot of humans in here that don't know about vamp—I mean us?" I said it like a question, voice barely a whisper.

She nodded, eyes wary.

"I thought this club was a blood donor hot spot." My lips fumbled for the straw in my drink.

"Abs, most of these clubs rely on humans for a lot of their business profits. They can't just shut them out because of that, so they designed these places for us to secretly coexist. Only "your kind" and the donors know about the back rooms where the feedings take place. There is heavy security throughout the club, mostly "your kind" since they can sense the difference between a donor and just a normal person. We never discuss anything about "your kind" or what we do with them unless it's someone we know. If anyone is ever caught slipping on this, you never see him or her again. None of us ever dare to risk it."

"That makes sense. Thanks for telling me. Bronx sort of forgot to mention that." Not that he needed to. He wouldn't give me a chance to talk to anyone that he didn't approve of, let alone some innocent human.

We sat in silence a few short minutes, smiling, people watching, and sipping our drinks. Then I saw Bronx get up and head my way. *Oh great. Here he comes to ruin my night.*

I flashed him a smile as he approached, hoping it would be a good move on my part. He smiled back and grabbed my hand, pulling me out of the barstool. "It is time for you to come with me." His gaze locked on me, and it felt like he was trying to use persuasion on me, warm invisible claws prying at my mind, but that feeling quickly passed as I stood up.

"Let me just say goodbye to Lily." Then I looked over at her with desperate eyes and leaned down to hug her. "See ya later."

Bronx yanked my arm, pulling me away.

Gee, how freaking rude. He couldn't wait two minutes for me to say goodbye to Lily? Even worse, he never acknowledged that she was there. She must have felt horrible. I decided to keep my thoughts to myself on this, storing them in the back of my mind. At the moment, it seemed like Bronx was easy to provoke, and that was the absolute last thing I wanted to do here at the club.

Bronx led me around the lounge area and I glimpsed Valentina sitting back next to Damon. She glared at me as we passed, of course, what else did I expect? We came to a narrow hallway where a security guard stood blocking it: dark skin, a little shorter than Bronx, stocky build. His black tee barely stretched around his muscles and he'd definitely been no stranger to the gym before he was made a vampire.

He must've recognized Bronx because he let us pass without speaking a single word. My captor led me a little farther down and then we turned into another hallway. Doors lined the walls, four on each side. Walking in the last door on the right, the room was big enough to hold two modern-looking black couches, a couple matching chairs, a few end tables, and two male blood donors. They were sitting on one of the couches. Blood-colored shag carpet covered the floor. Pictures of the Renaissance era with thick gaudy frames hung on the black lacquer walls.

Bronx waved an arm toward the empty couch. Listening like a good little girl, I sat down and immediately noticed a bottle of champagne in an iced wine bucket on a nearby end table. He grabbed the bubbly, a couple glasses, and then sat down next to me. The donors stared at us quietly as Bronx poured our drinks. "To us, and of course, your first night out," he said as he handed me an overfilled glass, fizzy white bubbles trickling down the side of it.

"Thanks." Our glasses clicked and then I chugged it down.

Bronx gave me a refill. "After we finish our champagne," he said, looking at me, then shifting his eyes toward the men across the table, "we will feed on these donors. You can choose which one you would like to be your first public donor." Bronx and both of the donors flashed smiles at me, all three of them seeming eager to get on with it. No reason to keep them waiting.

I let my nose decide which donor I wanted. The guy on the right had a clean, soapy-fresh scent so I got up and sat down beside him. He was slightly overweight, brunette, with thick eyebrows and dressed in black slacks and an egg-colored polo. "I want this one," I said.

In the blink of an eye Bronx was sitting next to the other donor; the four of us barely fit on the same couch. He smiled and then turned toward his donor. He was so quick to eat and never really made small talk with any of them. I, on the other hand, wanted to at least know my donor's name. "Hi, I'm Abby Tate." I reached out my hand.

Looking very confused he shook my hand and replied, "I'm, uh, D-Da-David."

"Don't be afraid, David. I just wanted to get to know you a little before biting you. It may seem strange to you, but I'm new at this."

"You're a, uh, a new vampire?" His eyes lit up and I felt a wave of excitement flow through him.

"Yup. One month old today."

"Wow, uh, I, uh, never, I never had a new one before."

Smiling at him I playfully responded, "Well, David, you're about to have yourself a new one. Is it okay if I go ahead and begin?"

Leaning closer, begging me with his eyes, David replied, "Puh, please go uh, a-ahead."

"Your wish is my command." I grabbed his head, tilted it to the side, and bit down into his neck. This donor was quiet but the vibrations in his body spoke volumes. I drank my fill, sealed the wound, and then laid him back onto the couch. In a flash I was on the other couch. I wasn't alone for long. Bronx was there and I didn't like the way he was looking at me.

"Abigail, enough of the games," he said. "I need you. Now, more than ever."

And that's when I really knew he was using it: persuasion. He was without a doubt trying to use it on me, its sharp claws scraping at the edge of my mind, the threat of him penetrating inside and gaining control increasing, intensifying. *My mind.* Panic and terror ripped through me. *He's not getting in! I won't let him in! It's my mind!* Fear turned to anger, heated waves swirling from my core, expanding in my chest. The room warped—like it had a pulse, growing and shrinking in a pumping rhythm. But then it stopped moving and my body relaxed slightly, the anger still lingering in the pit of my belly. I was still me. Bronx never got inside. And I wasn't sure what to do about that. To my knowledge, no one had ever been able to resist Bronx's persuasion, but I didn't have any more time to ponder that. I needed to act or Bronx would know his ability wasn't working.

Digging deep inside, I fought the urge to wince as I leaned forward and hugged him. Surely that would suffice and make him think he controlled me, but I was getting a sick feeling this time that wouldn't be enough. And he confirmed my fears by grabbing my hair, yanking my head back, and kissing me—hard, sloppy, and desperate smacks of his lips on mine.

My stomach twisted and my tongue folded on a gag. There was no way I could keep this up. The act was over.

I tried to push Bronx off but he wouldn't budge, his sloppy tongue moving all over my mouth, making my skin crawl with tension, my belly churn more violently. Still holding the hair on the back of my head with one hand, he grabbed the exposed part of my thigh with the other and started moving up. Up beyond the fabric of my dress, and it just kept going. I tried with all the strength I could muster to push him off, to no avail. Though I could obviously block his power of mind control, he was still so much stronger than me physically. With no other options, I screamed, "Stop it, you're hurting me, stop it, stop it now!"

But he didn't stop. His fingers reached the outer edge of the boy shorts that I wore under my baby doll dress. I just kept punching him and screaming for him to stop. The donors were out cold, enjoying their euphoria, not hearing my panicked cries, but I knew there was no way they could help me even if I could wake them up.

Bronx was too strong. He could take all three of us.

Slowly, his fingers crept under the elastic edge of my boy shorts. Desperation fell over me in a heavy wave. Still punching him with tight fists, I frantically screamed, "Please, Bronx, stop! Please don't do this!" between broken gasps.

In a blur he was on top of me, straddling me, pressing me deeper into the couch, his hands violating me in places they didn't belong. All that training had been for nothing. I couldn't stop him, my advanced strength failing me. Consumed by raw fear, a helpless feeling of being completely out of options, I cried, hard, tears falling in heavy streams down my cheeks.

Then suddenly, everything happened so fast. The door flew open and I could barely see the dark-skinned security guard that had allowed us back to this room. Bronx froze, grabbed his neck, and started gagging, like he was choking or his throat was caving in. As he held his neck, his body started to float up against the wall. Slowly. Until his head bumped into the ceiling. He remained frozen there, gagging. Terror preventing me from speaking, I looked over at the guard and boy did he look pissed. "You—come here," he demanded in a firm tone.

Without saying a word, I got up and walked over to him.

"I want you to stand in the hallway, right there." He pointed his finger to the spot. "Do not move until I get there!"

Nodding because I still couldn't talk, I did as he instructed and walked out into the hall, the door slamming shut behind me. That guard had special powers. Overwhelming powers. He'd overpowered Bronx. He'd saved me from being raped. I felt my body shudder as I replayed what just happened in my mind. Was he an Enforcer? But if so, why would he be working here at a nightclub? Watching Bronx overpowered was encouraging—maybe he would help me?

The door opened and the guard came out, face hard and stiff, saying "don't mess with me" with his eyes. I swallowed hard, my questions sticking in my throat. "Come with me." He grabbed my hand and pulled me down the hall. He stopped just before the hall ended, a different security guard now blocking the doorway. "That kinda crap ain't allowed in here. Your guy's gonna have to cool off before he can come out of that room. You're gonna need to go wait for him in the lounge. I'll have him show you where to sit."

Voice still paralyzed, I just stared at him and nodded, letting him know I understood. He then handed me off to the other security guard. This one was much smaller, about five ten, slender, his long brown hair pulled back in a ponytail, and he sported the same black-on-black attire that all other security guards wore. Pulling me by the arm across the lounge, he then sat me down in an unoccupied blue velvet love seat. "Just stay here until your boyfriend cools down, maybe an hour or so." His voice was sharp and very unfriendly.

With a shrug of my shoulders, my throat loosened and I finally found my voice. "He's not my boyfriend." Mustering more courage, I pressed on, "Do you realize what you guys just saved me from? I need help. Please. Can you help me?"

"Just shut the hell up and do what I said." His gaze hardened, as if to add more threat to his words, then he swung on his heel and marched away.

What kind of crap happened in those back rooms? Did they really think Bronx and I were just extremely aggressive lovers that beat each other for fun? Or was *that* what vampires really were like—overly sexual, kinky, provocative? I knew we did have animal instincts and super-human powers, so perhaps that was how some of them acted. I couldn't stop thinking about what would've happened if those security guards hadn't come in. Even though they were both assholes, which was probably part of their job description, I was still grateful to them. I just wished they'd let me leave before Bronx came out. Not that I knew where to go, but anywhere was better than being with him.

Feeling like crap, and wondering if I looked it too, I started combing my fingers through my hair. When I finished, a cocktail waitress made her way over to me. "Can I get you anything, honey?" she asked in a bubbly Southern accent. Her chestnut hair bobbed on her shoulders, full of curls. She wore a black mini skirt with a matching tube top.

"I'll have two Kettle club sodas. Make those doubles, please."

"No problem, darlin'." She turned around and started making her way to the bar, stopping to check on a few other customers.

I looked down at my lap, heavy in thought about everything that had happened, and worried sick about when Bronx would be released from the back room.

That was when I smelled something that could make everything worse. And before I could do anything, he was sitting right beside me.

67

"Hi, I'm Tyler Jensen," he said, hand extended out to me.

My senses were working overtime. This guy, this human guy, smelled amazing. There was one big problem, though. He was definitely not a donor.

8

Escape

I GAZED INTO HIS GREEN EYES, unable to move my mouth. Tyler Jensen was very good looking...I mean really, really good looking. His face was fresh-shaven with two full lips centered above his squared jawline, and his eyes so brilliant green they looked like jewels. His short brown hair was messy, as if he'd taken his hands and rubbed it both ways out of frustration, then locked it in place with some type of gel or hairspray. It was actually a great style for men who wore it well, which he did. His jeans were slightly faded, and his off-white, button-up shirt with dark gray stitching included a dragon head situated on his left pectoral. The sleeves were rolled just above his elbow, revealing a little muscle definition in his forearm. The top part of his chest peeked above an unfastened button, smooth and slightly sculpted. If Bronx came out here and saw me with this human, it would be huge trouble for us both.

My body cringed at the thought of Bronx. What a freaking monster he was—violent and evil. But what could I do about it? Here I sat, waiting for him to cool down enough to come out here and get me. When would that be? Would the security guards decide sooner rather than later to release him from that back room? Since my captor had been friendly with every vampire in here, certainly could allow him special privileges, and that meant he could be out here in just a few short minutes.

Panic iced my spine, twisted up my neck. This guy couldn't be sitting here. It was impossible for me to leave since the guards were watching me so I needed to do something quick to make him go away. But I was drawing blank, nothing coming to mind. With a shake of my head, I finally managed, "You can't sit here." But it didn't sound like I meant it: weak, not intimidating at all.

His head leaned sideways, probing me with his twin green orbs. His lips curved slightly, half smiling. "And why would that be?" His voice was deep, beautiful. And his hand still hovered in front of me, waiting for me to take it.

And why would that be? I didn't have an answer. Think fast. "Someone else is sitting there." Lie, lie, lie.

"Well, I can at least sit here until they get back. I'm sure whoever it is won't mind." He inched his hand a little closer.

I looked past him, toward the hallway in the back. The security guard was looking at someone's ID. Bronx wasn't coming yet. Glancing back at Tyler, I swallowed, hard, slow. "I'm um." My gaze fell to his waiting hand, then drew back up at his eyes. "I'm Abby Tate." Then I grabbed his hand.

Like a bomb exploding, shockwaves blasted through my body. My world was moving, pulsating, changing and suddenly I wasn't in the club anymore. I was somewhere else, dream-like but real.

Tyler and I were driving fast down a road that easily could've been a highway. There were bright lights all around us, flashing by as we passed. I was quietly sitting on the passenger's side. He was driving and talking about something that seemed pretty important. His eyebrows furrowed as he spoke. "It's the safest place we can go. I know you have a lot of questions and I promise I'll explain everything."

"I don't think you understand how serious this is. Bronx will find me. He'll track me down. There's really nowhere I can hide from him. You seem to know more than you should, so please explain to me why you're helping me. How do I even know I can trust you? What happened when I touched your hand?" I shoved my hair behind my ears, my eyes locked on him.

He glanced over. "Abby, you can trust me."

Then, with no warning, I was back in the club, sitting next to this mysterious human. "What the hell was that?" my voice trembled.

"What do you mean?" His face didn't match his question. He knew what I meant, it was evident in his eyes.

I didn't know which I wanted more—him to leave or to explain what the hell that was. "You know what I mean. I saw us going somewhere. Where?" Curiosity always wins. I just hoped I wouldn't turn out like the cat.

He looked away, staring down at the floor. His pulse sped up: I could sense each rapid pump of his heart, smell the increase of his blood flow.

The waitress returned. I signed the receipt (open tab on Bronx's credit card) and took the drinks from her. She hurried off with a few other beverages still on her tray.

"Are both of those yours?" Tyler asked and that's when I noticed he was looking at me again.

I answered with a slow nod.

He reached over and took one of the drinks out of my hand. "What are you doing?" I asked, a spark of anger igniting in my core, but I didn't take it back from him—yet.

His lips wrapped around the tiny black straw, then the icy beverage lowered inside the glass. "I love these," he said, the straw still in his mouth. "The soda water and lime make it such a crisp, refreshing drink. Can you taste them the same way I can?"

Forget the fact that he just rudely took one of my drinks. What the hell did his question mean? My stomach clenched, replacing my anger with fear.

He leaned in closer, lips traveling toward my ear. "You know, can vampires taste things the way people can?"

Something cold slithered up my spine, then it twisted into hot flames. I knew I needed to get away from this guy but my body was paralyzed by his question, that crazy vision. He knew about vampires, but he wasn't a donor. He'd called me out on being one. Denying it wouldn't get me answers, but admitting it could get us both killed. I went for the death wish. "How do you know that? Who are you?"

"I can explain all the details once you leave with me. I can help you, please trust me. We need to leave now."

"Leave? Are you crazy? They're watching me. They won't—" I scoped the club, the bar, the lounge, and the doorway to the hall. Nothing looked out of order. No one was paying attention to this guy and me. Nerves rolled circles in my gut, pushing the lead balloon up. "They won't let me leave." I started fidgeting with my hair. Stupid old human nerves, or I was the biggest scaredy-cat vampire ever.

He reached out his hand again, but I wasn't about to touch it this time. "I know you don't know me, but can you please try to find it inside yourself to trust me? I'm here to help you, I swear."

"How do you know me?" I demanded. "Why are you so confident that you can help me?" I stopped playing with my hair; my fists were balled, neatly lying on my lap.

He didn't look scared, intimidated, *squat*. His hand was still extended toward me, slightly waving. "Please just come with me. I promise all the answers you want."

I didn't want to touch that hand. No way. No freaking way. I stared at it as if it were the pink elephant in the room. "Like I said before, I can't leave. Not with you, not with anyone."

Tyler smiled. Then he started counting down: "five, four, three, two..." The instant he said "one," a fight broke out on the other side of the lounge near the bar. Two guys were swinging at each other, screaming obscenities. The bartender and a few security guards were running at human speed toward the brawl. The crowd began forming a half circle around the debacle, some fighting to get a better view by pushing their way through the sea of onlookers. Tyler grabbed my hand and stood up, pulling me up with him. "Come on, that's our cue. Time to go, now."

I had several reasons to follow him out of the bar. One: I needed to know what the hell he was talking about. Two: I needed to know how he knew about me. Three: I needed to know what that vision meant, what it even was. And four: What other choice did I have? Sit there and wait for Bronx to come get me? Yeah, that sounded real smart, didn't it?

As we hustled through the club, I was thankful no new visions appeared. Tyler kept a tight grip on my hand, pulling me behind him. We dodged other people as they ran past us in the opposite direction wanting to see what was going on. No one seemed to notice us running away from the fight, away from the crowd, and ultimately out the front doors.

He didn't let go of my hand until we came up to a silver 2008 Audi A4 in the back of the parking lot. There were parked cars all around us, providing some cover for our escape. He opened the door, hurried me into the passenger seat, and then quickly shut it. I watched him run around the front hood to the driver's side where he jumped in quick, fired up the engine as fast as humanly possible, and sped out of the parking lot, down a dark side street, and then turned onto a four-lane highway. Déjà vu. This was what I'd seen in that vision.

"Where are we going?" I demanded. My body was turned sideways in the seat, facing Tyler. He wore a seatbelt; I didn't. I guess I was a badass vampire after all.

"I showed you that vision so you would leave with me." He glanced at me, then back to the road, hands gripping the steering wheel so tight his arms shook. "We're going somewhere safe."

"Safe?" I said it like a question. "There *is* nowhere safe. Bronx will find me. He'll track me down. There's really nowhere I can hide from him." I turned around, staring out the window. Everything was blank, thoughts crowding my vision.

Tyler took my hand inside his. My world started moving, breathing, pulsing. I wasn't in the car anymore. I was inside his head. Or he was in mine.

It felt like I was really there but in my mind I knew I wasn't. It was like an outer body experience, based on what I'd heard about them. We were in a house, sitting on a dark brown leather sofa surrounded by plain white walls. We were staring at each other. Tyler was talking. "I know this is a lot to take in. It's a lot to believe. But you have to. I saw that you were in trouble. I get these premonitions, and then it's my choice if I try to change them or not. I try not to get involved unless it's really bad. Then I feel it's my duty to do something, to help out. So when I saw you, when I saw what that guy did to you, well, I knew I had to help."

"Premonitions?" I asked, looking deeper into his eyes. "You see things that happen in the future?"

He nodded. "Yes."

"But I saw it too. Were you showing it to me?"

He shrugged. "Yes I was." His eyes flitted around the room, then back to me.

"You know that I'm a vampire, but you still helped me? Why?"

He took a deep breath, held it for a moment, then slowly released it. "I learned about vampires a long time ago. Apparently, that's against your rules, but hey, I can't control what my premonitions show me. I know you won't hurt me. You're one of the good ones. Just don't tell on me either, okay?"

I swallowed, nodding. "So you've helped other vampires?"

"Just a couple. Mostly I've helped other people."

"Why are you helping me?" I asked again. "You know this could get you killed?"

He stared at me, eyebrows crimped up, voice soft, saying, "I saw how you became a vampire. I feel horrible that I couldn't stop that from happening. He kept you trapped in a house somewhere and the premonitions never revealed enough for me to find you...I needed to see the outside of the house, what the yard looked like, what the area around it looked like, but he never let you go outside. Then finally, I saw you at Pulse."

"So you're helping me because you feel sorry for me? That's not a good enough reason to die." I stood up and was across the room in one swift motion. There was a fireplace, an unburned log, red brick mantle. I stared into it, pacing back and forth, wooden floors creaking under my boots. I glanced over at Tyler, still sitting on the sofa. He watched me, a look in his eyes that shouldn't have been there. It wasn't pity. It wasn't fear. Both of those would've been expected. Desire, attraction, and passion blazed in his perfect green eyes.

"You're not telling me everything, are you, Tyler?" I kept pacing.

He nodded. "I've told you everything important. The parts you need to know."

I flashed across the room, standing over him, glaring down at his widened eyes, but surprisingly he didn't flinch as I knelt down, closer and closer. "You're a human that sees futuristic visions. That's all you can do. How are you going to help me? Bronx will find us and kill us both. He's stronger than me. He's evil. He's a monster." Anger surged, heating my entire body. Tingles crawled up my neck, on my head. My stomach clenched, mouth watering...it wasn't anger. Crap. Hunger. I needed blood. I gasped.

Tyler's brows drew together. "What's wrong?"

I stood up straight and stepped back. "I'm going to need blood soon."

In a snap, I was back in the car with Tyler. Quickly jerking my hand away, I rubbed it, trying to remove the residue from that vision. Obviously, our situation just got a whole lot worse. Unless, of course, Tyler knew a few blood donors. The look on his face, however, told me he didn't. Wasn't this just perfect?

9

Plan

WE WERE SOMEWHERE NEAR Savannah, Georgia when we finally pulled into the driveway of a small, colonial styled house with a cute little set of stairs leading up the front porch. Oak trees canopied above us and down the street as far as I could see, and a neatly trimmed row of bushes separated houses on both sides of this one. We slipped inside a two-car garage that looked more like a storage unit with only around thirty minutes to spare before dawn. Brown cardboard boxes were stacked in rows, some almost as high as the ceiling. His car was parked in the only opening. There was a workbench against the back wall, ambushed by more boxes. An access door, most likely leading inside the house, was straight in front of us.

Tyler got out, came around and opened my door, then extended his hand. I took it and let him lead me to the access door, which was conveniently unlocked. Still holding his hand, I followed him inside.

A dark laundry room greeted us. He walked as if he knew his way around, not bothering to turn on any lights. I didn't need it anyway. Following him down a narrow hallway—plain white walls, wooden floors—we passed an opening to a small kitchen, continuing straight ahead, though not for long. The hall opened onto a bigger room with two dark brown leather sofas sitting across from each other, a rectangular-shaped coffee table between them. A fireplace made up the back wall, accented by a red brick mantle, exactly how it looked from Tyler's vision. A shudder moved through my body, this whole situation beyond overwhelming, then I looked to the right and found a much bigger problem than confirming I'd already seen this room.

Behind one of the sofas, was a wall of big, open windows.

In a rush, Tyler pulled a cord and released the blinds. There were burgundy curtains, white flowers sewn on them, sweeping away from the windows and attached to the wall. Still hurrying, he unhooked them and they fell away from the wall, then he tugged them the rest of the way until the windows were fully covered. Coming back toward me, he hit a light switch, then motioned for me to have a seat on the sofa. I obeyed like a good little vampire.

On the rest of our drive to this house, Tyler had told me that he didn't know of any blood donors. Working with the two other vampires didn't give him any knowledge about where we got our food. He'd never known people willingly fed us until he saw premonitions of me doing it and all of those visions had been in Florida. Not really going to help us now that we'd left the state.

I leaned back on the sofa. "This is bad," I said.

He sat down beside me, keeping a little distance between us. "Why?"

Who said there weren't such things as stupid questions? "You really have to ask?"

He nodded, green eyes searching me. "The other vampires I worked with—er uh, helped—they could go long periods of time without blo...eating."

"They were probably a lot older than me. Young vampires need blood more often."

"How often?"

"I was drinking about two-to-three donors a night."

His face started to crumble. He now understood what I meant by saying this was bad.

"Can't you just drink from me?" he asked. Not needing *that* temptation at the moment, I was up and over by the fireplace in a flash. He gasped. "How'd you do that?"

"Vampire magic," I said, voice a little smart. "I can't take blood from you. You're an innocent. I've never had innocent blood."

"What's that mean?" He scratched his head, started to get up.

"Don't!" I yelled. "Please stay where you are."

He dropped back down on the sofa, eyes wide, hand on his chest. "This is officially the first time you've scared me. What do you mean by 'innocent blood'?"

"You're unbitten. Supposedly that means you'll taste better than any blood I've ever had. I don't think I should start sampling that with our current situation." I turned around and stared at the log in the fireplace. "My bite will make you useless to me anyway. And if you really can help me, then I need you, uh, sober." After further explaining how my bite would make him feel, an idea sparked in my mind. "I think there's someone I can call that can tell us where the blood donor clubs are around here."

"Really? There are blood donor clubs here?"

Taking a couple human steps toward him, I nodded. "Yes, they're everywhere. So are vampires."

Apparent relief flushed across his face and he leaned back so he could fish a cell phone from his pocket. "Who are you going to call?" he asked.

"There's a donor that I became friendly with. Surely she'd know how to help."

In a blink of time I was sitting on the sofa across from him, the windows at my back. He studied me, didn't hand me the phone. Watching him closely, I was unsure what else to say. After a minute of playing the staring game, he stood up, rounded the coffee table, and then sat down beside me, still keeping a little distance but not as much as before. With an outstretched arm, he handed me the cell. "Call her. If she can't help, we really need to know sooner than later."

I nodded, took the phone, then hesitated for a moment, trying to visualize her number from the time I'd called her before. Would it be enough to remember the number now? Closing my eyes, I started punching in her digits from memory, feeling hopeful. Until Tyler jerked the phone out of my hand.

"What the hell?" I demanded.

"You can't just call her without blocking the number. Most cell phones have Caller ID. What if...?"

"How do I block it?" Smart guy, that Tyler.

"First press the star button, then the number six, then seven." He handed the phone back to me with those three digits already entered. The small illuminated screen was waiting for me to enter Lily's number.

Pressing the highlighted numeric buttons with confidence, I was absolutely positive I'd got it right.

After three rings, she answered.

"Hello?"

"Lily, hey it's Abby."

"Abby? Oh my gosh, Abby! Are you okay? Where are you?"

"Listen, I can't tell you where I am. I'm okay. Don't worry." I gripped the phone tighter.

"Bronx is on a rampage looking for you. He questioned everyone at the club and no one seemed to notice you leave. The club's security is even helping him with the search, since it was their responsibility to keep an eye on you while they confined him."

Well, what had I expected her to say? Things were going just peachy? Yeah right. "I can't go into all the details right now," I said. "I have a favor to ask you."

Tyler scooted closer, reached over, and put his hand on my leg, just above my knee. A bold move on his part, but I chose not to do anything about it at the moment. He pressed his fingers gently into my skin, massaging in short, careful movements. Perhaps he was trying to help relax me and save his tiny cell phone from being squashed into a million pieces. Yeah sure—I remembered what I'd seen in his eyes. There was much more going on here and I wasn't going to be naïve about it.

Lily took a deep breath into the phone. "I'll help you if I can."

My body relaxed a little, and my grip loosened on the cell phone. "Do you know of blood donor clubs in other states? Is there a list of places, nationwide, that you could provide to me?"

"Ye—yeah, there is. It would be easier to know where you need one, though."

I could sense her desire to help me. And her fear of what would happen if she did, which was why I couldn't tell her where I was. She couldn't give away information if she didn't know it. "I just got off a plane but I doubt this is where I'll stay. Can you e-mail me a list of the top blood donor clubs in every state? That would be easiest since I don't know exactly where I'm going." I hated lying to her, but it would hopefully keep her safe.

"Why are you running? Where are you? I don't want anything to happen to you. He's pissed. Abby, please talk to me."

"You need to be careful around Bronx! He's crazy, and that's why I ran away. It's best that you not know where I am."

A few quiet moments passed as I silently prayed Lily would consider my request. Tyler removed his hand from my thigh. He lifted it up, behind me, pressing down into my shoulders, trailing up and down my back. It felt great. I couldn't even pretend that I didn't like it—I leaned forward just a little bit so he would have a better angle. Tingles spread over my body like tiny wildfires. Waves of relief washed over me. Should he really be doing this? Should I be allowing him to? I started to feel guilty and a little uncomfortable, but then Lily chimed back in and made me forget about Tyler's massage therapy.

"All right," she said with conviction. "There's a roster of info that all donors are given. Just in case we move around which a lot of us do. I'll e-mail that to you. What e-mail should I use?"

I looked over at Tyler and silently mouthed my need for an e-mail address. He got up, walked out of the room, and then returned with a notebook and pen. After writing it down, he handed me the notebook, an e-mail address written across the top of the paper. After reading it out loud to Lily, she repeated it back to me, confirming she'd got it right, then told me I'd have an e-mail within the hour. Since I trusted her, no second thoughts were given about the conversation. I knew Bronx was on her ass, but I also knew her loyalty was with me. As we said our good-byes, Tyler left the room again. A couple minutes later, he returned with a laptop and set it on the coffee table. He glanced over, eyes locking onto mine—penetrating, deep, bottomless. They were filled with so much more than just curiosity and a desire to help. There was a whole different kind of desire there. A danger field if I was reading them right, which I knew I was.

10

Determined

DAYBREAK WAS UPON US. The house had officially become my daytime prison. A bottle of Smart Water in tow, Tyler headed back into the living room. I sat on the sofa with the wall against my back, staring across the room at the burgundy curtains with white flowers. He sat down beside me and I glanced over at him. Clearly, he should have been asleep by now—his body must be running on pure adrenaline. At some point he was going to crash. "Aren't you tired yet?" I asked.

He gave a long sigh. "I'll lie down soon. Too amped up at the moment."

"Why don't you try lying down now? I'll keep an eye on the computer for Lily's e-mail. I'm not sure having someone come here is a good idea, so we'll most likely need to go to one of the clubs tonight. I won't be able to go much longer than that without blo...eating."

No response. He just gazed at me, eyes wanting, longing.

Turning away, I stared at the fireplace.

"Abby?" He said it like a question.

I didn't want to look at him, not into those beautiful green eyes. "What?"

"Can I see your fangs?"

You've got to be kidding me. I wanted to tell him there was absolutely no way I'd show him. But instead said, "Okay." Turning my gaze back toward him, I felt like a show-n-tell project. So I flashed a big smile hoping to get this over with. His eyes widened with obvious fascination and for some reason that embarrassed me. In a hurry, I dropped the smile and sealed my lips.

"Don't be embarrassed," he said. "You're beautiful." He leaned in a little closer, lifting his right hand to my mouth, stroking my lips with his fingers.

His touch brought an unexpected wave of excitement rushing through me, catching me off-guard. I chuckled, hoping to keep what I'd just felt concealed. Continuing their gentle exploration, the tips of his fingers crept a little bit inside my mouth. I could tell he was gauging me, waiting for some kind of reaction, and when I didn't give him one, he took that as permission to push all the way inside. As he traced along my oversized canines, I swallowed hard, slow. The possibility he'd cut his fingers was heavy in my mind and it made my worries tumble around in my belly like static rocks. If I smelled blood, could I resist it? Better not to test it at all. Carefully intervening, I put my hand on top of his, assisting his fingers around my mouth.

"Those are really sharp," an observation I already knew.

"It was really strange for me at first. I still haven't gotten used to them." I spoke softly, barely moving my mouth.

After allowing only a few more seconds of fang probing, I gently pulled his hand away. As I did, he laced his fingers with mine. My nerves racing, I tried to look at the bright side of at least not being sucked into another one of visions as I pondered when I should remove my hand altogether. "Look, Tyler, I really appreciate you helping me but I'm just not sure *this* can be anything else. You're human. I'm a vampire. Please don't take this the wrong way or as an insult. I just...we just need to stay focused. You need sleep. I need to figure out my next blood source." My free hand fidgeted with my hair, my stomach clenching tighter, which meant I was nervous.

That was really, really bad. How could I possibly like Tyler Jensen? Could I be feeling this way simply because of everything we'd been through the last twelve hours? Surely that had to be it. It had to be the adrenaline pumping through my veins, just like it was for him. Humans needed to be close in times of crisis and uncertainty, and that same feeling was amplified for vampires. I'd already learned how sexual vamps could be back at Pulse with Bronx, so that of course had to explain the weird feelings I was experiencing for Tyler.

He looked away, grip tightening around my hand, and stared down at the floor. Watching him take a few deep breaths as if there was something he wanted to say, but was unsure how to say it, I tensed, a feeling of dread blooming inside me. Another anxious moment passed, then he looked back up, his gaze hardened with determination, saying, "I feel like I've known you for months. That's how long I've had premonitions of you. Each one makes me feel closer, which is actually the reason why I had to help you."

Afraid to meet his eyes, but doing it regardless, I stole a few seconds to mull over what he said. Oddly, I *did* understand, but it wasn't wise to admit it out loud. Too many questions, too many problems; it was stupid to add more to the fire. "I've only seen two of your visions so I guess I can *try* to understand that a little, but the reality is that we just met. I've never seen you before tonight." Glancing down at our interlocked hands, my confusing feelings became a whirlwind of torment in my mind.

Time stretched, and he still hadn't said anything. When I looked back up, he was staring at me, his eyes saying things they probably shouldn't. He arched a brow, his lips compressing before he finally said, "I don't know how else to say this without just coming right out with it. I'm not expecting you to love me yet or anything, but you have to admit you do feel something."

Wasn't that straightforward and to the point? I'd always admired that trait in people, so why was it freaking me out right now? Oh maybe because he sort of just said the "L" word. My defenses shot up; invisible walls came crashing down. I tried to pull my hand away but his grip got even tighter. I knew I could break it, but I wasn't a monster. I didn't want to hurt him, fragile little human, amazingly good-looking human, but I wanted him in one piece. He'd helped me get away from Bronx. Didn't that make him my knight in shining armor? Surely that merited him a crazy pass right now. "So that's why you helped me?" I asked, stupid question.

He nodded, slowly. "I guess you could say that I fell in love with you through my premonitions. I can't control what I see. For three months all I saw was you, every night, everyday. After the first few weeks of watching you, I began to develop feelings for you. But I was afraid. You would definitely be a vampire by the time I found you, and I wasn't even sure how I could help you. I just knew I needed to try. I needed to find you and then we could figure things out from there. I couldn't just leave you trapped with him." His answer sank us further into that dangerous emotional quicksand and I was slipping right down with him. Just friggin' great.

Grasping for the right words, I said, "I really appreciate you helping me...I really do." The expectant look in his eyes caused my chest to tighten with guilt, but I couldn't bring myself to tell him what he wanted to hear. Everything was too new, happening so fast I couldn't feel my feet on the ground. "Tyler...I...*do* feel things right now, but let's face it, we both just had one hell of a night. It's not that I'm *not* attracted to you, but I just don't think we should get sidetracked right now. I mean...I'm already asking too much of you. And it's dangerous for you to be putting yourself in the middle of all this."

"I can't help you escape and then dump you off. I have feelings for you. Feelings that have grown over the past three months. I want to help you, and more than anything, I really want to be close to you, get to know you better. You're intriguing to me. There's already so much about you that turns me on. It's crazy, but I would never even know you're a vampire without having seen it in my premonition. You don't act like the other ones I helped. You seem so human...just like another person." A broad smile stretched across his face showing sparkling white teeth—just teeth, no fangs. He's human. I was a vampire. Did that even matter?

"You've had three months to get to know me," I reminded him sternly, "but I've only had one night of knowing you." Tears welling, a massive lump formed in my throat and I swallowed, fighting the tears that threatened to fall. The battle was short and they won, spilling down my cheeks in steady streams. Just friggin' great. Real badass vampire, that's me.

Tyler let go of my hand and wiped my tears with his thumb— gentle, caressing, soft, warm, and *alive*. Dammit! He looked at me like he couldn't believe vampires actually cried, like he didn't think it was even possible. And that made sense. It shouldn't be possible, it's such a baby thing to do. Not a powerful vampire thing to do. Beyond overwhelmed, my head fell onto his shoulder, barely registering the movement as I sobbed against him.

He rubbed my back with both hands, slow, gentle strokes. "Shhh, it's okay," he cooed, his warm breath tickling through my hair. "I promise it's gonna be okay."

"Wh-what el-else ha-have you se-een?" I sniffled, so hard to get the words out.

Tyler kept rubbing my back, calming me down a little. "Based on my premonitions, we stay here for a little while. I'm assuming you find food since you're smiling in a lot of those premonitions. I haven't seen anything else yet. Actually, I haven't seen anything new since I met you in person. Everything you saw I've already seen. I promise to tell you the second I get another one."

I lifted my head up and looked at him. His warm hands cupped my face and I could feel the pulse in his palms, tapping against my cheeks like raindrops. Softly, I placed my fingers on top of his, and through the tears, which thankfully had started to slow, I said, "I miss my life. I hate this. I hate what I am. It's not like I had that much going on when I was human, but I'd take that over this any day. I'm a freaking monster! How can you have feelings for me? You'd never have a normal life with me."

He snorted. "I don't have a normal life anyway. I haven't been close to anyone in years. Helping people requires me to move around a lot. I've been living here for a couple months on a month-to-month lease. Then I decided to help you and headed to Florida."

"Wait, this is your place? You shouldn't have brought me where you live. What if, what if Bronx finds us? You'll have to move..."

Tyler put his index finger on my mouth, hushing me. "Abby, don't you listen? I'm with you now. I'm a hundred percent committed to helping you. If we need to leave, we'll leave together."

That's when I knew I had to get up. He was going to kiss me if I didn't, and I just couldn't let that happen. Not yet. It was just too soon and I still had questions. Bronx was out there looking for me. I started to get up, to move away from him, but he grabbed my arm, pulling me back down beside him. I knew I was stronger than him. I knew I could easily get away, but I didn't want to hurt him, even though he was now starting to cross a blatant line—one I'd just drawn in the sand. Sand. Was that solid enough not to cross?

His face inched closer, steady and slow, eager eyes on me. My body sunk deeper into the cushions, the leather squeaking and groaning. I nervously swallowed, but the lump of emotions still clung to my throat. Tingles shot up my spine, cold and prickly along the back of my neck. Then the cold sensations morphed into heat and waves of fire flushed my face. Could I be blushing? Did vampires blush? My stomach was doing somersaults, a part of me wanting Tyler—to kiss him, hold him, feel close and safe: such a human thing to feel. Maybe vampires really were a lot like people. I scooted closer. He did too. My attraction for him reached a level I'd never felt before and I bit my bottom lip, instantly tasting blood. That jolted me out of the moment. *I can't do this! Get away from him now!*

In a rush, I jumped back, the sofa half-swallowing him as I pushed away. He gasped, eyes wide with fear. I was across the room the next instant, staring at the fireplace, wishing I could crawl in there with that unburned log.

"Abby," he called out. "I'm sorry."

I didn't look back; I couldn't, the lust I felt for him was still there. "Don't do that again," each word spoken slowly. "I could've hurt you." Oh my God, did I hurt him? I turned around fast, finding him on the sofa, and though he was frowning, he certainly didn't look hurt. But the next time he might not be so lucky. Next time? No way. There couldn't be a next time. Turning back around, I buried my face in my hands and cried.

Moments later, two strong arms encircled me from behind. I let out a deep, long sigh, turned around, and pressed my face against his chest. It was soft, warm, his heart beating fast, alive. It felt so good to be close to him, inside the circle of his arms. He gave me a tight squeeze as I reached my arms around his waist, pulling him closer still. My body relaxed, a calming wave washing through me that eased some of my tension. I felt the subtle movements of his chest as he breathed. A short time ago I'd wanted to be far away from him, but now it seemed I couldn't get close enough. At last my crying stopped, but I wasn't ready to let him go. So we stood there, holding each other for what seemed like an eternity.

"I know this is a lot for you to take in," his warm breath tickling my ear. "But please know I'm here to help you. I'm here for you. You can trust me."

Taking a minute to think about what he'd said, I realized how thankful I was for all his help, and the fact he was here with me so I wouldn't be alone. But so much was happening so fast. I needed some time to collect my thoughts and figure things out. "You really need to get some sleep. I'll keep an eye on things while you do. You want me to trust you, but you also need to trust me."

His grip loosened, and I let go of him. He took a few steps back toward the sofa. "You're right. I'll try. Will you please lie with me for a few minutes? Please?"

"You're not going to give up, are you?" I rolled my eyes, turned my attention back to the lonely log.

"No, I won't. But I promise to respect your space. I won't try to kiss you again."

"Ever again," I exclaimed through gritted teeth. "Do you even realize what happened to me tonight? Back at Pulse?" I swung around to glare at him.

He nodded, the features hardened on his face. "I saw the whole thing before it ever happened. That guy's a jerk. He would've tried again. And then he would've succeeded." Sitting down, he patted the empty cushion beside him. I wasn't sure why, but I listened to his invitation. Maybe I still needed to feel close, safe. Maybe vampires did get lonely, just like Bronx had said. I, on the other hand, had zero intention of turning Tyler into one of my kind for my own selfish reasons.

We sat in silence for a minute, and then he slowly laid his head on the cushiony armrest of the sofa. To give him room to get comfortable and stretch out his legs, I stood up. Once situated, he scooted over, making just enough room for me to squeeze in beside him. The sofa was big enough for both of us to lie next to each other as long as we were spooning. I nestled in behind him and draped my arm over his waist. This time, in the instant we connected, I was in another one of his visions.

Darkness danced with tiny flames as the room materialized in front of me. There were two red leather loveseats set adjacent to each other, dark blue walls, and there was a human man sitting directly across from me. Instantly, I knew I was in a back room at a donor club. A glass filled with a clear liquid sat on top of a dark wooden table positioned between the sofas. The floor was jet black and textured, perhaps an upgraded carpet. It felt like it had a thick, springy pad underneath. My boot squished further into it as I crossed my left leg over my right.

The human looked up at me and asked, "I don't mean to be rude, but aren't you gonna bite me?"

I was completely famished. Why hadn't I bitten into this donor yet? Getting up from the loveseat, I grabbed my drink and walked over to the man. "Sorry, I must've been lost in thought. I'm Abby Tate." My hand reached out for his, but he didn't return my friendly gesture. He sat there staring at me as if I needed to get on with things. "Well can you at least tell me what your name is?" Zero response; he just stared at me impatiently. By this time my need to eat had extended well beyond my ability to control it any longer. A meet and greet could easily be skipped.

This human obviously had nothing else to say to me. Remorse toyed with my emotions as I grabbed his head. Oh well, it wasn't my fault he didn't want to talk. He didn't fight me but he also didn't help me. I pulled him closer, and while doing so I leaned over him. His body was limp. No anticipation of my bite, no increased heart beat, nothing. My fangs located the vein in his neck and sunk into it. The blood from this inexpressive donor still quenched my thirst. He wasn't as sweet as Lily, but drinking from him was making me feel better by the second.

Finishing quickly, I laid the donor on his side. Tyler was out in the club waiting for me, and I needed to hurry up and get back to him so we could get out of here altogether. I couldn't risk someone that knew Bronx seeing me. Surely they'd turn me over to him without thinking twice. With cautious steps, I headed out of the VIP room and down a narrow hallway. Two security guards blocked my way into the main part of the club. They almost looked like twins—short, but still taller than me, and both had stocky builds. They sported shaved heads and the typical black-on-black attire.

"You're going to need to wait a minute, Blondie," one of the guards with a New York accent threatened.

"What do you mean?" Hoping that confidence was all that I exuded in my somewhat shaky voice.

The other security guard with a similar accent chimed in, "You heard him. You need to wait here for a minute."

There was no way I was getting around these two guards that appeared to be former UFC fighters. Old mottled and gray scars decorated their faces from injuries prior to being transformed into vampires. For whatever reason, you brought any old battle scars with you in your new vampire life. Anything on the exterior of the body— even tattoos. New injuries, however, would heal within seconds of infliction without any scarring at all. Any kind of internal issues would also mend, whether old or newly inflicted.

Desperate to understand what was going on, I demanded, "I think you need to tell me what the hell is going on here!"

The guard that spoke first pushed me back against the wall. "I think you need to shut the hell up!"

That movement was all I needed to see past these two morons and into the main area of the club. Tyler was sitting at the bar on the far side of the vast room. He sipped nervously at whatever he was drinking. Then suddenly, the bartender—a vampire—jumped over the counter and grabbed Tyler around the waist, flinging him to the ground, knocking two barstools over with him. I could hear a frantic cry escape Tyler's mouth as he hit the hard concrete floor. He demanded to know what was going on but no answers were given to him either. As I listened, anger coursed through me.

The bartender began securing Tyler's hands behind his back with some kind of rope. The other people in the club just stared. No one got involved. No one tried to help.

Heated rage unlike anything I'd ever felt erupted in my center and immediately rushed in tingly waves through my veins. My chest was tight, my throat constricted. Licking my dry lips, I ignored my new feelings and pushed all my focus on saving Tyler. Wait for it, I thought, remembering Bronx's instruction not to act on impulse and wait for an opportunity. There's always an opportunity. Concentrating harder on these two idiot security guards, relief flushed inside once I realized I was in. I could feel their minds. See their next moves. They wanted to hurt us, kill us, but I couldn't tell if Bronx was involved, or how they knew Tyler and I were together. But they knew and they meant us harm.

The second guard turned around, watching all the drama unfolding on the other side of the bar. Quickly, I grabbed the first guard's shoulders, his hands still pushing my back against the wall, and squeezed as hard as I could. My fingers pressed into his skin deep into muscle. He growled, fangs showing, eyes glaring at me. I jerked him to the side and then thrust him backwards. He flew away, gasping, eyes widened in surprise. He hit the ground hard and stayed down, though I knew that wouldn't last long, that he would heal quickly and come after me. But I took him down. Holy crap! I took him down!

Then his twin sidekick rushed me, but I was faster and dodged him completely. He charged and passed me, like a speeding bullet. His *head slammed into the wall, making a loud smacking sound, and blood splattered everywhere. Then he dropped to the ground slowly, leaving a crimson trail behind.*

Guard number one jumped up, snarling violently, spittle shooting through his teeth, and lunged at me. I flashed to the side, barely missing him, and his clothes brushed my skin as he soared past. He smacked the wall. Blood sprinkled about—a little less than the other guard—and then he joined his unconscious buddy on the floor.

Holy crap! I just knocked both security guards out. I didn't have long though. They'd be up and after me soon.

I flashed through the club to where Tyler was. Since everyone's attention was on Tyler and the bartender, no one had noticed my fight on the other side of the bar. Everyone loves watching a good fight—I couldn't believe they'd missed mine. Oh well, it's best they did miss it. I balled my right hand tight, rock hard, and then swung it at the bartender's face. It collided with his cheekbone, crunching and breaking bone, and he flew back a few feet. He crashed to the floor and stayed there. He was out—for now. I sighed deeply and shook my head. I'd just taken out three vampires back to back. That should be impossible, shouldn't it? These vampires weren't young like me. There was no way I'd just kicked their butts. But I had. I couldn't help the satisfied, small smile my lips pulled into.

In the back of the club, there was movement to one side. The twin security guards were standing up, glaring at me and ready to charge. I grabbed Tyler, his hands still bound behind his back, and threw him over my shoulder. Faster than lightning, I was out of the club, running far, far away.

The computer beeped, snapping me out of that vision. Still lying on the sofa next to Tyler, I sensed sleep had finally overpowered him. I pulled my arm away and sat up quick. He didn't move, obviously he was out cold. I shook my head. That vision. When would that happen? I couldn't let that happen. Too dangerous—anything could've gone wrong. And then everything would be worse, much worse.

After getting the laptop, I brushed my finger across the mouse pad, relieving the beach scene screen saver from its duty. There was a blank gray screen with a few small icons along the bottom. One of them was a mailbox. I clicked it twice and saw an e-mail address, Lily.Madison@gmail.com, with the subject line, *Here is the info you requested.* Highlighting that subject line, I then clicked open and a message materialized:

Abby,

*You'll need to download the attachment and that
should provide you with what you need. I'm still
really worried about you so please don't do anything
stupid! I mean anything ELSE stupid. Bronx called
here again wanting to know if any of us heard from you.
Adam is all over me, convinced I'm hiding something.*

I'll do my best to cover for you.

Lily

The file download didn't take long, alerting me when it was done and I clicked "open" to view it. It was a list of every blood donor club in the entire US. I quickly skimmed over it. There were six of them in Georgia. Four of the six were within an hour's driving distance. I wished Tyler's vision would have given me some kind of indication what club we were in. That one would be avoided at all costs.

Reading over the four closest options, there was: Brio on Saxon Street, FLIGHT on Herndon Avenue, 7 on Seventh Street, and Red Dragon on Bisby Lane. None of these streets made any sense to me, so I opened another browser and requested Google Maps. I plugged in each address and a little gold star pinpointed their locations on the interactive map. FLIGHT appeared to be closest to Tyler's house, and that seemed like the most probable one to go to. That must've been where that vision happened. That vision—what did it mean? I was able to overpower and escape three brute vampires that were all much older than me. How was that possible?

My thoughts started looping. I really didn't want to get stuck in one of those again. But it was kind of hard not to when you had more questions than answers. On a frustrated sigh, I slammed the computer shut, then put it back on the coffee table.

In a whir of motion, I was up and pacing. My hunger was growing more intense and I knew I couldn't last much longer without blood. Drinking from Tyler was not an option. What if we found a different donor club but the outcome was much worse than what I'd seen in that vision? I couldn't risk him getting hurt. He was no match for a vampire. But I had to go—I had to get blood. Somehow I needed to convince him to stay home on this one. It was the only way to keep him safe. But why did I have a gut feeling that fighting those security guards would be easier than convincing Tyler to stay home?

11

Must Find Blood

HOURS WENT BY BEFORE Tyler woke up. The sun would be setting soon, thanks to daylight savings. My hunger for blood was at a level I'd never experienced before, and it was escalating fast. I was worried, with tension building up around my neck and shoulders. I'd already caught myself staring at the vein in Tyler's neck twice while he slept. It had been hard to look away, but I'd forced myself to do it. I stood by the fireplace, the farthest point in this room from him. What if I lost control to these blood cravings? Was Tyler in even more danger here with me? I swallowed hard, shrugged my shoulders to loosen them. Tyler was waking up, yawning, arms stretched above his head. I took a few steps his way, stopping short, keeping a safe distance between us—at least I hoped. "Good morning, uh, evening," I said.

A smile stretched out of his yawning lips. "Hey, good morning." He stood up, walked past me, toward a hallway on the left. "Give me a few minutes to freshen up."

I nodded. Would a shower make me feel better? I used to love long hot showers, fruity-smelling soaps, and minty toothpastes. When there was more time, I was going to have to experiment with that. Bronx never did any of those things and tried to teach me his habits, but I'd do anything to feel human again. Vampires don't have to act like animals. We're not even alive like animals anyway.

Tyler returned to the living room smelling clean, fresh...tasty. He wore black boots, black denims, and a light blue dress shirt with the sleeves rolled halfway up his forearm. His hair was still soaking wet, little puddles all over the fabric covering shoulders. Walking past me, he took a seat on the sofa, holding a damp cloth in one hand, a hairbrush in the other.

"Come here. Let's get you cleaned up," he said.

I rolled my eyes. "What, I don't get to shower?"

"I didn't think you would want to. The sun's almost down anyway."

I walked over to the sofa, sat down beside him. "We need to talk."

He nodded. "Yes we do." Leaning over, he rubbed my face with the cloth—above my eyes, down my cheeks, across my chin. "Look, I know you saw my premonition and I don't want you to freak out, okay?"

"Don't want me to freak out? Are you crazy? How could you sleep after that anyway?" I stole a moment to calm myself a little, then added in a harsher tone, "You have no business going with me tonight. I need to go alone."

He moved the cloth down my neck, pressing just a little bit harder than before. "Well, you can forget that. You're not going anywhere alone," he said defiantly.

"I have to. I'm not putting you in danger if it can be avoided."

He reached behind my head with his other hand, lifting my hair, then slid the cloth back there and scrubbed my nape in tiny circular motions. "You're freaking out," he said in a level tone. "Please just relax. Listen, sometimes my premonitions come to me as dreams, like the one you saw earlier with me. You were snapped out of it before I was, though. We made it back home, Abby. No one saw where we went. A clean getaway."

His offered smile did little to ease my tension. Actually it seemed to make me more anxious. Shaking my head, I leaned back and exclaimed, "No way! There's no way in hell I'm going to put you in any kind of risk. Not one we're aware of and can avoid." I started fidgeting with my hair as a tsunami of anger washed over me. And of course it was no surprise my hunger intensified at that very moment, reminding me of my growing need for blood. "I need to eat...now." Panic surged. "Please, let me go, I'll be back before you notice."

"You're not going without me," he argued, "not when I know where we need to go."

"What do you mean?" I asked. His skin looked so soft and delicate, which only seemed to temp me more. I wondered what would his blood would taste like, wondered if innocent blood was really that much fresher than blood of the bitten. Would it be worth it just to have one small taste? Without thought, I was licking my dry lips. *No!* I mentally scolded myself, shaking my head rapidly, then bit down hard on my bottom lip, tasting blood—my blood. Tyler really *was* in more danger with me.

"My God, Ab..." he gasped and I could taste the fear in his voice. "...your eyes." He scooted sideways, moving away from me.

I knew my eyes were turning red, knew without a doubt that's what he saw. Getting up in a hurry, I was across the room in a flash, praying that distance would curb the hunger and keep him safe from me. "We don't have anymore time. You've got to tell me what club I need to go to. Please."

Tyler's pulse sped up. I could feel its rhythm from across the room. "The club we were at in my premonition was FLIGHT. If you don't want trouble, then we shouldn't go there. Even though the outcome was favorable. I'm assuming the info you needed was e-mailed?"

"Yes. Brio, 7, and Red Dragon are the next closest ones to us."

"7 is a donor club? I've been there before. It's actually a pretty cool place. Maybe we'll get a premonition on our way there." He grabbed his car keys off the table and stood up.

"You're not coming!" I was beyond anger at this point. I needed to see the map one more time to locate where Seventh Street was. Then I could run there myself. Vampires could run so fast, the need for a car didn't exist. Not only could I get there quicker, but if I went alone, Tyler would also be safer.

Crossing the room, I went for the laptop, but he knelt down and grabbed it first. How could he be faster than me? He must've known I needed it. "You don't want to risk fighting with me any longer, do you?" he said. "Quit wasting time, let's go." Turning on his heel, he hurried down the hall toward the garage.

"Fine," I mumbled, my raging hunger forcing me to follow him.

This time he didn't help me into the passenger side. I could sense his fear—thick and suffocating. It was unsettling to know he was *that* afraid of me, but I couldn't blame him. Needing a distraction, I rubbed my hands on the tops of my thighs. Any other time, the drive would've been shorter, but tonight it dragged along in slow motion. The good news was that we were finally pulling into a parking lot. No bad news...yet. There were several other cars parked around us. We pulled in next to a black Chevy pickup truck and I was opening the door before he cut the engine.

"Wait," Tyler called out. "We need a plan."

I nodded, hand gripping the half-open door.

"I'll go in first," he said, avoiding my eyes, staring at the steering wheel. "You wait a few minutes and then come in. Don't sit next to me."

"No, I go in first!"

He gave a long sigh as if he wanted to argue, so it surprised me when he said, "Okay. You go in first and I'll be a few minutes behind. Once you finish, uh, eating, you can leave ahead of me and I'll follow shortly after you."

That wasn't going to work either. Patience thinning, hunger accelerating, I needed to hurry up and finish this conversation. Through ground teeth, I told him, "No, I go in first, you leave first. You're not going to be in there without me." Without waiting for a response, I got out of the car and headed for the club with only one thing on my mind: *Blood. Blood. Blood.*

The sky was a starless, hazy-colored black, but the area was still lit up like a Christmas tree. Streetlamps provided some of the light, while the rest of it came from an assembly line of shops, restaurants, and businesses on the street. An old-fashioned, two-story brick structure stood eerily apart from the rest. A big black sign hung from the second balcony, the number 7 written across it in dripping red paint as if it were bleeding, which was probably the point. My mouth watered as I stared at the sign. Sucking on my bottom lip, I forced my gaze away, and with no guards at the door, I walked on in.

The inside was more expansive than the outer appearance suggested with several square-shaped wooden tables in the middle, a few big comfy booths along the walls. The ceiling soared up to the second floor with big iron light fixtures hanging down, illuminating red light throughout the space. Straight ahead, there were twin bars in the back, directly across from each other, with black marble counters, matching leather stools, and bottles of alcohol along the walls behind them. There were two humans sitting at the bar on the left. I headed that way and then sat down, keeping a few spaces between them and me.

The bartender was young, early twenties, about five seven, slender, with short brown hair cupping her heart-shaped face, and she was definitely a vampire. It didn't take long for her to come over. "What can I get ya tonight?" she asked, her voice a little scratchy but in that sexy kind of way.

"A vodka soda please."

"Sure thing." She smiled, lips tight, no show of fangs, and then turned around and started making my drink.

While her back was facing me, I leaned over the counter. "Can you please help me out? I need to get into one of the back rooms here." I kept my voice low and calm.

She turned around, slowly glancing me up and down. "I can see that you do."

I wasn't sure what to say so I just waited quietly as she stirred my drink and threw a lime wedge on top before handing it me. "Here ya go. Wait here. I'll be right back."

"Okay. Thank you."

Trepidation crawled through me as I watched her walk out of site behind the bar. If I didn't need blood, without a doubt I'd leave right now, but leaving wasn't an option. I slurped my drink until it was empty, then stared at the ice still in my glass.

"Come with me." The voice was deep, authoritative. I looked up. A guy stood in front of me—tall, at least six foot, with a narrow face, thin body, and long black hair pulled back in a ponytail. He was okay looking, but definitely not my type. The bartender stood beside him, gesturing with her eyes for me to go with him.

My hunger forced me to follow the black-haired vampire as he led me over toward the other bar, which wasn't empty anymore. Tyler was sitting there alone. His eyes flicked to me, then back down at his hands on the countertop. I followed Mr. Ponytail behind the wall of alcohol and down a short hallway. Straight ahead was a set of doors, painted the color of blood. Opening one of them, he motioned me inside. With him right behind me, I walked into another hallway of sorts, this one a little wider. The door closed behind us with a loud *thud* and I startled.

He grabbed me firmly by the shoulders, turning me around to face him. "You can't come in here looking like that! You'll give us all away. You're lucky I was the one working and not Eddie. He would've kicked you out of here. I should kick you out of here."

"I'm sorry. I'm still so new at this. Please forgive me. I'm just, I'm just so hungry," I said.

"Ah, a new vampire," his eyes softened as he let me go. "When? When were you transformed?"

"One month ago."

Stepping back, he tilted his head and studied me a moment. "Where's the one who made you?"

"He's not here. He's not with me anymore." I didn't want to lie and technically, I hadn't.

"Poor baby vampire," he said, and then gave a long sigh. "Abandoned just a month after birth. So sad." He walked around me and I followed. There was another set of red double doors ahead. He opened one of them, ushered me inside. "You'll find plenty of food to choose from in here, Baby Vampire."

I stood in a large, expansive room. The ceilings were high-vaulted, but not quite as high as the other part of the lounge. Smoke veiled the air like a thick fog and hazy red light filtered through it from a few hanging light fixtures. There were a few oversized red sofas, a handful of blood donors sitting comfortably on them. White shag carpeting covered the floor, yet surprisingly not a stain in sight.

"I'll be back to check on you," Mr. Ponytail said, and then he turned abruptly and left.

Unable to think of anything except blood, I smelled my way over to a younger guy sitting on one of the red sofas. He was short with a round face and a small, button-shaped nose. Sandy blond hair wisped sideways across his brow and his right leg was crossed over the left one. There was an Auto Week magazine in his hands, not that he could even see it in this minimal lighting. Peering above the page that supposedly held his attention, he looked up at me.

"Hey. How are you tonight?" I asked while sitting down next to him.

He gave a charming smile before closing the magazine and setting it on his lap.

The personable part of me, the side that loves to be cordial with my donors, was gone. This insane hunger now controlled me and I quickly grabbed his head and tilted it sideways—a lot more aggressively than how I usually did it. But hey, I was freaking starving. His shuddering body only made me hungrier, more excited. His neck was short, so I pressed his head down a little more, stretching it wider, then squeezed my face between his shoulder and chin, lowering my lips to the skin above the vein. My fangs extended and his blood spilled into my mouth before I even registered biting him. The more I drank, the better I felt, so I pulled from him until I was satisfied.

When finished, I sealed the wound and then laid him back onto the sofa. Gazing around, there were three other donors in here chatting amongst themselves and completely oblivious of me. And I was still the only other vampire, which meant I could easily take one more donor before leaving. But what if Tyler was in trouble? What if things weren't this smooth out in the bar, just like it was in that vision? That vision! I stood up and flashed out of the room.

No one waited for me behind either set of double doors, so I kept moving toward the public bar area. Tyler was sitting in the same spot, smiling and talking with the female bartender that had waited on me. My chest tightening, I swallowed hard, forcing myself to look away. Heading for the other bar, I passed him, then reclaimed my old seat. The two human customers that had been here earlier were gone, and that meant Tyler was the only non-donor in here. Panic seized me. That just double—no, triple—confirmed there was no way I'd leave this club before him. He'd better follow that pact we made—or else what, I just didn't know yet.

Tyler finished his drink and threw cash on the counter as he stood. A quick glance over his shoulder my way, and then he headed out of the club. Good boy, Tyler. I sighed with relief just as the female bartender was making her way back toward me, bouncing with each step, smiling. Would it look suspicious if I just left? Or should I order one more drink? Or maybe now that Tyler was out of here, I could go back and take one more blood donor. Hmm, what to do, what to do...?

Rounding the bar, she asked, "Can I get ya anything else?"

"Yeah, I think I'll have one more before I go." One more drink, not one more donor. Tempting though, I hated to admit.

She winked, grabbed a glass, and then turned around to make my drink. I scooted my seat a little closer to the bar while I waited, thankful it didn't take long. She twirled around in one swift motion as if she were a ballerina. "Here ya go," she said, voice like a song.

"Thanks."

After that, she got busy wiping some glassware with a clean rag. I took a few deep long sips, finishing the drink rather quickly, and then stood up. Some cash was stuffed in my bra so I fished it out, counted out sixty bucks, and threw it down on the countertop. It's vampire etiquette to tip for the time spent in the back room and since I wasn't sure how much my drinks were, I hoped that money covered everything. She nodded with a half smile, grabbed the cash, then shoved it in her pocket.

"Thanks again. I appreciate your help," I said.

She gave a slight nod and returned to the glassware, rag in hand.

I headed out of the club relieved, full, happy. Life was good. I was almost to the door when a hushed voice crawled along the back of my neck. "Baby Vampire, wait just a second."

I froze. Crap, crap, crap. My back stiffened with tension as I turned around and looked up at Mr. Ponytail, his gaze fixed on me. He smiled, slightly, glimpse of fangs touching his lips.

"Hi again," I said through a forced smile.

"You're leaving so soon? I hoped you were going to stay for a while tonight." Disappointment was evident in his voice.

"There are a few things I need to do now that I'm feeling much better. Thank you again." I was so anxious, and I pleaded with God that I didn't sound it.

"But you will come back, Baby Vampire? Won't you come back?"

Why did he care so much if I came back or not? And enough of that stupid nickname. Something was up. His tone was off—there was something in the way he was looking at me. He thought I was an abandoned vampire, and maybe that made him feel sorry for me. Pity, however, was not the only vibe I sensed from him. It was time to go.

"Why wouldn't I come back?" I turned around, started heading for the door in a brisk pace.

He was beside me in a flash—I hated when vampires did that. It's only cool when I do it. "I'm Brian," he said, suspicion gleaming in his eyes. "Please ask for me when you return. Tomorrow hopefully?"

"Okay...Brian. Very nice to meet you." I waved good-bye, rushed out the door. But I collided with something in the doorway, hard, solid like a concrete wall. It knocked me back a couple steps. But I was fine. No loss of balance.

Brian stood there, hand extended out in front of him. "I'm sorry. I don't recall getting your name."

I froze, stomach tightening, throat contracting. There was a hard knot in my throat, and no matter how hard I tried I couldn't swallow it down. It was just stuck there. What if he knew Bronx or had heard of the missing blond vampire? There was no way I could tell him my real name. "I'm Anna." I shook his hand reluctantly while desperately trying to keep it together and not piss this guy off.

He grinned, showing a broad, glistening expanse of teeth and fangs. "Anna, what a beautiful name for such a beautiful lady." His grip tightened around my hand. "What time tomorrow shall I expect you?"

Anger churned in my core—hot, fierce, and defensive. Was it going to come down to a fight? It was if this jerk didn't move out of my way. But I could sense he was much older than me. He would defeat me, hands down, no question about it. I needed to control my anger and try talking my way out of this somehow. "I should be here near seven tomorrow. If you'll excuse me, I really do need to get going."

I started to walk around him, but he backed up and threw his arms out to the sides, creating some kind of makeshift barricade, completely blocking the door.

My anger intensified and I balled my hands into tight little fists, holding them at my sides. "Is there anything else you'd like to ask me, Brian?"

He stared at me, fangs out, hands firmly gripping the doorjamb. He wasn't moving, which meant he was definitely trying to keep me from leaving. A growl built up deep in my throat, then spilled out of my mouth, snarling, challenging. Searching his eyes, I looked for his next move, but his mind was blank, empty. He was mentally blocking me too.

"Anna, Anna, calm down." His voice was like a cool wind in my head. "There's no reason for you to be upset. I mean you no harm. Please forgive me, I didn't mean to make you feel uncomfortable. I only wanted to ensure you felt welcome to return as often as you'd like." He dropped his arms, stepped to the side. His words were false; I could sense his lies. But could I make it out of the club? There was only one way to find out.

"You have a funny way of making me feel welcome," I said through clenched teeth. "I hope when I return it's not so confrontational." Then in a flash of movement, I was gone.

I used to hate running, would've done anything possible to avoid it. But this, if I could even call it running, was un-freaking-believable. It almost felt like flying except my feet were still on the ground, moving so fast I couldn't even feel them touch it. Blasts of air rushing my face felt like I was hanging my head out of the window of a speeding car, but way faster than that, and much more intense, as it whipped my hair directly behind me. The wind chilled my skin, and though my nose was like an ice cube, being cold simply didn't bother me anymore. As I put more distance between 7 and me, my panic eased, my anger simmered, and *that* allowed me to enjoy my first run as a vampire.

A vast woodsy area came into view straight ahead. The highway we'd traveled to get to the club was on my left, but cutting through the woods would be a more secretive way back to Tyler's. And it seemed like a better idea than following the highway that brought us to the club. Closing my eyes, I concentrated hard, listening to the sounds around me, licking my lips to taste the air, searching for any followers. But every scent I picked up was part of my current surroundings: old car exhaust and burnt rubber on worn asphalt, pollen, grass, and musky dirt from the woodlands. Hurrying into the woods, I continued at my amazingly swift pace. I ducked under low-hanging tree branches, curved around others that jutted out like long boney fingers. My footing was steady. My balance was perfect. I didn't run into anything, didn't trip, didn't fall. I just kept moving, purpose-driven, and confident, as if there was a built-in GPS system inside me. Up ahead was a stream—I could hear the rustling water, smell the dampness of the earth around it. But I didn't stop, didn't hesitate. Springing forward, I rode the air across the stream, landing perfectly on the other side. That had been too easy. I could've jumped higher, farther. Gasping aloud, I couldn't fight laughing. Maybe there were some perks to being a vampire after all. This was definitely one of them.

Tyler's house was getting closer, but I knew I couldn't go straight there. I wasn't being followed now, but what if my scent was tracked later? I couldn't lead the bad guys straight to us. There's no such thing as being too careful, so I kept moving.

After I was miles beyond his house, I turned around and backtracked another way until I arrived at his dimly lit back door. It was unlocked so I let myself inside, locked up behind me. The kitchen was small, cozy, with old wooden floors, matching wood cabinets, white-tiled countertops, older white appliances, and a small round café table in the corner with two tiny bistro-style chairs. Tyler's scent was all over. He had just been in here, perhaps unlocking the door for me. I let out a long sigh of relief. We'd made it home this time. We could worry about the other times later.

I walked out of the kitchen and into the hallway. Left took you to the garage; right led into the living room, where Tyler's scent was stronger. I followed it, with each step, the old wooden floors made creaking sounds. Note to self: Don't walk like a human if you want to surprise someone. Tyler jumped up from the sofa, tossed a magazine on the coffee table. He ran straight to me, arms open, lips stretched in a big smile. "You're okay!" he exclaimed. "Thank God!" He pulled me into a bear hug.

"I'm fine. Thank God you're okay too." I hugged him back, my face pressed against his chest, feeling the smoothness of his shirt, his hardened nipple underneath. He really was excited I'd made it home safe. Either that or he was freezing cold—hmmm.

"What happened back there? I saw you follow that guy behind the bar...it took everything in me not to get up and go after you. Thank God you came back out when you did." He let go of me, took a small step back, investigating me with his eyes, head tilting to the side. "You look different...better."

"I was taken to the back room for blo...I mean food. That's how they do it at the donor clubs." I shook my head, then shrugged. "I guess my eyes are their normal color again?"

"Yes. They're beautiful." He stepped forward, reached his arms around me, and pulled me into another warm, caring embrace. I hugged him back. It felt good, almost a perfect fit, and I knew that could mean trouble sooner rather than later.

Later was better, since there were more pertinent things to discuss right now. Dropping my arms to my sides, I pursed my lips, then said, "I don't think we can go back there."

He let me go, taking my hand inside his. No vision, still here with him in his living room. Good. He led me over to the sofa and I followed like a good little vampire. "Why?" he asked, astonishment plain in his voice. "It worked. We got in and out." He gave a long sigh as he sat down.

His grip tightened around my hand, pulling me down beside him. Close. No safe distance, our bodies almost touching. Was I the only one noticing how close we were? Our fingers interlaced, just like couples did when they held hands. It felt natural, good, right. An apparent distraction since I couldn't remember what he'd asked me. Finding his eyes, those beautiful gleaming green jewels, I could only stare. "Why can't we go back to that club?" said Tyler.

"That guy I followed to the back room, Brian, well he's not a guy, he's a vampire, but anyway he'll be looking for me if I go back."

Tyler grimaced. "What do you mean by that?"

I ran my fingers through my hair with my free hand, then told him everything that had happened at 7. Tyler listened intently, and it was clear he didn't like the last part, where Brian tried to prevent me from leaving.

"Why wouldn't that vampire let you leave? I knew I shouldn't have left you...dammit!" he said, voice deep, almost yelling.

"No, no. It was better that you did and luckily I handled the situation just fine." I looked away, stared down at the floor. "But there's something else. Something he knows, or something he wants. I'm not really sure. But I don't trust him. We can't go back."

Leaning toward me, he kissed my cheek. His lips were soft, moist, and that sensual touch sent tingles through my whole body. "Well," he whispered against my skin, "if you were that uncomfortable, then we're definitely not going back. I'll trust your intuition on this one, babe." He pulled his hand free of mine as he straightened, and though I wanted to, I didn't fight him. What the hell was up with my crazy hormones? A part of me wanted him, another part didn't. Sure, I wanted to be close, wanted to feel his skin on mine, relish the warmth of his human body. And as soon as I began cussing myself for thinking that, he wrapped me inside a hug, pulling me closer, squeezing me tighter.

Unable to fight the smile, I nestled against his chest. "Thanks. I appreciate that." A prickling heat blossomed in my center and I knew it wasn't just because I was attracted to Tyler. "I guess that puts us in our next dilemma," I told him.

"What's that?"

In a blur of motion, I was out of Tyler's arms, and a couple feet away from him on the sofa. "I hate this! I hate this, Ty!" My body started trembling uncontrollably, and I rocked back and forth trying to calm down, my hands balled into tight fists. "Now where am I going to go for bloo...food?"

He nodded, voice soft, saying, "Don't worry. We'll figure that out. Trust me." He inched closer, placing his hands on top of my fists, gently rubbing them with his fingers.

"I hope you're right. Our safety depends on that."

He didn't argue. He knew I was right.

12

New Identity

THE SUN PIERCED THE SKY with its killer rays, trapping me inside the house. Tyler had left almost an hour ago and I was drowning in anxiety waiting on him to get back. Pacing the living room sure wasn't helping. I was about to walk a hole in the wooden floors, with their continual creaking under the weight of my boots, the burgundy curtains with gaudy white flowers swaying as I passed them. Just when I couldn't take it another second, I heard a car pull into the garage.

Scurrying through the hallway, I rushed past the kitchen smelling of burnt toast and stale coffee. The laundry room was straight ahead, the garage beyond that. I came up to the closed door, grabbed the doorknob, then hesitated. A thin stream of light appeared along the bottom crease of the door. Right away, I jerked my hand back, and hopped a few steps away. A car door slammed shut seconds before the garage door made a swishing sound as it closed. Now, the light was gone, but I stayed where I was. Better safe than sorry. Footsteps approached, and I took a few more steps backwards, the odors from the kitchen assaulting my nose once more.

Tyler walked into the hallway, smiling, eyes sparkling like green stars. His hair was perfectly messy, and he wore relaxed fitted blue jeans with a heather gray hoodie. There were two large brown paper bags in each of his arms. "Hey babe. Miss me?" asked as he walked past me.

Not wanting to get too close to that smell, I stayed in the doorway. "Yes, of course I missed you, and I was worried sick. Did you find something for me to wear?"

"Come over here and see." He set the bags on the countertop.

I didn't move.

He glimpsed me over his shoulder. "What's the matter?"

"That smell. It's horrible. Just give me a minute to adjust."

"How about I just clean this mess up?"

I nodded; sounded like a great idea to me too.

After cleaning the kitchen as fast as humanly possible, he bagged up the trash and went to throw it in the bin in the garage. All the while, I waited patiently in the hall, watching him. As he jogged back in, he asked, "Is that better?"

I nodded, then followed him.

He grabbed the bags, carried them over to the café table, then pulled out a chair for me and we both sat down.

"All right. What did ya get me?" I asked.

Reaching into the bag closest to him, he pulled out a pair of faded, jeans and a short-sleeved, black button-up shirt. Then he returned to the bag, digging a little deeper. His hand came back out holding a pair of black pants and a royal blue V-neck shirt with thin spaghetti-strapped sleeves. He tossed everything into my lap.

I threw the skimpy royal blue top at him. "That's a little too sexy, don't ya think?"

Smiling mischievously as he caught it, he answered, "I thought you'd look hot in that. It's perfect for the clubs, but if you don't want to wear it out, that's fine with me." He chucked it back to me and then dug into the bag again. "Here, I knew you'd give me trouble over that shirt." He handed me a light blue V-neck tee.

Grabbing it, I said, "That's better."

He leaned back, half laughing. "Just be grateful you have a boyfriend that doesn't force you to hide those beautiful curves of yours."

Boyfriend. Tension churned inside while an argument built up on my tongue, but I just couldn't get the words to form. Did that mean he was my boyfriend? No friggin' way. Yet instead of correcting him, I asked, "What's in the other bag?" hoping to just change the subject altogether.

His right eyebrow arched. "Everything we need to change the way you look."

"Oh goody. Did you find some good wigs?"

He shook his head. "No, I didn't think that would work. You move so fast, what if it fell off?" He reached over, grabbed the other bag. He pulled out a pair of shiny silver scissors and one of those

106

hair colors in a box that you buy over-the-counter at most stores. There was a picture of a brunette woman on the cover. "You're going to look amazing as a brunette."

My widened gaze on the scissors, I swallowed hard. "What are those for?"

"Bangs."

Anxiety flared through me. "No friggin' way!"

"Yes friggin' way." He was smiling. Why the heck was he smiling?

"You're enjoying this too much," I told him.

He stood up, held out his hand for me. "Yes I am."

Reluctantly, I took his hand. "Fine."

He ignored my pouting all the way to the bathroom. Sitting on the counter next to the sink was a small lamp glowing yellow light. Almost everything else was white: the tile floors, cabinets, slick marble countertop, textured walls. Tyler pulled the sheer white shower curtain to the side, revealing a matching porcelain tub with tiny square tiles on the walls. A big square piece of wood was nailed on top of what must've been a small window, preventing any light from getting in.

He got a few towels out of the cabinet under the sink and laid them on the ground in front of the tub. "Get on your knees and hang your head over the tub," he instructed. "I'll run the water through your hair to dampen it." He slipped the detachable showerhead out of its base and brought it down to his side.

"I don't think you get hair wet before you put color on it. Read the directions." But I went ahead and got on my knees just in case.

He paged through the pamphlet, a little too quickly for my taste. "You're right. Glad I thought to check that," he smarted. "Hang your head over the tub anyway, just incase I get this crap anywhere besides your hair."

Using the tube-shaped applicator, he squirted the hair color all over my head, running his hands through my hair, blending in the cold, sticky gel. It stunk to high heaven, but it was still better than burnt toast and stale coffee. When he finally finished, he twisted my hair in a bun and told me I could sit up. It was going to take at least twenty minutes for the color to process. While he washed his hands, I got up and sat on the toilet lid. He told me about his shopping trip as we waited, and by the time he finished sharing almost every detail, it was time to rinse my hair. Water splashed everywhere, completely soaking me. Thank God I had new clothes to change into.

I grabbed a towel, dried off the best I could, and then walked over to the mirror, barely recognizing the brunette girl looking back at me. I couldn't believe how different I looked simply by changing my hair color. This identity change really *was* going to work.

Tyler got a comb, started working it through the knots. "Bang time," he said, and leaned down to get the scissors.

Maybe he grabbed them too hard, or perhaps they were just too sharp, but I smelled the blood before I heard him gasp.

Staring in the mirror, I watched that dark red ring form in my eyes. "Get out of here! Now! I mean it! Go!"

Tyler made a run for it and I was thankful for once that he didn't argue. I gripped the sink, my fingers pressing hard against the marble as I fought the swelling temptation to go after him. The scent of his blood was all over me—sweet, fresh, *unbitten*—and it smelled better than I'd ever imagined. My mouth watered, I shook my head and swallowed it back several times, but it was pointless. Nothing was helping. I couldn't refocus my thoughts, all I could think about was Tyler's blood. Tears welled at the realization that I *was* the monster I'd always denied being. And there was no way I could fight it anymore. A taste, just one simple taste was all I needed, and surely then I'd be able to gain better control. Releasing the sink, I rushed after him, following his sweet, metallic aroma.

By the sink in the kitchen was where I found him standing, carefully wrapping a Band-Aid around his finger. A moment of clarity hit me and I held onto the sides of the doorway, my fingers pressing against the textured drywall. Drywall? I needed something more solid, because surely my tight hold would break this in a minute's time. Panic surged inside me. "What are you still doing in the house?" a hysterical scream of words. My stomach churning, I added more levelly, "You have to leave...now...get out of here."

"Abby, you're better than this. Fight it. Resist it."

What was he doing? Why wouldn't he leave? I couldn't fight it. There was no way I could stop. The hunger grew, raging inside every piece of my being. Grip loosening, my feet inched closer toward him, and I absently registered drywall clumping under my fingernails as I scraped it, trying to keep my hold, but it just wasn't enough to stop me. "I can't control it! I can't control myself! Ty, please!"

Still he didn't move. He stood there, green eyes staring at me, holding his injured finger in the other hand. My tears burst into a full-blown waterworks show as I mentally prayed that I wouldn't hurt him.

At that moment, the hunger won and I whirled straight for him.

"Abby, I love you! Don't be mad!" Tyler reached above the sink and pulled open the thick burgundy curtain. Rays of light burst through the tiny window and instantly my exposed skin burst into flames. I screamed, deep and loud, wailing like a banshee as I waved my arms, trying to ease the burn. Smoke seeped from my pores, searing my flesh. Fangs extended, I let out a threatening growl as anger swelled inside me to the point I was seeing red in my mind, but there was nothing I could do. The sunlight hurt too much, its heat agonizingly intense. Leaping back, I retreated to the safety of the dark living room, now wanting more than just his blood, but to also hurt him for what he'd done. The flames now extinguished, I held my arms out, looking down at them. Skin was peeling, and there were oozing pussy blisters and sores that made me think of one of the lepers the Bible spoke of. I forced a breath, and then another, each time getting a little more air inside lungs that no longer needed it.

"Abby," Tyler called out. "Are you okay?"

A growl built up deep in my throat before rolling off my tongue. "That wasn't very smart." I didn't recognize my voice. It was evil, pure evil.

"I had to protect myself. You were coming after me."

There were footsteps approaching the living room. "Don't come any closer," I hissed.

"I'm sorry." His voice was closer and I swung around to see where he was, anxious, ready to jump at him again. He stood in the hallway, light from the kitchen glowing behind him. "Please. You're better than this. Fight it. You've got to try." He sounded choked up, like he was about to cry.

I shook my head, mortified by my behavior but completely helpless to it. Knowing I needed to get a grip, I willed myself to calm down as I took a few more breaths hoping that would help relax me. A cool sensation crawled up my nape, onto my head, followed by tingles that raced up and down my skin like static-charged ants. Chills flushed my exposed areas as if I was standing in front of an open freezer, and I glanced down at my arms again. They were already healing, open sores were sealing up, the blisters disappearing beneath the surface. Noticing my thirst for blood wasn't as strong as before, some of my tension eased. I could resist it now, didn't need it as badly anymore, and I wondered if my ability to heal was offsetting the blood craving. At last, the fog of hunger evaporated from my mind and I exclaimed, "Ty! I'm sorry! Are you okay?"

"Y-Yes. I'm okay! Are you?" He inched a little closer, his right foot entering the living room.

I held out a hand to stop him. "Don't you dare come closer to me. Not yet. I can still smell your blood."

"What should I do?"

"You really need to leave and give that wound some time to heal before coming back."

Eyes widening, he nodded, saying, "Okay." Then, turned abruptly and left without another word.

How could I have been so close to biting him? Did he hate me for that? I certainly deserved it if he did, yet right as I was about to bite him, he'd professed his love for me. Dammit! *God I hated being a vampire!* Why couldn't I control myself? His blood had created a raging hunger that I'd been completely lost to. Could it be that my attraction to him intensified the desire to drink from him?

Back in the bathroom, the weight of my thoughts throbbed in my skull and I let out a frustrated sigh that did little to ease the pressure. Retrieving the scissors, I carefully cut some bangs, a glimpse in the mirror showed they looked okay—as good as bangs can look anyways. Absently staring at the new me another moment, I watched as my face slowly crumbled, a quiver of my lips, the thin creases in my glabella as I fought the tears that threatened to come. After a few rough shakes of my head, I turned away from the mirror, my hatred for the girl staring back at me making it too difficult to look at myself any longer. Dropping down to the floor, I wrapped my arms around my legs, and completely lost it.

It seemed like hours had passed. My remnant tears were now dried, leaving a sticky residue on my face. I rubbed under my eyes a few times, then slid my fingers back to my nape and pressed firmly on the tightness beneath my skin, but unfortunately not finding any relief. There was a sour taste in the back of my throat, a bitter knot in the pit of my stomach. In the next instant I was at the sink, splashing water on my face a few times, then taking a few gulps, feeling the soothing chill in my mouth as it helped wash away the acidic flavor. But as my knees buckled and my stomach clenched tighter, I knew my moment of strength was short lived. On the floor once more, I tucked my legs against my chest and buried my face in my hands.

Time seemed to stand still, and when I first picked up Tyler's amazing scent, I wondered if it were real. But when I heard movement, and his smell got stronger, I knew he was somewhere in the house. How had he slipped in without me noticing before now? The thought only brought on more of a pity party as I imagined being the only vampire alive that a human could get the slip on. A door slammed shut, pulling my attention to the footsteps getting closer and closer. Sharpening my senses, I couldn't detect any more blood. Relief rushed through me in waves just as there was a knock at the door, but a flash memory of chasing after him, desperate for his blood, kept me paralyzed on the floor. Another knock, and after a click of the knob, the door slowly swung open. I could feel his gaze on me, but I was still too humiliated to look up at him, keeping my lasered focus on the tops of my knees.

"Hey," he said softly.

"Hey."

"Are you okay?"

Very slowly, I turned and looked up at him. "I don't know."

To my surprise, he smiled. "Come here."

"I don't think that's a good idea."

"Sure it is. No more blood. Promise."

Hesitantly, I got up and walked over to him. He wrapped his arms around me like a warm winter blanket and pulled me against his chest. Being inside his tight hold was comforting and wonderful. But I didn't deserve it.

"I'm so sorry. I'm sorry." I stammered, words rushing off my tongue faster than I could think them. "I didn't mean to—"

"It's okay." He squeezed his arms tighter around me. "It was an accident. I should've been more careful."

"What if another accident happens? I'm a monster! You're not safe with me around."

"It's no safer without you around." He let go of me and stepped back, then cupped my cheeks as he fixed his beautiful green gaze on mine. "I'm not going anywhere and neither are you, unless it's together. I'm not losing you over a stupid cut on my finger."

My shoulders slumped. "But I can't control myself. I couldn't stop...your blood. It smelled incredible. I've never smelled anything like it." I searched his eyes looking for a sign of fear, or resentment, or anything like that, but none of those emotions were there.

"Maybe that's because you love me?" He leaned down, his lips creeping closer.

A tight ball of heat formed in my lower belly and expanded slowly from my core sending gooseflesh racing on my arms. He inched closer, his breath warm and gentle on my face, and I licked my lips with anticipation, tasting his closeness, then in a panic, I bit down on my bottom lip hard enough to draw blood. In a gasp, I stepped back, freeing my face from his hands. "No," I breathed. "We can't do this."

He stood there for an uncomfortable moment, the air tense and restless. "I'm sorry. I didn't mean to do that." Running his fingers through his hair, he surveyed the bathroom, then said, "I'll get this cleaned up."

"I can do that. It's the least I can do after everything that's happened."

Since neither of us would obey the other's offer, we cleaned the bathroom together, working in complete silence.

After it was sparkling clean and filled with the aroma of Lysol, he pointed to his bedroom and said, "I'll bring you the new clothes. You can change in my room for privacy." He flashed me a wolfish grin. "Unless, of course, you'd like to..."

"Your room is fine." Because I definitely wasn't changing out here in front of him, and he wasn't coming in there for a peep show either. I got ready lickety-split and came back out to find him waiting for me in the living room. Since we still had some time to kill before nightfall, we used an empty dining room to practice a few basic defensive fighting moves. Tyler brought some of his own experience, but we both quickly found that I was much better—and not only because I was a vampire. I taught some moves that could easily be done by a human, and I could tell he was pushing himself to succeed. Occasionally I'd use some of my incredible senses to escape his swinging fists or flying feet. Fortunately I barely felt it when he did land a blow, and when he finally reached the point of exhaustion, we ended our training session.

After moseying back into the living room, Tyler brought me up to speed on some research he'd done earlier while he was out. Since he had taken his laptop, he used the Wi-Fi at Starbucks and researched some donor clubs outside of Georgia. He'd narrowed it down to Rayver's Pub or ex-RAYNE, both located in Hilton Head, South Carolina. But since Tyler hadn't gotten anymore of his futuristic visions, we had absolutely no idea which club would be our safest bet. Unfortunately he couldn't force his premonitions to happen, which meant there was a chance we'd have to make the choice on our own. Seemed like gambling to me, and I'd never been any good at that.

13

Predicament

RAYVER'S PUB WAS LOCATED IN an expansive, one-story building that stretched down an entire block. Several other businesses shared the space, but most of them didn't look open at this hour. Making a similar pact as before—ever so reluctantly on his end—Tyler waited in the parking lot across the street, giving me a generous head start. After a cautious gaze around, and not seeing anyone else, I took the last few steps separating me from the donor club. The entry door was held open by a wooden barstool and I couldn't help the nervous twitch when my fingers brushed across the rotted doorjamb as I walked inside. Three square-shaped metal tables, each with four chairs, were situated straight ahead, and the bar was in the very back, clearly visible from where I stood since the area wasn't as big as the outside appearance had led me to believe.

A woman sat on the left side of the bar, so I made a beeline for the right. After all, she was human, and I could sense she was innocent, which actually made me feel better knowing she was here since Tyler would be walking in soon. Glancing over, she flashed me a small smile. She looked approximately my age, with shoulder-length blond hair heavily streaked with dark lowlights, and she wore a red-ribbed tank with a pair of skin-tight jeans. One curvy thigh stretched over the other and her sun-kissed skin betrayed endless summer days at the beach. Since Hilton Head was a beach town, that wasn't so surprising.

Returning her smile, I sat down leaving a couple of empty seats between us. She looked away, stealing a few sips of her beer before returning to the magazine that had previously held her attention. The bartender was an older man, fifty-something, slim, with thinning salt-and-pepper hair and super tan skin that could pass for leather. But what was strange about him was the fact I sensed he wasn't a donor. What in the heck was he doing working at a donor club? Nerves racing, I swallowed them back the best I could and gave him my drink order. Thankfully, he flashed me a genuine smile and got busy with my request.

A few minutes stretched along before he handed over my drink, and after he set it in front of me, I watched him turn around and head toward the side of the bar, where it seemed a hallway of sorts twisted out of sight behind it. Thinking that must have been where the VIP rooms were located, I coughed, pretending to clear my throat but really hoping to get his attention, and when he stopped at the edge of the doorway and looked back, I let out a sigh of relief seconds before my anxiety rushed back. But I knew I needed to just get on with my request. The sooner I did, the sooner I would hopefully have some blood in my belly. And then I could get the hell out of here with Tyler. "Excuse me, sir," I called out at last, "I kind of need your help with something."

He took a few steps back my way. "What ken I help ya wit', honey?" His voice was deep and raspy.

"Um, it's um, kind of personal, could you come here?" I used a teeny weenie bit of my persuasion on him to be sure there would be no suspicious delay. It worked perfectly and he walked right up to me. A quick glimpse at the blond woman confirmed she was still looking at her magazine, not at me and the bartender, thank goodness.

He leaned down, face to face. "If der's a way I ken help ya, I'm happy to do it. Just as long as it ain't illegal or any utter kind of trouble." I smelled whisky on his breath.

"No trouble," I whispered, "I just need access to your back room, please."

"Oh, well dat's an easy one, honey. What's yer name and I'll let my boss know yer here? Oh and I'm Quinn." A huge grin flashed across his face exposing his teeth for the first time. All of them were perfectly shaped and bright white—not really what I'd expected.

"I'm Anna. I really appreciate your help, Quinn." I smiled back.

"I'll be back in a jiffy, Anna. Just wait right here." He turned around and headed behind the bar.

At that moment, I sensed Tyler behind me. Within seconds he was sitting down on my right, leaving an empty barstool between us. He pretended to barely notice me, or the human girl beside me. He wore faded jeans and a long-sleeved, gray button-up shirt. His leg impatiently rocked back and forth, tapping against one of the stool's wooden legs.

There was movement and voices behind the bar, pulling my attention that way just as Quinn popped out from behind the bar, grinning as he headed toward me. "I'll be right wit ya, sir." He politely motioned to Tyler and then looked at me. "Anna, my boss Stone said to meet him in duh back for dat meetin of ya'lls. I can take ya der now."

Meeting? It must be a story he concocted since Tyler and the other woman were in here. Going along with him, I said, "All right, great. Thanks." Then got up and followed him behind the bar without looking back.

I was led through a small hallway illuminated by canned lights in the ceiling, and we quickly approached an oversized wooden door. Quinn knocked three times and then turned the handle. The door creaked as it opened, then I followed him inside. The room was long and narrow, with black painted walls and old wooden floors. It reminded me of a studio apartment, but without the bedroom. There were two black sofas in the front, sitting adjacent from each other, and in the back there was a wide, rectangular-shaped table with six chairs. Just beyond that against the wall was a built-in cabinet with sink.

A male vampire—Stone, I presumed—sat on the right-hand sofa with his feet propped up on a small table in front of him. He was very good looking, so attractive, in fact, that I felt embarrassed for even looking at him. He was tall and slender with eyes like azure skies, and light brown hair that fell just below his ears. He wore black boots, black jeans, and a tight long-sleeved, red cotton shirt that showed off his well-shaped body. He patted the cushion beside him and with slow, cautious steps I walked over and sat down. The door creaked and I looked back that way to find that Quinn was gone. I was officially alone with the vampire boss. Oh goody for me.

He inspected me with those gorgeous blue eyes and I couldn't help the discomfort that brought me, or the flaring tension in my chest. "It's nice to meet you, Anna. I'm Stone Rayver."

"Hi, it's very nice to meet you." I reached out my hand.

He firmly grabbed it.

"Quinn will be back shortly with another round of whatever you were drinking. I hope you don't mind having a drink with me before *dinner*." He pulled my hand close to his mouth and then kissed the back of my palm.

A drink before dinner? Why was it these club bosses loved making me feel obligated to hang with them? That Brian guy had done it, and now here Stone was doing it too. But since I hadn't gotten any blood yet, and the fact he was still holding my hand, it left me little choice but to go along with it. "A drink sounds good." I told him at last as I nervously watched him.

He smiled, showing off his fangs. "I can sense you are anxious...and very young."

I nodded, tugged my hand away. "I was transformed a month ago." Butterflies started dancing in my stomach, and it wasn't just from hunger.

"One month, huh?" He gently stroked my cheek and I fought the urge to cringe away. "You are a very beautiful woman. Where is the one who made you?"

"We, uh, decided to go our separate ways." Part truth, part lie. I just hoped Stone couldn't sense the lie part.

"How on Earth could your maker abandon such beauty? I cannot imagine what drove him or her to that decision." He leaned in close and sniffed my neck. "Your human essence still lingers within you." He reached down and grabbed my hand again. "May I?"

I didn't know what he wanted. Hoping that my young age would buy my naivety, I said, "I'm sorry but I don't understand."

"May I taste you? I've never tasted one that still carries the essence of human life." He brought my hand up to his mouth and licked it. "Mmm, you're delicious," he sighed.

The door creaked, interrupting my need to answer Stone's question. Quinn came in, drinks in hand, and made his way over to us. Setting them on the small table, he asked, "Ken I do anyting else for ya sir?"

"Please send the donor back here in about ten minutes. That will be all for now." Stone looked away from Quinn and back at me. "Sorry for the interruption. Now where were we?"

117

I watched Quinn leave the room, wishing that he'd stayed instead. I wasn't sure what Stone wanted, but I was afraid that if I told him no he wouldn't allow me to have the blood that I came for. And to make matters worse, I was only getting hungrier by the minute.

"Quinn is human," a nervous statement of the facts.

"Yes he is," said Stone matter-of-factly.

"But he's not a donor."

"No he isn't. Is that a problem?"

"Isn't that forbidden? What about the Enforcers? Doesn't Quinn have to be a donor to know about us?" My hair fell to the side as I leaned forward, setting my drink on the table.

Stone took a few sips of his golden beverage, then replied, "I guess in a way that's true. The Head Council is strict about our secrecy." He tilted his head to the side. "However, Quinn and I have an arrangement. There is nothing to worry about with him. Our secret is safe."

"Head Council? Who is that?" because surely Bronx hadn't mentioned them. Fidgeting with my hair, I leaned forward again and retrieved my drink.

"Aren't *you* the one telling me about vampire code and conduct?" His crisp tone pulled my attention his way. He raised a brow, no doubt at the way I gawked at him. "You don't know who our own Head Council is?"

Nope. I'd never heard about the Head Council. Clearly, Bronx had forgotten to mention them when he was educating me on vampire politics, and it made me wonder what other things my evil captor never told me. Shaking my head, perplexed, I replied in a soft voice, "Sorry, I must have been misinformed." Not that I would instantly trust this guy, but knowing Bronx was a liar made it that much easier to believe someone else.

Stone reached over and pulled my hand out of my hair, giving it a tight squeeze. "The members of the Head Council are the oldest, strongest vampires that are *unalive* today." He chuckled, most likely at the way he said unalive if the change in his tone were anything to go by. "They employ the service of all gifted vampires, calling them Enforcers, and ensure that we all keep a low profile and, of course, that all donor clubs pay the appropriate business fees to the Head Council, much like paying taxes. These payments also ensure Enforcer security at the donor clubs. Just think about it, who else could keep a vampire on their best behavior?"

That explained the powerful security guard at Pulse that overpowered Bronx and detained him in the back room. He had to have been an Enforcer. But if all vamps with special abilities were Enforcers, did that mean Bronx was one too? With every detail I uncovered, it felt like I was only left with more questions, and it frustrated me beyond words.

Interrupting my thoughts, Stone asked tersely, "If you don't mind, I'd like to get back to what I asked you. May I taste you?" He let me go and set his drink on the table.

Unsure how to answer him since I had absolutely no idea what the hell "taste me" meant, I nibbled my bottom lip. The need for blood was what kept me rooted in my seat, but I was also curious to learn more about my kind and it seemed Stone had the answers I wanted. Then the thought of Tyler anxiously waiting for me at the bar flashed in my mind and the tension in my chest thickened. The need to get on with things pushed me to finally say, "Okay." Hoping like hell I wouldn't regret that answer.

"Yes, I may taste you?" asked as if he needed clarification. Taking my hand, he lifted it to his mouth, his lips brushing across my skin.

Tingles raced from his soft touch, unexpected anticipation blossoming inside me. "Y-yes." I gripped my drink tighter with my other hand, bracing myself for whatever would happen next.

"Anna," he breathed, "you're absolutely adorable."

His fangs pierced through my skin and slowly entered the vein in my wrist. I could feel the flow of my blood in a head lightening rhythm, and everything around me seemed to be moving, warping. The black walls were getting closer, threatening to cave in on me, and I stifled a scream, my raw fear becoming almost tangible. It felt as though my feet were sinking into the floor as I tried to watch Stone, but it was impossible to focus. Coherent thought was challenged, but I tried to reassure myself that this was something vampires did, perhaps even naturally, though I'd never witnessed a vamp drink from another one of their kind before. My attempts of counting to ten didn't calm me at all, and the fact that I couldn't keep track of what number I was on wasn't helping. Panic surged and I knew I was going to completely lose it. And just as I was about to rip my arm away from him, it was over.

As he raised his head and leaned back, the walls slowly retreated, giving me some much-needed space. I released a long sigh then freed my arm from his hold, his inquisitive gaze hardening on me as I rubbed the tender spot on my wrist where he'd bitten.

"Amazing," he said through a smile. "I've never tasted anything like that. Your blood..." His eyebrows drew together. "You're not being completely honest with me, are you, Anna? Or should I call you Abby?"

In a flash, I was at the door, a gasp of sheer terror stuck in my throat, but as I reached for the knob, Stone was already there, blocking me. "I won't hurt you," he assured. "Please, you can trust me. I can explain."

Body trembling, I stayed frozen where I was, staring at him. He seemed sincere, I couldn't see even a hint of a lie in his gaze, but I wasn't sure if I could trust myself after the weirdness I'd just experienced when he drank my blood. *Blood.* The irony of that epiphany made my gut twist and I knew without a doubt that I couldn't risk leaving this club without feeding. It would be too dangerous for Tyler and because I didn't sense anything hostile from Stone, I had no choice but to hear him out. Crossing my arms in resignation, I said, "I'm listening."

"I had no idea you were hiding so much. I was only interested in finding out where you're from and how long you might stay here. Please forgive my intrusion of your privacy." He reached for my hand, took it inside his. "I promise your secrets are safe with me. You have nothing to worry about."

Nothing to worry about? He obviously didn't learn very much when he drank from me. I studied his eyes more intently, still trying to see signs of dishonesty, but there wasn't any. Instead all I sensed was that he meant me no harm, which was a little reassuring.

"Please sit back down with me." He walked pulled me back toward the sofa and I followed. What else could I do?

He said, "Thank you," as he sat down.

"Can you do that with anyone?" I slowly moved in beside him, keeping a small distance between us. "You know, taste their blood and get information about them? How does that work?" And did that mean if I drank from him I could do the same thing?

He smiled shyly, charmed. "Yes. It is my gift. I'm able to read people by tasting their blood. Similar to the way psychics can read your palm." His gaze flicked to the floor, then back to my eyes. "Abby—"the use of my real name sent chills through my body— "you are very special. I've never tasted anything like that before."

That statement unnerved me. "What else did my blood tell you?" *And why don't you go ahead and tell me more about yourself since I won't be able to gain those details by drinking your blood*, I thought.

"Something awful happened. That's why you can't use your real name."

A knock at the door startled me. I looked over just as Quinn walked in with the girl from the bar following right behind him, which confused me. She was an innocent human and had no business in the back room of a donor club—unless she was...

"Hello again, Britney," said Stone, snapping my attention on him as he motioned for her to sit on the sofa across from us. "Quinn, please grab us another round. We'll wait for you to bring it before we begin."

"Yea, sir," Quinn replied, "be right back wit dem." He nodded and left the room.

I watched Britney sit down, then looked at Stone and exclaimed, "What is she doing back here? She's innocent!"

"No, you don't understand," he said. "Britney has been patiently waiting for this and I promised her that I would drink from her tonight before the others show up. But since you are here, and your bite is much stronger than mine, maybe you wouldn't mind doing it? After all, aren't you in a hurry to leave? This will be your quickest way."

Britney flashed both of us a huge smile with an apparent gleam in her expectant eyes.

"But I just can't do that to her," I told him. "I can't be the one that gets her addicted to this. I'm sorry."

Britney's smile faded and in a screeching tone, she cried, "You promised! You swore tonight would be the night!"

Stone waved a hand to silence her, and then directed his attention to me. "Are you really hesitant for her benefit or your own? There is no reason to fear drinking the blood of an innocent."

There wasn't? "That's not it" was what I replied with instead, anger surging through me. "I just don't think it's right." And I really didn't.

"Fine. Whatever you say." Stone grinned, half laughing. "But this decision has already been made. If you don't want to do it, then I will. I'm not going back on my word. Besides," a nonchalant shrug, "Quinn has given his blessing for this."

"Why would you need Quinn's blessing?" I asked.

"Because Britney is his daughter. I would never touch her without his permission, but as I told you, Quinn and I have an arrangement."

Britney opened her mouth to say something but Stone waved his hand again, and she kept quiet. Smart girl.

No one said a word the next few minutes and I was seconds away from freaking out. I couldn't just get up and leave without getting blood, though I wished I could. And clearly Stone knew that too. But could I really take it from her? It was obvious her fate had already been decided. If I didn't bite her, Stone without a doubt would.

"Britney," Stone broke the silence. "Did you know that Anna is only one month old?"

Her eyes brightened. "Are you kidding me? Just one month?" She looked at me with a huge smile. "Oh please, will you be the one to bite me? Please? Please, Anna?"

I was left with an incredibly tough decision. Either I bite this innocent girl, turn her into a donor, and risk getting addicted to innocent blood just so I could leave sooner. Or stay here and watch Stone do it, while I wait for another donor to arrive. No telling when that would be and what danger I could possibly get into before that.

My gaze flitting from Stone to Britney, I couldn't help but notice the look in her eyes was practically begging me to do it. Pressure tightened in my chest and unease churned in my belly. This girl would become a blood donor with or without me, and I really needed to get Tyler out of here. That was when I finally came to grips with what I needed to do. "I can't promise my bite is still as potent as it used to be," I said.

Britney's head moved up and down like a bobblehead doll. "Does that mean you will? You'll be the one to bite me first? Oh I never could've dreamed of this," she replied in a shrill voice.

Mentally collecting myself, I gulped down the rest of my drink, set the empty glass on the table, and got up. In slow steps, I headed over to Britney. Unfortunately she wasn't that far away, and I got to her faster than I'd wanted.

"I'm pleased you are doing this," Stone said. "I will return the favor to you."

"Yes you will," I snapped. "Our conversation is far from over. I want to know what you haven't told me."

"Done. Whatever you want to know. I promise."

Unsure if I could trust him but completely positive I needed blood now, I knelt down and gently grabbed Britney's face with both of my hands, tilting it to the side. Her body shuddered as I drifted closer, her scent calling to the animal inside me, and I wondered if this would be easier than I'd thought it would be. My fear became excitement; anxiety turned to eagerness as I hovered over her for a brief moment, then brushed my lips against her neck. It was soft like cashmere, warm and alive.

This was her last chance to change her mind.

She didn't. I sunk my fangs deep beneath her skin and tightened my grip on her as she tried to jerk away. But it was hopeless for her now; the taste of her refreshing, untainted, blood was already on my tongue. Biting harder, her vein released a heavier flow and I pulled it from her in frenzy. Eventually her attempts to struggle lessened, and I felt her body fall into that blissful state that all blood donors find themselves in during the bite of a vampire.

14

Warned

THE BLOOD OF AN INNOCENT really was everything Bronx had said it was—sweeter, fresher, tastier. The finest of delicacies. I wished I didn't like it so much, kind of like wishing you didn't like caviar the first time you tried it. But maybe now that I'd had it, I wouldn't want to drink Tyler's blood anymore. Fat chance, I'm sure. We'd just have to see how good my willpower was the next time he cut his finger. Actually, he was probably better off just not bleeding around me.

Britney was lying on her side, sprawled out on the sofa. Her arms were tucked up against her chest and clumps of blond hair streaked with darker pieces of a chestnut color hung over her face like multifaceted curtains. She had been out cold for several minutes and she'd stay that way at least a couple more hours.

I was sitting next to Stone, waves of adrenaline from the blood feast finally wearing off. "I can't believe how good that was," I said through a smile as I looked at him.

"The fresh blood of an innocent is always better than the tainted blood of an experienced donor." He chuckled and then took a sip of his golden beverage.

"I wish I didn't know that." I looked away momentarily, filled with a renewed sense of worry for Tyler. Regardless of how good Britney was, there was no way I could make a habit out of biting innocents. I feared there would be no turning back if I did, and I couldn't risk putting Tyler in such a dangerous situation—or any other innocent human. "So why didn't you keep her for yourself then?" I swung my gaze back at him.

"Because you needed blood much more than I did and there is more nourishment in drinking from an innocent. Is it so hard to believe that I did something nice for you?"

Mulling that over, I shrugged. "I guess I owe you my gratitude then. Thank you."

He grinned. "It was my pleasure."

"Do you mind getting back to where we left off, please?" I leaned forward, reaching for my drink on the table.

"You're feisty after you eat. Aren't you?" he said, playfully teasing.

"I'm not being feisty. You promised me some answers." My impatience was coming across in my voice. "You know my real name. I won't deny that any more. You know something bad happened. You also said you can sense the essence of my human life. What the hell does that mean and what else do you know?"

"Calm down, Abby. Calm down, please." He reached over and grabbed my hand and I pulled it away. "Is it okay if I call you Abby?"

I took a big gulp of my drink, which I hoped would calm me a little. It didn't. A huge part of me wanted to go grab Tyler and get the hell out of here. But I needed answers and there was no way I could get them if I left. Glaring at Stone, I stood up then started pacing the area between the sofas and the door. For a short while, the shuffle of my boots and Britney's deep breaths was all I could hear.

"Can we please start over?" asked Stone. "You seem very angry. And I didn't mean to upset you. I will tell you everything you want to know. Please sit back down."

Lips compressed, I kept pacing a little longer. Every time I stole a glimpse at Stone, he was smiling. "Fine," I said, feeling defeated. Then I plopped back down next to him.

He chugged the rest of his drink and set down the empty glass. "I think your human essence is still strong because of how you were transformed into a vampire. It's against the rules to be forced into this life, and unheard of to be done without the approval of the Head Council." He stopped talking, appearing deep in thought, then went on, "You were brought into this life with no knowledge of it. The one who made you used a high level of persuasion on you to lure you away from the protection of the outside world." He ran his fingers through his hair, tucking both sides behind his ears. "You're a very special woman."

We were silent the next few moments as I absorbed what he'd told me, gripped by fear that he already knew too much. What if he knew Bronx? Or what if he saw Tyler save me? Britney moaned; the sofa groaned and squeaked as she shifted her position on it, and I watched her for a short while, unsure what to do next. Should I leave, or keep asking questions? There were so many things I didn't know, or had been told lies about, and I really wanted to learn the truth. And since I didn't sense hostility or anything suspicious from Stone, I hoped staying just a little longer wouldn't hurt.

Looking his way, I was a little taken aback by his stare. There was something in those beautiful azure eyes—mystery, intrigue, attraction—that caused my stomach to clench. He reached for my hand again, gently squeezing it inside of his. This time I didn't pull away. "Don't worry," he said. "I didn't get his name. But I do know he made numerous attempts to force you to love him. None of them ever worked. Actually quite the opposite." A low snicker escaped his lips. "You hate him. An opportunity came for you to escape and you took off, never looking back. You've changed your identity hoping to prevent him from finding you."

I could do nothing but stare at him. Everything he just said was one hundred percent true, and if his ability of reading blood had showed him all of that, then surely he knew more...possibly even the face of my captor. "Is there anything else?" I finally asked.

There was a flicker in his eyes and instantly my spine was iced with tension. "You don't really think you can hide from him forever, do you?"

At his question, my unsettled fear was now a roiling storm inside my body. *Could I really hide from him forever*? I'd surely hoped I could. Without a plan, Tyler and I would be running forever, and that realization slammed into me, hard, and it was something I couldn't accept. In an effort to calm down, I balled my fist, but Stone held on, curving his hand to stay around mine. "I hope I don't have to," I mumbled at last as I fought the tears welling in my eyes. I needed to get out of here. There was absolutely no way I was going to cry in front of the vampire club boss.

Pulling my hand away, I got up. Stone's gaze was on me, I could feel it, but I refused to look at him and confirm it. There was more to his story, but I definitely couldn't stay any longer to hear it tonight. If he was telling the truth then he knew nothing about Tyler, thank God, or that Bronx was the one I was running from. But I couldn't ask him to be sure, I was too afraid my question would give away details he might not know. I had no reason not to trust Stone, of course; no reason to put my trust in him either. Besides, as far as I could tell, he'd kept his word. He'd answered my questions, and given me details that make this whole situation more dangerous. The changes I'd made so I wouldn't be recognized weren't foolproof. Stone had just proved that—though he claimed he didn't know who was after me. But that was no guarantee he didn't know who Bronx was. Surely if he did know Bronx, he would have already heard from him. He would've been told about the young vampire on the run and to keep an eye out for her. Would Bronx offer some kind of reward for my safe return? Based on Lily's e-mail, he would do anything to get me back. I knew that much was true.

The lies Bronx told me kept piling up. Why hadn't he mentioned the Head Council? Why had his explanation of the Enforcers been so different from Stone's? My mind was reeling with confusion, still so far away from the answers I sought. My chest tightened as I took a few steps toward the door—my only way out of this back room. A quick glimpse of Stone over my shoulder, and I knew it was time for me to get moving.

"Are you leaving?"

A simple question, so why was my voice stuck on the lump in my throat. I looked away, stared down at the floor and took another step.

"You're leaving?" asked again, no hint of anything sinister in the question, the distance of his voice proving he was still sitting on the couch.

I swallowed hard as I inched closer to the door. "Thank you for taking the time to answer my questions. I really do need to get going now."

When he didn't say anything, I couldn't fight the urge to look back at him. His face was expressionless, eyes were blank. I couldn't tell what he was thinking or what he was going to do. My fear was morphing into anger, defensively charging my body. If he was going to try to prevent me from leaving, it was time to find that out.

He stood up, took a few steps toward me. I froze, contemplating my next move. "Abby, the pleasure of having you

127

here has been all mine." A smile stretched across his face as he reached out his arms.

Panic seized me. I gave in to it, stepped back.

His hands lowering, "I don't mean to frighten you."

"I'm not scared," I lied, my voice level. "I hope I can trust this information to stay with you and you alone."

"I give you my word. I will tell no one of our visit."

He wouldn't? Could I trust that? "Thank you," I told him as I turned and grabbed the doorknob.

"Wait!" Stone shouted, my fingers in a death grip. "You'll need a safe place to feed. Please know you are welcome to come here anytime you need. The donors usually arrive around midnight." He took slow human steps, removing the small distance between us then grabbed my hand gently, caressingly. Pulling it to his lips, he kissed the back of my palm again, and after he let go, his touch lingered on my skin like a soft perfume.

I smiled shyly, feeling a chill flush my cheeks. "I appreciate that. Thank you again." Then I turned back around, opened the door, and walked out.

In hurried steps, I was in the public bar area. With Britney now in the back room, Tyler was the only customer out here, and for that, I was extremely thankful. Quinn was whistling to himself as he washed some glasses in the tiny sink stationed at the bar. "Anna," he said as I walked by, "I hope er'tang went good back der wit Stone."

"It sure did. Thanks again for your help."

My mind raced to think of the best and fastest way to get Tyler out of here, without any delays, and with little other options and time not on our side, I knew I'd have to use persuasion on him. Looking over at Tyler, I let out a sigh as our eyes met. This was my chance. Our gazes now locked, I focused, concentrating as hard as I could and to my surprise, it happened instantly—almost effortless. I was inside his mind, pushing encouraging thoughts for him to throw the cash he owed for his drinks on the counter and leave immediately. I watched with relief as he obeyed and I didn't take my eyes off of him until he was out of the pub. It should only take another minute or two for him to make it to his car, which felt like an eternity waiting for them to pass, all the while hoping my effect wouldn't wear off before he made it back to his house.

At last, I began my descent from Rayver's Pub, successfully making it to the doorway. Quinn was still whistling away in the background. Without looking back, I flashed away.

This time when I ran, my speed wasn't even close to before, each step seeming slow and sluggish. My mind was drowning in all the new information I'd learned from Stone. And if it were possible, I hated Bronx even more. Why was I so shocked to keep finding out more lies he'd told me? It seemed to me that my old captor should be in a heap of trouble with the Head Council, since, to my knowledge, he'd secretly turned me into a vampire. Maybe that was the reason he'd never told me about those ancient rulers in the first place. Or perhaps he didn't know of the Council either, though I found that hard to swallow with his detailed descriptions of the Enforcers, who according to Stone, worked directly under the Head Council. I couldn't be naïve to this. Bronx was too old not to know about them. So it seemed obvious that he'd been trying to keep the whole thing a secret from me? And since the Enforcers were gifted vampires, that had to mean Bronx was one of them. And Stone too. But could I trust what the vampire club owner told me? So far, I didn't really have a choice.

You don't really think you can hide from him forever, do you? Why would he imply that Bronx would find me? Clearly he knew something more and I wondered again if he knew who my old captor was. There was only one way for me to find out, though, which meant I'd have to go back to Rayver's Pub.

A beep pulled my attention to the laptop on the table, and I found myself standing in the living room without even registering I'd come in the house. Sensing I was alone, on a sigh, I walked over to the sofa and sat down. Leaning over, I grabbed the computer and set it on my lap, wiggling my finger over the mouse pad to bring it to life. The home screen materialized just as I heard a car pulling into the driveway. Tyler was here at last.

A door slammed shut before I heard footsteps stomping the wood floors in their hurried approach. "What the hell was that?" he all but spat at me. "What in the hell do you think you're doing?"

"What are you talking about?" And I really had no idea.

"You know darn well what I'm talking about! You used that vampire hokey pokey on me—hypnosis, persuasion, whatever you call it!" Now standing over me, he crossed his arms in front of his chest, and glared at me so intensely I thought I saw flames in his eyes.

Swallowing hard, I leaned to the side and put the laptop back on the coffee table. Then I slowly stood up and grabbed both of his hands. "Look Ty, I needed to get us out of there. Would you have preferred I talk to you right there in front of the bartender? That definitely would've gotten us the wrong attention, which I'm afraid I'd already done."

Tyler's mouth gaped open. "What do you mean? How?"

"The vampire owner in the back of the pub, Stone, well he's kind of psychic." I stared deep into Tyler's beautiful, fiery green eyes and watched them soften a little.

Raising a brow, he asked, "Psychic as in he knows things? Like things that are going to happen?" He squeezed my hands.

"Um, well yes and no." I nibbled my bottom lip and took a small step closer to Tyler, now feeling his warm, steady breath on my forehead with our proximity. He released my hands and stretched his arms around me, crushing me in a bear hug against his chest. I stood there for a short while and listened to the melodic drumming of his heartbeat. It was relaxing, soothing. But reality loomed around it and my shoulders stiffened with tension once more. "He found out everything about me by drinking my blood." I swallowed slowly as I felt Ty's body tense. "I don't know if he can see anything in the future. Everything he told me had already happened. But he also cleared up some of the lies Bronx told me. And I'm convinced he knows more."

Yanking his arms away, Tyler stepped back and eyed me with suspicion. "He drank your blood? Why would he drink your blood?"

The jealousy radiating from him was at an insane level, which instantly threw me into a defensive mode. "Ty, listen to me. There is no reason to be upset. You need to trust me. Stone wanted to drink my blood and I only allowed him to do it to gain access to a blood donor. That's it! I had no idea that he could read things about me by drinking my blood. I swear it."

He raked his fingers through his hair. "Why would you let him do that to you? We could've found a blood donor somewhere else." He rolled his eyes and looked away.

I leaned into him, reached for his hand, but he pulled it away. "Stop this," I exclaimed. "Please stop this! What's wrong with you? I needed blood. There wasn't time to find another donor and I couldn't risk putting you in danger like that." Tears formed in my eyes and I wasn't sure if it was because of this stupid fight with Tyler or everything I'd been thinking about before he got here. Maybe both.

He grimaced. "I just don't understand why you would let him touch you like that. Him biting you sounds pretty intimate to me."

"There is no reason for you to be jealous. Vampire behavior..."

"I. Am. Not. Jealous."

I grabbed his shoulders and shook him gently until he looked at me. "You're going to listen to every word I have to say or I am out of here...out of here for good."

His eyes widened, then he shook his head, saying, "Okay," in a soft voice.

I waited a minute to confirm his silence was genuine and when he didn't say anything else, I pressed, "We're not together, we're not a couple. But even if we were, there was nothing I did that was wrong. I'm not going to lie and say I don't feel anything for you, but it's too dangerous for us to allow anything to happen. Do you understand?"

He nodded.

"We cannot be together. Not now, maybe not ever. I'm a vampire. You're human. We're on the run from an evil monster that, if he catches us, will probably kill us both. *This* can't be anything. We have to ignore it at all costs. So cut the jealous crap. Why would it be so surprising that a vampire bit me? I bite people every night. It's gross and very animalistic but it's a part of who I am, what I am. All Bronx did was fill me with lies and I have to find out the truth my own way now."

He didn't say anything at first, only stared at me with those big green eyes. But I'd said my part and the ball was now officially in his court. "You're right," he eventually said. "It's just so hard. I care so much. I didn't mean to get jealous. This vampire stuff is new to me but I accept it, all of it. I promise I'll handle things better from now on." Wrapping his arms around me again, he pulled me against him. His breath on my ear was warm, heavy, and I waited for him to say something else.

But he didn't.

He started nibbling on my earlobe—gentle, soft, wet. The slow stroke of his tongue teased me, sucking me up in a whirlwind of emotion that at first I couldn't escape. Only his touch mattered, only the tangible feel of his hard, sturdy body surrounding mine as his licks sent hot and cold flashes everywhere inside me. Somewhere in my center, a fire came to life, burning and expanding. "Abby, I'm so sorry," he breathed. "Please forgive me."

His mouth lowering, he kissed a trail from my ear to my neck. He pressed his hands harder in my back, fingers digging into the tense muscles there. Blinded by the sensation, I pulled him closer and his warm body felt incredible against mine. But it was too much, too fast, and slowly the haze of our connection lifted and caution set back in.

"Ty, we can't—"

Suddenly, he bit down hard into my neck, almost breaking the skin, and I was sucked into that emotional vortex all over again. My body felt like a weightless inferno, and I thought at any second I was going to explode. Nibbling my bottom lip, I held him even tighter as I tried to regain clarity, but his touch had become a distraction too intense to get past. Just now registering he'd stopped biting me, his mouth drifted up my neck, across my chin, up a little higher. "I've wanted this for so long," he panted. His breathing deep, his lips barely an inch away from kissing me.

Shutting my eyes and squeezing them as hard as I could, I fought the burning need inside my body and rasped, "No, we can't do this." I tried to step back and shimmy away from him, but his grip on me only tightened, trapping me against him. If I were just human, I wouldn't be able to move. But I wasn't. So I used a little bit of my vampire strength to pull out of his embrace, leaving him gasping as I flashed over by the fireplace.

After regaining his balance from nearly falling, he swung an astonished look at me then said, "I don't know where that came from. I'm so sorry. Please don't be mad. I'm sorry." He took a few steps toward me.

He'd bitten me as if *he* were a vampire and my body still wanted him—bad. I held out a shaky hand to stop him. "No," I croaked. "Don't come any closer. Please."

He waved his arms in surrender. "Okay. I'm gonna go in the kitchen and get a drink."

More words wouldn't form, so I just nodded then watched him walk out of the room. I'm not sure how long it was before he called out and asked me if I wanted a drink, but thankfully I'd cooled back down and felt like myself again. He brought out a couple glasses of water and took a seat on the sofa. As he set the glasses next to the laptop, he asked me to fill him in on everything else that had happened at the pub. I sat down next to him—but not too close— and told him everything he wanted to know. His eyes grew wide when I got to the part about biting an innocent. They grew even wider when I told him how delicious she was.

There was one piece of information that I purposely withheld from telling him, since there was no way I could risk arguing again. The fact that I'd be returning to Rayver's Pub alone would not go over so well, but my decision to go without him was final. The right time to tell him was still undecided. Was there ever really a right time?

The laptop beeped again, alerting there was an unopened message waiting. In the heat of our discussion, I'd forgotten all about it. Tyler leaned forward and got the computer, then after a few clicks, the email was on the screen.

Abby,

I was thinking of you. I'm so worried. Bronx
has gone crazy. He's looking for you everywhere.
He doesn't believe you're in Florida anymore. He
has other vampires helping him search for you. I
overheard him say something about Texas. Are
you in Texas? Be careful. Don't trust anyone.
They could be working with him.

Please write back and just let me know you're okay.

Lily

Tyler and I simultaneously looked away from the laptop and stared at each other. What the hell was I going to do now? Bronx was starting to look for me outside of Florida. But oddly, why would Texas be the next place he'd look? Did that mean Savannah

133

was safe for now? Not that I believed any place was really safe—not until Bronx was no longer after me.

But would his death be the only way to stop him? And more importantly, could I really kill him if it came down to it? I'd never killed anyone or anything before in my entire life, or afterlife. If divine intervention allowed an opportunity for me to kill my old captor, what if I couldn't? What if I froze and let him get the best of me in that moment?

All I could go on right now was a gut feeling that I would be safest right where I was, at least for a little while longer.

15

Ability

TYLER SLEPT FOR NEARLY SIX hours before awakening abruptly due to another vision. His shrieking cry interrupted a love song by George Acosta that I'd downloaded from Beatport.com. Alarmed, I rushed to his side and found him sitting against the bed's headboard, a sheen of sweat coating his skin. The vision—or premonition as he would call it—showed Bronx finding me on a night I went to one of the donor clubs alone. The location and time frame as to when that happened remained a mystery. Going back to Rayver's Pub without Tyler tonight, then, just got more challenging. Putting those thoughts aside, I sat down on the edge of the bed and firmly wrapped my arms around him. My face pressed into his cool, moist tee as I nestled into his chest. Beads of sweat dripped from his chin to the top of my head.

I held him tight, reassuring him the best I could as he tried to regain control over his breathing. Unable to pull himself together, he pushed me away and stormed out of the bedroom. Like a shadow, I trailed after him. "I just wish I knew where it was. What club you were at, and when it happens." His bare feet slapped the wooden floors all the way to the kitchen.

Lingering in the hallway, I tried to encourage him. "Maybe you'll get another vision. One that will fill in those blanks."

He looked at me, eyebrows raised, mouth crimped, and replied, "Maybe? I have this stupid gift of seeing the future and the best I can offer right now is 'maybe'? Maybe I can help you, or maybe not. It depends if my stupid gift works again!" He grabbed a coffee cup out of the cabinet next to the fridge and chucked it across the room. It hit the wall with a *bang*, and shattered into a million pieces. Instead of moving to pick it up, Tyler hunched over the sink, staring into it.

Edging closer to him, I reached for his back and nervously rubbed it. Regardless of the unsettled mood, I felt a small fire spark to life inside me. "Just calm down," I cooed, pressing harder into his back. "Try to relax. Anger never helps anything."

Without looking away from the sink, he ground out, "We only have a couple of hours before you're going to need blood. How will we know what club to go to? I can't risk him finding you."

My stomach churned with the need to feel close to him, and I quickly pulled away, stepped to the side. Shaking that sensation off the best I could, I retrieved another mug and set it on the counter beside him. Keeping my hands to myself this time, since clearly touching him was doing crazy things to my libido, I said, "I appreciate your concern for me, I really do." I started fidgeting with my hair. "That's why I know you'll understand that I have to go back to Rayver's Pub tonight. Not just for blood, but for information. And I need to go alone. I can't risk putting you in danger."

He looked at me, eyes widening, "You're what?"

"I need to know what Stone's not telling me. He's holding out on me and I need to know why."

"I'm going with you," he snapped. "You're not going back there alone."

"Yes I am. I have to. Don't you see that's the only way to find out what Stone knows? You. Can't. Come." I walked over to the café table and started pacing in front of it, that familiar anger trickling inside and replacing those previous feelings of attraction.

"What if something happens?" he exclaimed, throwing his hands up in the air and waving them at me. "How will I know? How can I help you if I'm not there? What if Bronx is there? Then what will you do? You're absolutely not going anywhere without me tonight. Do you understand that?"

I stopped moving and glared. "What the hell would you do if Bronx was there? Fight him? How? He would kick your ass *before* you took your first swing at him. What protection can you possibly offer me?"

Tyler didn't back down for a second. "Regardless of what you think, I know how to fight!" he yelled. "Without me there, he'd just take off with you. I could at least provide a distraction and give you an opportunity to escape."

Anger surged hot in my veins and I could feel my fangs extending. "Escape? And then what? Just leave you there with him? I'd end up needing to save you...along with myself."

His eyes drilled into mine. "I'm coming with you or you're not going! And you're not going to scare me away with those fangs of yours."

That got my blood boiling to the point where I was about to explode. I could feel the burn in my eyes—hot, stinging fire. "I can't risk that! You can't come with me!"

He stared at me, frozen, and perhaps fearful as my raging glare challenged him to say another word. I sensed the vein in his neck thumping rapidly, and I licked my lips as I imagined how good he would taste, most likely better than Britney. Shivers danced on my spine, and I squeezed my fists into tight balls. I couldn't bite Tyler. It wasn't worth it—I cared about him too much. Afraid if I didn't put space between us I'd lose myself to the blood lust, I flashed out to the living room, shoulders slumped, head low.

He didn't follow. The coffee maker started steaming and puffing. Shortly after, I could hear it pouring into the mug. Hopefully he was thinking things through and realizing I'd made a good point. At the end of the day, what protection could Tyler offer me beyond his ability to see the future? No offense to his male ego, but he had to know I was right. Since I wasn't entirely convinced of that, though, I paced in front of the fireplace, occasionally noticing that lonely log. Gradually, the anger melted away, the blood lust eased up, and my eyes no longer burned.

Even though his footsteps were soft, the wooden floors still creaked. He stood in the doorway, coffee cup in hand, staring at me with those beautiful green eyes. The expression on his face was softer now, but I was still afraid he might set off my anger again. Because of that, I decided to stay by the fireplace.

"I don't agree with you"—he took a sip of his coffee—"I don't think you should go without me. I want to be there for you. I don't like this at all but because you feel so strongly about it, I respect your wishes and will let you go without any more arguing."

Had he just conceded? I stood there frozen, mouth open but unable to speak. His truce was totally unexpected, yet so very appreciated, and I found myself wondering if I'd really heard him say that or if in fact, I'd imagined it. But with him still standing there and looking at me expectantly, I knew he'd really said it. Relief engulfed me and soothed my lingering anger. Gazing at him with quiet gratitude, I could sense a slew of emotions bundled inside him: sincerity, attraction, concern, uncertainty, fear. And it made me admire his surrender that much more. I wouldn't have been able to do it. Such a hypocrite, I know.

Walking toward him in slow, steady, human steps until we were only a foot apart, I caught a good whiff of his coffee and my nose twitched. Ignoring the smell, I gazed at him, keeping my focus on his eyes. "Thank you," I whispered. "Thank you for trusting me on this." I grabbed his hand, gave it a tight squeeze.

"I'm going to be worried sick until you get back here. Worried sick! Please don't be gone long. In and out."

"I can handle that." I was on my tiptoes, kissing him on the cheek, then rushing back to the other side of the room.

"As tough as you are, it's hilarious that coffee can send you fleeing for your life." He chuckled, then went back to the kitchen.

While Ty made something to eat, I stayed in the living room, sitting on the sofa against the wall, blankly staring at the laptop. More questions looped in my head while I made unsuccessful attempts to answer them, from that strange e-mail Lily had sent to the mysterious club boss and his secrets. There was definitely more to his story, and it was driving me crazy not knowing. The overwhelming thoughts were drowning me, and getting the answers was the only way I'd ever reach the surface and get that breath. Right now, though, I was a long way from that. Plus I still didn't know what I was going to do about Bronx. I knew I couldn't hide from him forever.

By the time Tyler made it into the living room, I was mentally fried.

"You should change out of those clothes so I can wash them. It'll give me something to do while you're gone," he suggested. He sat down next to me, gently rubbing my thigh.

That familiar warmth ignited in my gut, crept up my chest. I gave him a mild shrug. "Okay."

"Did you respond to that e-mail yet?" He stopped rubbing and scooped up my hand.

"No. But I will before I leave tonight," I assured him. Gently pulling free, I stood up and headed out of the room. The warm tingles inside me relaxed. When I glanced back at him, a trace of sorrow glimmered in his eyes, and I shook my head, feeling a sorrow of my own. I didn't want to upset Tyler. Actually, I felt bad about it. But there were so many other things to deal with—things more important than some silly love affair. Love affair? What in the world was I thinking? We couldn't afford to get distracted right now. It could cost us our lives, and I wasn't willing to pay that price...again.

Sitting down on the edge of Tyler's bed, I let out a long, troubled sigh. Aside from the Tyler, Stone, and Bronx problems, I couldn't shake my worries for Lily either. She'd been in the back of my mind ever since I left the club. Our friendship was no secret and I knew Bronx would use that to his advantage to find me. Even though she didn't know where I was, there were still other ways he could use her to get me back. They say don't borrow trouble, but I had a feeling the trouble was already there, whether borrowed or not.

I overheard him say something about Texas. Are you in Texas? Lily had asked it, but was the question really coming from her? How could she overhear him say something about Texas without him knowing? It was impossible. Bronx was too smart to allow that. My stomach rolled over, clamping, tightening. I didn't want to believe that Bronx had already gotten to her, using his gift of persuasion to control her as if she were his puppet and he was the puppet master. But it made too much sense to ignore. If Bronx had Lily, and I believed he did, then that meant she was in danger. And I had to help her.

In a hurry, I got up and changed into a blue V-neck tee and black pants, then ran a brush through my hair. A quick glance in the mirror showed that I looked okay and I gave my reflection a brief smile before heading out to the living room.

"You look beautiful," Tyler murmured as he groped me with his eyes.

I felt that warm sensation spark to life inside me again, spreading all over from my head to my toes. "Thanks. You do too." It was amazing how good he looked in blue and white striped pajama bottoms and a comfy-looking, white cotton tee shirt.

Sitting down beside him, the leather groaned against my weight. I grabbed the laptop and shook away the screen saver with my finger. The tiny clock in the top right corner said it was seven fifty-one in the evening. Tyler slid his hand behind me, rubbing my shoulders while I typed a response to Lily. I was getting more worried for her by the minute, but revealing that in this e-mail would be a horrible mistake. I was certain that the message would ultimately end up being read by Bronx. So I decided to keep my response to her short and sweet, confident that I'd hear back from her (Bronx pretending to be her) pretty soon.

Lily,

I'm ok. Don't worry about me. Please take care of yourself! I promise to keep in touch.
Your Friend,

Abby

I shut the laptop and placed it back on the coffee table. No longer rubbing my shoulders, Tyler scooped up my hand, and when I tried to stand, I was met with resistance. When I tugged, his grip only tightened. Even though I was much stronger and could easily break free, I sank back into the sofa and leaned over into his chest. His other arm wrapped around me, almost making me forget about everything. The warmth from his body, his amazing scent, his tender touch—I loved it all. With soft, caressing movements, he stroked my hair with his fingertips. My body tingling with delight, I craned my neck and looked up at his face. His eyes were glossy, moist, barely holding back tears, and seeing that got me choked up. Ducking my head back into the safety of his chest, I could hear the beat of his heart speeding up.

"Abby," he said in a timid voice. "Please be careful."

"I will. I promise." I wasn't sure if I was reassuring him or myself.

My eyes met his as I pulled out of our embrace. He palmed my cheek while his other hand intertwined with mine. His face lowered, slowly erasing the small gap between us. Charged butterflies started fluttering inside my stomach and the hot sensation returned in my core. Mentally I knew to pull away. I knew I shouldn't do it. I knew it would put too much of a strain on us. Our focus would become blurred and our efforts would become more challenging. This was the moment that actions would speak volumes louder than my false words.

The warmth of his lips on mine sent static chills coursing through my body. He let go of my hand and aggressively tugged my hair as the kiss deepened into a sensual teasing that had me opening my mouth for him to come in and explore. His tongue eased inside and began moving around in slow, arousing movements. My arms snaked around him and I was digging my fingernails in his back the next instant, completely caught up with the way he tasted, the warmth radiating from his perfect body. He gasped, his shuddered breath tickling my tongue with pleasure that only intensified when he dropped his hands to my waist and slipped them under my shirt. His fingers fumbling with the button of my pants, he kissed me harder, his tongue moving more boldly, and a moan escaped my mouth that I barely recognized—carnal, hungry. Several flicks of his wrist, but my button didn't seem to be budging, then his eager fingers skimmed across my waistline, causing my whole body to tremble. My fangs slowly emerged as I opened my mouth and delicately nibbled his bottom lip before reengaging in a kiss that would've stolen my breath if I'd still been human. *Human.* A silent warning rose between us, but it quickly faded as he clamped down on my bottom lip with his teeth. Instantly, I tasted my blood, which sent me spiraling out of control as he pulled back and lowered to my neck, where he continued inspecting me with his mouth. The pleasure of his kisses could not be described by words, intensified by the metallic flavor pooling in my mouth. As I grabbed his hair and tugged his head to the side, he sucked in a deep breath. I licked my lips as I lowered them, closer and closer, until they brushed against his skin where his racing pulse only teased me further. Opening my mouth, I could feel the tips of my fangs resting just above the vein in his skin. A growl formed in my throat and spilled out of my mouth just as I attempted to bite down into him, but he jerked out of my hands and I bit air instead. There was a part of me that wanted to try again, needed to sample how he tasted, but when his frightened eyes met mine, something snapped in my head and I needed to get away from him.

I startled, full of shame and contrition, and was across the room in a blur of motion. Glancing back, I found Tyler still gaping at me, and that brought a turbulent wave of regret. There was no need for him to say a word because I could read it in his eyes; I could see it all over his face. Though he was afraid, he still wanted me, and that meant I needed to get the hell out of here—for more reasons than before. I needed to get back to the mission at hand, which was to keep Tyler safe, find out what Stone wasn't telling me, and somehow help Lily. "I gotta go," I announced in a rush of words, then flashed away without waiting to hear if he said anything back.

With the need to clear my head taking longer than I'd thought it would, it took me twice as long to arrive at Rayver's Pub. The attraction I felt for Tyler was becoming too difficult to fight, and I either needed to find a way to deal with it or get away from him altogether. The thought of the latter stung; the fact I'd almost bitten him stung worse. Using every bit of energy I had, I temporarily made myself forget about what had happened, even though the heat of that kiss still lingered on my lips as I made my way through the front door of the pub. Instantly, I picked up the scent of three humans sitting at the bar. One of them was Britney, the new blood donor, who had just glanced back my way, her eyes widening with glee when she saw me. "You guys, this is her," she squealed while standing up and running to embrace me. After hugging her back, I walked with her to the bar.

"Hi." I smiled at her two innocent human friends.

"Anna"—Britney was still under the impression that was my name—"this is Mac and Sara. Mac and Sara, this is Anna. She is the amazing one I told you about." Mac was a stocky guy with short auburn hair and heavy freckles sprinkled on his skin. He wore loose-fitted jeans and a navy blue tee. Sara was the epitome of a cheerleader, tall and slender with a little curve in her butt and thighs, and straight honey blond hair falling just below her shoulders. Both of them looked to be in their mid-to late twenties.

"When you guys do it, you gotta let Anna be the one," Britney explained.

"I'm ready. Especially if she's gonna do it!" Mac said, voice loud and excited.

Sara scowled and rolled her light hazel eyes. "I thought you were going to wait, Mackey?"

Britney slurped her drink and then looked over at Sara. "Trust me, it's the most amazing thing ever. Stone said that because Anna's still a baby, it's way more intense."

"Wait just a second," I scolded. "I'm not here for you. I'm here to speak with Stone." *And maybe the two unbitten wannabe's*, I thought.

Britney grimaced. "We'll see about that."

Quinn appeared from behind the bar, and his eyes lit up when he noticed me. "Anna, yer right on time. Stone was just askin 'bout ya."

Ignoring Britney and who I assumed were her soon-to-be blood donor friends, I headed toward the back room. As I did, I felt three sets of eyes burning holes in my back, but I didn't turn around to confirm it. I quickly embraced Quinn as I passed by. He was such a sweet man and I admired his patience for that annoying daughter of his. Her insistence on getting her own way was quite irritating, which was most likely the reason he'd caved and allowed her to become a blood donor in the first place.

The canned hallway ceiling lights weren't turned on but my eyes easily showed me to the door, the only thing separating me from Stone Rayver, vampire club boss and possible Enforcer. I raised my hand to knock, but before I did I heard Stone call out, "Please come in."

With a twist of the knob, I walked inside the dimly lit room and went over to where Stone sat. "More innocents for the evening?" I asked, taking a seat beside the club owner.

His familiar black jeans and boots were now paired with a gray long-sleeved shirt, and his hair was parted down the middle with a glossy finish. In one hand was a cocktail glass containing the golden liquid he enjoyed drinking, while his other hand swiftly grabbed mine and brought it to his lips.

"Who do I smell on you? You naughty girl!" he scolded, lips curling into a smirk.

"That is none of your business!" I yanked my hand away. "You know why I'm here, let's stick to that."

He sipped his drink. "Oh, Abby, jealousy is such a horrible emotion. Please accept my apologies."

More jealousy? What was it with men and their jealous emotions? "You barely know me," I told him crisply. "There's no way you could be jealous."

He gave a mild shrug, took another swallow. "You want to know what I haven't told you." Good, he was getting straight to the reason I was here.

I crossed my arms in front of my chest. "Yes. Weren't you supposed to tell me everything yesterday?"

He tilted his head to the side. "How can you question me when you were the one in a hurry to leave? And now I know why," he snickered. "You've done well keeping his identity a secret. I should've discovered that first when I tasted you. How in the world did you keep that from me?"

Ignoring his attempt to find out about Tyler, I got back to the reason I was here. "I have time tonight. I want to know more about the Head Council and their connection to the one who transformed me."

"I can't answer that without knowing who *he* is." Stone nestled his back against the sofa.

Feeling cornered and wanting desperately to push my way out, I decided to spill Bronx's name with hopes it would not come back to bite me in the butt.

Reaching over, I grabbed the drink out of his hand. The alcohol, definitely some kind of scotch, burned as I chugged down its entire contents, then with a clank, I set the empty beverage glass on the table. Trepidation coiled through me, making it difficult to speak. But then with the memory of everything my old captor had done to me, that familiar heated sensation of anger surged inside, and because of that, I was able to push his horrible name off my tongue.

"Bronx." My throat loosened and my fiery anger increased. "His name is Bronx."

Stone's eyes gave it away instantly. He knew Bronx, and now I assumed a lot more than just that. Realizing this sent my anger into a frenzy and it felt like I was going to explode from the inside out.

At first my eyes burned. But it wasn't long before my hands sizzled like they were holding lit embers, and yet oddly it didn't hurt. I didn't feel pain. Glancing down at them, I gasped aloud. My hands were glowing bright orange, and in seeing that, panic immediately seized me. I jumped up, waving my arms in front of me. "What's happening to me?"

Stone got up too, stepping away from me. "Abby," he shouted, "It's getting too hot in here. You need to calm down!"

A bubble of heat was still around my hands, warming the room, and though I could feel the hotness, it didn't burn me. But it was obviously affecting him. "I don't know! I can't control it!" a clambering of words as I watched Stone back away a little further. Not wanting to hurt him, I moved backward too until my butt collided with the wall. Then suddenly the orange glow burst into flames with flickering tips, and when that happened, it also got hotter. Scared out of my mind, I cried out, unsure of what to do or how to stop the fire. But I needed to figure something out because Stone's bewildered gaze surely meant he had no clue how to help me. When waving my arms again only seemed to intensify the fires on my hands, I sunk my head low, feeling defeated. "It won't stop. I can't control it."

Stone made an effort to come toward me, but the growing heat forced him back. Desperately, I gulped at the air around me as I tried to focus on regaining control of my body. That's when a sudden wave of dizziness moved through me, and I felt something even stranger, something I hadn't felt since becoming a vampire. My heart was beating. I could feel my rapid pulse in my ears as tingling sensations coursed through my veins. In that same instant, the flames spread up my arms, but strangely the only heat I felt was coming from somewhere in my chest, swelling in my lungs with a burning thickness and making me gulp at the air. I glimpsed Stone helplessly watching from across the room, his eyes wide with panic, and I was certain mine were too. My throat tickled with each massive breath I inhaled, and in releasing them, I realized that I was actually breathing too. Really breathing. How was that possible? And with every puff I took the glowing fire on me seemed to fade. Sweat pooled at my nape and across my brow as the intense heat slowly cooled, the visible fires extinguished.

Another attempt to reach me was a success, and Stone rubbed my back in a soothing motion once there. "You're breathing," he stated with awe. "The essence of your human life must be acting out right before our eyes."

"What does that mean?" I asked, placing my hand on my chest and feeling the *thump, thump* of my heart beating. How was it possible that I could feel those human things again? Though it was wonderful and something I'd wanted since being turned into a vampire, it still terrified me. "Feel this." I grabbed Stone's hand and placed his fingers on the pulse in my neck. "Not only am I breathing again, but my heart is beating too."

He pressed down. "It's beating. It's really beating."

Excitement seized me as beads of sweat dripped from my brow and I couldn't believe what my body was doing. Or why it was doing any of this. But my excitement quickly faded, replaced by fear, confusion, and shock. Was this proof that I was part human? Was that even possible? Stone kept rubbing my back, keeping me calmer that I would've been, and though I hated to admit it, I actually enjoyed his touch. Stone, not Tyler. The thought of Tyler brought a rush of guilt to the surface and I wondered what he would think about all of this. Stone being a vampire, I assumed that meant he'd handled this fire thing much better than Tyler would have since he was human, and I was glad I'd been at the pub when it happened. Yet just another complex reminder there simply wasn't time for love, lust, whatever, no matter who it was with. And that meant no more slips like earlier with Ty.

Then the jumble of thoughts in my mind went blank, my body became limber. The sound of my heartbeat slowly faded and I could sense it'd stopped beating altogether. With a constricted throat, my breathing slowed as well, and then ceased too. And though I wasn't sweating anymore, there were damp rings under my armpits and around the collar of my shirt. I looked up at Stone's face and his eyes widened. "Are you okay?" he asked.

Shaking my head I answered, "I don't know." And I really didn't.

"I've never seen anything like that before. You were, you were..."

I sighed. "Whatever that was, thank God it's over now." I walked over to the sofa and fell into it. Stone followed my lead and resumed his usual spot beside me, propping his feet on the table.

"When I tasted you last night..." He ran his fingers through his hair, his forehead wrinkled in concentration. "You're different than any other vampire I've tasted. I don't exactly know what that means, but it might be the beginning of an explanation here."

Suddenly, hunger unlike anything I'd felt before tore through me, and I felt my fangs burst out of my mouth. I couldn't think about anything but blood. Blood, blood, blood. Remembering that Britney was at the bar, I begged Stone to send her back to me. Regardless of what I'd just gone through, there was absolutely no way I was drinking from another innocent—especially after what almost happened with Tyler.

Without speaking a word, Stone flashed out of the room. I was alone for just a few seconds before the canned lights in the ceiling brightened as he came in with Britney and one of her friends, Mac. Oh great. Just great. He brought an innocent back here. Dammit! Fight it, Abby. Maybe Britney's blood would still taste as good as it did last night? After all, I was the one that tainted it in the first place.

All three of them sat across from me—Stone in the middle, Britney on his left, Mac on his right. Eager, smiling, ready. In the next instant, I was sitting beside Britney, never even felt myself move. I was just there, controlled by an insatiable hunger, mindful of Mac sitting just two bodies away from me. When I grabbed Britney's face, she gasped, then I twisted it sideways, ignoring Mac's amazing scent as my fangs burst through her skin and sunk into her juicy vein. The flow of her blood reenergized me while she wailed and moaned from the intense pleasure of my bite. When finished, I licked her neck, sealing the wound and picking up any remnant drops of blood, then laid her head on the armrest. Glancing over at Stone, he was just laying Mac against the other armrest. Apparently, he'd wanted some innocent blood this evening, and fortunately for him, I was in no mood to judge. I might even have been a little jealous.

Afterwards, we met each other across the room, back on the other sofa. He swallowed hard, took my hand inside his. "Because I like you, I will not lie to you. But it will not be easy for me to be so forthcoming. You will not like what I have to say, but you must control your emotions so they don't get the best of you again."

I stared at his deep blue eyes remembering the recognition I'd seen in there at saying Bronx's name. Immediately after that, my hands had been covered in glowing bubbles of heat. "I don't want that to happen again either, but I need to know what you know about Bronx."

"I know Bronx very well," he admitted. "We shared an interest in Meredith and I needed him gone. Three had become a crowd, if you know what I mean."

"What? You also knew Meredith?"

"Yes. I had just discovered my ability, seeing inside someone's essence while drinking their blood, and I offered my services to the Head Council just as any gifted vampire should. I did many tasks for them, and by doing so it created a higher ranking for me amongst some of the other Enforcers. I tried to use my reputation by asking the Head Council to help Meredith and I *permanently* remove Bronx as an Enforcer, only they changed our deal halfway through by not killing him. They overrode Bronx's death and relocated him to Florida because Bronx offered his services to them as well: his secret ability of mind control. You see, our use of persuasion is limited. We can only use it on humans. Some are more talented with this than others. But Bronx can use it on humans and vampires, gaining complete control of their minds. The Head Council saw value in letting him live and serve with them."

"The Head Council will kill simply because they are asked to?"

"Yes," he said. "Sometimes they do not even need to be asked.

"You're an Enforcer?"

He nodded. "But I haven't had any special assignments since Bronx was relocated. All I have to do is run this club, pay them their money."

"What about Meredith?" Great, just what I needed. Another scorned ex-lover. Or wannabe ex-lover like Valentina was.

"Meredith no longer wanted me after she discovered what Bronx could do. She left me to go be with him, but he rejected her and cursed her existence. I went after her and arrived just in time to witness him using his mind control on her. He led her outside in the heat of the sun and watched as she slowly burned to death. Fear of him giving me the same fate kept me from trying to save her. I fled from Florida and came to this town wanting to start over." He shook his head. "I was such a coward."

His face looked sincere—I could see the lingering pain in his eyes. He was telling the truth. Every single word he said. I could feel it, sense it. But, of course, now I had more questions. "If Bronx is an Enforcer, then why would he allow a security guard to overpower him? That was the only reason I was able to escape him."

Stone met my eyes, stared for a moment. "There's a reason he chose you, Abby. You're special. More special than you even realize, and the power emanating from you—it's unlike anything I've ever seen. I don't know all the answers, but I do know you're going to be a very powerful vampire."

The use of Stone's word "special" sent my mind straight back to my father and the insane phone calls he'd made to me. *Abby, you're special. He knows and he's coming for you.* Was it possible that my father knew about all of this? Did he know about Bronx and what he would do to me? But if so, that meant he knew about vampires. And if he knew about vampires, was that why he left my mother and me so many years ago?

I needed to keep probing Stone. As long as he was talking, I was listening. "What do you mean by special?" Because really, how could I possibly be such a powerful vampire?

Delight beamed on his face, the muscles in his cheeks pulling up into a smile. "Don't you feel it? A very powerful ability, or maybe it's more than one. Maybe it's multiple abilities, growing within you. That has to be why your arms burst into flames."

"What? I'm getting an ability?" I straightened. "That's what's happening to me?" Excitement flowed, but the ghost of my father's voice drowned it out. *Abby, you're special. He's coming for you.* My father was sounding less like a lunatic and more like a person who knew a lot more than I'd ever imagined.

Then I thought of Tyler and a sense of urgency consumed me. How long had it been since I left him at the house? I needed to get back before he came looking for me. In a hurry, I stood up.

Stone reached for my hand. "Wait," he said.

I looked down at him, and his grip tightened. "Let me taste you again. Maybe it will uncover more of this mystery." He slowly brought my hand to his mouth.

I was torn between wanting to get back to Tyler and the excitement of the possibility of getting my own powerful ability. The decision had been easier to make than I'd thought it would be. Tyler would have to wait just a little bit longer. Stone's lips were already tickling the skin on my wrist as I sat back down. This time, there was no delay—his fangs immediately ripped into me. And my body tensed as he eagerly drank, savoring my powerful blood.

16

Introduced

I HAD NEVER FELT MORE ALIVE since becoming a vampire. Laughter roared off my tongue as I carelessly raced back to Tyler's house. My feet were light as feathers as they tracked over dirt, stones, fallen branches, and muck. A musty smell filled the woods, perhaps because of the day's scattered showers, and my hair was damp from the surrounding branches that brushed it while flashing by. The confirmation that I was getting an extremely powerful ability, or perhaps multiple abilities, consumed my mind as I reflected back on what Stone had told me. Pyrokinesis was the power he'd tasted the most, my freakish experience with glowing heat capable of burning anyone or anything that touched them was evidence this ability was rapidly manifesting within me. When Stone had read my blood, he was startled to discover that the intensity of my gift of fire was merely the beginning of whatever else was coming. But unfortunately, he couldn't uncover why I became sort of human when the pyrokinesis flared up.

When Stone finished drinking from me, there was fear and excitement in his gaze, which had led him to his explanation of the only two ways a vampire could be killed. Burning to death was one; decapitation was the other. Wooden stakes through the heart was just another myth about our species, as was silver chains and holy water, which old folklore would blatantly contradict. So here I was, a "walking flame thrower" Stone called it, and once I mastered that new ability, I'd become the biggest threat and most deadly weapon to all vampires. It would take several Enforcers and perhaps the entire Head Council, working together as one to defeat me—if that would even be possible at all. Not that I was looking to fight those ancient rulers, it had just been Stone's way of letting me know the depths of my gift. He'd also begged me to practice with the fire a little more before leaving the pub. Fear of another unexpected outburst had made me agree, even though I knew Tyler would be worried sick.

At first, gaining any control whatsoever of the pyrokinesis was impossible, and had sent Stone to the back of the room numerous times. But thankfully, before giving up, I finally started to get the swing of it. Filled with a renewed confidence, and after a big hug from Stone, I took off. The anticipation of seeing Tyler and telling him everything that had happened, sat impatiently on the tip of my tongue.

Out of nowhere, my father crossed my mind, as I approached the back door of the house. His possible knowledge of all of this seemed more likely and a pang inside my chest reaffirmed how brokenhearted I was over him. If I hadn't hung up the phone, would I have gotten more information from him? Perhaps I should've listened to him and not accused him of being insane. It was hard to stop my assumption that he possibly knew about vampires, and that fact alone being the reason he'd left me, but I couldn't tell Tyler about it—not yet anyway. I wasn't sure how I felt, or what I believed, but I didn't want to make my father look crazy if he wasn't.

Placing all thoughts about my father in the very back corner of my mind, I let myself inside the house. Tyler was sitting at the café table in the corner of the kitchen. Beaming with delight, I rushed over and sat in the empty chair beside him, and was unnerved when he didn't express happiness to see me. As a matter of fact, his hardened expression revealed the opposite, anger boiling in the depths of his eyes, and it caused me to momentarily forget about everything wonderful happening to me.

"Ty, what's wrong?" I croaked. How could his obvious bad mood send me spiraling straight down with him? Unfortunately I already knew that answer and I refused to acknowledge it.

"I'm glad you're okay," he said flatly.

Tension mounting, I said, "I'm sorry. I'm sorry I left like that, but it was for the best." Jumping up from my seat, I flickered into his lap, but his uncrossed arms acted like a barricade to keep me away. But instead of retreating, I leaned against them. At least the gray hoodie he wore was soft and inviting.

He didn't say anything, didn't move, which led me to think I'd really upset him, but he shouldn't be this angry just because I'd left the way I did. Should he?

"I'm getting an ability," I mumbled against his arms, hoping that he'd be just as excited as me and open them up. "A powerful one. And maybe I'll end up with multiple abilities." I leaned back and cupped his face, forcing him to look at me, and it alarmed me to see that he didn't appear surprised by what I'd just told him.

We played a silent stare-off for several minutes. His face stayed hard, eyes glistening with anger. Since I wasn't a mind reader, there was no way for me to know what was wrong with him. So I told him everything that happened back at the pub, hoping to get a more encouraging reaction and praying he wouldn't be any more jealous of Stone.

He let out a heavy sigh and finally opened up his arms, letting me fall against him. "Oh Abby," he breathed, "what am I going to do with you?"

What the hell did he mean by that? Since I wasn't sure, I kept quiet and waited for him to continue. He swallowed hard, tightening his arms around me. "I got a premonition right after you left."

"What? What'd you see?" My throat constricted and my stomach twisted in knots. I knew based on his actions this couldn't be good.

He shook his head, arms squeezing harder around me, as he rasped, "It's going to kill you. I watched you die." A big fat tear splashed on my head, followed by the sound of his muffled sobs.

"No. That's not going to happen." I lifted out of his arms, staring at his face, green eyes heavily stung by those salty tears. "I'm going to learn how to control this power and I'm going to defeat Bronx with it. I promise."

"That's not what I saw," he answered right back.

Palming his face, I locked my gaze with his. "I'm already starting to control it."

His eyebrows scrunched, confused. "What do you mean?"

"Watch me."

In a flash I was in the empty seat beside him, holding my right hand out in front of me, fingers together, palm up. I closed my eyes, concentrating hard, emptying my mind of rambling thoughts, distracting feelings—exactly the way I'd practiced with Stone before he would let me leave the pub. I summoned the energy inside me, calling it forth, demanding its presence and submission. Squeezing my eyelids, I kept a steady focus on my pyrokinesis and soon enough, my chest flushed warm. And then it got hotter as it spread through my body like a wildfire. Hot shivers crept up my spine, then the heat intensified, now a raging inferno inside me. Mouth open, I gulped huge breaths, the crisp flow of oxygen only making my body burn even hotter. But just like before, it didn't hurt me. I wasn't in pain. The fire was still solely inside of me and since I hadn't released it out yet, Tyler was perfectly safe. Everything was fine.

My heart rumbled to life, beating, pumping, and I couldn't help the satisfied smile that pulled at my mouth. It was time for the fire to come out, but on my terms only. I willed all my energy into my awaiting hand, and the fire obeyed, moving there instantaneous like lighting. Tyler gasped, but I blocked him out of my mind to hold my concentration. As long as I was in control, he was safe and everything would be okay. Taking another deep, slow breath, I opened my eyes at last, and saw that familiar orange glow radiating off my palm as if a bright flashlight were under my skin.

"How are you doing that?" he asked.

"I'm isolating the energy to my hand. As long as I stay focused, that's where it will stay. My hand is so hot it will scorch anything it touches." I glanced up at his face and then quickly back to my hand.

"Wow. That's incredible..."

"Isn't it?" I chuckled. I was proud of my new ability—more than proud, I was inebriated by the reality of having pyrokinesis and more so by the fact that I was now able to control it. "We've got to celebrate. Bronx can't hurt us anymore. I'm not afraid anymore!" Jumping out of the chair, I twirled around, holding the glowing bubble of heat safely in my hand. Then I closed my fingers and balled my hand into a fist, thin streams of smoke wafting from it. The fire was out. Cool prickles rushed all over my body as my breathing slowed, my heart stopped beating. I was a normal vampire once more.

I skipped over to the fridge, pulled out two Chimays, and then popped the tops off with my teeth—yep, my teeth. I would've never done that when human, not that I couldn't, but because I'd be too afraid to even try it. But now I felt fearless. A whole new form of confidence was taking over and it made my feet feel light, as if they were floating above the floor. Grinning, big and wide, I swooped back into Tyler's lap and handed him a beer. He took it, smiling shyly, perhaps a little nervous, unsure of everything happening to me, to us. I held out my beer. He hesitated briefly, and then clinked his bottle into mine. The celebration had begun.

After finishing our first round, I retrieved another. Tyler eased up, seeming happier, a little less cautious. Contagious giggles alternated between us, and light chatter declaring my freedom and the fact we were no longer on the run, soared off our lips. Perhaps Tyler was finally becoming a believer. That or he was at least acting like he was. Either way was fine for now, though I sensed there was something a little off about him, but I easily put it out of my mind. The carefree atmosphere was revitalizing. All of our worries and fears were silenced. We moved into the living room, turned on some music, then danced around to the beautiful lyrics and melody. Everything was absolutely perfect.

When the song ended, we plopped down on the sofa together. Tyler leaned in closer, staring at me, eyes full of something I couldn't quite place, attraction, lust...maybe even lo—. No, I wouldn't say it.

"I was thinking," said Ty, "That maybe we, maybe there could be, something between us now. Maybe we can be together and not fight it anymore?" He reached for my hand, gave it a tight squeeze.

Those warm tingly feelings returned, scattering all around inside me. Knots formed in my stomach, then expanded into my chest. I should've known this would be coming. "I just don't think that's a good idea." I shook my head back and forth—rapid movements. "We don't even know how the Head Council will receive me. And Bronx is still out there and—"

He licked his lips then sealed them over mine and kissed me so deeply, I whimpered. At first, I didn't move, his passion consuming me and setting me aflame with suppressed desire, my body spinning and immobile all at once as I struggled to form a coherent thought. Caution flared like a red light in my mind, but my body wanted the opposite—wanted to feel close, to kiss him back. His kisses grew rougher, his full lips pressing hard against my mouth, enticing me further with a slow, wet swipe of his tongue. Still I couldn't pull away, I liked how it felt way too much. The muddled voice inside my head was being drowned out, taken over by a raging lust for him. Grabbing the back of his head, I pulled him closer, tangling my fingers in his hair as I finally surrendered.

Several blissful moments passed, head-lightening pleasure coursing through my body with the firm press of his fingers in my back. His tongue darted out again, and this time I parted my lips right away, allowing him access to come on inside and explore. His shuddered breaths tickled as he entered, and the hair on my nape rose. I let go of his hair, hands rushing down his neck, shoulders, and back, before pulling him closer with an aggressive tug. Then suddenly, the fear of being too rough and hurting him gripped my spine and I knew I needed to stop, *we* needed to stop. It couldn't happen like this, not yet, not so soon. I let go, dropped my hands to my sides, and leaned back. He gaped at me, his eyes desperate and wanting. Shaking my head, overwhelmed by emotion, I looked away. My body was hot for him and it didn't want to stop, but caution wouldn't ease from my mind. Conflicted, I nibbled my bottom lip, now watching his face coming closer, his lips lowering towards mine in a slow, steady movement. But we couldn't. We had to stop before things got out of control, so I threw out an arm to block him from coming any closer. "Please don't," a hoarse plea of words. "We can't. This is happening so fast."

A sudden heat slid through my veins at the way he stared at me with a determined gaze. He didn't speak a word, and with the way his emotion shown in his beautiful green eyes, he didn't have to. But I knew this couldn't happen, not yet, not like this. Not when there were still so many unknowns. The worry of how the Head Council would react to me once they learned of my pyro still lingered in my mind, along with the fear of how they'd react to me loving a human. *Loving a human?* A mental war waged in my head as I stood there looking into the depths of his eyes, his unwavering gaze a mirror of the passion still simmering between us. And as I stared harder, I couldn't help but wonder if somehow, in fact, I had *fallen* for him. After all, he'd been my savior from the beginning and I owed him everything for getting me away from Bronx. Bronx. Just thinking that name sent liquid ice down my spine. He was still out there, hunting me, and until my old captor was stopped once and for all, neither one of us were truly safe.

And then there was Lily, and if my suspicions were right—and I knew they were—then she desperately needed me to help her. I swallowed a lump of emotion in my throat as I realized I'd have to face Bronx, fight him and destroy him. All of a sudden, the night wasn't looking so great anymore. Even using my amazing new power wouldn't really guarantee my victory. Sure my gift of fire was unheard of, but he might have an advantage with his mind controlling ability.

With so many things still unresolved, was it possible to find love in the midst of it all? Love? It had to be lust, a sexual longing, a need to feel close during challenging times. Whatever I wanted to call it, it didn't matter. My body still ached for him and from the way he looked at me; he wanted me just as bad, if not worse. The spark of emotion between us was growing too difficult to ignore and that meant the crossroad I'd come to was either completely opening up to Tyler or running away from him—right now. Which one would it be? Tick tock. My body would decide for me if I didn't act fast. On a long swallow, I closed my eyes with resignation, then threw my arms around him, instantly resuming right where we'd left off. My decision was made at last, sealed by the way his lips were all over me, and it wasn't just love or lust, but savage ownership. And I welcomed the roughness.

Hours had passed. Both of us showered and dressed, then regrouped at the café table in the kitchen before heading out. Even though I thought it was a really bad idea, Tyler had convinced me to let him come to the pub to meet Stone.

"You look beautiful." He stretched around the table and kissed my cheek, and I hoped I wasn't pushing the limits with the sexy royal blue top I wore with spaghetti straps for sleeves.

Letting my gaze roam over his soft gray sweater and black slacks, I smiled sweetly an said, "Thanks, so do you."

"Ready to go?" He hopped up and grabbed his car keys off the kitchen counter.

"Ready as I'll ever be." I rubbed my hands on my jeans. "Let's do it."

We held hands and listened to Katy Perry the entire way to the pub. Unable to ignore that little voice cautioning me about bringing Tyler with me, I silently prayed that Stone wouldn't overreact—and that Tyler wouldn't get jealous. Yeah sure, if I believed that, then I really was a fool in love. *Love*?? Why do I keep calling it that? By the time we parked, my nerves were doing flips in my belly. Tyler got out and came around to my side to open the door. Taking his awaiting hand, I let him lead me across the street, still holding hands as we walked through the entrance of the pub.

Here goes nothing, I thought.

We strolled inside, heading straight for the bar. Britney was sitting on the left, in her usual seat, and thankfully she was alone. Tonight, she wore white jeans and a green hoodie. Her and Quinn were in a heated discussion about something, but they hushed right away, and I missed whatever it was. Quinn's eyes beamed the moment he looked me. "Hey Anna," he said. "Welcome back. Stone'll be glad to know yer here."

Britney quickly turned around and exclaimed, "Hey An..." freezing when she saw me holding hands with Tyler. The smile evaporated from her face and she did a very obvious roll of her eyes. "I guess you don't need me," she pouted.

Realizing she must think Tyler was my donor, I decided to have a little fun with it and keep my mouth shut. There was a good chance Britney would turn out to be my donor tonight regardless, but there was no reason to give that away to her now—not after her bratty attitude. "Britney, this is Tyler," I told her.

Tyler and Britney shook hands, her face still pouting, and then I introduced him to Quinn. The older man's lips compressed as he studied Ty a moment, and I thought maybe he recognized him from the other night. "I'll go let Stone know yer here. Would ya like sometin' to drink before I go back der?"

Tyler respectfully answered, "We'll both have a vodka with a splash of soda water and a lime please, sir."

"No problem, son," Quinn replied and flashed me a quick smile. He moved quickly for his age, and as Tyler and I got situated in the barstools next to Britney, the drinks clanked on the countertop in front of us.

"Thanks," I said, then turned my attention to the gorgeous man sitting on my right. I could feel Britney's eyes on the back of my head and I really hoped I was driving her as crazy as she drove me.

Tyler and I did another rendition of cheers with our cocktails and I heard Britney puff an annoyed sigh behind me. Completely ignoring her, and feeling proud of myself for pissing her off, I drank my tasty beverage and then set the glass down. Moving my gaze back to Ty's, a huge smile stretched across his face. He leaned toward me, his lips hovering around my ear. His breath was warm on my skin and it tickled my lobe. *Oh please don't kiss me. Not here,* I silently prayed. And thankfully he didn't. He gave a long sigh and said, "I love you, Abby."

My eyes instantly filled up with tears, but this would be a horrible place to cry, so I fought it, choking it back the best I could. *Dammit!* How could I care so much about this man that I would burst into tears at the sound of those sweet words? I wanted to say it back, but for some reason, I couldn't. Not now, not here. So I flashed him a smile. What else could I do?

"Hey Anna," Stone called out as he approached from behind the bar. His smile vanished, face crumbled as he glared at Ty. "You must be her boy toy," he smarted.

Staring daggers at Stone, Tyler replied, "And you must be that jackass she told me about."

Stone's glare hardened and his fangs extended. In that moment my fears were confirmed as I sensed the building testosterone around me. I heard Britney laughing and I looked over, daring her to continue. Then forgetting about her, I looked back at Tyler, then the club owner, both still staring daggers at each other. From the depths of his throat, Stone growled—deep and guttural—fixing his predator eyes on his prey. But instead of backing down, Tyler jumped up, pushing the barstool behind him, holding his balled fists in front of him. Stone inched forward, and I knew he would pounce at any moment, and that meant I needed to do something, now.

Throwing myself in front of Tyler and extending my arm out to keep Stone back, I shouted, "Enough of this crap. If you guys can't get along, then I'm out of here!" I looked back at Ty. "And you're coming with me."

He inhaled deeply, softening his position as he stepped back. "You're right. This is stupid." Ty shook his head, but kept a wary gaze on his enemy.

I glanced back at Stone. "He wanted to meet you, not fight with you. If you're not capable of being friendly with him, then we're leaving," my tone seething with threat.

Stone relaxed a little and concealed his fangs. "I'm sorry. I don't have a problem with it as long as he stays out here."

"Wait just a minute," Tyler argued, running his fingers through his hair, "Wherever she goes, I go."

My gaze back on Ty I said, "I don't think it's a good idea for you to come in the back room anyway." It would be embarrassing to let him watch me feed, let alone the discussion I needed to have with Stone. "I won't be long. Please, just wait out here for me?"

Britney clapped her hands. "Oh goody for me."

"Shut the hell up!" I yelled.

"No, we stay together," Tyler snapped.

"Like hell," challenged Stone, eyes slanting back into a glare.

Here we go again, I thought, wishing desperately that Tyler would just listen. Keeping my stance between the two males about to rip each other's throats apart, I said, "Ty, I'll be quick. I'm not particularly excited about you watching that anyway. Please. Please do this for me."

A few tense moments passed as I waited for his answer. Then thankfully he nodded. "All right. I'll do this for you. But you better be back fast or I'm coming back there."

A wave of relief washed over me. After thanking Ty with a quick peck on the cheek, I flashed Britney a look that demanded she come with me. Without arguing, she jumped up out of her chair and as we rounded the bar, I called out, "Stone, I'm trusting—"

"Oh don't you worry," his voice was directly behind me, "Quinn will take great care of your boy."

I knew Tyler must have been using every bit of strength he had to refrain from following me, and for that, I was extremely thankful. The thought of him watching me feed was disturbing, and the more I thought about it, the more I realized I wasn't ready for him to see that side of me. Despite his ability to "see" me eating in his visions, I was nowhere near prepared to willingly put on a show of it. Perhaps his patience on that would be demanded indefinitely. The three of us entered the back room and found our places on the sofas: Britney on the left one, Stone and I on the right. As she unzipped her hoodie, revealing a hideous green-colored tank top, she demanded, "What the hell was that all about?"

Oh God, please shut her up. In a flash, I was across the room and sitting next to her. As Britney crossed her arms over her chest, Stone started laughing. Rolling my eyes at him and then swinging them back to Britney, I asked, "Do you want to sit here and chitchat or do you want me to bite you?"

Britney's eyes grew wide with delight, and an oversized smile spread across her face. "I want you to bite me," she panted.

"And I don't want to keep you waiting," I replied smartly, then leaned down and bit into the plump vein inside her neck. She gasped, and moments later, moans escaped her mouth until she was finally silenced by the intense pleasure of my bite. A little while later, I was licking the last few drops from her skin.

After that, I got up and headed back over to Stone. He was giving me one of "those" looks. "Don't say it," I challenged.

"Don't say what?" he replied, voice playful.

"You know what."

"Like the fact he's human and knows about us."

He had me there, but if he could have an arrangement with Quinn, then I should be able to have one with Tyler. "We have an arrangement," I informed. "And I don't have much time, so perhaps we could talk about something of importance?"

He propped his feet on the table, keeping a watchful eye on me. "My dear sweet Abby, I would do anything for you. But you must know that guy is bad news, I can smell it."

"Smelling is not your gift, so keep your opinion to yourself."

"But I'm telling you, something is way off with that human."

"There is something special about him, but that is none of your business." Oddly, I had sensed something strange about Tyler earlier. Maybe Stone noticed it too? Or maybe it was his gift of premonitions that he sensed? But whatever it was, I shook off the thought; thankful he wasn't making the human thing an issue.

Stone chuckled and tilted his head to the side. "Fine. Mum's the word, my love, but only if I can have a little taste?"

Of course he had to request that, didn't he? I was beginning to believe that I was supplying him all the blood he needed. And I also couldn't help but notice that he'd dressed up for me again. His hair was styled similar to the way it had been last night, and he wore dark fitted jeans and a black button-up shirt.

Shaking my head, I replied, "I don't think that's a good idea tonight. Unless, of course, you can now see the future and want to look into mine."

"Perhaps I could tell you more about your new ability? That would be something worth hearing about."

"*Perhaps* you're right. But what I really need at the moment is complete control over my pyrokinesis. When I'm not pissed off, I have no problem with it, but I fear that if incited I'll come apart like I did before." I leaned forward and ran my fingers through my hair.

"Controlling it will take lots of practice," he cautioned. "You can't expect quick results with it, but I'm happy to help you anyway I can."

"But I don't have a lot of time. I need to be able to control it now." I stood up and paced the area between the sofas and the door and muttered, "It's my only chance."

I glimpsed Stone watching me, his features sharp with concern. "No way! You can't do that, Abby! You can't go after him. You're not ready. Not even close."

I shook my head, fighting the waterworks show that was seconds away from going off, the tormenting memories of my captivity pushing to the front of my mind and making it harder to control the emotion. "But I have to! He has my friend and he's using her to find me. If she doesn't lead him to me, then what will he do to her? I can't let anything bad happen to her."

Stone got up and walked over to me. I stopped pacing, and he grabbed my shoulders and turned me around to face him. "You can't go after him alone," he murmured.

I couldn't fight it any longer, the unshed tears finally spilling down my cheeks. "That's the only way I'm going. I'm not risking putting anyone else in danger."

He shook me gently. "What if he overpowers you, if he gains control over your mind? Then no one will be able to stop him. He'll force you to use your abilities for his victory over anyone who tries to stop him." He pulled me into a caring embrace, whispering in my ear, "I don't want that to happen to you. I care too much about you."

Burrowing my face in his chest, I cried harder. There was no doubt that he was concerned for me, but I couldn't think about that right now. Dealing with Tyler would be challenge enough. I couldn't handle arguing with either of them over something they obviously didn't understand. Lily was my friend, not theirs. So to ensure my own safety, it was easy for them to feel she was dispensable. But I, on the other hand, felt the polar opposite. I couldn't just sit back and let Bronx use her. I needed to do something. Lily needed me. If I could release the full potential of my new ability, I could easily take my old captor down.

But could I kill him if it came to it? He would never give up and just let me live without him. He'd made it very clear that I would be his eternal lover. *Eternal lover*...I cringed at the memory and the realization that his death was my only assurance for my afterlife. If Tyler or Stone were to help me, what would Bronx do to them? The guilt I'd feel if either of them was hurt would destroy me.

Even though the back room was barely lit by the overhead canned lights, suddenly in my mind, brightness shot through it. I hugged Stone tighter, hoping to conceal the glimmer of my thoughts. There could definitely be no reading of my blood tonight.

My final decision to help Lily was made. And I'd be doing it alone.

17

Left

I WATCHED TYLER'S STEADY BREATHING as he slept peacefully on the sofa, still dressed in last night's clothes. Exhaustion had taken him as soon as we'd arrived back to his house, and his head lay comfortably on the armrest, his feet draped over my lap. An e-mail had come in while we'd been out, and it was now weighing heavily on my mind. With the laptop beside me on the other armrest, I skimmed over it for the sixth time:

Abby,

I really need to talk to you. Have you heard of the donor club Ice? It's in Lake Mary, about an hour away from Clermont. Bronx has already looked for you there so it should be a safe place for us to meet. It's really important.

I'll be there tonight at midnight.

Lily

In my heart, I knew this message was written by Bronx. Frustrated, I shut the laptop, then lifted Tyler's feet so I could get up. After gently returning them to the sofa, I flashed to his bedroom and shut the door behind me. The room was dark, but my eyes easily led me to the center of it. Dropping to the ground, I crossed my legs and sat Indian style, holding both hands out in front of me, palms up. The room around me went black as I closed my eyes and began to concentrate on my pyrokinesis.

Slowly, as the flow of oxygen penetrated my lungs, the vibrations of my heartbeat rattled inside my chest. Inhaling deep breaths, I focused on all the energy within me, instantly creating a rush of heat. It surged toward my awaiting hands—where I purposely directed it to go. My fingertips tingled and hot shivers raced down my spine. I concentrated harder, demanding full control over my power, practicing the use and dominance of it, not because of any fear of harming myself, but the sheer terror that I would hurt or even kill someone I loved.

At the moment, feeling confidently in charge of my pyrokinesis, I opened my eyes and stared at the softball-sized glowing orb inside my cupped hands. Using all the mental power I could gather, I encouraged the round orb to float above my cradling hands and then circle around the room. It did as I commanded, lighting the area around it with vibrant shades of both fire and ice, casting shadows on the walls as it passed. Consistent bright orange illuminations and flashes of dazzling white beams pulsated with the sedate movement of the orb. After making its journey around the bedroom, it returned to my awaiting hands like a good little ball of fire.

Though my body felt weaker, my mind pushed harder, mediating, thinking, fighting to keep my focus solely on the fire. Using this gift drained me slowly. My advanced strength was still there, just not as much as before. But there was an incentive, a little extra motivation. I kind of liked the human traits I got while using my power. Okay, I liked it a lot. Unfortunately the reason that happened was still a mystery, but we were getting closer to uncovering it every time Stone drank from me.

I ordered the burning ball to circle around the room a few more times. As it traveled, I inhaled enormous breaths of warm air, filling my lungs with oxygen. Beads of sweat started filling my pores as the smoldering globe returned to me. Now it was time to push a little further with my capacity to control it. I still had my strength. There was still plenty of time. My mind homed in on Lily and what I could do to save her. Reminding myself that Bronx was using his mind control on her, I felt the orb grow bigger. My cupped hands opened up to allow its larger size, which was now about as big as a basketball. Dwelling on my hatred for Bronx and my concern for Lily, I forced the ball to travel once again around the room. I could feel its desire to grow bigger, hotter, but I fought back, keeping my control over it. It would disintegrate anything it touched, anything it got close to. Amazingly, I was able to forbid the heat from increasing further and also maintain its basketball size as I directed it to continue circling the room until I finally summoned it back.

As I watched it obey me, I grew more confident I was ready to help Lily and perhaps kill Bronx while doing so. The last time he'd tried to use his persuasion on me—or "mind control" as Stone would call it—he'd been unsuccessful. I felt him trying to break into my mind, but I'd been unscathed by his attempts. How could I be immune to Bronx's ability when Tyler and Stone had no problem using theirs on me? Was it possible that I could block someone from using their ability on me? Knowing what Bronx could do after his admitting he had a heightened persuasion, I was able to block his efforts of using it on me again. Perhaps I could test it on Tyler or Stone to be sure. And if I was right, that meant a second ability was already in motion within me. Surely, I would be powerful enough not to have to worry about Bronx, the Head Council, or any Enforcers.

Closing my hands around the heated orange ball, I extinguished it, leaving behind a puff of smoke, which quickly blew away. My breathing slowed, my heartbeat halted abruptly. I stood up, a little weakened but recharging quickly, a renewed sense of confidence sifting through me as I walked out of the bedroom.

All decisions were now made as to what I was going to do about Lily, her last e-mail to me, and Bronx. Later tonight, after a quick visit to the pub, I would be heading to Ice to meet Lily...AKA "Bronx disguised as Lily". I could be there in a couple hours. If things went as planned, then Bronx would be dead and Lily could go on with her life without him torturing her any longer. I should be able to return to Savannah long before Tyler would even worry about my absence.

But before I could go, I needed to swing by the pub not only to feed, but to also test my power-blocking theory on Stone. If I was wrong and I couldn't block him from reading my blood, then he would see my plan and keep me from going. The stakes were high.

Unfortunately, I was going to have to lie to Tyler—it was the only way to keep him safe. If he knew what I was planning, he'd kill me, and just knowing that brought a hefty feeling of guilt. When you love someone...*love*! I didn't want to think about that, since clearly I'd do nothing but over analyze it. When you care about someone, it makes it that much more difficult to keep secrets from them unless you're trying to prevent them from getting hurt, which I was. So in my mind, that was all the justification I needed to move forward with the only plan I had, even though there was a risk of losing Tyler altogether by lying to him. Could he forgive me? Would he trust me again? At least he'd be safe and alive. And for that, I'd pay any price. Even if it meant losing him.

It was two minutes past six in the evening and Tyler was still asleep. I stood by the fireplace, watching him from across the room. I decided that not responding to Lily's e-mail would be best. It indicated she'd be at Ice to meet me, and I was convinced that both she and Bronx would be there. No reason to give away the fact I'd be coming, so hopefully the surprise factor would still play out on my side of things. The instant I saw Bronx, I would surge every bit of heat into him and burn him from the inside out. His death would be quick. His remaining ashes would blow away in the wind. Lily and I would be free of him forever and we could finally live our lives without fear. Hopefully there wouldn't be any Enforcers with him. That would make my efforts much easier. Confidence in my plan boomed inside me. I was so close to destroying the one who'd made me into a monster, the one who'd ruined my humanity and robbed my soul.

Tyler stirred to life on the sofa, arms stretching over his head and his eyelashes fluttering. "Abby," he called out through a yawn.

I flickered to him from across the room, gazing down at his face. "I'm here."

He sat up and patted the cushion beside him and once I was seated, he asked, "So, do ya wanna try somewhere new tonight?"

Wanting to avoid eye contact, I looked away. "I really think the pub is the best place for us to go. We know it's safe. Stone is a friend."

"Your friend," he snapped, "not mine."

Beyond catering to that jealous crap of his, I stood up, and headed off to his bedroom.

"I'm sorry," he called out, "wait."

167

Looking at him, I replied, "I can't believe you still talk like that. After all the discussions we've had. I honestly just don't get it...perhaps I never will." I furiously fidgeted with my hair, twisting brown wispy strands around my finger. "I'm going to the pub alone. I'll be leaving in an hour." I stormed the rest of the way to his room, slamming the door shut behind me.

The last thing I wanted to do was argue. Not tonight. Not right before I left to go battle Bronx. Truth be told, though, I had to admit it happened at such a convenient time. Now my going pub to the pub alone wouldn't need an explanation. Tyler knew that his jealousy frustrated me and now I could use that to my advantage. I guess this made me just as bad as any other manipulative girl out there. The only difference being that I was a manipulating vampire badass. *That* had to make it a little better. Maybe if I kept telling myself that, I'd eventually believe it.

It didn't take long to pick out the perfect outfit. The worn and torn jeans from last night and the baby blue V-neck tee were a comfy choice for such an uncomfortable night ahead. I dressed quickly and returned to the living room only to find Tyler running back into it from the hallway.

"Where'd you go?" suspicion dripping in my tone. I walked over by the coffee table, standing in front of him, hands on my hips.

He chuckled. *"Nowhere."* His hands were concealed behind his back, and I sensed that strange vibe I picked up before. Without a doubt, I knew he was hiding something.

"Don't lie to me." And I knew he was, the way he didn't look me in the eyes only confirming it more.

He stepped closer, swinging his hands in full view, revealing a small box—a baby blue box tied with a glossy white ribbon so many girls dreamed of getting. "What's that?" I asked.

"Just a little something to express my love for you." He smiled and handed it to me.

Hesitantly, I took it. "You really shouldn't have. When did you even have time to shop for this?"

He leaned forward, kissed my cheek. His lips were soft, warm, and alive. They drifted away from my cheek, over to my ear. "I care about you." His voice a faint whisper. "I love you. That's why I had to. Just act excited and open it, will ya?"

I forced a breath to reign in the millions of emotions eating at me. I cared so much about him too, but I couldn't say it. The swelling cloud of guilt helped extinguish any romantic emotions anyway. Staring at the blue box, then looking up at him, I reluctantly decided to go ahead and open it. There was a baby blue satchel inside. I picked it up and felt something hard beneath the soft cloth surface. A quick glance up at Ty's face and he nodded at me, encouraging me to keep going, so I did. After pulling the strings that sealed the bag, I turned it upside down and shook the contents into my hand. A glistening silver chain spilled out with an oval pendant in the center engraved "Tiffany & Co."

I gasped. "Ty, it's beautiful!"

He smiled, took the necklace, unfastened the oversized clasp. I lifted my hair out of his way and let him fasten it around my neck. Releasing my hair, I threw my arms around him, saying, "Thank you! Thank you! Thank you!"

"You're welcome, you're welcome, you're welcome," he said while pulling me into a warm hug. My face sunk into his soft, cottony sweater. His arms squeezed tighter around me. "Don't be long tonight, okay?"

I gave a shaky nod against his chest. There was absolutely no way I would be quick this evening, even though my silent prayers were filled with that same request. Then out of nowhere, the strange feeling that something wasn't right weighed down on me. I tried to focus on it, willing my powers to help me figure out what it was, but nothing happened. Still that strange feeling of something being wrong lingered and I wondered if it was my own guilt rearing up, leaving me conflicted and confused. The sooner I left, the sooner I got this over with. My tension mounting, I pulled away from Tyler and let the lie flow straight off my lips. "I won't. See ya soon."

I didn't linger. After a quick kiss good-bye, I was out the door racing purposefully toward the pub, eager to test my theory and get on with the big plan. Stone would be all too willing to drink my blood, only to discover that there was nothing to read at all. *That* at least was the result I was hoping for. Once I got my proof, and of course, my fill of delicious blood, I'd be on my way to Lily in Florida. Bronx was just hours away from his final death. It would be fitting for him to take my human life from me and in return, for me to take away his afterlife. An eye for eye, some called it. Soon, vengeance would be mine.

18

Theory

THE PUB WAS HOPPING WITH humans and vampires, not a single available seat in the place. Britney and Stone were sitting at one of the square-shaped tables in the front, along with two vamps I'd never met before. One of them was an older blond female with a bob-style haircut. Her dark washed skinny jeans were like a second skin around her long, thin legs and a white midriff tube top showed off her slender arms. The other was a younger-looking male, maybe early twenties, with short, spiky, copper-colored hair around a cute, pudgy face. He wore black cargos and a turquoise button-up shirt. Another glimpse around and I still didn't notice Britney's friends from the other night, Mac and Sara, but I was certain they were here. Their scent was fresh; perhaps they were in the back room, either passed out from the bites of vampires or anxiously awaiting to be.

Looking well-groomed as always in his favorite black jeans, and a sleek gray button-up shirt, Stone's wandering eyes quickly found me. He got up right away and walked over. Pulling me in a caring embrace, he brought his lips down to my ear. "I'm glad you're here alone. You are alone, aren't you?"

"Yes I am," I admitted, my cheeks pulling up into a smile. "I need to meet with you privately, please."

"I was hoping you'd ask me that." Giving my hand a tight squeeze, he directed me toward the table where he'd been sitting. "A quick introduction with some old friends of mine and then we'll head to the back."

Britney's eyes lit up when she saw me, perhaps because she too noticed that I was alone. "Anna," she exclaimed and then jumped up and hugged me. Her green button-up shirtdress flowed with her movement and felt soft on my skin as I returned her embrace.

"Hansel and Mary, this is my friend Ab...Anna," Stone said, catching himself. "Anna, these are my dear old friends, Hansel and Mary."

Mary got up first, her pumps crunching on the wooden floors. Her short hair looked like soft feathers framing her petite, oval face. Deep, dark eyes threatened to seduce me as she pranced over to me like a cat balancing on a ledge. "It's very nice to meet you, Anna." Her French accent was heavy but her words were definitely English. "I knew Stone was hiding someone from me. I could read it all over his face when I asked if he had a lady love." She reached out and embraced me, kissing my cheeks one at a time, and then returned to her seat. When I looked over at Stone, I caught him rolling his eyes at her. Deciding that the less I said the quicker this meet-and-greet would be, I politely smiled at her and then turned toward Stone's other friend.

Hansel stood, thin lips curved into a smile while his pudgy fingers grabbed my hand. Then he kissed the back of my palm just like Stone had done many times in the past. "Such a pleasure to meet you," he purred.

As he returned to his seat I replied, "It's really nice to meet you both."

"Please excuse us, Anna and I have a meeting," Stone told them. "We will be back shortly."

"We shall enjoy the company of the lovely Britney until your return," Mary replied, winking at Britney, whose cheeks had flushed bright pink. Regardless of her blushing, I was certain she was eating up the attention.

Stone held my hand as we headed to the back room. I looked back toward Mary, Hansel, and Britney and waved good-bye. All of them smiled and then returned to whatever discussion had been taking place prior to my arrival. No one sitting at the bar looked up at us, and I was thankful there would be no other introductions. Not on this night. The end all, be all of Bronx and all his threats, lies, and entrapments.

We rounded the bar and started down the short hallway. The canned ceiling lights were faintly lit and incense was burning ahead of us—patchouli scented and very strong. Patchouli was a fragrance you either loved or hated. I hadn't been fond of it as a human, but now it didn't bother me as much.

"You remember Britney's friends, don't you?" Stone asked. "Will they be in our way if they're in here?"

"I knew Mac and Sara were here somewhere. Have they already been bitten?"

He gave a graceful shrug. "No, not yet. Would you like to?"

"Sounds good to me."

He let go of me to open the door, our boots shuffled as we walked in. Sara and Mac were laughing about something but quickly stopped once they saw me and Stone. They were sitting on the sofa on the left side of the room, and Stone and I sat down across from them.

A big smile stretched across Mac's face. "Hey Stone! Hey Anna!" he exclaimed. "We were just waiting for the first round of vampires, wasn't expecting it to be you two." He was wearing faded blue jeans and a dark gray tee. Shadows danced on his face as he shifted in his seat, making his auburn hair look almost black.

"Sorry to disappoint you," Stone snickered, "but Anna and I will have to do."

Without hesitation Mac responded, "No disappointment at all. I was wondering if I'd ever get a chance to have Anna." He leaned forward and tugged at his tee, evening out some of the wrinkles. "Britney always gets her and never shares."

Sara couldn't have looked more disappointed if she'd tried. She slumped back in the sofa, bottom lip plumped out, pouting. Her honey blond hair was tied in a ponytail with lots of wispy strands flowing freely around her face and she wore an oversized gray sweater that threatened to swallow her up. Perhaps it belonged to Mac.

"I was kinda hoping to get Sara this time," I said through a smile.

She gazed at me with astonishment while Mac looked like I'd burst his bubble.

"That sounds great," he finally replied, disappointment evident in his tone. "Sara, you should take her up on that offer."

She nodded. "Thank you, Anna."

"You're welcome."

Sara's blood was incredible. It wasn't quite as fresh as Britney's (that first time I drank from her), but it was close. I sucked and gulped until my appetite was sated, then licked her neck one last time to seal the wound before gently laying her to the side. I went back to the other sofa, while Stone was still drinking from the vein in Mac's arm. Did the blood flow as freely from there? I made a mental note to try that sometime.

Waiting for Stone to finish left me with nothing to do but think. And the only thing on my mind was the grueling night ahead. When I got to Lily, would Bronx be hiding or would he instantly reveal himself? Would he be surprised that I would show up, alone and ready to destroy him?

Absently, I ran my fingers over the thick silver chain hugging my neck, and once it registered in my mind, I couldn't stop the barrage of guilt that came. Tyler would kill me if he found out. He'd done nothing but help me since the day we met, which was part of the reason I was going alone tonight. I cared very deeply for him— so much I didn't want to see him get hurt. But did I love him? The attraction was undeniable and I wanted to say those three precious words to him. But did any of that even matter? After tonight, everything would be different, except the fact that he was a human and I was a creature of the night.

Stone sat down beside me, pulling me out of those heavy thoughts. "So what can I do for you tonight?" he asked.

Time to lie some more and hope he'd ask to taste me. "I feel horrible for bringing Tyler here. I want to apologize for that. He just doesn't fit in with our kind."

He flashed me one of those "I told you so" looks. "Oh Abby, didn't I already tell you that?" He chuckled lightly. "Now please tell me you no longer require his attention."

"I wish it were that easy. You know, to just shut off your feelings." My fingers traced along my collarbone, then nervously tugged at some of my hair that had fallen over my shoulder. "Shouldn't stuff like that be easier now?"

Stone's brows drew together, wrinkles forming in between them. He rubbed my back sympathetically. "It *should* be easier but it isn't."

"Well hopefully I can get an ability that makes it easier."

174

He didn't respond at first. He watched me with a heavy fascination, shaking his head. "You're welcome to stay here as long as you need. We can work on controlling your pyrokinesis and then I'll go with you to end this bullcrap with Bronx once and for all. We'll destroy him together. Nothing would bring me more satisfaction than seeing him perish."

Giving him a mild shrug, I said, "That sounds nice. Thank you."

Stone's eyes lit up. "So you're moving in as of tonight?"

That question rattled me a little. I really did need somewhere to go, some place safe and preferably with other vampires so I could learn more about my kind. Tyler would never forgive me for what I was about to do in Florida, but would Stone hold a grudge? Would this invitation still be here for me once he found out? "I don't know. I have a lot to figure out tonight. I'm not really sure how it will go with Tyler."

"Well, the invitation is always open."

"Thanks."

"I'm sorry to ask this," Stone said, voice cautious. He looked down at his lap for a moment and then back at me. "Did he promise to keep our secret, or is your arrangement with him compromised?"

"Our secret is safe," I said right away, and I truly believed it was. "There's nothing to worry about. He's known about our kind for a while now. Please don't make that an issue."

Stone smiled gently, nodding. "I won't mention it again." He lifted my hand to his lips and kissed it. He should ask to taste me any moment now, just any second. The anxiety was almost unbearable, Stone's lips trailing away from my hand, grazing across my wrist. "Just a little taste before you go? Maybe we will discover a new ability?"

Bingo! I nodded with a smile, hoping he couldn't sense my relief and excitement.

His fangs were in my wrist the instant, the room already shifting and warping, just like it had every time before. Then I felt it creeping through me, Stone's powerful attempt to dig out my deepest darkest mysteries. Concentrating hard to block it, I could feel it swirling at the edge of my mind and yet I was able to stop its invasion inside. It reminded me of when Bronx tried to use his persuasion on me at Pulse. How I'd deflected his power then, and I was doing the same with Stone's now, with little effort at all. I was really doing it!

Stone kept sucking down my blood and I could sense his swelling attempt to penetrate beyond my shield, but he wasn't making a bit of progress. "That's enough," I rasped. When he didn't stop I repeated it louder, but instead of stopping, he just sucked harder. I tried to pull away from him but his grip was firm, and I couldn't budge an inch. Why wouldn't he stop? He was taking too much blood. Shadows lurked in my surroundings; my eyes struggling to keep focus. "Stone, stop! You're hurting me." Fear shot through me at the weak sound of my voice.

Back and forth, I wobbled, as the room got darker, Stone's grip tightening as my body gave way and fell backwards. It felt like I'd been swallowed into the sofa, which might be better than Stone draining me dry. Another surge of panic, then my consciousness wavered, blinking in and out a few times before I was lost in a bubble of nothingness.

Something wet, warm, and tangy drizzled down my throat, slowly restoring my energy. It somewhat reminded me of the time that I died as a human, but without bright lights or any type of euphoria. Surprisingly, it was easy to focus when I opened my eyes. The sleeve of Stone's gray button-up was rolled up his forearm, and his wrist was pressed down on my mouth. Relief colored his features when we made eye contact.

"Abby, my God, are you okay?" he asked with concern.

Reluctant to stop drinking, I nodded my head, and as I lay there, memories began swirling. *Lily! Crap! How long was I out?* Instantly sitting up and pushing Stone's arm out of my way, I gasped, "How long? How long was I out?"

Flashing a bewildered gaze, "Not long, about ten minutes or so. Are you okay? What the hell happened?"

"I don't...I don't know." I nervously rubbed my face, around my lips, above my eyes, as I tried to make sense of what just happened.

Stone reached over and gave my hand a tight squeeze, his face filled with shock. "I wasn't able to read your blood. That's never happened to me before." He shook his head. "Then I felt you try to pull away. I tried to stop drinking from you but I couldn't. Something came over me. I don't know what it was or even how to explain it. I'm so sorry."

"I'm fine...I think." But I was more than fine. I was ecstatic. I'd blocked Stone's ability, which meant I could do the same to Bronx when I saw him tonight. He wouldn't have any mind-controlling advantage now.

"Abby," Stone murmured, "I was so scared that I'd hurt you."

"It's okay. I'm okay. Maybe tonight is just not my night. I'm stressed out. There's so much on my mind." Pulling my hand free of Stone's grasp, I got up and took a couple steps toward the door. "I should probably go."

In a flash Stone was beside me, his body between the door and me. "But we don't know what happened! What if that, whatever it was, happens again?"

A few soft moans erupted from Mac, reminding me that him and Sara were still in the room. I looked up into Stone's worry-filled eyes. I sensed just how much he cared about me and how much tonight had really scared him. His concern weighed heavy on my heart, and I was very thankful to have him as a friend. And that motivated me even more to keep him out of my messy situation. Grabbing his hand, I gently squeezed it. "I'll be back soon. Promise. Please don't worry. We'll figure this out."

He stretched his arms around me and pulled me close. "All right. You better return soon. And you better be okay."

I hugged him back and then walked out of the back room. He didn't follow right away. Muffled voices grew louder as I made my way into the bar area. It was busier than when I'd first arrived—so busy that some were standing now because there still weren't enough places to sit. That made it very easy for me to slip right out of the pub without one word from Britney or the vampires she was sitting with. I was thankful for that, since my mind was working overtime rejoicing in my success and worrying about why Stone couldn't stop drinking from me. And more importantly, what if something like that happened again when encountering Bronx in just a few short hours?

19

Caught

I RAN WITH IMMEASURABLE speed through the night, heading back to Florida, back into the mouth of the monster that made me. I tried to stay focused on my primary goal: save Lily, kill Bronx. It was useless to worry about things I didn't understand or couldn't control. There would be no reason for Bronx to drink my blood. That wasn't the way his mind-control gift worked. And the last time I blocked Bronx's powers, nothing had happened to me at all. The only reason I got weak and fainted back at the pub must have been because Stone couldn't stop drinking from me. Perhaps I just needed to practice that new ability of mine a little more.

Zipping past the Georgia-Florida line, the chilly air swept against my face as my feet swiftly proceeded through the heavily treed forest. Then, hearing an odd growling noise coming from somewhere ahead of me, caution bloomed in the pit of my tummy. I slowed my pace and closed my eyes, letting my senses home in on whatever was up there, the urgency to hurry back on my way still a cinder in my mind. But oddly I couldn't identify the scent. Moving closer, the growling got louder, then some bushes nearby started rustling. With lasered focus, I followed the sound. It was close, maybe just a few yards in front of me. But there was still no scent. I froze in my tracks, fear gripping my spine. What in the hell could be out there that I wouldn't be able to sense as a vampire? Surely whatever hid behind those bushes was nothing that could overpower me and there was no reason for me to be afraid.

When human, I'd loved animals, which I still did, but it wasn't the same since all of them were terrified of me. Regaining my confidence, I slowly started toward the bushes. The sooner I unveiled what hid behind them, the sooner I could get moving. Inching closer, slow and steady, I was careful not to make a sound.

But one of my steps was off and it crunched down on a pile of dead leaves. Instantly, the bushes stopped shaking and an eerie feeling crept over me, that kind where you know you're not alone. My ears tweaked, my nose twitched. Nothing. No scent. No sound. The little voice inside my head was screaming, *just run. Get out of there!* In a full-blown panic, I jumped back away from the bushes and took off like a bat out of hell.

Out of nowhere, something hit me—no, collided into me—and I fell hard to the ground, landing on my face. Molten coppery liquid mixed with dirt and cracked leaves filled my mouth. What hit me? Facing the ground, I used my hands to push up, but as I did something hard rammed into my stomach. I gasped in pain as it rammed me again, causing me to spit the dirty blood from my mouth. There was pressure on my back, like something was on top of me, smashing me harder into the ground below.

Where were my powers? Where were my advanced strength and senses? Dammit! Did blocking Stone's powers cause me to become powerless? Multiple failed attempts to use my pyrokinesis only led me to mental exhaustion. Terror flaring, I tried to lift up again, pushing as hard as I could. Nothing. What could possibly be holding me down? I tried again to get up but still couldn't budge. Maybe if I could get a glimpse of what the hell was holding me down, I could figure out how to get it off. Straining, I turned my head to the side, and as I did pain shot through the back of my neck—torturous, agonizing, throbbing. And I knew something was trying to rip off my head.

Waves of tormenting pain spread all over my body. A prickling burn seared my skin—everywhere, all over. I couldn't take it anymore. It was excruciating. Then my spine crunched, but I couldn't tell if it had broken. All I knew was that I couldn't move anymore. But at least I wasn't dead. Feeling pain, no matter how bad it was, meant I was still alive. If the intentions of whatever, whoever, held me down were to kill me, then surely I'd be long gone by now.

Something grabbed the hair on the back of my head, low by my neck. Was it a hand? *Someone's* hand. Jumbling my thoughts, it yanked up hard and pain tore through my skull. I screamed, then my face dropped back against the ground when it released me. As I lay there a minute, unable to move, I realized something even more terrifying—my body hadn't started healing yet. I forced a breath to control the panic, but it didn't work. How was I going to get out of this mess? Think, just think. But I couldn't focus through the thrusts of adrenaline rushing through my body, and the longer I laid here, the more intense it became.

Shuffling movement, I could feel it moving closer, pressing down harder against my back, then something wet slithered across my earlobe. My whole body cringed, but I couldn't move anymore than that, not that I wasn't trying. Sensations like ants crawling up my spine made me shiver, then my stomach wretched when excruciating aches ripped through my every limb.

Breaking through the white noise of pain, I heard a voice—low, hushed, deep. "Hello Abigail. It has been too long since we last saw each other. Far too long indeed."

20

Betrayed

I HAD NEVER FELT SO WEAK, or been in this much pain, since becoming a vampire. After hearing that all too familiar voice, I was knocked unconscious, and I have no idea how long I was out. Now, I found myself locked up in a room with no windows and absolutely no other way to escape. The door actually felt like steel when I kicked it, and the dark gray walls must've been made of iron. Yep, that pretty much removed any doubt that my powers were gone. Yippy for me.

I studied the room—or should I call it my prison?—and felt a vague familiarity. I'd been here before, but when? Maybe when I was human? Or maybe it was more recent? It was too hard to concentrate, my mind wavering between hysterical and delusional. I knelt down onto the rustic wood floors. Two metal-looking chairs and a small table were in the corner of the room, just a short distance away. I thought about crawling over to one of the chairs, but it seemed like too much work so I stayed where I was. I rolled over onto my back, not finding any comfort whatsoever, and stared at the ceiling. If it weren't for those dimmed canned lights in the ceiling, I'd be lying here completely blind. Just like a helpless human, which at any other moment in my life I would've embraced with open arms.

Countless times I tried tapping into my pyrokinesis, and any of my other abilities, all to no avail. Why hadn't I thought to check this before leaving the pub? Becoming a vampire sure didn't make you any smarter. Obviously. I lay there a little longer, a full-on pity party in my head. Eventually I realized it wasn't going to help me, so I rolled over, got on all fours, and crawled to the closest wall where I sat against it for support and crossed my legs. The only thing I hadn't tried yet was prayer. With nothing else to lose, I folded my hands together and closed my eyes, praying, meditating, and occasionally freaking out altogether, in no particular order.

The doorknob turned, startling me out of those deep thoughts. I peered at it like I had X-ray vision, but since I didn't, all I saw was the door swing open. More light gleamed in hurting my eyes so I looked away, then I heard heavy footsteps slowly get closer and closer. I shuddered and pressed back into the wall, but there was no escape, nowhere for me to hide. Glimpsing back where he stood, I found him staring down at me, smiling, a broad glistening expanse of teeth and fangs. His dark eyes sucked me into them like a whirlpool I couldn't fight.

"Why are you sitting down there on the floor, Abigail? These chairs are in here for your comfort. Please get up and sit in one." His words were deep and slow and very intimidating. He took a few steps closer and reached out his hand. "Let me help you up."

Even though I was terrified, the words "no thank you" escaped my mouth as I lowered my face toward the floor, not wanting to make eye contact any longer.

In a blur I was raised and pinned against the wall, his hand around my neck. My feet dangled beneath me, and he held me level with his cold eyes that were like black winter ice. His smile now gone and when next he spoke, it was so loud I wanted to cover my ears but was afraid if I took my hands off his death grip around my throat, he'd crush my vocal cords. "I did not ask you. I told you. I told you to sit on those chairs and I told you to let me help you up. You will obey me! Do you understand?"

Unable to verbally answer him, I nodded my head, or at least tried to. To be sure he understood me, I blinked my eyes up and down. They were trying to say, "Yes we understand, yes we will listen."

The features on his face softened and he released me. Sliding down the wall, I rubbed my sore neck, then without hesitation, I walked over toward the chairs. Each step was forced, like heavy weights were tied to my feet. After what felt like an eternity, I was finally sitting and glaring up at him through my lashes. I wanted to slap that prideful expression right off his face. Fat chance right now, I knew. His movements were nothing but lethal grace as he moved swiftly until he was sitting down interrogation style beside me.

He leaned over and pointed at my stomach, his finger just a few inches away. I didn't move. "There is blood all over you. I will bring you some fresh clothes in a moment. I never meant for you to bleed so badly."

My eyes welled up with tears. Just perfect. Now I was going to cry like a baby *and* not have my powers.

"What…have…you…done…to…me…Bronx?" I fought back tears between each word.

A smirk puckered his full lips. Slowly, he pulled his pointing finger away. "Now Abigail, if I told you that, I would have to kill you. And it is very important that you stay alive for me. My plan cannot work without you."

"What plan?" I demanded. Then remembered what Stone had warned me about. *He'll overpower you and use you with his mind control. He must need you for something, Abby, that's why he turned you into one of us. No vampire has ever developed powers as great as yours.*

"You will be with me forever. What part of that did you not understand?" His eyes slanted, piercing me with a spiteful glare.

"Where's Lily?" I blinked once and a few tears spilled. I cradled my arms around my chest and held on tight, hoping I could find some comfort. So far, it wasn't helping at all.

"Do not worry about your donor friend. She is unharmed and will remain that way as long as you cooperate with me." He leaned over and slid his thumb across my cheek, his touch repulsing as he rubbed away my tears. But more fell and replaced what he wiped. "There is no need for you to cry. I will not hurt you again. I needed to be certain that you were powerless. Knocking you unconscious was the only way." He cupped my face and I let him, too weak to pull away.

"How? How did you strip away my powers, my advanced senses? Am I human again?"

"Do not be ridiculous," he said through an amused chuckle. "You are still a vampire. You will be a vampire forever, unless, of course, you are killed. You can never be human again." He slipped his hands away and leaned back in the chair. "I am not sure what you know, but I am certain you know how powerful you are. So tell me, what does your pyrokinesis feel like when you use it?"

Feeling my eyes widen, I quickly glanced down at the floor. "What are you talking about?"

"You hold no secrets, Abigail. Do not waste time lying to me." He gripped my chin and forced me to look at him. "Answer my question."

"How?" I asked, my voice steady. "How do you know what power I have? How did you know?" I shook my head until he let go. "You targeted me! You turned me into a vampire because you knew I would become this. How the hell did you know?" A bitter accusation and the only thing that seemed logical at this point.

"Now that is a question that I would love to answer for you." He burst into a sinister laughter, raking me with his gaze. "The truth will hurt you, Abigail, which I do feel you deserve. You are mine and I will never share you with anyone else."

I couldn't speak. Anger and despair was coiling within me, slowly oozing to the surface and all I could do was stare at him.

There was a knock on the door, the sound rippling through the silence. My tummy clenched at the way Bronx grinned. "You may enter."

Trepidation moved through me and my gaze fell to the floor. Footsteps shuffled closer and closer, but that didn't identify my new visitor. Nor were my senses picking up on anything. Slowly I raised my head and froze, one hand touching my chest. Oh my God, what the hell was he doing in here? I shook my head, unable to grasp what I saw, who I saw. "Oh...my...God!" Each word stretched out. I couldn't believe my eyes. We stared at one another as if we both were trying to figure out what the other was thinking. It surely didn't look like he was here to help me escape and even worse, he didn't look scared of Bronx. "What. Are. You. Doing. Here?"

Tyler stood a few feet away from Bronx. "I'm sorry, Abby." He frowned, looked down at his feet.

Whatever I might have been feeling, it was dying and the numbness was left in its wake. I simply couldn't handle this, my mind couldn't process any of it. "Get out...now! Both of you. Get out..." I cradled my knees against my chest, rocking back and forth, unable to say another word, unable to think, unable to feel. I was hollow inside and nothing Ty could possibly say to me would make this okay, would enable me to understand why. Why he betrayed me, why he lied to me.

I heard receding footsteps and the door closing behind them. Gripping tighter around my legs, my body trembled with raw emotion, my eyes burned with unshed tears. What in the hell was Tyler doing with Bronx? They seemed too familiar with each other to have recently met. But how far back did they go? Was Tyler working with Bronx when he'd kissed me? When he'd told me he loved me? But if that were the case, then wouldn't my vampire senses have picked up it? Wouldn't I have noticed something was off? *Off!* I gasped, sitting up straighter in the chair. Something had been strange. Stone had noticed it too, but I'd shaken it off, blaming Ty's ability. I'd even blamed my own guilt, giving Tyler the benefit of the doubt. But those weird vibes had been right in front of me the whole time and I'd ignored them. How could I have been so blind? Dammit! I'd trusted him! I'd let my guard down with him, and I'd told him everything—well, almost everything. What I didn't tell him, I bet he just saw in one of his futuristic visions and then he conveyed everything to Bronx.

Tyler, Tyler, Tyler. Just thinking his name sent pain ripping through every fiber of my being. He was nothing more than a liar, no better than Bronx. He used me and then betrayed me to the one person on this earth that I needed salvation from. He never loved me. His touch, his kisses, his words. I'd been such a fool. My chest tightened with despair—perhaps the closest thing I could feel to a broken heart, and it hurt like hell.

There were moments, while sitting alone in the dimly lit hellhole, when I'd try to convince myself that Tyler was just one of Bronx's puppets and that he was under the influence of Bronx's mind control. But I knew that wasn't the truth. For Bronx's mind control to work, he would need to be in close proximity to the one he was using it on. And I knew for a fact that he was nowhere near Tyler and I when we fled to Savannah. I would've sensed him if he had been.

I was swirling in a cyclone of confusion. The facts that I'd uncovered, willingly or not, cut into me and I knew no matter what happened next, the scar of this betrayal would always remain. And that was if I actually lived through this. Then my thoughts shifted over to Lily and my chest ached for her. She'd been thrown in the middle of this madness like a fishing lure, and I'd taken the damned bait. Surely, Tyler had known this would have happened all along thanks to his nifty little gift of premonitions. And I couldn't help but wonder if this was playing out exactly as he'd seen it. What a fool I was for believing his feelings were sincere. But to my defense, his jealousy of Stone had seemed real. The vengeance he'd promised to help me achieve had been so believable. The feelings he'd provoked inside me had been...nothing. Everything he'd said was a lie. His actions were empty. He'd been in alliance with Bronx all along. But why would Bronx allow Tyler to take me away in the first place? It just didn't make sense that he'd willingly let another man take me away from him. Unless, somehow, Tyler had used his visions to convince Bronx that this would help his master plan, whatever that was, and that meant Tyler was even more involved in all of this.

I let go of my legs and grabbed my head, pressing into the temples, trying to ease some of the pressure. Anger, sadness, and worry turned my mind inside out. And to top it all off, I was growing weaker.

After fleeing from Bronx, I'd developed my powers and learned how to use them. If I'd been with Bronx when that happened, I could've easily escaped. And perhaps killed him in the process. Had Tyler's visions show that to Bronx? Maybe Tyler had only gained my trust to give Bronx time to figure out how to take away my powers. And with that knowledge, I was ambushed in the woods— because Tyler had already seen me traveling there in his visions. That's the only way Bronx would've known where to find me. Nothing else could explain it. And that meant Tyler really *did* have a huge role in all of this.

Wrapping my arms back around my legs, I rocked back and forth. The truth about Tyler blared out brighter than the sun, or at least as bright as I remembered it. All the tender moments we'd shared weren't real. The passionate kisses really meant nothing. Flashbacks of the time spent together in his Savannah house—if it was even his house at all—tore through me like a raging tornado. Bronx would've never allowed Tyler to kiss me or tell me he loved me unless it was only to gain my trust, which he'd done successfully. But Tyler had earned my trust without all those things. I guess he'd just used the romance to keep me distracted from sensing the truth.

My insides were a pit of emptiness, hollow and numb. I was weak and needed blood, but didn't care if I ever tasted it again. I tried to get up but felt dizzy and sat back down. My fingers rubbed my eyes, which burned and stung, but at least I wasn't crying. My neck and shoulders felt heavy; tension straining the muscles beneath the skin. It really sucked not being able to heal myself. And that wouldn't even begin to happen unless I got blood—a lot of blood. So to relieve some of that pressure, I started to massage my neck, working my fingers deep into tender flesh. Something hard and cold whisked across my fingertips. The necklace Tyler gave me. Remembering the loving moment when he gave this to me made my stomach roil and my tongue fold with nausea. Frantically, my fingers traced the necklace, searching for the clasp so I could remove this horrible gift and throw it at him or Bronx the next time I saw either of them.

Tugging and shifting the silver chain seemed endless—the clasp never made its way around. Maybe my fingers skipped over it, so easy to do since the clasp was about the same size as the rest of the chain pieces. And I was getting weaker by the second; that surely wasn't helping me. Then I felt something sharp, a tiny prick on my finger. The clasp. I strained to pull the chain forward so I could get a good enough grip on the lever, but it wouldn't budge. *What the hell?* I tried again, nothing.

The doorknob rattled, then the door slowly swung open, an eerie creaking noise that you'd hear in a horror movie. All that was missing was the scary music. I froze in a panic, quickly dropping my hands to my knees. The last thing I wanted was to be caught touching that stupid necklace, not until I got it off and could use it as a flying projectile. I watched my fingers nervously trace and poke at the holes in my jeans.

"Abigail, come with me." Bronx commanded.

I slowly raised my head up, avoiding his eyes. "I'm not sure I can get up. I've already tried." Then, I tried again anyway to prove I was telling the truth. Placing my boots on the floor and my hands on the seat of the chair, I pushed with all my strength but barely moved at all. Completely exhausted, I leaned back.

Bronx walked over to me and bent down, then cradled his arms around me like I was a baby, one arm around my back, the other under my knees. In a flash, he rose and my head fell backwards as he did. I tried to lift it up but was too fatigued. "I am going to get you cleaned up. Please do not get any ideas of escape while we are away from this room," he warned.

I wasn't sure where he took me, but I assumed it was a bathroom. He sat me on a short bench with my back against the wall. I leaned sideways against something cold and hard that reminded me of a bathtub. After numerous failed attempts to focus, I decided that closing my eyes would be best. The back of my lids looked like curtains in a dark movie theater—only I knew the motion picture wouldn't be playing soon, the weight of the curtains too heavy to lift.

Something damp, and a little rough, wiped my face. "You are worse off than I thought," Bronx said, his voice soft. "Can you hear me?"

My lips slightly parted to answer him, but I couldn't speak. I forced a little noise out of my throat that sounded like a hoarse growl. Every minute that passed, I was progressively getting weaker. I felt sick, so sick, unlike any cold or virus I'd ever experienced when human. Thoughts of a final death floated to the surface of my mind. Every moment that passed, I was one step closer.

"Tyler, come in here! Now!"

Clambering loud footsteps rushed in. "What is it, Boss?" His breathing was deep and short and I envisioned the vein on his neck pumping with each gasp. Oh, how easily I would bite him now, after everything he'd done to me. I no longer cared to preserve his innocence, which he'd already showed was nonexistent due to his alliance with Bronx.

"What is wrong with her? She is not supposed to be so sick." Bronx continued to wipe my face, neck, and arms with the cloth.

"She's been trying...powers...every time she tries...the weaker she will get..." My consciousness was fading in and out and his answer came out broken.

"But I need...healthier...this!"

"Then you'll...feed her. Should I...get...girl?"

An eerie moment of silence filled the room. A brief moment of clarity regained, but I still felt horrible. Bronx finished wiping me and began to pick at my hair with what felt like a comb. "This hair color is horrid! Why did you allow her to do this?"

"It seemed like the right thing to do at the time."

"Then you should not have a problem changing it back." Bronx was making progress with the comb as strands of hair began to flow through its teeth, tickling the side of my face.

"Yes, sir."

"Go get the girl."

"If you want her hair color changed, shouldn't I do that before she feeds?" Tyler's tone was suspicious.

"No, go get the girl now."

"But sir," Tyler begged, "I can't be in a room with her after she feeds. She'll kill me after everything she just found out!"

"Yes. She. Will." Bronx burst into that sinister laugh, and my consciousness started wavering again. "I never said...you would not...punished for...advances...if she chooses...kill you...then...is your sentence."

The last thing I remember thinking was if Tyler would return with "the girl" before it was too late. Or maybe it already was.

21

Face-to-Face

HER MELODIC VOICE WAS LIKE that of an angel, and her tender touch on my cheek felt like silk. "Are you okay? Abby, it's me. Wake up. Wake up and bite me."

I couldn't move, my eyes were sealed shut, and I didn't want to bite her anyway. Why live? Why should I want to live? To be Bronx's slave all over again. He would use my power and I'd never be able to defend myself.

What had Tyler done to me? How had I become so helpless, so defenseless? After all that fighting and training, I couldn't even use those moves. Would drinking from Lily change that? Mostly likely not. Bronx had demolished me in the woods; whatever was happening to me had already taken me down. No powers, no senses, and no longer a will to fight.

"Abby, please," Lily begged, "please Abby, bite me. I need you, don't leave me here." She brushed her neck against my lips, back and forth, trying to taunt me.

Her skin was so warm, inviting, *alive*. Vibrations moved through her neck as her pulse pumped rapidly. My tongue swelled, saliva moistening it and I couldn't help licking my dry lips, accidently grazing my tongue across her skin. The next instant, I was set aflame with a hunger so intense it controlled me, and there was no way I could stop now. My mouth opened and in one swift movement I bit down, hard, her gasp giving away her surprise. The warm delicious liquid flowed like a river and my stomach was the mouth to the ocean. I could feel Lily's body trembling and I raised my hands, tangling my fingers through her soft brown hair as I gripped her scalp. I was relieved at how my arms moved with ease, my strength being enough to hold her steady, and that meant I was healing. Feverishly, I drank and with each pull I felt better, stronger, and once it was time to stop or I'd take too much blood from her, I sealed the wound and gently laid her on the floor. To gather myself and get my bearings, I gazed around, immediately recognizing where I was: the master bathroom at Bronx's house. Memories of trying on clothes, laughing, and talking with Lily flashed in my mind. Noticing my advanced senses were back, I could detect her soft vanilla fragrance beneath the metallic scent of her blood, the musty smell of my dirt- and blood-stained clothes, and Bronx. He was somewhere in the master bedroom, most likely waiting to see me when I came out. At least he'd let me enjoy a meal before making me sick all over again.

No reason to delay this confrontation—better to just get it over with. Scooping Lily up in my arms, her gray chiffon dress crumpling against me, I walked out of the bathroom, each step careful, cautious. Bronx sat in the corner, on the plush leather chair that I used to sit on when I had my "alone time." He gazed at me with eager eyes and muscles pulled his cheeks into a grin. I eased Lily onto the large canopy bed, which was easier to do with all those sheer white curtains removed. The bed looked more like a shell of a canopy bed now—basic, plain, undecorated. As I stood by Lily, I kept my eyes locked on Bronx.

"Do not try to use your powers or you will become weak and frail again." His voice full of warning as he leaned forward in the chair but didn't get up.

My mind raced with everything I'd learned about him, all the things Stone had told me. And how Bronx had actually killed Meredith—a woman he'd claimed to love—simply because she'd been in his way. "You're a murderer," my tone seething, "and a liar! You killed Meredith...you killed her then lied to me about loving her...lied to me about her still being alive and sending you away...to this place with the aid of Enforcers. Enforcers who work for a Head Council of vampires that you never thought to mention to me as you proclaimed your undying love for me. And now what? Whatever you love, you kill, so is that your plan for me too?"

He got up and stalked toward me in human steps, the grin washed off his face and his nostrils flaring. "It seems you already know too much."

"So it's true!" Because he surely hadn't denied any of it. Stepping back, I bumped into the bed. There was nowhere to go but on the bed, and I definitely wasn't going there.

"I guess there is no reason to keep it from you now," he said and snickered. "Yes. Yes, I killed Meredith. She would have stood in the way of us, Abigail. I could not allow that. Once I discovered you, I wanted only you. If Meredith would have respected my wishes, she would still be alive."

Anger surged inside me, so intense it would've stolen my breath away if I had it. Trying to calm myself, I closed my eyes, willing my emotions to get under control. I wanted desperately to access my powers and destroy him that very minute, but the fragile condition it would put me in held me back. "You don't want me. All you want is control over my powers, and you plan on using your ability of mind control to gain it." I opened my eyes and stared at the floor a moment, collecting myself a little more before raising my gaze to his. "So now that you have me, Bronx, why don't you go ahead and control me? What are you waiting for, an invitation? Well go ahead, you evil bastard, go ahead and steal my powers."

Taking another step in my direction, stopping just a foot or two from me, he responded loudly, "You are not in any position to tell me what to do or how to do it! Do you understand me? You are not the one in control here!" In a blur, he lunged forward and thrust out his fist, punching me in the face so hard I saw stars and fell sideways, blood pooling in my mouth as I bounced off the mattress. Pushing off the bed I flashed back around without thinking, accidentally using my senses, and glared at him, fangs extended. A growl rumbled out of my throat, my tongue massaging the inside of my cheek where the blood was leaking. A cool sensation swept through me—I was starting to heal. There was no way to stop it. *That* fact left just one thing to do if my abilities were automatic. If I was going to get run down for it, I might as well go out with a bang.

A roar of laughter rumbled off my lips as I pumped myself up for what I was about to do. In the blink of an eye I sprung up, swinging my fist right at his pretty little face, just missing him when he dodged out of my way. I landed light on my feet, then turned and leapt up, airborne, fist aimed, with razor-sharp focus. He lunged forward and swung back, his fist colliding into mine with a crunch of bone that sent me flying backwards. Another cool sensation spread through me and I knew my body was already healing my hand as I landed on the floor, on the other side of the bed. A little dizzy, I shook my head to control the spin then tried to get up. Nausea flooded through me right away and I stayed down—weak, pathetic, defeated. My eyes stung with unshed tears as I looked up at him.

He stood over me, his hard gaze blazing with anger. "What did I just finish telling you?" I winced at his harsh tone and he laughed so loud it pierced my eardrums. "You cannot use your powers or you will become weak again. Do you really want to be in that state when you encounter Tyler?" His laughter trailed behind him as he flashed to the door and left the room.

His words left me angry, confused, and most of all, hurt. Tyler would be coming in here? Bronx left me alone so I would have to face Tyler again? A sudden iciness slid through my veins and I wrapped my arms around myself, chilled to the bones. I tucked my knees closer against me and prayed the next person I'd see would not be the one who'd betrayed me. But I was quickly learning this wasn't my day.

The door creaked open, then soft footsteps approached. His scent flooded my senses, and I realized some of my strength was back. Getting up in one swift movement, I glared at him through my lashes, masking all other emotion inside. There was no way he was going to see the pain he'd caused me.

He smiled shyly, nervous. "A-Abby." He looked down at his feet a few seconds then back up at me. "I am so sorry. I never meant to hurt you. I never meant for us to—"

"Just shut up!" There was nothing he could say to me that I wanted to hear, nothing that would make any of this okay. "You're a liar and I will never believe another word from your mouth. You are no better than Bronx." My fangs swelled in my mouth and I took a small step back.

He stood there completely dumbfounded, speechless. His smile was gone and his green eyes looked glossy, sad. Unwelcome images of his arms around me, his lips kissing me, the sweet words he'd said, tortured me, each second dragging out, throbbing inside my head. *God, Tyler! Why? Why did you do this to me? How could you do this to me?* But I wouldn't ask, I wouldn't let him see the pain he'd caused by demanding answers. I refused to let him even think

I cared enough to know. My whole body tensed as I fought to suppress the memories. Fingernails dug into my palms as I squeezed my hands into tight fists. After everything I'd been through with my ex-boyfriend John cheating on me with my BFF Mandy, I'd still opened my heart to Ty. After everything Bronx had done, I'd still let Tyler in. And that meant I was a complete idiot vampire, not the badass I'd been pumping myself up to be.

Tyler nervously ran his fingers through his messy hair. Oh how sexy I used to think that was. Now I'd love to rip every single strand from his head one by one. I stepped forward slowly and he flinched, stepped back, his eyes widened with obvious fear. Good. He *should* be afraid of me. I inched closer and again he retreated a step. Sick of the game, I flashed straight to him, now standing a couple inches away.

He startled but didn't move this time. "Please, please let me explain. I know you don't want to hear it and you have every right not to believe me anymore, but please at least listen to me."

"What's in it for you, Ty? Why are you helping him?"

He let out a deep sigh. "I am working for Bronx, yes that part is true."

"Tell me something I don't already know!"

"But I never expected to get feelings for you. That wasn't part of the plan."

"Save it," I hissed. "You're a liar! All of that was just part of your game."

He waved a hand to the side. "That's not true! I care about you! I love you! I swear it!"

After rolling my eyes, I glared harder at him. "Cut the crap. I don't care about any of that. All I want to know is *why* you're helping him?"

His arms hung loosely at his sides and I watched movement in his throat as he swallowed. "Bronx hired me several years ago after he heard about my premonitions. In exchange for my help, he paid me money, lots of money. Abby, I was broke and had nothing, and then all of a sudden this incredible offer just falls in my lap. How could I say no?" He closed his eyes slowly and then opened them. Stealing another deep breath, he continued, "He wanted me to help find the most powerful vampire. Since most vampires don't have special powers, it was easy to eliminate most of those found in my premonitions. But then there you were. The powers I saw you using in the future left Bronx speechless. Apparently no one had ever heard of a vampire with such extraordinary powers. He asked me to find you for him and I did. I thought my job was finished—"

"Wait a minute. I wasn't a vampire? I wasn't a vampire when you led him straight to me? That's why he turned me? Because of you!" A lump formed in my throat, anger searing my spine. Without a doubt, I could kill Tyler. I bit down hard on my bottom lip, hoping to somehow keep control.

He stared down at his feet and nodded, voice soft, saying, "Yes. I led him to you." He sniffled. Was he crying? Those fake tears wouldn't get any sympathy from me.

"You are worse than Bronx. You're dead to me." Through a snarl, I added, "You're lucky I don't rip you apart right now."

Slowly he raised his head up, eyes locked on mine. He lifted his hand, placed it on my shoulder. I growled a warning and stepped back, but he leaned in, and his hand moved with me, grip tightening. "I didn't know you then. I never thought I would fall in love with you. I swear I wanted to tell you the truth, I wanted to tell you everything, but I couldn't. I knew you would hate me if you knew—"

"And what is it I should feel for you now, Tyler? Forgiveness? Understanding? Compassion? Why the hell do you deserve any of that? You're the reason I'm a monster. And you're the reason that Bronx has me now. *You*! You knew how desperate I was to get away from him and yet you led him straight to me. How? How could you do that to me? That is not love!" I ripped out of his hold and was back near Lily in a blur of motion. Anger was red in my mind and I knew I was capable of hurting him—or even killing him.

"That's not true! I did love you! I still love you! I'm sorry. I'm so sorry." He moved closer, a hand reaching out, but all I could do was back further away. "Abby, please, I never meant to betray you."

I balled my fists tighter, wanting desperately to break his pretty little face, but instead they hung frozen at my sides. The pain was so intense, the anger so overwhelming, and all I wanted was for him to feel it, all of it—the betrayal, the broken heart, the lies. Seething with rage to the point of numbness, I let the emptiness fill me up until I felt hollow inside, then bit out, "I don't love you. You are dead to me."

Even though I sounded scary and intimidating, a part of me, somewhere deep down in there, called me out on my own lies.

22

More Confusion

HE STARED AT ME, SPEECHLESS, with dread all over his face, but I still found it impossible to find pity for him. Not after everything he'd just told me. He was the reason Bronx turned me into a vampire. He was the reason Bronx now held me prisoner. Everything was Tyler's fault. I needed him out of here, before I completely lost it. Anger surging, I glared at him. "Please leave."

He sucked in a breath, then murmured somewhat absently, "I can't leave."

I blinked in confusion, but his gaze quickly sharpened and his lips compressed in a tight line. "Why not?" I asked harshly. "I want you out of here. Now!"

"I have to change your hair color back to blond" was what he answered with, though he certainly didn't look thrilled about it.

"You what?" There was no way in hell I was letting him touch my hair again.

"Bronx sent me in here to do it because he can't stand looking at you with brown hair. I'm sorry. Please, let's just do this and then I can get out of here as you asked."

"I owe you nothing," my tone absolute. I saw the fear in his green eyes, which fueled me a little. "I don't care what Bronx thinks of my hair. Either leave willingly or I'll throw you out." My anger was starting to rupture and I knew I needed to relax or my body would automatically try to bring forth the fire. And if that happened, I'd get sick and fragile all over again. Personally, I'd already had about enough of that.

He shook his head slowly, reluctantly, and I could taste the fear oozing from him. "Please don't use any of your powers. It'll make you weak just like you were before," he informed grimly. "Only blood can help restore some of your vampire senses, and Lily is the only donor here. There's no way you can drink from her again anytime soon."

I licked my lips. "Lily may be the only donor here, but she is not the only *human* here." I watched the muscle twitch in his jaw and smiled, letting him squirm a minute longer. Then, "What happened to my powers?" I asked him pointedly. "You at least owe me that." And so much more.

"I'm sorry. I don't know—"

"Save it," I snapped, "you *do* know, I can see it all over your face."

"No, I don't know what happened to your powers."

"Swear it to me, to my face! Look me in the eyes and swear you know nothing." As good a liar as he was, I probably wouldn't be able to tell truth from fiction. But dammit, he owed me after everything he'd done to me.

"We're running low on time, please let me help you change your hair back. If he returns and it isn't done, we'll both be screwed." He turned around and headed toward the bathroom, never once looking back to see if I'd followed.

Watching him swagger away only seemed to piss me off more, his obvious confidence I wouldn't jump him from behind adding more fuel to the already raging fire of anger inside. But it was an easy guess that he must've already seen this in a vision, which totally sucked he had such an advantage on his side. A part of me really did want to shred him to pieces, but another part—perhaps bigger part—didn't want to be a monster. And aside from that, I couldn't help wondering why he wouldn't swear to my face he didn't know what had happened to my powers? Did that actually confirm he knew? Maybe I really did scare him bad enough that he didn't want to lie anymore, not that he was so forthcoming with the truth. But obviously, he also knew Bronx would kill him if he talked to me, so here he was—stuck between two pissed off and deadly vampires.

Beyond frustrated, I stomped to the bathroom in a huff. Tyler was looking for something under the sink and he didn't stop to look up as I came in.

"What are you doing?" I asked.

"Getting the hair color and stripping crap out."

"What are you, an experienced hair colorist now?"

198

"No, I googled the info I needed to make you blond again." His voice was a little too smart for my taste.

"Look, I really don't need your help. I can do this myself. Please just go in the bedroom and let me handle this alone. You owe me that after everything I just found out."

"Abby, please let me—" He reached out and grabbed my hand. I started to pull away but was instantly pulled inside one of his visions.

Bronx was in a gothic-style building, castle-like with gray stone floors and walls. Enormous wrought-iron chandeliers hung from the thirty-foot-high ceiling, casting eerie shadows with their soft light. The massive hall he walked down led to arched wooden double doors. He forcefully pushed his way inside. A massive formal room with similar décor as in the hallway materialized. There was a large round table with six chairs circling it. Occupying five of the chairs were vampires. I could sense they were very old vampires, even though a few of them looked no older than me. All of them wore elegant black suits, but each had their own unique undershirt of different styles and colors, beneath their silken jackets. They were playing some kind of card game.

Bronx slowly approached the vampire in the center of the table with his back facing him. His hair was white as snow and draped down just past his shoulders. Without turning away from his card game, he addressed the new visitor. "Ah. Bronx Granger. It has been such a long time since we last met in person. Whatever has brought you here?"

"Elliott." Bronx slowly dropped down on one knee and then bowed his head. "I have an important issue to address, and I am confident that with your help I will be able to take care of it."

Elliott turned around, giving me a view of his face. It was smooth and youthful, unlike what I'd expected. His cheeks were slightly sunken and his chin was a little pointy, much like his nose. His eyebrows matched his hair. He wore a black button-up undershirt. Cocking his head, he said, "Is this not something that you can handle with your amazing gift of mind control?"

Bronx raised his head and stood back up. He patted Elliott's shoulder with a hand. "I can handle it," he assured, "but I will need you to charm this and infuse it with a power so great that it will prevent the one who wears it from using their powers."

I struggled to see what was in Bronx's hand.

"I fold," called out one of the younger-looking vampires. His hair was dark brown and spiky. His undershirt was a teal cotton tee.

"You fold every hand, Jeffrey," scoffed another youthful-looking vampire. His hair was dirty blond, thick, and wavy. His jacket was unbuttoned, revealing a picture of the Tasmanian devil on an orange colored tee shirt. Turning his attention to Bronx he said, "I apologize for being rude. We should have taken a break from this agonizing game the moment we picked up your scent."

"Thank you, Trace. But I am the one that has barged in here requesting your assistance. Please accept my apologies for disrupting your game." Trace nodded an approving look at him.

Elliott held out an open hand. Bronx held it briefly, then released it and stepped back. There was something shiny in the old vamp's hand and I stared at it in disbelief. It was that Tiffany & Co. necklace that Tyler gave me!

The vision stopped and I was in the bathroom again, sitting on a towel folded on the floor with my back against the tub. I stared at Tyler, speechless, confused, and a terrible constriction wrenched around my chest. Had I just uncovered more betrayal from Tyler? I opened my mouth to say something, but his fingers pressed into my lips. His head shook, his gaze urging me not to say anything. Frowning, I nodded and with a wink of his eye, he got to work on my hair.

Since there was really nothing for me to do except sit here and wait, I started fondling the necklace. What a mess this little gift had turned out to be. Tyler leaned down, his breath warm on my ear. "You can't take it off. Only he can remove it."

I gave a shaky nod. With every detail uncovered, it seemed the puzzle only grew more pieces to find. And for the life of me, I still couldn't figure out what Tyler's role was in all of this. It was easy to let myself believe he was trying to help me since why else would he have shown me that vision. But on the other hand, seeing that had proven just how deep his alliance had been with Bronx and it incriminated him further. Or did it? Was there something I wasn't seeing, something I'd missed that he'd hoped I'd seen? And if that were the case, then what the hell was I supposed to be looking for? I didn't have deep pockets so I couldn't pay him like Bronx was. So he was either pissed at Bronx and wanted to get revenge by helping me, or he really did have feelings for me. A bitter knot lodged in my chest, and I was nowhere close to relaxing it.

My thoughts looped in a dreaded circle with no sign of slowing as I struggled to understand. Maybe at first, I was just another job for Tyler. But something happened, changing everything. The way he'd looked at me, all googly-eyed and full of emotion, it had to have been real. The way he'd kissed me, passionate, intense, so full of emotions that couldn't be faked. It had been real, dammit! It had to have been. There was no way I could've read that wrong. None of those romantic moments would've worked if there hadn't been real feelings behind them. But regardless of that logic, I could never be close to him again. Once broken, I'd already learned trust was never possible to be regained. He'd be lucky if I found forgiveness and sent him on his merry way. Of course, he could make that a whole lot easier if he'd just help me get this stupid necklace off. After all, he was the one who put it on in the first place.

Tyler got up and grabbed a towel, pulling my attention to him. He tossed it down at me. "Your clothes are still in the closet. Bronx wants you to change into the red dress and gold sandals."

"What the hell am I dressing up for?"

"I don't know, please just do it." Turning abruptly, he went for the door. He glanced back, hand on the doorknob, eyes glistening with the knowledge of things he hadn't yet revealed, and winked again. Without a doubt, I knew he was up to something, but was it going to get both of us killed?

23

Aggravated

I REMAINED SITTING IN THE BATHROOM, my mind swarming with questions. How was I going to get out of this mess? Tyler was definitely up to something. That much I knew for sure. But what could it be and could I even trust him? After how bad he'd backstabbed me, how could I even consider it? Little other options—so far none—I guess that made me a glutton for punishment. Or a glutton that wanted to get the hell out of here.

Only he can remove it. Dammit! How was I going to convince Bronx to remove the stupid necklace so that I could get my powers back and kill him? *That* wasn't going to be easy—yeah sure, more like impossible. But if Tyler could remove it then that would certainly be a huge help. But even if he could, how in the hell was I supposed to make him take it off? Just the thought of using my powers seemed to drain me of energy. There was no way I could use them to force his hand. Once I'd exhausted that subject, other questions surfaced. Obviously when Bronx had asked that group of ancient vampires in suits to *infuse the necklace with a power so great that the one who wore it would be powerless*, he'd been referring to me all along. Were those old vamps Enforcers? Actually from what Stone had told me, they matched the description of the Head Council, and I was willing to believe him over anything my captor had told me. So assuming it was the Head Council, did them charming the necklace mean they had access to magic? Or was it just one of their powerful gifts? Even deeper than that, though, why would they use their powers or magic against me? The only law I'd broken was not coming straight to them once I discovered my special gifts. But give me a break. I'd had quite the distraction and surely after I explained myself, they'd understand. The fact they'd been working with Bronx unnerved me though and perhaps that meant they weren't fair and just leaders of the vampire race after all. Maybe they were power hungry killers just like my captor. Where were they now? In hiding somewhere? Lurking until the perfect moment to strike me down? Or maybe, just maybe, I knew as much about them as they knew about me and Bronx had been keeping our existence from each other secret all along. But why?

Abby, you're the most powerful vampire I've ever seen. Stone's words echoed through my mind as I struggled to remember anything else he may have told me. Perhaps it was possible the Head Council was afraid of me since they were supposed to be the strongest, deadliest vamps, and clearly my gift of fire could challenge that. But if that were really the case, why wouldn't they demand Bronx to bring me to them? Unless, of course, they didn't know about me, and that meant they didn't know Bronx had me. What if my captor wanted my powers to defeat them and be the leader of the vampire race? I threw a hand over my mouth to stifle my gasp. He was going to use me to bring down the Head Council. It made perfect sense. Stone had been right.

Startling me, there was a loud knock on the bedroom door, then it opened wide. "Abigail, are you ready?" Bronx walked in the room and scowled when he saw me sitting on the bathroom floor.

Fear gripped me as I slowly stood up. "Um, no," I croaked.

In a swish of movement Bronx was in front of me. I didn't even see him walk in. He was just there—black suit, black-buttoned undershirt with the top few buttons missing. The exposed part of his chest looked like a sheet of white ice, pale and shiny. His eyes formed tiny slants as he glared daggers at me, then he backhanded me across the face so hard that I stepped back twice to regain my balance. Blood pooled in the corner of my mouth and I licked it, tangy and wet. Without thinking, I drew out my fangs and growled. "You're a jerk," my tone seething, then I instantly felt a wave of nausea and I knew the necklace was weakening me. Anger churned and it was difficult to see through the fury that hazed my vision. I held my fists as my sides, trying to regain my composure and calm down.

"Be careful what you do. The more power and strength you use, the sooner you will become frail. Is that what you want?" His voice was taunting, his words mocking, and more than anything I wanted to slap the smirk right off his face.

But instead, I stayed still and glared at him. I couldn't afford to get weak again and not have a blood source to replenish my strength. Lily would be waking up soon, but her body wouldn't be ready for another feeding. I was still undecided about taking blood from Tyler—against his will of course. So I looked away from Bronx—because if I kept looking at him I was going to crack—and stared at the doorjamb, fighting to ease my anger. Until I found a way to get this necklace off, I needed to act...well...human. The one thing I'd thought I wanted more than anything, and now twice I'd had that wish come true and regretted it, wanting my vampire life back again. They say you always want what you don't have and I was sick of proving that true.

Bronx grabbed my arm tightly and pulled me out of the bathroom. I followed because I had too. "Five minutes," he turned and threatened me further with his gaze. "I will be back in here to get you in five minutes. You better be ready!"

I swallowed hard, hoping to get that imaginary heart out of my throat, and nodded—slowly up, even slower back down. A cold swish of movement and he was gone, door shutting behind him. Lily stirred on the bed as I walked past her in human steps back toward the bathroom, stopping at the closet just before it. She sighed and cleared her throat and when I glanced back, her eyes were open and she was flashing me one of those charming smiles. I wanted to return the gesture, but I couldn't get my lips to cooperate, so I got busy looking for that stupid red dress.

"Abby?" she called out and when I didn't respond she said my name again. Stopping my search, I glimpsed back at her again. She was sitting up, back supported by two fluffy pillows against the wall, her beautiful brown hair a tangled mess from sleeping on it. "What are you doing?" Her face was full of curiosity.

With a frustrated shrug of my shoulders, I was rifling through the closet again. "You've got to be kidding me," a grumble of words as I pulled out the only red dress I could find and held it up. "I'm supposed to put this on?" I stomped over to the bed then tossed the dress on the mattress next to Lily. "Bronx wants me to change into this. God I wish I had my powers. I would give him a piece of my mind."

Lily reached over and grabbed the dress, its soft satin material folding neatly over her fingers. "Only you could wear that and get away with it." She tossed it back on the bed. "At least it'll cover your boobs."

And that was Lily bringing a positive point to light. What in the hell was I dressing up for, anyway? The reason for even putting this dress on was a complete mystery to me. What was Bronx up to? *Be ready in five minutes.* My stomach heaved since it'd probably already been five minutes. He'd be back to get me in any second and unless I wanted to get bitch-slapped again, or worse, I needed to change into this stupid dress.

I peeled off my disgusting, dirty clothes and realized I'd need to clean up with a sponge. Blood and dirt stains were all over my skin. I used my advanced senses, unthinkingly, to flash into the bathroom and scrub my body as rapidly as possible. Rushing back to Lily and the bed where the infamous red dress waited, I felt a wave of exhaustion and nausea come over me, making me dizzy. Just great. I desperately needed more blood, but that wasn't an option, so I pushed forward with putting the dress on, fighting the urge to vomit all over it.

I squeezed into it, literally, and was thankful Lily helped me. The dress was short and tight, with a tank-styled top and a low back line.

"I hate to say it, but you look hot," Lily said, her voice soft and tired. She was still recovering from the loss of blood and needed more rest.

"Lie back on that pillow." I gently pushed her backward. "Don't force yourself to do anything else until you have your strength back."

"I'll be fine."

"Please just listen to me."

She looked at me with small, lazy eyes and nodded. "Okay."

I walked back over to the closet and fished out the gold sandals. They were kind of chic and I actually liked the wedged heel. They fit perfectly. "Look, you may be my only blood source and I need you to be strong." I turned around to face her. "I don't want to drain you. I won't. If you don't rest, then I don't drink."

She nodded, eyes filling up with tears. "What are we going to do?" she asked, her voice cracking. She inhaled a huge, shaky breath. "We've got to get out of here."

"I'll get us out of this. I'll find a way." I ran my fingers through my damp hair. "Don't worry about anything except resting." My voice sounded both confident and believable, even to me. And I had no idea where it came from.

A loud pounding at the door sent chills crawling up my spine. Bronx came in, tongue darting across his lips and eyes glistening in the faint light of the room, loaded with expectations. "You look more beautiful than I imagined, Abigail."

I swallowed the lump in my throat and went to him with heavy steps. My whole body tensed as his arm slid across my back and wrapped around me. His suit jacket was crisp, pressed, and smelled brand new. "Your natural hair looks much better on you," he said. "Thank you for changing it back for me."

Biting a slew of retorts on my tongue, I let him lead me out of the room, down the hallway, and through the living room. I tugged at the bottom of my dress hoping to lengthen it, but no such luck yet. Those hideous gargoyle statues watched me as if following my every move and I made a mental note to shatter those things once I got my powers back. Candlelight flickered around me, casting tiny shadows on the walls. A scent, vaguely familiar, fluttered across my nose. I licked my lips, tasting something or someone from my past, my recent past. It wasn't human. It was stale, dead, empty—definitely a vampire.

Bronx pulled me tighter into him as we entered the dining room and I felt the vibrations of his muted laughter against my arm. A wrought-iron chandelier with lightbulbs that looked like candle flames hung from the ceiling, radiating subdued light, illuminating the body of the mystery vampire lying helpless on the table below it. Massive silver chains held his arms and legs. His back was to me, dark hair matted, tangled, and bloody. His black pants were ripped up, clumps of dry blood scattered around what was left. Also covered in blood was his shirt and I had no idea what color it used to be. Six oversized iron-looking chairs were organized around the rectangular-shaped table. Tyler sat in one backing the wall, his face blank, eyes steady. He wore a black suit similar to Bronx's but his undershirt wasn't black, it was red. Why were they dressed like those old vampires from my vision? I had a bad feeling I was about to find out.

Bronx turned right, dragging me along with him. He pulled out a chair, diagonal from Tyler, and pushed me down into it. Then he moved to the head of the table, standing tall and proud with a big, brilliant grin. I looked away, fear of the unknown clawing through my chest. I stared at the poor, helpless, imprisoned vampire just a foot or two away from me. Those chains shouldn't be holding him down like that since we weren't affected by silver. But as I'd already learned the hard way, we *are* affected by special abilities and magic, powerful magic wielded by the Head Council. But what did this vampire lying before me have to do with Bronx wanting my powers?

His musky scent—where had I smelled it? I knew him from somewhere, but where? The mystery was raking on my already raw nerves. Bronx stood like a statue, a mocking grin plastered across his face, and I couldn't help the image of me slapping that right off of him and then throwing those magic chains around his neck and pulling until his head popped off.

Bronx finally broke the silence pulling me out of those murderous thoughts. "This night is a special night for all of us. A turning point for vampires and whom they will call their leader. Most everyone in this room will benefit from this new ruling. And I will see to it that the one who tried to prevent me from rising as king will painfully perish from his existence."

I assumed that the "one whom tried to prevent" Bronx from becoming the king was this poor vampire chained to the table. I felt sorry for him and wished with all my heart that the necklace would fall off so I could get my powers back. If only that would happen, I could save this vampire and destroy Bronx. But wishful thinking had done nothing for me yet. I didn't expect it to start now.

I looked beyond the prisoner and locked eyes with Tyler momentarily before his gaze flitted to the vampire on the table, then back at me, eyebrows drawn together like he was trying to tell me something, but I didn't understand. Bronx was still talking, distracting me. "...I will rise up and those who serve me shall be allowed to live. Those who oppose me, well, let us just agree that we all know what will happen to them. We are about to witness it right here. A true sacrifice and powers beyond that of what anyone could conceive will sanctify me as the king above all others..."

Blah, blah, blah. At this point I completely shut Bronx out— you've heard one jerk's leadership routine, I'm sure you've heard them all. With my concentration now fully on Tyler and the prisoner, that familiar scent danced intensely on my tongue. Then, suddenly, I got a much-needed break. The vampire turned his head and looked straight at me. I gasped aloud, interrupting Bronx and causing silence to fill the room. Immediately I knew who it was, though I couldn't believe my eyes. I'd never forget that face after the interrogation he had put me through back at 7.

Brian's eyes widened, recognizing me instantly. He looked weak and hungry, like he hadn't had blood in days, or maybe longer.

"Abigail, this is Brian," Bronx said. "I believe you two have already met. He never should have tried to help you. Soon he will pay for that. Very soon." He laughed—deep, horrible, evil.

I didn't understand how Brian had helped me. If anything, he'd intimidated me. "What are you talking about? This man didn't help me in any way!" I slapped the table, anger growing, heat weaving up my spine. "All he did was give me access to a blood donor. What crime was that?"

"This poor vampire knows too much. If you would have returned to his donor club, he would have told you everything and spoiled my plans for you."

I knew Brian had been up to something. But why didn't he tell me that the first night? What had he been waiting for? "But you have me now," I pleaded with Bronx. "There is no reason to kill him for something he did not do...please."

Bronx lowered his hands to the table, his hardened gaze glaring down at me. My stomach clenched as I waited for whatever twisted bullcrap was coming next. After what seemed like an eternity of silence, he finally spoke. "Oh Abigail, it is not me who will kill this vampire. *You* will be the one to sacrifice him for me."

24

Missing Pieces

"I WILL NOT KILL HIM for you. I won't kill anyone for you, ever! I will never do anything you ask of me!" I pushed up out of that chair so fast—too fast—and a wave of dizziness swept through me. But I couldn't stop the anger. It hit like a tsunami and I was drowning in it. And no matter how hard I fought to regain control, fatigue was already setting in.

"Abby's right," Tyler said. "You have her now. There's no need to kill—"

"Silence! You will not speak again. You are here to observe, and you are lucky that your fate will not be the same as this idiotic vampire after what you have done with Abigail," Bronx's voice roared. He looked back at me, his eyes glossed over with rage. "Enough of this delay. It is time to take what is mine."

Bronx charged over to me and grabbed me by the back of my hair, instantly lifting me off my feet and bringing my eyes level to his. I kicked and swung my fists, causing sharp pains to scatter around my head, but nothing seemed to faze him. I was too weak. Then I remembered he would need to look into my eyes for his mind control to fully work. Against the pain in my scalp, I looked away.

"We will just try this a different way!" In a flash, I was pinned against a wall, both of his hands holding my head. I couldn't look away now, I couldn't even move. He was holding me too tight. So I did the only thing I could think of. I closed my eyes.

He jerked my head forward and slammed it back into the wall. And then he did it again. And again. The angrier I got, the weaker I got, and him slamming me into the wall was only making it worse. I knew once he locked eyes with me, it would all be over, so I kept them closed, squeezing tighter and tighter. I had to fight. I had to resist. Lily needed me. The vampire community needed me. Backstabbing Tyler needed me. And oddly, this stranger, the dark-haired vampire from 7, needed me.

For the life of me I couldn't understand what Brian could possibly know that would put him in so much danger. How had he gotten involved in the first place? Obviously he wasn't working with Bronx. No, that dirty job belonged to Tyler. The puzzle pieces kept coming, and the puzzle was so close to becoming something I could make out. Either that, or the whole thing was about to blow apart. If Bronx got control over my mind and then forced me to kill Brian, I'd never find out the truth. It would die with the mystery vampire from 7.

My head wasn't slamming against the wall anymore, but there were starbursts in my mind and an annoying ringing in my ears. Bronx dragged me by my hair, taking swift steps. I put up a bit of a struggle but it got me nowhere. He forced me down on the table, in some awkward backbend position, smashing my head into the wood. "Open her eyes! Open her eyes, now!" Bronx's voice was full of rage and impatience.

Familiar fingers gently touched my face, tracing around my eyes, then tugging them open. I was too weak to fight back anymore. Tyler's lips mouthing "I'm sorry" was the first thing I saw. Then Bronx's eyes were there, those black bottomless pits threatening to suck me inside. I watched him (because I didn't have a choice!) while I waited for his mighty power to subdue me. Eerie waves of pressure soared around in my head like nitrous gas at the dentist's office. Here he came. This was it. I swallowed hard, dread building. My eyes were dry and I tried desperately to blink but to no avail. The pressure became more intense, the heat in my core growing thicker, hotter. And just when I couldn't take it anymore, a scream tore from my throat. I screamed again. Loud—so loud, my voice crackled. Biting down on my bottom lip, I instantly tasted blood. *My blood! It's still me! I'm not Bronx!* Then surprisingly, the pressure slowly pulled back, easing more and more until it was completely gone.

Seemingly unaware that I wasn't affected, Bronx still loomed over me holding me in that awkward position. He pushed me harder into the table, mashing my shoulders to the point I thought they'd break. And if that happened, my body would instantly start healing. Fear iced my spine. There was no way I could afford to be weak, especially once Bronx realized his mind control wasn't working on me. Tyler gasped, distracting my captor to the point that he released my shoulders, but it didn't matter—I still couldn't move with Bronx on top of me. However, I was able to turn my head just enough to get a glimpse of Tyler. His facial expression was beyond horrified: eyes wide, mouth gaping.

"It. Is. Not. Working! Why Is She Not Responding To Me?" Bronx shouted at Ty and my gut wrenched as I waited to see what he'd do to me next. In one swift motion, he picked me up and tossed me across the room like a rag doll. My back hit the wall with a loud *smack,* and then I fell face first to the floor. I rolled to the side, attempted to get up, but wobbled and stopped short. That dreaded nauseous feeling came at me in a rush, and the only thing I could do was lay there on the ground, waiting, trying to anticipate his next move. But he wasn't coming for me. His attention was on Tyler.

"I don't know. It should work," Tyler said. "I saw it in my premonition. We've done everything exactly as it should've been." He pushed his chair back, hitting the wall, and stood up.

Bronx flashed to Tyler and backhanded him across the face, all in one whirlwind movement, and Tyler flew across the room until he landed in a crumpled heap a few feet away from me. "YOU ARE NOT TELLING ME EVERYTHING!" My captor's voice was so loud it rang through my eardrums. "I HAVE NO REASON NOT TO KILL YOU IF THERE IS NOTHING MORE YOU CAN HELP ME WITH." In a blur of motion, he grabbed Tyler by the head and slammed him straight into the wall. It happened so fast, I barely saw any of it. I tried to get up, to help Tyler, but it was already too late. He lay motionless on the floor, the scent of his blood flooding over me.

Leaning against the wall for support, I began to painfully pull myself up. Hunger burned in the pit of my belly and I closed my eyes momentarily, fighting against the snapshots of crawling to Tyler and drinking his blood flashing vividly in my head. Hustling footsteps caused me to open my eyes. In a rush, Bronx closed in on Tyler, his eyes still filled with vengeance, rage, and death. If I couldn't snap out of the blood haze and stop my captor, then he would kill Ty right now in front of me. But oh he was still very much alive right now, his blood so sweet, tempting, *unbitten.* "Stop. Please stop!" I managed, barely recognizing my own voice. "I will help you. Don't kill him." I tugged the bottom of my red dress as I straightened and glared at Bronx.

His hand was fisted, arm ready to swing and finish Ty off, but instead he hesitated. Through the pain, through the waves of dizziness, I could feel a tinge of relief that he'd listened. But then strangely, his gaze hardened and flitted around the room. I followed his trail of sight, but didn't see anything, though I could tell he sensed something. He looked disturbed, afraid even and he finally looked at me and said, "Your offer is not appealing to me in the slightest, Abigail. I do not trust you. You would never work for me unless I controlled you."

I couldn't deny that he was right. *If* he took this stupid necklace off, I'd kill him. No question about it. But the question I couldn't shake was: why hadn't he been able to gain control over me? The necklace was on, which meant I couldn't prevent him with my ability to block powers. Suddenly, a flashback of being at Stone's and thinking I'd blocked his ability when, in fact, I'd been wearing the necklace then too, and I threw a hand over my mouth to stifle my gasp. The only thing I could think to make any sense whatsoever was perhaps I was powerless as long as I wore the necklace, but somehow, some way, the necklace not only made me powerless, it also prevented powers from being used on me—a two-way power blocker. Was that what Bronx had just realized too?

Could it be that the only way for Bronx to gain control of my mind was to remove the necklace? But if he did, I'd be waiting. Ready to fight back with all the power of fire I could harness. Was that why Tyler had winked at me? He knew all along that even though he would turn me over to Bronx, there was no way for him to control me. He had to of known it when he put the necklace around my neck.

"Come," Bronx demanded, "now!"

Still feeling weak but fueled by the latest discovery, I slowly moved toward him, tugging at my dress with each step. I tossed my head to the side, getting some of my hair out of my eyes, and looked up at Bronx who appeared to be listening for something. His eyes were looking in my direction, but they seemed to look past me. I chose not to interrupt him and waited for further instruction—or perhaps another ass beating.

After a short quiet moment, his eyes were no longer distant. His full attention was back on me. "I should kill him right now," he roared. "No one lies to me and lives!" Spittle sprayed between his exposed teeth and fangs, some of it hitting my face.

Cringing, I exclaimed, "But he works for you." I glanced down at Tyler, fighting the urge to get on my knees and check on him, and then looked back at Bronx. "How can you blame him for this? He was following *your* orders."

"That is what I will find out. You can trust me on that. If you want him to live, then you need to find a way to carry him to the bedroom. Now. My mind can change on this decision at any minute." He turned abruptly, threw the helpless vampire over his shoulder (chains and all), and left the room.

Instantly, I went over to Tyler, dropping down on my knees, his blood tempting me like Godiva to a chocoholic. "Wake up, please." I checked his pulse. It was steady. I gently shook him a few times and then rolled him onto his back. His face was bloody and I had to fight the temptation to lick it, just before sinking my teeth in his throat. Shaking that thought away, I inspected him another moment and wasn't sure if anything was broken or if everything was, but at least he was alive. "Tyler, can you hear me?"

Nothing. No response. And I was out of time. Praying my strength wouldn't give out on me, I scooped him up in my arms, holding under his knees and across his back, and pushed up with my legs until I was standing. I waited a couple seconds to ensure I was balanced, but unfortunately that's when I noticed his blood on my arms. *I don't want his blood. I don't want his blood. I can do this.* The nausea wasn't making this any easier either, or maybe it was because it seemed to pull me out of the haze of hunger. It might still be too soon, but I'd have no choice but to feed from Lily. Just a little shouldn't hurt her, and it would help me tremendously.

The gargoyle statues still stared me down as I walked through the living room, taking slow, cautious steps. What the hell were they looking at? Up ahead I heard movement in the bedroom and that worried me. Lily was in there alone. Picking up the pace, I rushed through the hall, and with the master door open, I walked right on in. Lily still lay on the bed with her back propped up by pillows. Very gently, I laid Tyler down next to her. I fought the urge to lick his blood off my arms, surely I'd never be able to stop there once tasting his innocence, and looked back at Lily. Her widened brown eyes moved to the right and then back at me, like they were directing me toward the bathroom. I followed her lead and saw Bronx.

He walked past me and stopped a few feet from the bedroom door, then glared at me over his shoulder. "There is no escape for any of you. This room is secure just like the last one you were held in, Abigail. I will be back soon and when I return, you will be mine. At that time I will decide Tyler's fate." He burst into a sinister laughter, turned abruptly, and headed out.

"Where are you going?" I shouted after him but my only response was the lock engaging on the door.

"Abby, who's that guy he put in the bathroom?" Lily started to get up.

"No. Please. Lie back. Relax. I know it hasn't been long enough, but I need blood." I searched her eyes as I cupped her cheeks. "Do you think you could handle me taking just a little from you?"

"I think so. But what's going on?" She placed her hands on top of mine. "Abs, I'm scared."

"I don't know how long Bronx will be gone, but there's so much I need to figure out while he his. I'll explain everything to you later. I think that vampire in the bathroom can fill in some of the missing blanks, and then if I can just get Tyler to wake up, he'll hopefully fill in the rest. I'm going to get you out of here."

"Okay. I trust you." Lily turned her head sideways, exposing her neck, then leaned back into the pillows waiting for my bite.

25

Answers

AFTER TAKING JUST A LITTLE of the blood I needed from Lily, I quickly stood up and headed for the bathroom, led by a burning curiosity. There were so many questions and so little time to get their answers. I was also worried about Brian's condition; part of that was my own selfishness, the other part, actual concern. I glanced back at Tyler. He was hurt pretty bad, but hopefully he'd be okay for now. There wasn't really anything I could do for him at the moment anyway and his blood was too tempting. It was best to keep a safe distance for now, though I couldn't help but wonder why I even still cared.

Secured by bloody, silver chains, Brian laid in the bathtub. His head was propped up against the tiled wall, and his knees were bent so he'd fit within the small space. I sat down on the bench next to the tub. "Brian, can you hear me? Brian?" I reached over and gently nudged him. His head tilted slightly in my direction and I saw that his eyes were sealed shut by blood—thick, dried, crusty. Frantically I pulled at the chains, hoping to get them off, but my efforts were useless. Whatever "infused magic" kept him from breaking free, also made it impossible for me to break him out. "Please. Wake. Up." I shook harder. Nothing. *Dammit! What was I going to do?* Then I remembered how Lily's blood had made me feel better and I knew without a doubt he needed to feed.

With no available donor, my fangs extended as I lifted my wrist to my mouth. Stone had always seemed somewhat sated after drinking from me and I hoped the same would apply for Brian. The skin ripped away from my wrist, quick and precise. Blood trickled down my arm like crimson syrup and I hurriedly slapped my wrist to Brian's mouth, pressing hard against his lips, silently praying it would work. But when he didn't move, anxiety curled through my insides. Impatiently, I waited, counting the seconds in my head, and then something happened that would only make this bad situation worse. A cooling sensation flushed through me, tingling all over my skin and I cursed as the healing process had already begun. For whatever reason, I'd thought there would be more time before my wound closed up, and I wasn't sure if I'd have the energy to go through that again without getting more blood from Lily. *That* was definitely not an option right now.

"Drink, dammit! Drink!" Still nothing happened and in a full panic I pressed my wrist harder through his lips to where I felt the prick of his fangs. Turning my arm, the sharp points of his teeth reopened the gash and I winced as the healing sensation intensified, compressing my chest and the temperature getting colder.

Despair set in, the intensity of it quivering deep into my bones. And just as I was about to lose hope altogether, there was a little suction on my wrist—delicate, slow. Brian's lips opened wider, his teeth grazing my skin before his fangs ripped into me and he sucked harder, more violently. I laughed, tears streaming down my face as he grabbed my wrist, pressed it harder against his mouth, slurping down more of my blood. I let him take from me until I couldn't afford to lose another drop, then pulled free of his hold in a bloody whir of movement. Brian scrambled around, his body jerking. "Can you hear me?" I asked. "Are you okay?"

It took him a minute to relax, the rush of my blood bringing life back inside him. He heaved and opened his eyes, little crusties of blood left behind. "Hi, Baby Vampire," he mumbled, voice soft and weak.

"Look, we don't have much time," I told him. "What do you know about me? Why does Bronx want to kill you for it?"

He closed his eyes, as if trying to think of what to say, and then blinked a few times, slowly. On a deep sigh, he said, "I do know you." He tried to sit up straight, but his body wasn't strong enough to hold it so he slumped back down. Using a teensy weensy bit of my advanced strength, I reached forward, pulled him into a better sitting position, and then leaned his back against the wall. "I did not know who this Bronx person was until he sabotaged my club and kidnapped me," Brian said. "I did not even know why I was here until I saw you."

"What? What are you talking about? Why would I be the reason you'd be here if you weren't working for Bronx?" I nervously twirled strands of my hair, my eyes focused sharply on Brian.

"Conrad called me the other day and told me about this crazy vampire that tried to kill him. He barely escaped—"

"Who the hell is Conrad?" I demanded. "And what does he have to do with any of this?"

"Conrad told me that he called and tried to warn you before you were transformed. That's when he was attacked."

"Wait, what did you say? Conrad tried to warn me? Conrad who? D-d-do you mean...?"

With his weak, raspy voice, Brian told me the unthinkable. "Conrad Tate."

Conrad Tate, my infamous father. My mouth gaped open, completely dumbstruck. That's why my father had called me? He'd known about Bronx? *Abigail, you're in danger. He's coming to find you. Somehow, I'm not sure how, but he figured it out. He knows how special you are. You can't let him find you.* Had that meant he knew of the powers I'd obtain once becoming a vampire? Was that the reason he'd left me, because he knew this all along?

Cutting into my thoughts I heard Brian still talking. "...but Conrad was in Texas when he called me, and there was no way to connect me to him—"

"Texas?" I exclaimed. That had to be why Lily asked me if I was in Texas.

Once I'd escaped Bronx and took off with Tyler, I'd have nowhere to go, no one to trust. So Bronx must've thought I'd try to find my father. He could've easily gotten help from an Enforcer, or the Head Council themselves, to track down my father's whereabouts. But none of that explained how my father knew about me, or how he knew that Bronx was after me, or what his involvement in all of this was. All that time Bronx held me prisoner, he'd never once mentioned my father. Tyler never said anything about him either. The answers were on the tip of my tongue, but I couldn't spit them out just yet. I needed to talk to Tyler.

Brian watched me silently.

"What else do you know?" I asked.

"Not much."

"So Bronx wants to kill you because you know my father?"

"Yes. Bronx and Conrad have been at war ever since the discovery."

"What discovery?" I scooted closer, my face almost touching Brian's.

He hesitated, voice thin with fear. "Your powers, Baby Vampire. Your amazing powers."

"But I was powerless when my father called me! How did he know?"

"I don't know. I swear. I swear on my life he never told me anything else."

I searched his face for lies, but he was telling the truth. I wouldn't get anything else out of him, and I was running out of time to keep trying anyway. I got up—fast. Gazing down at Brian, I asked, "Is there a way to help heal a human?"

Brian gaped at me. "Are you talking about the human working with that monster?"

My stomach clenched at hearing those words. Ty *was* working with a monster—the same monster that kidnapped me and turned me into a vampire. "Yes," I admitted both to him and to myself. But the fact remained I still needed answers and Ty seemed to be the only one who could tell me. "Please. I don't expect you to understand, but if there's a way to help him..."

"Baby Vampire, all you have to do is feed him some of your blood. But I must warn you that as long as your blood flows through him, he will possess your advanced strength."

That was interesting. "For how long?"

"A few days, at least that. Maybe more. Before you give him any of though, you better be sure you can trust him." He rotated his head to the side, turning away from me.

The burning question of the night: Could I trust Tyler? If I gave him my super strength, would he at least be honest with me? There were no guarantees on that, but I was certain Bronx would kill him once he returned. Which was why I couldn't leave him in his current beaten and mangled condition, whether he told me the truth or not. At least he could use my advanced senses to get the hell out of here (why did I care about that?) and hopefully take Lily with him. He would do that for me, wouldn't he? After all, he did owe me. With time almost out, it was at least worth a try.

"I'll be back in a minute," I told Brian, feeling a little optimistic. "Thank you."

"I hope you know what you're doing," he muttered.

"I hope so too." In a swish of movement, I was standing over Tyler. His body was still, quiet, lifeless, but I could sense his pulse and knew he was alive. His suit was ragged and torn, and there were dark stains on his shirt. Blood. The light silver comforter was covered in his blood too. The sight of it alone could easily snap me into a frenzy, the haze of my hunger for his innocent blood almost impossible to resist. But I had to fight it. I needed to be strong. And for extra assurance I reminded myself that I couldn't afford to have him passed out for hours anyway. Not if he was going to help me...and save Lily. But he needed me too. At this point we were both screwed if we didn't work together and I hoped like hell he wouldn't prove me to be a stupid fool (again) once I gave him my blood.

Nerves racing, I closed my eyes tightly and bit down into my wrist.

26

Twist of Fate

TYLER'S BEAUTIFUL GREEN EYES stared back at me. Relieved, I pulled my wrist away. "What did you do to me?" he asked, sitting up. "I feel different."

"You should. I gave you some of my blood."

"You what?" He gasped, and in a blur he was standing a few feet away from me. "Holy crap! How did I do that?"

"I hope you don't prove to me I made the wrong choice in helping you." I straightened and took a careful step toward him, studying him.

"I can move as fast as you," excitement in his tone, then he raised a brow and asked, "Your blood is doing that to me?"

"Yes. By drinking my blood your body was able to heal quickly, but it also gave you my advanced abilities for a few days."

He took a deep, long breath, then released it very slowly. I could tell he was adjusting to the new senses as they bombarded him. Senses so strong that worry instantly set in. What if he couldn't handle them? "This is crazy," he blurted, flapping his arms. "I feel weightless!"

I put my hands on my hips and smirked. "Well you kinda are weightless."

A smile stretched across his face like he'd just won a million dollars. Then, in the blink of an eye, he was across the room near the closet and doing pushups. "I can't believe you never gave me your blood before. This is so awesome!" After several long moments and God only knew how many pushups, he finally stopped. With steady breaths, he stood back up and looked at me.

Lily shifted around on the bed and I knew I needed to hurry up and press Tyler for information, then get him to take her out of here. Fast. Before Bronx came back. "Tyler, there's no time for fun and games." My voice was firm, urgent. "We don't have a lot of time. Bronx will be back soon, and—"

He chuckled. "So? What can he do to me? I can take him *now.*"

I took a few human steps toward him. "Not if he gains control of your mind!"

He blinked, then flashed me a wry grin. "His mind control won't work on me."

"His...what? Wait a minute, what'd you say?" Because I couldn't have heard him right. If he wasn't affected by Bronx's mind control then that meant he'd betrayed me all on his own, with no outside influence like I'd originally thought. Swallowing the emotion in my throat, we stared at one another for a moment.

His brows drew together, then he waved a hand, saying, "I'm really, really sorry. For everything." He shrugged, stared down at the floor, then met my gaze levelly. "I wanted to tell you everything from the beginning, but I couldn't. Bronx would've killed me; hell, I bet he already wants to considering how many times I kissed you and how close we got. That was never part of the plan—*his* plan. Abby, I had to help him. I didn't have a choice. I never meant to fall in love with you. I never wanted to lie to you. I swear it. You've got to know that I'm telling you the truth."

Anger pushed to the surface of my body—fuming, hot, intense. Followed closely by a wave of nausea. My knees buckled, and I hit the floor with a loud *thud.* In a flash, Tyler was there, pulling me into his lap. "Are you okay?"

I couldn't answer right away. Dizziness flooded my head and my stomach churned violently. The room around me started warping like it had a pulse of its own. I remembered this had happened to me back at the pub, when Stone tried using his gift on me. "The necklace," I croaked. "Get it off..." I grabbed it, yanking as hard as I could but it wouldn't budge.

Tyler helped me pull at it, but he got as far as I did: nowhere. "I want to get it off, but only he can. I'm so sorry." He scooped me up in his arms and carried me over to the bed, setting me down next to Lily.

As I got situated in a position that didn't seem to hurt as much, for whatever reason my thoughts flashed back to what Brian had just told me in the bathroom, how Conrad—my father—had tried to warn me about Bronx before it was too late and how that call almost cost him his life. I couldn't help but wonder what else, if anything, he'd known, since clearly it was about to cost Brian, his supposed friend, his life. If Tyler knew anything about my dad, I needed to know. "What do you know about my father?" My voice was bolder and I was thankful to be feeling a little better.

His face started to crumble and he looked away.

"Tyler, answer me!" I said, teeth clenched.

Keeping his eyes on the floor, he walked over to the closet and started rummaging through it. Clearly, he was ignoring my question, which didn't matter now anyways. We were out of time and he needed to get Lily out of here. Feeling defeated, I said, "If there's no other way to remove this necklace, then I'm as good as dead." I fidgeted with the clasp. "Please go. And get Lily out of here."

Tossing a pair of faded jeans and a black tee shirt at me, he replied, "I'm not leaving you. Put these on."

"You have to leave. Bronx will be back soon."

"You're right. He will. So hurry up."

Tyler turned around, giving me some privacy and since I hated that stupid red dress, I changed as fast as I could without the use of my advanced speed. "What are we going to do?" I asked while slipping on my boots.

"There's only one other way to get that necklace off of you. It's risky, but we have to go to the Head Council."

"But I thought they were working with Bronx?"

"They are, kind of. But they don't know he has you. He never told them that part." Tyler rushed to me and grabbed my hand, pulling me along with him.

"Did my father work for Bronx?"

"You're persistent and stubborn," he grumbled. "We don't have time to talk about that right now. Come on, let's go. We'll discuss it later, I promise." In the blink of an eye we were at the door, and Tyler dislodged it from the doorframe, hinges hanging, splintered pieces of wood falling about. He seemed to be getting pretty good with my abilities.

"I'm not leaving Lily," I argued, "and what about Brian? We can't just leave him either…"

"We don't have a choice!" Tyler picked me up and slung me over his shoulders.

Immediately I was hit with crazy intense pressure all over, uncomfortable prickly sensations beneath my skin, down in my bones. And if that hadn't been bad enough, the nausea returned. Since I wasn't even using my powers, then why was I feeling so horrible? "Tyler, something's wrong."

He didn't reply, just pushed forward through the door. But suddenly something hard slammed into me, knocking me out of his arms and flinging me back several feet. I landed hard on the floor, my tailbone breaking the fall. Recovering as quickly as possible, I turned sideways and looked up at Tyler. He was standing in the hallway, gaping at me.

Shaking my head to ease the spin, I slowly stood up. "What the hell was that?" Those strange feelings were thankfully starting to ease up.

"Well, I guess that plan is out," Tyler muttered and stalked back into the bedroom. Gently placing a hand on my back, he asked, "Are you okay?"

"Yeah. I think so. What happened?" I eyed the doorway as if I expected it to answer me.

"Bronx must've added an entrapment clause to the necklace. He can confine you to any location he wants and the necklace will hold you there." Tyler turned and started pacing between me and the door, raking his hands through his hair.

"But I didn't see that in your vision."

He stopped moving and looked around warily, sniffing the air. "Did you hear that?" His head tilted to the side. "He's out there. He's back!"

I went to him and grabbed his hand. Squeezing it tightly, I whispered, "You. Need. To. Run."

"I can't leave you here. Not after everything I've done to you." A trace of sorrow flashed in his eyes. "I can take him on. I'm strong enough now."

A desperate part of me agreed with him. But that wasn't an option. Trying to keep my voice steady I said, "You have to leave. Please take Lily and get her out of here. You owe me. This is what I want...please."

He knew I was right. It was pointless for him to stay and fight especially when I still needed Bronx to get that stupid necklace off.

"Fine. I'll go," his voice a monotone of resignation. "But I'm going to them for help." He turned to leave.

Stopping him, my fingers tightened around his. "The Head Council is too far away—"

"No they're not. They're here, in town. All five of them."

"What? What about Lily?"

"There's no time," he breathed. In a swish of cloth, he pulled free of my hold and was gone.

A door slammed, distracting me from all the anger and hurt I felt for Ty not helping Lily. Bronx was definitely back and after checking on Lily, I went into bathroom. Brian still lay sideways in the tub with his back facing me. Taking a seat on the bench, I leaned over and said in a soft voice, "Bronx is back."

He slowly turned his head, then looked straight into my eyes. "And the human, is he going to help us?"

"Yes," I said, somewhat hopeful. "He's going to the Head Council. They're here, in town."

Brian sighed. "Conrad. Thanks to Conrad."

"What are you talking about?"

"Conrad would've gone to them for help the minute I went missing. Or they must have information leading them here in Florida. They do not enjoy visiting this place so there would be no other business for them here."

"They—"

Suddenly, out of nowhere, Bronx grabbed me by the throat and jerked me off the bench. With a flick of his wrist, he tossed me across the room like a rag doll. I smacked the wall and dropped to the floor. Shaking it off, I pushed myself up but he was on me again, wrestling me back down to the ground. "You little bitch," he roared, "I should kill you now!" He pinned my arms above my head with one hand and gripped my neck with the other, then lifted up and slammed me back down with the force of a battering ram. Pain exploded throughout my head, and I took a deep breath praying my body wouldn't start healing yet. *Where. Is. Tyler?*" Bronx shouted, saliva dripping from his exposed fangs.

"He took off. I don't know where he went." My head was throbbing, but at least he didn't slam it again. But then just as I dreaded, my healing ability fired up. The weakened state I was in was discouraging and without a doubt, I needed more blood. But there was nowhere to get it. Not without killing Lily.

Glaring down at me, eyes sharp with fury, Bronx said, "Are you going to work with me, Abigail, or will everyone in this room have to die because of you?" In the next instant he was standing by lily and a gasp caught in my throat. Snatching her ankles, he pulled her down flat on the bed. Then he grabbed a pillow and pressed it over her face. Slowly, he pushed harder and harder as he stared daggers at me from across the room.

"No!" I screamed, and though I was weakened, I still flashed up so fast that horrible nausea flared instantly. But thankfully, my adrenaline was pumping so hard I was able to fight through it. "Leave her alone! Stop it!" I charged after Bronx and collided straight into him. He fell sideways, but caught himself fast and flashed back to her, pushing the pillow down again. I grabbed his arm, yanking with all my strength. "Please! Please don't do this! I'll do what you want! I promise! I'll do whatever you want!"

"If you try anything, anything at all, she is dead!" Bronx tossed the pillow across the room, grabbed my arm, and pulled me to the big plush chair in the corner. He pushed me down into it, the cushions threatening to swallow me with the force. He bent down, his face right there in front of mine, big red eyes glaring. "I mean it, Abigail! You better not pull anything!" He reached behind me, eyes threatening, challenging, and gave the necklace a few tugs. It constricted around my neck, tighter and tighter. I swallowed hard. And then finally he stood up, holding that awful silver chain in his hand. I was free. Holy crap. *I'm free.*

An avalanche of power surged through me. It was intoxicating and wonderful and exuberating all at once. Sure, I was still weak, but at least I was weak with full access to all my awesome powers. I shrugged to loosen my shoulders, rotated my neck until it popped, then slowly looked up at my captor. He was leaning down again, staring at me levelly, and said in a near whisper, "Now, you are mine."

Instantly, those familiar warm tingly sensations of his mind control clawed at the edges of my mind, distracting me from the rush of my own power as it restored. In a full panic, I closed my eyes, squeezed them shut, and tried to focus on blocking him out, but it was too late. He was still there, slithering closer and closer, the pull of his gift threatening to take over completely. He was too strong; my ability to block him wasn't working, and despair settled through me as I prepared for him to take over, which I feared would be any second now. But before giving up, I tried one more time, willing my ability to prevent him from gaining access to my mind. *My mind.* I was the only one strong enough to take him and I couldn't let him win. Straining against the weight of his intrusion, I felt sweat beading across my brow and my chest compressed with pressure so fierce that I feared at any moment it would burst. His eyes narrowed, as he kept pushing inside, unrelentingly inching deeper into me in such a violating way. A flashback of when he'd tried to rape me at the club and the hair on my nape rose as trepidation curled through my stomach and I gave one last mental thrust to shove him back.

A loud *snap* erupted in my head, the force so intense it rocked me back in the chair. My head throbbed, disorienting me, bright white spots scattering on the backs of my lids. A few flutters of my eyes and then I opened them all the way. At first everything around me was fuzzy and I blinked a couple more times, then tried focusing again, this time taking in Bronx looming straight in front of me. I startled at seeing him so close, but was also amazed at how crystal clear my vision was. It was just like it'd been before my powers had been drained by that stupid necklace, and a quick mental assessment of the rest of my senses confirmed everything was working again perfectly too. I curled my toes and fisted my hands, stifling a gasp of excitement as I realized I was still me. Bronx's mind control didn't get me! I *did* have the ability of blocking powers. And now it was showtime. I guess I wouldn't be doing what Bronxy boy wanted after all.

Bronx's fist struck the side of my face so hard it flung me out of the chair and across the room. Mostly unfazed, I shook off the lingering starbursts in my head and got up. No waves of nausea or overall weakness holding me back, I licked my lips, tasting blood I hadn't realized was there, and glared at him. He held his ground and didn't approach clearly knowing *I* was in control. Not him. "You little bitch!" he roared.

"I don't think you're in a position to call me names," I replied through a smile.

"I may not be able to control you, but I can still destroy you!"

Narrowing my gaze, I said, "By all means, come and get me."

He charged at me fast, fist flying through the air. I dodged it, stepped sideways, and hurled my hand out, landing my open palm on his nose. Blood splattered everywhere—on the floor, on me, and all over him. He leaped to the side, screaming something intangible with all the blood pooling in his mouth, but I was quite certain it was something to do with him killing me. Then he moved to attack again, thrusting out both arms, but in a whir of movement I was behind him. I grabbed his shoulders hard, fingers digging into skin and muscle, and launched him across the room. Seconds later, he slammed into the wall and dropped to the ground. He'd be out for a few seconds, but then I knew he'd be back for more. He wouldn't stop until one of us was dead. Better him than me.

This was my moment. The one I'd waited for since the day he turned me into a vampire. Closing my eyes, I focused on getting centered and ready for him. I sucked at the air, finding nothing at first, but then trickles of warm breath slithered through my nose and down my throat, raising my chest and coaxing my heart to start beating. Each pump was slow at first, then it quickly picked up speed and danced along with my breathing pattern. Something hot sparked in my core and spread out through my veins, searing beneath my skin. My fire. It was there: obedient, waiting, and ready.

That's when Bronx made his move. In one hurried motion, he rolled to the side, sprung up, and rushed toward me. I held out my arms, inhaling a deep breath, and as I released it, the fire pushed up to the surface. My hands glowed bright orange and a brilliant white ice all at once. Bronx froze, took a careful step backwards. The heat was hotter, more intense than I'd ever felt it before, blurring my vision and causing my whole body to break out in a cold sweat. My eyes stung and tears immediately fell out of them. Suddenly, Bronx's scream tore through my ears, though I couldn't make out what he was saying. For the first time ever, he actually sounded scared, and his fear only seemed to fuel my fire. Footsteps ran for the door, but I screamed out, "You're not going anywhere!" and in that moment, I released all the fire inside me.

Icy hot flames of intense red and orange morphed into deep blue and white scorching infernos, covering his body from head to toe. The fire was so hot and bright, you could barely look at it. Now I understood why my vision went blurry—my body was protecting itself from the fire. Bronx dropped to the ground, shrieking in agony. He rolled over and over again, but the flames burned hotter, bigger, more radiant. I focused harder on controlling my pyrokinesis and I could feel the energy was eager to obey me. Until this very moment, I'd had no idea how powerful I was.

My breathing sped up, and my heartbeat thumped harder, faster. The fire penetrated my pores, oozing out in watercolors of blue, white, orange, and red. The flames over Bronx started swelling up, consuming part of the room. Heat rose toward the ceiling as everything around me started to burn. Gray and white ashes fell down like a snowstorm. The smell of burning wood, cloth, hair, and skin was so pungent my tongue folded and I gagged, swallowing the bile back down. Lily started coughing violently, and I realized the heat had spread too close to where she was. Whether Bronx was dead or not, there was no other choice but to reign in my fire. If I didn't, Lily would die. And I refused to let that happen.

I squeezed my eyes shut, straining to control the pyrokinesis. Taking several breaths, deep and slow, I concentrated so hard my brain hurt, but I didn't give in—I forced myself to keep pushing. The heat raged inside me, but it was starting to ease just a little. It was working. I kept thinking and fighting for control. Control over me and my power. I opened my eyes steadily, cautiously. My vision was crystal clear. A wave of relief washed over me, tingles scattering over my skin as the flames went out. Smoke drifted around the room like a heavy fog. But all the fire was gone. Where was Bronx? I searched the room in a panic, but I couldn't find him anywhere. How in the hell had he slipped past me and escaped? Lily coughed again and I was beside her the next instant, checking her pulse. She was fine, her heart beating strong. She let out another slew of coughs and I knew I had to get her out of here. I heaved her over my shoulder as she wheezed for air, a fresh breath. But as I flashed for the door, I remembered Brian. In one swift movement, he was on my other shoulder, and I was carrying them both out of the room, surprised I was able to use that much strength without feeding. Especially after all the energy I'd just exerted using my pyro.

"Conrad was right about you," Brian mumbled, voice soft.

Unsure of what that meant, but having a hunch it was about my powers, I rushed down the hallway. There wasn't any soot or smoke out here in the living room, so I set Brian and Lily on the sofa and went back to the bedroom to find Bronx. I could hear Brian still going on about Conrad being right. Goody for Conrad.

The bedroom was thick with smoke and filled with fumes that would suffocate any human. Overhead, ashes still rained down. Led by my advanced senses, I walked over to where Bronx had been ablaze. Suddenly I couldn't fight the surge of emotions that came over me and I dropped to the ground, a hand over my mouth to stifle my sobbing. When I grazed my fingers across a pile of ashes, shockwaves shot through my entire body, confirming what I'd already felt to be true. It was Bronx—or at least all that was left of him.

27

Open Mind

WHEN I WAS HUMAN and faced grueling circumstances, my life and everything going on in it would flash before my eyes. The day my father walked out on me. Then later when my mother disowned me. Those memories played over and over like a bad home video. Oh, and let's not forget that special day when I walked in on John, the love of my life (yeah right!), sleeping with Mandy, the closest girlfriend I'd ever had. The pain from that moment was still sharp, and I couldn't help wondering why we thought about crap like that after a life-or-death situation. Tough times were like magnets. They attract each other when they're present. Why didn't good times seem to do that?

Now Bronx was dead—and so were all of his well-kept secrets. Tyler knew more than he was telling me, but he was probably long gone by now. Unless he really did go for help, but I doubted it. He'd taken off and I'd be lucky if I ever saw him again.

I stood up and brushed my hands across my jeans, dusting off any pieces of Bronx that may have gotten on them. The thought of it grossed me out. I crossed my arms over my chest and held tightly, feeling dirty, empty, and numb. No matter what horrible things happened in my past, nothing compared to murdering someone, nothing at all. Even though Bronx deserved it, and I had no other choice, it still felt wrong, strange, and repulsive. It was self-defense. He would've killed me. Him or me? I chose me.

"Abby. Abby!" Lily called, and I could hear the fear in her voice.

Turning around, I went to the doorway. "I'm coming!" I glanced back at Bronx's little mountain of ashes—actually more like a hill. *You got what you deserved, you bastard!*

I left the room, heavy in thought, but certain I did the right thing. With every slow step, it felt like cinderblocks held down my feet. My advanced senses were working, but not at full power. I needed blood—very, very soon. Using my pyrokinesis always seemed to leave me ravenous, like a bear waking up from its hibernation. I didn't think Lily could handle losing any more blood yet, so I was going to have to wait.

As I walked into the living room, Lily got up, but quickly fell back onto the sofa. "You're too weak, sweetie," I said as I went to her, gently placing my hand on her back, and massaging it in comforting small circles.

On the same sofa, Brian was a short distance away. He stared at me—big eyes and smiling—a broad glistening expanse of teeth and fangs. "Is he dead?" he asked.

I nodded, didn't speak.

"Bronx is dead?" Lily asked in a small voice.

Glancing down and finding her peering up at me, I gave a slight nod and her eyes instantly filled with tears, then, as if it was contagious, my eyes welled too. Looking away, my gaze settled on Brian, still tied up with those bloody, silver chains. I walked over to him and with a firm yank of my wrist he was freed. Bronx's death must have undone the dark magic used on them.

Brian stood up and hugged me. "Thank you. Thank you," he whispered in my ear.

"Are you going to be okay? I've got to get her—"I motioned to Lily with my eyes—"out of here."

"No, I'm fine. I promise," Lily argued. She tried to get up, and again it didn't work. I gave her one of those "I told you so" looks and then turned back to Brian.

"Yes, yes. I'm fine," he told me, "better than fine. Thanks to you. Where will you go?"

"Don't worry, I have a place to go."

He didn't press me to find out where that was. Thank God.

"Can you tell me anything else about my father? Do you know where he is?"

He shook his head. "I'm sure Conrad will find you when he's ready." A huge, warm smile stretched across his face and he bowed down like I was his queen. Then in a swish of bloody cloth, he was gone. I had no doubt he was rushing back to 7 and I made a mental note that if I ever wanted to see my father again, that would definitely be the place to start. It was time for me to get the hell out of here.

I went to Lily, knelt down to pick her up, but hesitated. An eerie wave of energy crept through the air like an invisible fog and I cocked my head sideways, using my advanced senses to figure out what it was. There was an intense musky odor, but it wasn't familiar to me. My nose twitched and the smell got stronger. Anxiety curled through me as I looked down at Lily. She smiled, completely clueless. At that moment, my guard shot up and I felt extremely protective of her. And that meant whatever was out there might not be friendly. Suddenly a loud boom shook the house and it sounded like the front door was blown off its hinges. Without thinking, I was between her and that horrible sound.

"What was that?" Lily asked.

"Shhh."

"Ab-by?"

"Be quiet," I said through a loud whisper.

Out of nowhere, four vampires were standing in the room no more than six feet away from me and Lily. I hadn't seen them come in. They were just there. I could feel the intensity of their power prickling on my skin unlike anything I'd ever felt before, yet there was something familiar about them. They all wore perfectly tailored black suits, each with their own unique undershirt and shoes. Without a doubt, I'd seen them before. They were the ancient vampires in Tyler's vision. Though I wasn't sure where the fifth one was, but these four were definitely members of the Head Council.

Tyler really had gone straight to them for help. But now where was he?

The oldest-looking vampire with milky-white hair that fell to his shoulders stepped forward and extended his hand. "What we heard about you is true," he said in a neutral tone. His liquidy eyes were like twin sapphire pools and he wore a black undershirt with a pair of matching boots. "I am Elliott, and it truly is a pleasure to finally meet you."

I swallowed hard, feeling tension curl through my insides like sharp, twisting wires, and shook his hand. It was strong, hard, and his power vibrated up my arm. "It's nice to meet you," spoken through a nervous smile as I gazed at him a moment and then took in the other vamps standing just behind him. They nodded, faint smiles tugging up their lips.

"She looks so much like her," said the brunet with the fresh spiky haircut (Jeffrey, I think). He looked to be in his late twenties when he'd been turned and wore an aqua tee under his suit jacket and black Sketchers sneakers.

"Yes...yes she does." The youthful-looking vamp with dirty blond hair and beautiful cornflower blue eyes inched closer. He wore a white tee with a picture of Cap'n Crunch visible through his open jacket, and I remembered Bronx had called him Trace in Tyler's vision.

"But how is that possible?" the last vampire asked—I didn't recall overhearing his name. He looked forty-something (in human years), with a rugged face, deep voice, dark hair streaked with gray and slicked back with gel—very *Miami Vice.* His undershirt was a baby blue button-up dress shirt. It matched his shiny black dress shoes.

Tension mounting, I stepped back and eyed them warily. "What are you talking about? Who do I look like?"

Elliott said in a near whisper, "Madelaine DuMonde."

"What do you mean?" I asked. "Who is that?"

"That is your mother." In a blink, Trace was only a couple inches away, standing about a head taller than me. He was absolutely gorgeous with radiantly creamy skin and dirty blond hair that was a mass of thick, glossy waves falling just below his ears. As he curiously gazed down at me, his beautiful baby blues seemed to pull me inside them, and I couldn't look away.

Forcing a few shakes of my head, I said, "That's not my mother's name. Evelyn...Evelyn was my mother's name..."

"No," Trace replied firmly. "Evelyn was your father's blood supplier."

"What? What are you talking about?" I demanded, because clearly they had their facts mixed up.

"Trace," Elliott said. "I do not think she knows anything about this. I can sense her discomfort and lack of understanding."

"Yes, that's right," Jeffrey agreed, voice soft.

"Abby." Trace tilted his head to the side and his brows stitched together. "May I please take your hand?"

"Why? What are you going to do?"

"I won't hurt you. I promise. We are on your side." Trace reached for me and scooped up my hand, regardless of the stiffness in my arm, and laced his fingers with mine. Instantly, everything around me was calm, tranquil, and I relaxed into his hold, my body leaning closer toward him, like I was in his spell. "Do you feel that?" he asked.

"Yes. What is it?"

"It is the feeling of truth. I want you to know that what I'm telling you is true and I will use my gift of discerning to prove it."

I nodded. He was telling the truth, I knew it without a doubt in my mind. "Okay. I'm ready."

"You are the daughter of the most powerful sorceress ever to live. She gave us the ability to use magic and loyally worked with us to maintain order and conduct among the vampires. Everyone loved her, but not everyone could have her. She chose to be with Conrad Tate over all other vampires."

"What...wait! My father is a vampire?"

Trace nodded, eyes still focused on mine. "This caused jealously and hatred among a small group of Enforcers. They formed an alliance and attempted to assassinate him, except their plan didn't go as expected and Madelaine was murdered instead. We were outraged and stricken with grief at the news of her passing. We ordered the death of all the Enforcers responsible. The loss of our sorceress was a huge blow to the vampire community and to this day, we still mourn her death."

"But—" I couldn't finish my thought. Swirling tranquil emotions rested on my tongue, numbing it like Novocain at a dentist's office. Trace's truth serum was still in full effect, making me eager to listen to him.

"Recently we discovered the impossible. Somehow Conrad impregnated Madelaine. It is inconceivable for vampires to reproduce. The only way that could've happened was through Madelaine's powers. By giving birth to you, she passed along her powerful bloodline and somehow she was able to prevent Conrad's vampire strain from crossing into you at birth. Madelaine wanted you to have a normal life. To be just a normal human girl. Her powers would've stayed dormant in your blood forever—unless, of course, you were transformed into a vampire. Bronx took it upon himself to bring you over, giving you all the advanced strength and senses of a vampire and awakening the powerful sorceress blood inside you. A hybrid, if you will. *That* is why Bronx wanted you. I don't know how he learned about you, but he wants to gain control of your mind and use you against us. We are here to stop him—permanently."

Trace squeezed my hand a little tighter, ethereal vibrations trailing up my arm. He wasn't lying. I knew it, could feel it down in my bones.

A couple more moments passed and then at last he released my hand. I was myself again, normal, aware, and restless. The weight of the truth he'd told me was almost too heavy to bear and I almost wished he were still holding my hand. "How do you know this?"

"Because Madelaine appeared to Elliott and told him."

"But you said she was dead!" I looked at the other vampires who were standing still, motionless as statues.

"She is," Trace replied. "Elliott's gift is talking to the dead."

"O-o-o-kay." I couldn't help but think how handy that gift was going to be when they found out about my old captor. I glanced back at Lily who was sitting quietly and listening intently to my exchange with the Council. After flashing her a nervous smile, I returned my attention to the group of ancient vamps.

"Abigail," Elliott said.

"Call me Abby. Please."

The old vampire gave a graceful shrug. "Abby, where is Bronx? We have followed his scent all over Florida." Then he added with annoyance, "It has been quite challenging to locate him."

That was why Bronx had left earlier. He'd been trying to hide from the Head Council until he gained control over my powers. When he realized how close they were, he'd fled from the house, most likely hoping to throw them off and create a false trail as to where he was. "He, um, he's..." Should I tell them the truth? It sounded like they wanted him dead anyway. And yet what if him being dead pissed them off? Maybe they wanted to punish Bronx.

Tension gripped me, angry and hot. I heard shuffling behind me, then Lily marched to my side—brave, defiant, maybe stupid. She was either feeling better or acting on pure adrenaline. "He's dead! Bronx is dead!" she exclaimed. "He was going to kill us. He was going to use Abby to kill us all. It was self-defense. She didn't mean to do it. She was protecting all of us." Her rich brown hair was a tangled mass with clumps of it sticking to the sides of her face. She stared at the Head Council, eyes wide, fearless. She placed her hands on her hips and then I noticed tears falling in tiny streams down her puffy pink cheeks.

Miami Vice spoke up first. "Is this true?" He looked at me, his gaze hard, unfathomable.

"Yes," I answered right away. "Everything Lily said is true."

"Where?" Trace asked, his face unreadable.

"He's in the bedroom back there." I pointed to the hallway behind me.

Elliott looked at Jeffrey for a couple seconds. Without a word, Jeffrey nodded, then in a blur, he took off, presumably to look for Bronx. I reached over, grabbed Lily's hand, and squeezed. She flinched and I eased up a little, knowing my grip had been too tight. Holding her hand brought comfort—a little anyways. And right now I needed all I could get. Almighty powerful vampire, hybrid thingy—yep that's me.

"Will I be punished for killing him?" I asked.

Now her fingers dug into mine. Yet it was nothing I couldn't handle. "But you can't punish Ab—" I elbowed her in the stomach (which thankfully shut her up) and she shot me a nasty look. The glare I swung back at her, however, dared her to say another word.

Then Jeffrey returned from the bedroom and confirmed Bronx's death. The four vampires urgently spoke amongst themselves in a hushed chatter, and though I should have been able to, I couldn't make out a single word. It sort of sounded like the teacher on *Charlie Brown*. I concentrated on hearing them, trying to focus my weakened, but not expended, advanced senses. Nothing happened, but it should've. And of course it was easy to assume that someone had the ability to prevent others from hearing them, which gave the Council the option to communicate privately anywhere they were. Oh, how handy that must come in. *But not when you're with a vampire that can block your powers.*

Even though I was weak and desperately needed blood, it was still worth it to try. I needed to know what they were saying because if the situation was grim, I'd need to get Lily the hell out of here. Closing my eyes, I focused my energy on blocking their power, or whatever they were using to leave me deaf to their private discussion. Right away, tingles shot through my body, prickly and painful. Waves of pressure built up in my head, making it feel heavy on my shoulders. I strained, and kept pushing, forcing my power to the surface until I could feel it starting to work. Hoping I wouldn't appear suspicious, I opened my eyes. Lily squeezed my hand again—encouraging, supportive. But she was clueless to what I was doing. Or was she? I felt tiny waves of energy flowing from her hand to mine. It tickled my fingers, brought warmth to my hands. I glanced at her. She was looking at them, eyes wide with fear. Well, maybe I was taking some of her energy, though I wasn't sure exactly how, but she definitely didn't have a clue what I was doing. The voices of the Head Council were coming in crystal clear now. They were arguing...about me.

"But she'd be an asset to us," mumbled Trace. He tugged at his tee shirt and ran his fingers through his dirty blond hair.

"You do not know if we can trust her!" hissed Miami Vice, face hard, resistant.

"We have no reason to condemn her. We wanted this fate for Bronx. She only made it that much easier for us." Elliott's words were eloquent, sincere.

"But she gave blood to that human, and if Tristan doesn't capture him we may never know what he is and the extent of his involvement..." Jeffrey looked uneasy. Were they afraid of Tyler? Why would they be afraid of a human—unless, of course, Tyler had kept more information from me. Big surprise.

Elliott looked at Jeffrey, lips unmoving, voice soft but optimistic. "We can make that an issue or we can overlook it. Abigail is the most impressive our kind has ever seen. If we condemn her for something as trivial as giving a human our blood, how can we expect her to willingly work with us?"

"Jeffrey, Elliott's right." Trace stepped closer to the huddled group of vampires. "We need her with us, not against us. Remember what Madelaine told us?"

"Yes. We need to get that human," Jeffrey scoffed.

"Enough of this! The decision is made!" Miami Vice threw up his hands. At once, their minds silenced and I couldn't hear another word. What decision? They hadn't said. I felt like a sitting duck, with four hunters stalking me with loaded guns. One of them was bound to hit me, so I braced myself as they all turned to look at me.

237

Miami Vice stepped forward, arms open, voice level, saying, "Abigail, there will be no punishment for the death of Bronx Granger. We wanted this fate for him long ago, and we are grateful for your assistance with it." His eyes dropped to the floor for a moment, then back to me. His hands folded together, then he continued, "Also, there will be no punishment for giving vampire blood to a human"—there was an eerie silence like he was thinking what to say next—"because I am assuming that you do not have a problem helping us track him. Once you locate the human, you will bring him to us."

A rush of anger blazed through me. What the hell did they want Tyler for? And better yet, why did it piss me off so bad? I shouldn't have cared if or why they wanted him, and yet I did, very much so. As screwed up as it was, I was not over him, even though his lies continued to unravel before my eyes. I needed to know what they wanted, though, and more than that I had to know they wouldn't hurt him. "The human that I gave blood to helped me tonight. I wouldn't have been successful without him. Why would you want me to bring him to you?" I stepped forward, surprised by the challenge in my voice. Lily grabbed my hand, pulled me back, but I slipped away from her, using a small fraction of my vampire strength.

Elliott came closer, placing his hand on Miami Vice's shoulder. "I apologize for Charles' tone. Like you, we just have a few questions." He raised an inquisitive brow. "Don't you want to know the truth about that man, if that's what he even is?"

"What do you mean?" I demanded, glancing back at Lily. She hadn't moved, quietly standing behind me. Probably scared out of her mind.

"He is gifted with abilities beyond what any human is capable of having." Elliott's face stiffened. "We have also linked him to a few rogue vampires."

Tyler had mentioned helping a couple other vampires. But he'd never said anything about them being rogue. "What rogue vampires?"

Miami Vice scowled. "That is not your concern. We have already dealt with them."

I didn't like the way he said that. His tone gave away how they'd dealt with those vampires and it was most likely something I

238

didn't want to know about. But what did that mean for Tyler? Would they "deal" with him the same way? And when he mentioned Tyler had gifts, was he referring to the visions he saw or did they think Tyler had more abilities? If that were true, why would Tyler keep it from me? Oh sure, right, that's the stupidest question of them all. Whether or not I found Tyler wasn't the question at this point. Actually, it was whether or not I'd turn him over to the Head Council once I did.

Elliott took a small step forward, his sapphire gaze expectant. Miami Vice's features hardened—if that were even possible. The other two vampires were watching me very steadily. Everyone was waiting for my answer.

I swallowed hard, feeling pressure strong enough to choke me had I still been human. "I will help you look for him under two conditions." Thank God I didn't sound as nervous and uncertain as I felt. "One. You will not kill him or hurt him or anything comparable. Two. You will tell me where I can find Conrad Tate."

Elliott looked shocked, eyes widening as he glanced back at the others. Then he quickly regained his composure, turned back to me, his gaze once again normal as though nothing had ever happened. He reached out his hand and said, "We have a deal."

Even though I shook his hand, I wasn't sure if I could trust him.

28

Reunited

LILY DECIDED TO STAY IN FLORIDA, for now anyway. Since there was no way I was going to put her in danger as I tried to find both Tyler and my father, her multiple requests to come with me had been denied. The Head Council mentioned a few places my father was known to spend time at; however, they also cautioned me that Conrad Tate was a very dangerous vampire. Yep, he wasn't just a vampire, but also a very dangerous one. I was still trying to swallow all of that. And all that crap about my real mom being some powerful, dead, sorceress.

Taking Lily back to Pulse had assured her safety and quenched my blood thirst. Saying good-bye to her proved more difficult than I'd thought it would be. Her parting words still floated about inside my mind as I raced against the sun back to Hilton Head.

"But Abs, I don't want you to go alone," she argued through tears. "What if something happens to you? We've already seen how easy it is for someone to hurt you."

"Don't worry about me. The Head Council won't be using any magic against me. They need my help. I think we can trust them for now." I reached out and grabbed her, pulling her into an embrace. Her body was warm, inviting. "You're my best friend and I promise to return to you."

She nestled into me, burying her face in my shoulder. "How can you trust them?"

"I believe what Trace told me. His gift of discerning is genuine, I could feel it." I stroked her soft brown hair slowly, hoping to comfort her.

We stood there for several minutes, not speaking, our cheeks moist from tears. Eventually our time was up and I stepped back, gazing into her big, beautiful, brown eyes, as she smiled fondly, reassuring me. My throat choked up, tears returning to my eyes as I kissed her cheek. It was warm, soft, and alive. Then, in a flash of movement, I was gone, never looking back.

With the threat of sunrise mere minutes away, Rayver's Pub finally came into view. Streetlamps spewed faint light like hazy round balls. The sidewalks were empty of people, the streets barren of cars and bikes. The air was damp and stuck to my skin, clothes, and hair with a cool, sticky texture. I hurried to the pub's entrance, my daylight clock ticking internally as if it were a time bomb, which, in a way, it was.

Quinn and Britney were on their way out, leaving the vampires behind for a restful day full of sunshine, I was sure. "Hey, Anna." Britney waved as they passed me, then crossed her arms around her chest. A jean jacket was draped over her green shirtdress, all the buttons done, her body shivering in the bone-chilling air. Quinn smiled shyly, wrapped his arm around his daughter, huddled closer to her, and then they disappeared out of the pub. I was going to have to tell them my real name the next time I saw them. Or maybe they could just keep calling me Anna. Sounded close enough.

Stone sat at the bar alone, his back slumped over, elbows on the countertop, his head resting on the backs of his hands. I took the seat next to him and he didn't even bother looking my way. His hair was unkempt and his black shirt was unbuttoned, exposing his perfectly sculpted chest—stunning. He stared at a glass filled with ice, a golden thin puddle hovering at the bottom. "I wondered if you'd return," his focus heavy on the empty drink.

"Please don't tell me you're *that* pissed off?" I nervously ran my fingers through my hair, which was still damp. The thought of a shower was tempting and I wondered if there was a full bathroom somewhere at the pub.

"You think it's funny that you just vanished without a trace? I tracked you to North Florida and then, just like you, your scent disappeared." He still wouldn't look at me.

I grabbed his arm, tugging gently. After resisting a short while, he finally, very slowly, turned to me. He was frowning. "I'm sorry," I offered softly. "I didn't want you, or anyone else to get hurt. It's over now. I'm okay. Bronx is dead."

"You killed Bronx?" His frown vanished and he raked me with a disbelieving gaze.

241

I nodded, smiling.

"With your pyrokinesis?"

I nodded again.

"I don't believe it!" He grinned—dazzling, incredible.

"Well, it's true." My head tilted to the side, hair falling over my shoulder, cascading slightly over my face. Those pesky bangs felt stuck to my forehead.

Stone swept his fingers across my brow, moving some of my hair out of my eyes. "You're blond."

"It's my natural color."

"I like it."

"Me too." I stared down at the countertop and then told him everything that happened. How Bronx captured me and held me prisoner, along with the vampire from 7, and how it was all Tyler's fault. Then Tyler ended up changing sides and trying to help me. Stone's face lit up like Christmas morning when we got to the part about Bronx's death, so I made sure to tell him all the details. It was still hard to believe that I'd actually killed him. Even though Bronx deserved it, something didn't sit right with me about it. I was a murderer now—no matter what my reasons were. But at least I wouldn't be punished for it. There's always a silver lining on every cloud. Right?

I told him all about the Head Council, my real mother, my vampire father, and how I'm some kind of hybrid species. He laughed when I said that. "What's so funny?" I asked.

"The hybrid thing sounds kind of weird."

Yeah it kind of did. "Did you know about the sorceress?"

He nodded. "I've heard about her. But she died a long time ago. No one really mentions her anymore. I would've never dreamed that you were her daughter."

I started fidgeting with some of the hair that had fallen over my shoulder. "Well, that's what Trace told me."

"Did he use his gift on you?"

He obviously knew about the sexy Council member's ability to discern the truth. "Yes."

"Then whatever he told you is true. So you're definitely a hybrid thingy." Stone playfully nudged my shoulder.

"Ha ha. Very funny." I stopped messing with my hair and tucked some of it behind my ears.

"So what about Tyler?" Stone took my hand inside his, holding it gently.

"One of the Head Council, Tristan I think, is tracking him." I bit my bottom lip and looked at Stone. "But they want me to help find him too."

Stone frowned, face full of disappointment. "Are you going to?"

I swallowed hard. "I kind of made a deal with them. I don't have a choice."

Stone picked up his ice-filled glass. "Want something to drink?" He reached behind the bar and grabbed a bottle of Glen Levitt.

"Sure. That's probably a good idea," I said.

He twisted the cap off and drank a big gulp straight from the bottle. "You're not going alone. Promise me you won't." He sounded very serious.

I jerked the bottle out of his hands. "I can take care of myself. Did you not hear anything I just told you?" Bringing the bottle to my lips, I chugged down the warm, pungent, liquid that burned all the way down my throat. I definitely preferred it on ice.

"I know how strong you are, but you're not emotionally bulletproof. You will need someone to help you. Both with your father"—he paused as if trying to figure out the best words to say—"and with that human." He slipped the Glen Levitt out of my hands.

What he just said stung like a slap in the face. He was right. Emotionally I *was* unstable and seeing Tyler again would stir up all kinds of feelings. Combine that with a possible father-daughter reunion and it could equal a disaster. "All right. Fair enough," I said. "And if I don't go alone, does that mean you're coming with?"

"Who else do you think?" he snickered.

I stole a moment to think about it. It really would be nice to have someone with me, helping me, supporting me. And I knew I could count on Stone for that. "Okay."

"Okay what?"

"We're doing this together, you and me. And you better not get yourself killed." With a straight face, I stared at him.

Both of us burst into laughter, and I grabbed my stomach to ease the twisted knots. He did the same. It felt so good to feel happy, momentarily carefree. Stone reached over, slid his arms around me, and pulled me into a caring embrace. "I was so freaking worried about you," he quietly murmured, lips tickling through my hair. "Thank you for doing it my way this time. It's only because I care, you know?"

Here came the tears, filling up my eyes like an impending flood. My throat constricted, trying to fight them back. Stone's grasp tightened around me, which at least was comforting. For the first time since becoming a vampire, I truly felt safe. And that accelerated my tears like gasoline on a fire. I tucked my head under his chin and buried my face into his chest. It felt like home, the closest thing I had to it anyway. Sighing, I slipped my arms around him and held him back.

"I know you care. And I appreciate that you want to help me," the weight of emotions making my voice crackle.

His grip loosened and we both sat back, gazing intently at each other.

"So when do we leave?" he asked.

I mulled it over in my head for a moment. "I don't know."

"Did the Head Council give you a time frame?"

"Not really. But I know I don't have forever."

He half laughed, rolling his eyes. "So I guess that means we'll find the human first."

"Pretty much. I don't really think they care about Conrad." I grabbed the bottle of scotch and took a couple sips, then wiped my mouth with the back of my hand. "I'm the one that wants to find him. I have questions that only he can answer."

He took the bottle from me, chugged down a hefty amount. "What if he doesn't want to be found?"

"It's really not up to him. I deserve to know more about my *real* mother...who I really am...my heritage..."

Stone's eyes grew wide, then he swung around, his lasered gaze on the entrance.

"What is it?" I asked, following the direction of his view but didn't see anything at first. Then I picked up *his* scent and didn't have to.

"I know you're there!" Stone called out, standing up from the barstool, eyes narrowing.

I jumped up and placed my hands on his chest. "Please don't. Let me talk to him."

"This is my bar! He's not welcome here, unless he's turning himself in."

I pressed harder against Stone's chest, then glanced back at the entrance. No one came in. Nothing happened...yet. I flicked my eyes back to Stone's. "Please. Do this for me. Give me five minutes to find out what he wants. If I don't like it, we take him down...together."

Stone's face was full of anger. He looked down at me and it softened just a little. "You know we should bag him now and take him to the Head Council."

Swallowing hard, I silently begged him with my eyes. I'd made a deal with the Council and I was under their strict orders. And yet I knew for a fact *he* wasn't here to turn himself in. Based on how angry Stone looked, he knew it too.

"You have five minutes." Stone kissed my cheek and then vanished behind the bar.

I watched the door—nothing there, no movement, no noise.

"Abby." Warm air tickled the back of my neck like a feather brushing skin.

In a hurry, I turned around to find Tyler standing right there. How the hell had he gotten behind me? "What are you doing here?"

He reached up and palmed my cheeks. I flinched but didn't pull away. After a brief moment, I relaxed a little, resting my face more comfortably against his soft, warm grip. "I had to see you," he said, voice soft, his beautiful green eyes threatening to hypnotize me. "I couldn't leave without seeing you again. I knew you'd be here...even though I know he's here too." He frowned and let go of my face.

"Stone is the least of your worries."

"I know. A member of the Council is tracking me." His muscles pulled his cheeks into a sly grin. "I lost him hours ago though."

I shrugged, which did little to ease my tension. "I'm supposed to help find you. And turn you into them when I do." Why was I even telling him that? "They may have acquired more Enforcers to help with the search." I stared at him a moment, his face a mask of indifference, then I pressed, "Why do they want you so bad? Were you helping rogue vampires?" Because I needed to know if he'd lied to me about that too.

There was a shift in his body, muscles in play but he remained utterly still. Then he ran a hand through his hair and said, "I want to tell you everything. I really do." He stepped forward, reaching for me.

My mistake may have been not backing away from him, but as he encircled his me in his arms, I held my hands tight at my sides. That at least was my attempt of holding my ground, though the lump of emotion in my throat was becoming harder to swallow, and I knew my resolve was shaky at best. My stomach clenched and I choked back the threat of tears. No matter how angry I was, why did it feel so good inside his arms? And why was there a pang of guilt when thinking about that deal I'd made with those ancient vampire rulers? "I can't let you leave." My voice was muffled against his chest, which actually made it easier to hide the few sniffles that escaped. "I have to take you to them. They promise your safety."

Tyler let me go and took a small step back, just enough to look down at me. He caressed my chin with his fingers and lifted it gently, slowly, so that we were looking at each other. His face lowered, lips closer and closer. His eyes were burning green flames in search of oxygen, and I was the oxygen. His breathing sped up, deep, warm puffs on my face. I didn't step away—even though I should have. Then, he closed his mouth over mine and kissed me hard, awakening a fury of need within me that I hadn't even realized existed. I grabbed him by the back of his head with both hands, tangling my fingers through his messy hair, and jerked him closer. His hands slid down my back, then crawled their way under the edge of my shirt. His fingertips slid across my skin, leaving a sizzling trail in their wake. I let go of his hair, eased my grip on the back of his neck and dug my fingers into the tense knots I found there. He sucked at the air as my mouth pressed harder against his and I ground my lower body against him, arching my back to get closer. Passion consumed me and set me aflame, and feeling that jolt of heat was like dousing my fire with a reality check of cold water. *I can't do this! Need to stop it! Now!*

I seized him by the shoulders and pushed back, using just a little extra force. Since he was fueled by my powers, he was tougher to budge, and I gaped at him with that realization.

"Are you going to turn me in, Abby?" He was still out of breath from kissing me, and I was almost envious of that since I'd halted my gift of fire before my breathing had begun.

"Give me one reason, *one reason* I shouldn't take you to them. I deserve the truth. No more lies."

He inched closer and I leapt several feet back, crashing into a chair and knocking it over. "I never wanted to lie to you. I wanted to tell you everything. I love you…I swear it." Tiny streams of tears dripped down his cheeks.

"So tell me now," as he moved closer I threw up a hand. "No, please. Stay where you are. And just tell me, Ty. What do you know about my father? Why does the Head Council want you?"

He swallowed hard. "Abby." He stared down at the floor. This must be bad. He couldn't even look at me.

"Spit it out!"

He let out a long sigh. "Your father is dead."

I froze. My whole body went numb. That couldn't be true. "But he called me. He was trying to warn me about Bronx."

Tyler ran a nervous hand through his hair. "Bronx almost got him then. Your father got away, though. Bronx was beyond pissed off about that."

My mouth dropped open as the pieces of the puzzle connected. Tyler must have helped Bronx find my father using his gift of premonitions. And if that were the case, and Conrad was really dead, then it was Ty's fault. "You helped him," my voice dripping with accusation. "You helped him find my father and kill him."

"No!" Tyler exclaimed, arms rising. "Bronx wasn't going to kill him. He just wanted to keep him quiet. He was supposed to chain him up like that other vampire." He took a moment to collect his thoughts. I waited impatiently, anger seeping through my pores. "It was an accident. Your father was too strong. He fought back. I'm sorry. I'm so sorry."

I dropped to the floor as if a wrecking ball just crashed into me. I couldn't handle hearing this, not yet, not now. Slamming my fists repeatedly against the floor, I replayed the words Tyler had just spoken. Just a few short minutes ago I was going to find my father, talk to him, get answers, and see him again with my own two eyes. But now that hope was lost, gone forever.

Tyler's hands rubbed my back, soft and hesitant. When I didn't react, he drew closer, wrapping me up like a baby, pulling me against him, and gently rocking me. I lost myself in his arms and cried harder than I ever had before as we sat there on the floor of the pub.

Gradually, the tears eased up, sticky trails left behind on my cheeks. I leaned back, just enough to look at Tyler. His face was soft, sincere, and so damned beautiful it almost hurt to look at it. When your hand gets stuck in the cookie jar, there's no way to get it out without letting go of the cookies. But I wasn't ready to let go. I didn't know why it was so hard. Why do feelings have to get in the way of your conscience?

"The Head Council doesn't know my father is dead?" I said it like a question, though I was pretty sure they didn't.

He nodded slowly. "I worked with a couple friends of Bronx's. Those are the rogue vampires the Council told you about. *That's* how I met Bronx in the first place." He grabbed my chin, gently tugged it, making sure my eyes stayed on his. "But Abby I swear, I swear I didn't know they were bad. I would've never helped them, or Bronx, if I had known."

I shook my head to slow the spin. The Head Council had no intention of keeping Tyler unharmed and alive. That was why I'd gotten the suspicious look from Elliott. There would be no way to clear his name since his involvement in all of this was too easy to prove. And once they discovered my father's death and the fact that he helped Bronx get him, it would be all over. My whole body hurt, tension building so thick in my chest if felt like I needed my ears to pop. Realizing I cared too much to turn him in only made everything that much harder to handle. It was a struggle to see his innocence in all of this, but a part of me believed it was there. I didn't have Trace's discerning ability, but I could feel the truth from Tyler's words. He'd finally come clean and admitted everything. And though he was involved—very involved—none of it was his fault. He'd been lied to just like me.

"You need to leave." I'd said it, but a big part of me didn't really mean it. Empty, meaningless words. But I knew Stone would be back out here any minute.

"Come with me."

"I can't."

His eyebrow arched. "Why?"

"Because the only way to find out more about my mother is by speaking to her myself. And the only way to do that is through the Head Council."

Tyler nodded and then looked away. A brief moment of silence passed and then he got up, pulling me with him. "Before I go, I need to hear it. I need to hear that you believe me. Abby, I would never hurt you intentionally. I love you. I really, really love you. I'm sorry for everything."

I closed my eyes and slowly opened them back up. He looked at me expectantly, his eyes drilling me for an answer. Stepping closer, I grabbed his face, and kissed him—hard. All the passion I could ever dream of still burned alive with the touch of our lips and static charged butterflies took flight in my belly. Sliding a trail of baby kisses all the way to his ear, I whispered, "I believe you."

"Thank you," a breath of words spoken through a sigh of relief.

We held each other a little bit longer then suddenly his body tensed. Slowly, he pulled out of my arms, and stepped back cautiously, his gaze flicking between me and the entrance. "I really do have to go now."

I knew right away Tyler saw something, one of his visions. "What? What's there? What did you see?"

"That vampire, the one that's tracking me. He's almost here."

My stomach tightened with worry. Obviously the Head Council didn't trust me. And I guess I shouldn't blame them for that. "Go. I'll cover for you," I said. "But I don't think they will stop looking...until they get you."

"Don't worry. I have a few good hiding places." He swooped in, kissed me on the cheek, and took off.

"Ty wait!" I shouted, bringing my wrist to my mouth and ripping it open with my fangs. Blood pooled from the puncture marks and dripped down my arm. In a blur of movement, he was next to me, gripping my wrist, his lips parted slightly as he brought it to his mouth. After he finished drinking, he kissed me one last time, the metallic tang of my blood interspersed with his spicy male flavor filling my taste buds, then he flashed away for good.

Fighting back the tears that threatened to choke me, I mumbled, "I love you, too."

###

About the author:

2013 National Indie Excellence Awards Finalist
2012 Voted Best New Author by Popular Book Blog Nose Graze

Ashley Robertson resides in sunny Orlando, Florida, and loves writing about anything paranormal. She also composes poems and songs, though she learned long ago she doesn't have a singing voice. When she isn't writing you'll find her spending time with family and friends, sharing personal training and nutrition advice via **ExtremeMakeovers.com**, traveling and exploring new places, and drinking fine wines and gourmet coffees from her Nespresso machine.

Visit her website to learn about her upcoming releases, guest blog posts, and featured giveaways at: **AshleyRobertsonBooks.com**

Want to read more?
Here's a sneak peek of Crimson Flames—Book #2 in
the Crimson Series.

Crimson Flames

By Ashley Robertson

1

The Deal

MY STOMACH CLENCHED as I sensed the vampire's approach. He was close. So close I could feel the thrum of his power vibrating along my skin. The hairs on the back of my neck rose, and I knew if I was going to use my power for defense, then I needed to bring it forth now. I closed my eyes, forcing myself to breathe as deeply as I could—which thankfully had gotten easier with practice. I focused on the energy inside me, willing it to the surface, and as I felt it swelling, building like an approaching storm, I threw out my hand, gripped Stone's shirtsleeve, and urged him to the floor. "Get down! He's here!"

Stone raked me with a look that told me he was not too pleased, but then fear swept over his face when he realized just how little time we had.

The wooden door to the pub suddenly burst open—bits of wood and dust raining down from the force. Even though Stone should've cowered behind me—since his gift of reading blood wasn't something he could fight with—somehow he'd found some bravery and boldly stood by my side. Though I appreciated it, I didn't like it, and desperately wished he had listened to me. But I couldn't think about that *and* call forth the fire within me at the same time. So I pushed Stone to the back of my mind with the silent promise of dealing with him later. Then I returned my attention to the power building inside me. One last deep breath and my heart shuddered to life inside my chest, making a rhythmic pattern with my faux breathing. A tingling warmth spread from head to toe, then settled on my awaiting hands. Seconds later, there was a glowing orb of fire (about the size of a basketball) cupped inside my palms. And just as the vampire appeared through the settling fog, I called out, "Not another step, Tristan, or it will be your last!"

"I think you should reconsider your threat," Tristan shot back. "We are on the same side."

That I sincerely doubted, but I knew killing a member of the Head Council would definitely put me on the "Most Wanted" list. Which I might already be on, since I'd helped the human this vampire was here to claim escape.

"She's not bluffing!" Stone said through a snarl. I wanted to glare him into silence, but I refused to take my eyes off of the vampire standing in the broken doorway, wearing a black Armani-looking suit—now lightly covered with dust. It was a custom for all members of the Head Council to wear black suits, but each of them would wear shoes and an undershirt of their own choosing. I guess it was a way to express their individual personalities. Yet this one seemed to express himself through his spiked, platinum blond hair, not the basic black undershirt and matching boots—which were much more boring compared to what I'd seen a few of the other Council members wearing. But this vampire was far from boring. He was a tracker for the Council—one of the best hunters on earth. And he was after my human boyfriend.

"You know why I'm here, Abigail," Tristan bit out. "The human was here."

I felt my gaze narrow as I carefully took a step forward, the ball of flames growing hotter in my hands. "Yes, he was. It's my fault he wasn't captured."

"That's not exactly true," said Stone as he moved up beside me.

I stole a few deep breaths, fighting the urge to throw my fireball at him instead of the blond vampire in the suit.

"Please explain!" Tristan ordered with impatience. But as Stone attempted a reply, he was cut off. "Not you! I want to hear this directly from Abigail!"

"Abby," I corrected, feeling sweat forming above my brows and pooling between my breasts.

The blond vampire smirked, folding his arms in front of his chest.

"I did not restrain him because I do not believe he will be kept safe once in your hands," I went on. "And until I can prove his innocence in all of this, I feel it's best that he stay far away from *you*."

A tinge of red formed a ring around Tristan's irises as he scowled. "That is not your decision. He must pay for his involvement with those rogue vampires, including Bronx. He cannot get away with helping them try to destroy our stronghold."

"I made an agreement with the other Council members," I reminded him. "Doesn't that count for something? Your word is nothing if your actions do not back up what you say." My voice was getting louder, my patience thinning. And the angrier I got, the more difficult it became to control the fire in my hands.

"Yes. We have a deal," Tristan assured. "We will not kill him or harm him—just as we told you—but that does not mean he won't be punished some other way."

"I don't believe you," I snapped.

Stone put his hand on my shoulder. "Abby, maybe you should—"

In a flash of movement, the vampire closed the distance between us and held Stone in a headlock from behind with his fangs hovering over my friend's neck. And since it wasn't to drink Stone's blood, since Stone was also a vampire, then that meant it was a threat to rip out my friend's jugular. From there it would be too easy to finish Stone by ripping off his head. And that's when my patience snapped. There were only two ways to kill a vampire—burning to death or decapitation—and he was about to find out firsthand just how very dangerous I was. Sure, he could threaten to kill my friend, but he'd be burned alive before Stone's head hit the ground. I placed all my focus on the orb of heat in my hand, willing it to retract to half its size while intensifying, growing hotter, then I thrust it at Tristan's face. In a blur of motion, he ducked, throwing Stone to the floor as the fireball grazed over his head, singeing the soft tips of his hair. A snarl erupted from his throat as his fiery gaze locked onto mine. There was a brief hesitation, burnt hair and musk filling my senses, then something similar to curiosity flashed over his eyes and he was airborne, plunging straight for me. My body shuddered as heat blasted out of every pore, radiating from me like invisible steam. Throwing his arms over his face, the vampire faltered midair and fell sideways, then jumped back once he landed and retreated by the door from which he'd entered. Satisfied I'd made my point, I pulled all the heat back inside me, then rushed over to Stone and helped him up. "You okay?" I asked.

He nodded by way of an answer, then ran his hand through his coffee-colored hair—which was completely messed up now.

My eyes narrowing, I fixed my gaze on Tristan across the bar by the door. "Do that again and I'll kill you," I warned.

Tristan brushed some of the dust off of his pants. "Abigail, I'd rather not have to repeat that again. Hopefully I've made my point by now," he said, his mouth curling into an amused grin that nearly reached his eyes. The hints of crimson were gone—for now anyway. "I would not have harmed your friend, as I'm sure Mr. Rayver here is already aware." He glanced at my disheveled friend, a smirk still pulling at his lips; then his gaze slid back to me. "Your powers make you far greater than just any other Enforcer. You are an equal with us. We should work side by side, you making the sixth, and final member, of the Council. But you must not argue with our protocol. If rules are broken, there are, and will always be, consequences. There are no exceptions to this. Ever. The rules of our kind are ageless. It's been that way for centuries and shall remain that way indefinitely."

Well that was news to me. I knew the Head Council wanted my services, but I'd thought they just wanted me to be one of their many Enforcers. Enforcers were gifted vampires like me. Well, kind of. A few months ago I'd been kidnapped by an evil vampire named Bronx and turned against my will, which awakened the sorceress's bloodline inside me, unbeknownst to me. But Bronx knew all about it, and he'd planned to use my powers to defeat the Head Council. Only I'd killed him before he got the chance. Later on, I'd learned about my real mother being an all-powerful sorceress and how she'd used her magic to impregnate her vampire lover—my father. So I never really was just another vampire. Or even an Enforcer. I was always more than that. A whole new species altogether, a hybrid, and a hot commodity among the vampire world—since there was no other like me. Yet if the Head Council really wanted my partnership, then I just gained a whole lot of leverage. Anxiety curled through my belly. "If you want me to work with you, and of course the others, then I will need you to be more flexible. Rules are always in place for guidance, but we both know they are not in stone. Especially when I believe innocence is a key component."

"When there is proof of one's innocence, then we have a trial," Tristan explained. "But there is no proof of that with this human."

I thought about that for a moment. Sure, I didn't have "proof" per se, but I had Tyler's word. And though he'd lied to me about his

255

alliance with Bronx, and the fact he'd known about my father's death all along, for some crazy reason I believed him now. "Allow me the time to find the proof you require and I will consider partnering with you."

Tristan shot me a lasered glare. His face softened but I had absolutely no idea what his thoughts were. Mind reading wasn't one of my gifts—yet. Since no one could predict what other gifts I'd inherit.

"How can you possibly believe this human didn't help those rogue vampires?" he asked at last.

Keeping my eyes on Tristan's, I shook my head. "He was involved. I'm not saying I can prove that differently. He's innocent of knowing what Bronx's intentions were, what those rogue vampires' intentions were." I paused a moment to suppress some of the heat inside me, though I didn't completely extinguish it just in case things got hostile again. "He thought he was helping them," I went on. "He thought they were in trouble. He didn't realize he was working for the bad guys until...until it was too late."

Stone snorted in disbelief, but kept his mouth shut. Smart vampire.

Tristan's eyes widened. "How can you possibly believe that? He must have you brainwashed!"

"That isn't possible," I told him.

"What are you speaking of?"—confusion in Tristan's voice. "Bronx would have claimed you with his mind control had you not killed him first."

"No, it's not possible to brainwash me," I explained. "And that is how I *was* able to kill Bronx." Saying that struck a pang inside my chest: I didn't want to be a murderer any more than I wanted to be a vampire, err hybrid. "I have the ability of blocking powers."

A wave of surprise flashed over Tristan's face. "There is so much to learn about you, Abigail," he said.

"So do we have a deal?" I asked, taking a couple steps toward him.

Tristan raised a brow. "How much time are you asking for?"

"As long as it takes," I replied instantly. "I have a feeling you and the others will delay me, since we are all curious to learn more about my powers."

Tristan closed his eyes momentarily, presumably using his telepathic powers to confer with the other members of the Council. I stole a moment to look at Stone. He was shaking his head slowly, azure eyes with hints of red wide with shock. I shrugged my shoulders warily, knowing fully that to keep Tyler safe, I'd break this deal and the neck of anyone who attacked him. Obviously Stone knew that too.

"We have a deal," Tristan finally announced.

I smiled. Relief flushed through me as the remnant heat within finally extinguished. Moments later, my breathing slowed and my heartbeat completely stopped. Oh the joys of being a vampire hybrid. "I have one more favor to ask," I said, a whole new confidence exuding in my voice.

Stone called out, "Abby, what are you—"

"Silence, Mr. Rayver," Tristan stated. "I am very interested in what Abigail will ask for now."

"I want to speak to Madelaine. Will Elliott do that for me?" My real sorceress mother, Madelaine, had died long ago, and I'd never even had the chance to meet her. My father and one of his female blood donors, all the while believing she was my mother, had raised me. And though I'd love for Elliott to connect me to my father, I simply couldn't risk giving away the fact he was dead too. Who knew how that little piece of info would affect the deal I'd just made, or the innocence I wanted to prove for Tyler. Bronx killed my father. But it was because of Tyler's gift of premonition that Bronx was able to find my dad in the first place. So I guess you could say Tyler did carry some of the blame. But he'd sworn that he never thought Bronx would've killed him. And I believed him, hopefully not foolishly. So far I was taking the news of my father's death okay. Maybe my estranged relationship with him was helping me through the mourning process. After all, he'd left me when I was ten. Fifteen years later, I'd finally gotten a phone call from him, warning me I was in danger. I never had a chance to thank him for trying to help me...or see him again.

"Abigail," Tristan said, bringing me out of those thoughts. "You're going to make a great addition to our team. You're already very good at negotiations." He chuckled lightly. "It will be our pleasure to call upon Madelaine for you and an honor to introduce you to your real mother." Holding out his hand, he moved closer, giving me a good view of his violet eyes speckled with the deepest of cobalt, not a trace of crimson in them, which calmed me further. "So we have a deal?"

I nodded, taking his hand inside mine. "We have a deal." Then I asked, "When do we leave?"

His answer was one simple word: "Dusk."

I felt my chest tighten as he said it, even though I'd somewhat expected that to be his answer. Moving to where Stone was behind me, I threw my arms around his neck and buried my face against the softness of his tee, yet I could feel the ridged lines of muscle just beneath. "I know I just got back here, but I promise we'll have more time once this is all over. I will miss you," I told him, my voice muffled.

He gently grabbed my shoulders and pushed me back, just enough for him to look at my face. "What in the hell are you talking about? Do you actually think you can get rid of me that easy?"

"What do you mean?" I asked, feeling confused.

"I'm coming with you."

"No, you're not!" Tristan shouted from behind me.

I shrugged as a plan formed in my mind. "Wait a second. I think it's a great idea for Stone to come."

"No," Tristan repeated.

"Actually, sir," Stone said, "I can be of help to both Abby and the Council. I can help look for the information Abby seeks to clear her human while she is tied up with business affairs with you. It would make her that much more available."

I felt my eyes widen. That was actually better than my plan. "But you hate Tyler." And he did—with a passion.

"Oh I still hate him, but I think the world of you." Stone gently gripped my chin, caressing it between his thumb and forefinger.

A lone tear I hadn't felt before dripped from my eye as I smiled. Stone let go to wipe it and I glanced over at Tristan. "Please allow Stone to come with us. He would be a true asset. And he is my friend. Please."

Tristan was quiet for a short moment, face hard, eyes studying us intently. "Very well."

"Where are we going exactly?" I asked.

"Boston," Tristan replied. "We have a few stronghold locations, but we are operating out of Boston right now. It's good to move around. Staying in the same place for centuries can get quite boring. And it's not as safe."

I nodded. I'd never been to Boston before, but I'd heard it was an interesting place. A huge part of me was looking forward to seeing it, checking out all the historic monuments, buildings, and the statue of Sam Adams, if there would be any time for sightseeing. With Stone coming, we would certainly accomplish twice as much, twice as fast. I trusted that he would work diligently on finding a way to prove Tyler's innocence. Though Stone despised Tyler, I was certain that he cared enough about me to do as he said he would. Yet Stone wouldn't be upset in the slightest if he was unable to find the proof we needed to clear Tyler's name.

There was also the uncertainty over what kind of situation I'd be getting myself into with the Head Council. Learning vampire politics and more about the new species I'd become when Bronx turned me...well, that could take more time from me than I could ever imagine. Plus meeting my mother for the first time and finding out more about her set my emotions swirling with anxiety.

I closed my eyes and let out a deep, long sigh. *Just take one thing at a time, Abby. One thing at a time. Quit worrying about things that haven't happened yet.* Bronx was dead. Tyler was alive and pardoned for the moment. Lily, my closest human friend and old blood donor, was okay. Stone was here with me now and would stay with me at the Head Council's stronghold. And I'd gotten pretty good control over my amazing, awesome, and insanely strong powers. I'd say my life, afterlife, whatever, was going pretty darn well at the moment. Yet, at the time, I had no idea just how quickly everything was about to change.

More Books by Ashley...

CRIMSON FLAMES
Book 2 of the Crimson Series
Half-vampire Abby Tate's newly discovered powers are the key to the Council's victory over a group of evil vamps who will do anything possible to remove the hybrid threat. With no other options, Abby is forced to rely on the aid of the Council, yet can she trust them? Even worse, can she fight the unwelcome attraction that's growing between her and one of those ancient vampire rulers?

Add it to your Good Reads shelf now: http://www.goodreads.com/book/show/17287650-crimson-flames

Buy now on Amazon: http://www.amazon.com/dp/B00BLKTJG4

UNGUARDED
2013 NATIONAL INDIE EXCELLENCE AWARDS FINALIST (in the Fantasy genre)
Guardian angel Selene was close to becoming an archangel—until she fell in love with a vampire. Now her dark lover has been kidnapped and the only way to save him is by abandoning her human charge. But her choice to save him doesn't come without a price. Selene must push her diminishing angel abilities to where she risks becoming fallen, praying she can save the ones she loves before her fate is sealed.

Add it to your Good Reads shelf now: http://www.goodreads.com/book/show/15356720-unguarded

Buy now on Amazon: http://www.amazon.com/UnGuarded-ebook/dp/B008G3N9H4

DEATH DEALER
A Death Angel Novella—Book 1
Death: a word Mia Baron knew too well since the murder of her parents. Her drive for vengeance was why she became a Death Dealer, signing her life away in her own blood. Deacon Gage craves justice for his own horrific tragedy that forced him into the same life as Mia. A new job threatens to destroy her and he realizes he's the only one who can save her...at a price that might be too much to pay.

Add it to your Good Reads shelf now: http://www.goodreads.com/book/show/18098934-death-dealer

Buy now on Amazon: http://www.amazon.com/Death-Dealer-Angel-Novella-Book-ebook/dp/B00DQ1J9PW

Still want to read more??

Here's another Sneak Peek ☺

Death Dealer
A Death Angel Novella—Book 1

<u>1</u>

The full moon's reflection gleamed brightly in the iridescent glass pane of the first-floor nursing-home window, framed by chunky, weathered slats that had been painted white at some time in their existence. Crowding just below the glowing orb's mirrored image was a mass of thick shrubs, uneven in shape and slightly overgrown with pinkish flowers still dangling from a few branches, the tips of their petals browning as if touched by death. *Death.* A word Mia Baron knew all too well. She inhaled deeply, the cool air tickling the back of her throat and forcing her to stifle a cough. The last thing she needed was to get caught snooping outside the PB Retirement Community. Her need to see the person just beyond the reflecting glass of the window yearned deep in her heart. Realization that this was the last time she'd ever see this person clenched her stomach with grief.

Crouching low to the green herbaceous cover that was a mix of soft, straw-like grass and spurge—a type of weed that grew in places the ground was kept moist—Mia shimmied through a small opening in the shrubs that was probably created by her comings and goings over time, and once she reached the gray brick exterior wall of the nursing home, she turned left and crept until the window she sought was directly above her. Slowly rising, she placed her hands on the sill and peered through the crystal-clear glass at an angle where the moon no longer obstructed her view. Though slightly darkened with tint, which would have made it difficult for the average person to see through, she gazed longingly at the old woman reclined in a twin-sized, remote-controlled bed that elevated her upper body. A tray table was suspended over her waist, most likely rolled there from across the room when the nurse brought her dinner. Leftovers of what appeared to be mashed potatoes were piled in the corner of her plate, and the remnants of green Jell-O were in the compartment directly above that, which surprised Mia because the old lady usually ate all of those disgusting, wiggly squares.

The door opened and a middle-aged nurse walked in. Her eyes looked tired with dark circles her cover-up did a poor job of concealing, and her smock was the blandest color of blue Mia had ever seen—matching the nurse's mood, no doubt. Flashing a forced smile at the old woman, the caregiver ran a hand through her short, auburn hair, then retrieved the plate of leftover dinner and any other trash from the tray table before rolling it back to the corner of the room. "Don't be up too late watching television. You know that stuff just rots your brain," she called over her shoulder as she walked out, pulling the door shut behind her.

A normal person wouldn't have been able to hear any of that—unless they could read lips, which Mia couldn't do very well at all. No, the reason that her hearing and vision were so precise didn't have anything to do with normal, because Mia Baron was far from *normal*. A fact she'd gotten accustomed to.

It pissed Mia off that the nurse hadn't asked the old woman if she were feeling okay, or if she needed anything else, but those questions had only been asked the first week the old woman had been admitted. The politeness had worn off after that, blending in with the stale environment of the place a lot of older folks would spend their last days. What saddened Mia more was the fact that she'd always wished those she came for would be of this age, where they'd already lived their lives to the fullest and now were trapped in an existence where death would be welcomed. But most of the ones she came for didn't live at the PB Retirement Community, or any other retirement community for that matter. No, most of the people she came for were younger and should have had so much more life ahead of them.

Which was why it should have been a blessed night that Mia was finally getting her wish. Only the weathered person she stared at through the window wasn't just some old woman who was going to die—it was the one person who'd raised her since she was a little girl.

Lifting her hand from the sill to place it on the cool glass surface of the pane, Mia was momentarily lost in her past, the memories flooding in with snapshots of images long forgotten. Catching butterflies in an open field with wildflowers spread across the ground, the old woman, petite and pretty for a woman in her sixties, her hair a mixture of gray and white cut short with small curls set tightly to her head, laughed as she watched a six-year-old Mia swoop her brand-new butterfly net over the tops of several flowers and come back with a beautiful monarch. Sitting on a wooden swing that hung in the corner of a wraparound porch, watching the cars zip by on the highway just up the manicured hill, ten-year-old Mia's head nestled on the old woman's shoulder. Mia driving the 1966 soft yellow Ford Thunderbird with booger-green interior for the first time on her own, glimpsing the old woman in the rearview mirror wearing a red-and-white-striped apron over her floral sundress, waving and shouting to Mia as she maneuvered up the rocky driveway and onto the smooth, paved surface of the street.

It became harder to breathe as Mia fought the tears that had, unbeknownst to her until now, welled up in her eyes while she'd been lost in thought. Surprise flitted through her mind as she wondered when the last time she'd cried even was. But tears didn't matter—she knew that with certainty. Nothing could change what was coming and Mia dreaded it with every ounce of her being. The only comfort she could take was in knowing that at least the old woman would be asleep when it happened. No more pain. No more sadness. No more nursing home. Soon, all of that would be gone, taken away by her death.

So when the hand that held the remote went slack and the old woman's head drooped slightly into the pillow, Mia knew it was time. Trepidation tightened in her chest as she gripped the top wood frame of the window and pushed upward, using some extra power in the movement to ensure the window would open—even if it were locked. With a *snap, pop, creak* the pane shuddered ajar. The wood, swollen with moisture, forced Mia to stop, not because her advanced strength was tested, but she simply didn't want to make any noise that would awaken the old woman. It would be better that way—for both of their sakes.

Now with a gap about three inches tall, Mia stopped her efforts and lowered her hands to her sides. This was more space than she needed, and she quietly chuckled to herself, sometimes underestimating her own power. She glanced at her surroundings once more to ensure she was alone and then closed her eyes and concentrated on being inside the room. Her whole body prickled with energy seconds before the pain sliced through her like sharp, twisting metal that attached to her insides and squeezed around each part. Sweat broke out across her brow and pooled between her breasts—like it had every time before this one—as her physical body slowly broke down, piece by piece, disintegrating into an opaque gray mist that now hovered just outside the window, drawn inside by the three-inch opening and the person sleeping unawares. After entering the room on a current of cool air, she floated to the side of the bed, still in mist form, letting her senses fill of the old woman. Peppermint, most likely the mouthwash she'd used, was most dominant, but under that was the soft aroma of roses and thyme, her favorite perfume, and just beneath that was the bite of body odor that confirmed it'd been days since she'd been properly bathed. A growl rippled through the opaque haze of Mia's misty shape as anger surged red in her mind, drowning out the television that played an old rerun of *Bonanza*. *No more of this shit*, Mia thought, *I'm taking you away from here—far, far away from this God-forsaken hellhole.*

Mia materialized back into her physical body, her skin a light shade of tan as if the sun had gently kissed it, but it wasn't the sun that had given her that color—it had been her father's half-Mexican lineage mixed with her mother's small percentage of native Indian, which also gave her high cheekbones, brought her height to five and a half feet, and there was a touch of a widow's peak centered above her brow and sweeping back to the luminous chestnut waves that fell behind her shoulders and landed in the middle of her back. After swiping her palms down the thighs of her black leather pants, she leaned over the bed and carefully slipped the remote from the old woman's boney grip—a hand that was once so much younger with smooth, creamy skin now uneven with bumps and raised veins that looked like blue tunnels beneath the paper-thin surface of her flesh, fingers once elongated and beautiful now with a crooked arch and swollen, rounded knuckles that her gold wedding band would never be able to slip over. A lump barreled its way up Mia's throat as she set the remote on an end table that was littered with used tissues and plastic cups of half-filled water before focusing her attention back on the old woman. Bending over and stretching her body so her lips were closer to the old woman's ear, Mia whispered, "I love you, Grandma," the strain in her tone evident in the soft sound of those words.

It still stung deep in Mia's heart that she had been unable to make it during most visiting times, which were inconveniently between the hours of ten in the morning and four in the afternoon, and because of that, she'd always wondered if by chance things had been different, her grandma would've remembered who she was just one more time while still alive. Four years ago, Alzheimer's had stolen away Mia's beloved grandmother, yet the old woman's body remained a fragile shell to the soul that resided within.

And now Mia was here to collect it—just like all Death Dealers did.

Though she had a hunch her grandma's soul would gleam bright white, the color that indicated the path of the Light Gate, she would only know for sure after it separated from the host body— the delicate human shell that belonged to the woman she loved like a mother.

A tear slicked down Mia's cheek and dropped off the edge of her chin, a big splash landing on the pillow mere inches from her grandma's sleeping face. Stepping back, Mia did the best to collect herself, fighting back an avalanche of emotions she'd somewhat expected. Though when her boss and Death Angel, Abram, had given her the task of guiding her grandma's soul to the gates of whatever realm her spirit would move into, Mia had no choice but to accept. She owed it to the woman who'd cared for her after her parents died, twenty years ago that felt like an eternity of time with so much that had changed since then. At the young age of four was

265

when Grandma had told Mia her parents were in heaven, that they were now angels watching over her from somewhere above the clouds during the day. And at nighttime, Mia would help her grandma pick out which stars she thought her parents were. While younger, it had been easier for her grandma to shield her from what happened, home-schooling her until the news went stale and the town hushed its gossip. It wasn't until fifth grade that Mia first attended a real school and for several years she'd stayed to herself, sat alone at lunch and in the back of the classrooms, and had gone straight home after school. Sure, some would speak with her, but it had always been short and sweet. No real lasting friendships made. But it was the end of seventh grade when Benji Barnes said something to her, something she'd fought to forget but now the information grated her heart. He'd asked her if she was the daughter of the murdered couple, the one whose body parts had been found all over the house, carefully hidden for the investigators to slowly find, some pieces to this day never recovered.

Mia had never recovered either.

After that, Mia did a lot of her own research, finding everything Benji had said to be true, not one bit of it an exaggeration which would be expected of a young, popular middle-school boy. *The police are still looking for leads in the Eduardo and Natalie Baron gruesome murder. These loving, doting parents leave behind a beautiful four-year-old little girl who has been taken into protective custody. Investigators believe this was a random act of violence and have yet been unable to acquire any suspects, though they believe it could be cult related. But nothing explains why the bodies were chopped up and hidden in various places throughout their Manhattan Beach area home and police have yet to locate all of the pieces.*

More tears fell as Mia shook away the memory, the one reason she'd become what she was. Being a Death Dealer was supposed to bring Mia closure, finally give her the vengeance she sought in righting her parents' grizzly murder, and when Mia turned eighteen, she'd finally signed her name on the dotted line with her own blood. However, Abram had yet to deliver her the name of the person or persons responsible, but it was his promise of doing just that that had sold her into this dark afterlife. After guiding her grandma's soul to the proper gate, she planned on bringing it up to her boss...again.

Glancing down at the cherished old woman, Mia carefully placed the palm of her hand across her grandma's forehead. With one last tear streaming down her cheek, Mia took a deep breath and whispered, "It's time."

###

~<u>Acknowledgements</u>~

I'm so thankful to God for the amazing opportunity of following my dreams of being an author. And to my incredibly supportive husband, Baron, who without I would never have been able to follow this journey.

To my wonderful mom and dad for all their encouragement and support—not only for my dreams of being an author, but for every endeavor I've gone for.

To my sister, Allison—I love you so much and I appreciate you reading and loving my books. Your support means the world to me.

Stephen Delaney (Close Reader Editing Services), your professional touch and eagle eyes are beyond appreciated. Because of you, this book is the best it could possibly be. Thank you.

Stephanie with Once Upon A Time Covers designed the awesome cover and it's a perfect fit to this book. Thank you for making this cover look so good and for the smooth process of working together.

To each and every one of my friends, and the many book bloggers I've developed wonderful blogationships with. I freaking love you guys!!! For buying my books, reading them, reviewing them, and following along with me on this journey. From the bottom of my paranormal loving heart, Thank you.

And a huge virtual hug and special thank you to all my fans. I'm beyond honored that you like my books enough to buy them and share them with your friends.

More about the author can be found at
www.AshleyRobertsonBooks.com

* 9 7 8 0 6 1 5 5 3 1 7 6 2 *